Praise for *Little Fires Everywhere*

"Witty, wise, and tender. It's a marvel."

—Paula Hawkins, author of *The Girl on the Train*
and *Into the Water*

"Witnessing these two families as they commingle and clash is an utterly engrossing, often heartbreaking, deeply empathetic experience. . . . It's this vast and complex network of moral affiliations . . . that make this novel even more ambitious and accomplished than her debut. . . . It is a thrillingly democratic use of omniscience, and, for a novel about class, race, family, and the dangers of the status quo, brilliantly apt. . . . The magic of this novel lies in its power to implicate all of its characters—and likely many of its readers—in that innocent delusion [of a post-racial America]. Who set the little fires everywhere? We keep reading to find out, even as we suspect that it could be us with ash on our hands."

—*The New York Times Book Review*

examination of motherhood, identity, family, privilege, perfectionism, obsession, and the secrets about ourselves we try to hide."   —*Buzzfeed*

"Engrossing . . . With each revelation, *Little Fires Everywhere* grows more propulsive and insightful, boring through the placid surface of American suburbia."

—*The Dallas Morning News*

"Ng has one-upped herself. . . . A finely wrought meditation on the nature of motherhood and the dangers of privilege and a cautionary tale about how even the tiniest of secrets can rip families apart. . . . Ng is a master at pushing us to look at our personal and societal flaws in the face and see them with new eyes. . . . If *Little Fires Everywhere* doesn't give you pause and help you think differently about humanity and this country's current state of affairs, start over from the beginning and read the book again."   —*San Francisco Chronicle*

"As she did so well in *Everything I Never Told You*, Ng crafts sympathetic backstories for the characters that make their decisions understandable if not entirely acceptable. She . . . raise[s] questions about what mothers can give and what their children need when no one can stick to the rules."

—*St. Louis Post-Dispatch*

"A haunting, layered story of mothers and daughters, and how they attract and repel each other."   —*The Seattle Times*

"A multilayered, tightly focused and expertly plotted narrative . . . A deeply impressive novel with the power to provoke and entrance."   —*Minneapolis Star Tribune*

"One of the best novels of the fall . . . *Everything I Never Told You* was good, but this is better."   —AARP.org

"Once again, Ng has delivered a near-perfect novel."
                    —BookRiot

"An intricate and captivating portrait of an eerily perfect suburban town with its dark undertones not-quite-hidden from view . . . Ng explores the complexities of adoption, surrogacy, abortion, privacy, and class, questioning all the while who earns, who claims, and who loses the right to be called a mother. . . . An impressive accomplishment."
                    —*Publishers Weekly* (starred review)

"Ng's stunning second novel is a multilayered examination of how identities are forged and maintained, how families are formed and friendships tested, and how the notion of motherhood is far more fluid than bloodlines would suggest. . . . [A] tour de force."   —*Booklist* (starred review)

"This incandescent portrait of suburbia and family, creativity, and consumerism burns bright. . . . The characters she creates here are wonderfully appealing, and watching their paths connect—like little trails of flame leading inexorably toward one another to create a big inferno—is mesmerizing, casting into new light ideas about creativity and consumerism, parenthood and privilege."   —*Kirkus Reviews* (starred review)

"Spectacular sophomore work . . . a magnificent, multilayered epic that's perfect for eager readers and destined for major award lists."   —*Library Journal* (starred review)

"With brilliance and beauty, Celeste Ng dissects a microcosm of American society just when we need to see it beneath the microscope: how do questions of race stack up against the comfort of privilege, and what role does that play in parenting? Is motherhood a bond forged by blood, or by love? And perhaps most importantly: do the faults of our past determine what we deserve in the future? Be ready to be wowed by Ng's writing—and unsettled by the mirror held up to one's own beliefs."

—Jodi Picoult, *New York Times* bestselling author of *Small Great Things* and *Leaving Time*

"*Little Fires Everywhere* takes us deep into other people's homes and lives and darkest corners. Along the way, Celeste Ng is always witty, engrossing, unsparing, and original."

—Meg Wolitzer, author of *The Interestings*

"*Little Fires Everywhere* is a dazzlingly protean work—a comedy of manners that doubles as a social novel and reads like a thriller. By turns wry, heartrending, and gimlet-eyed, it confirms Celeste Ng's genius for gripping literary fiction."

—Peter Ho Davies, author of *The Fortunes*

"*Little Fires Everywhere* showcases what makes Celeste Ng such a masterful writer. . . . By looking so closely at this community, she opens up the entire world."

—Kevin Wilson, author of *The Family Fang* and *Perfect Little World*

"[A] powerful work about parenthood and politics, adolescent strife and artistic ambition, and the stark choice between conformity and community."

—Rumaan Alam, author of *Rich and Pretty*

"I cracked open this book mid-morning and did not even move again until it was time to turn on a light. What a joy it was to be so thoroughly taken. . . . *Little Fires Everywhere* is a deft, smoldering masterpiece."

—Mira Jacob, author of *The Sleepwalker's Guide to Dancing*

"As I read Celeste Ng's second novel I found myself thinking, again and again: How does she know so much? About all of us? How does she write with such perception, such marvelous grace, such daring and generosity? *Little Fires Everywhere* has the irresistible pace of an expertly tuned thriller, and the observational brilliance of lasting literature. It marks Celeste Ng as a writer of the first rank, among the very best in her generation."

—Joe Hill, author of *The Fireman* and *Heart-Shaped Box*

"Celeste Ng is a powerful and poignant writer whose attention to detail is pitch-perfect. Her intuitive rendering of how and why people behave in such unflattering ways is important."

—Terry McMillan, author of *I Almost Forgot About You*

"Un-put-downable . . . A must read for book clubs."

—POPSUGAR

PENGUIN BOOKS

LITTLE FIRES EVERYWHERE

Celeste Ng grew up in Pittsburgh, Pennsylvania, and Shaker Heights, Ohio. She graduated from Harvard University and earned an MFA from the University of Michigan. Her debut novel, *Everything I Never Told You*, was a *New York Times* bestseller and winner of the Massachusetts Book Award, the Asian/Pacific American Award for Literature, and the ALA's Alex Award. *Little Fires Everywhere*, Ng's second novel, was a *New York Times* bestseller, winner of the Ohioana Book Award, and named a best book of the year by over twenty-five publications. Her books have been translated into more than thirty languages, and she was the recipient of a fellowship from the National Endowment for the Arts. She lives in Cambridge, Massachusetts.

ALSO BY CELESTE NG

Everything I Never Told You

LITTLE

FIRES

EVERYWHERE

CELESTE NG

PENGUIN BOOKS

PENGUIN BOOKS
An imprint of Penguin Random House LLC
penguinrandomhouse.com

First published in the United States of America by Penguin Press,
an imprint of Penguin Random House LLC, 2017
Published in Penguin Books 2018
This edition published 2020

ISBN 9780735224292 (hardcover)
ISBN 9780735224315 (paperback)
ISBN 9780143135166 (paperback movie tie-in)
ISBN 9780143135661 (mass market movie tie-in)
ISBN 9780735224308 (ebook)

Printed in the United States of America
3 5 7 9 10 8 6 4 2

BOOK DESIGN BY LUCIA BERNARD

To those out on their own paths,
setting little fires

Whether you buy a homesite in the School Section, broad acres in the Shaker Country Estates, or one of the houses offered by this company in a choice of neighborhoods, your purchase includes facilities for golf, riding, tennis, boating; it includes unexcelled schools; and it includes protection forever against depreciation and unwelcome change.

—Advertisement, The Van Sweringen Company, Creators and Developers of Shaker Village

><

Actually, though, all things considered, people from Shaker Heights are basically pretty much like people everywhere else in America. They may have three or four cars instead of one or two, and they may have two television sets instead of one, and when a Shaker Heights girl gets married she may have a reception for eight hundred, with the Meyer Davis band flown in from New York, instead of a wedding reception for a hundred with a local band, but these are all differences of degree rather than fundamental differences. "We're friendly people and we have a wonderful time!" said a woman at the Shaker Heights Country Club recently, and she was right, for the inhabitants of Utopia do, in fact, appear to lead a rather happy life.

—"The Good Life in Shaker Heights," *Cosmopolitan*, March 1963

LITTLE

FIRES

EVERYWHERE

1

Everyone in Shaker Heights was talking about it that summer: how Isabelle, the last of the Richardson children, had finally gone around the bend and burned the house down. All spring the gossip had been about little Mirabelle McCullough—or, depending which side you were on, May Ling Chow—and now, at last, there was something new and sensational to discuss. A little after noon on that Saturday in May, the shoppers pushing their grocery carts in Heinen's heard the fire engines wail to life and careen away, toward the duck pond. By a quarter after twelve there were four of them parked in a haphazard red line along Parkland Drive, where all six bedrooms of the Richardson house were ablaze, and everyone within a half mile could see the smoke rising over the trees like a dense black thundercloud. Later people would say that the signs had been there all along: that Izzy was a little lunatic, that there had always been something *off* about the Richardson family, that as soon as they heard the sirens that morning they *knew* something terrible had happened. By then, of course, Izzy would be long gone, leaving no one to defend her, and people could—and did—say whatever they liked. At the moment the fire trucks arrived, though, and for quite a while afterward, no one knew what was happening. Neighbors clustered as close to the makeshift barrier—a police cruiser, parked crosswise a few hundred yards away—as they could and watched the firefighters unreel their hoses with the grim faces of men who recognized a hopeless cause. Across the street, the geese at the pond ducked their heads underwater for weeds, wholly unruffled by the commotion.

Mrs. Richardson stood on the tree lawn, clutching the neck of her pale blue robe closed. Although it was already afternoon, she had still been asleep when the smoke detectors had sounded. She had gone to bed late, and had slept in on purpose, telling herself she deserved it after a rather difficult day. The night before, she had watched from an upstairs window as a car had finally pulled up in front of the house. The driveway was long and circular, a deep horseshoe arc bending from the curb to the front door and back—so the street was a good hundred feet away, too far for her to see clearly, and even in May, at eight o'clock it was almost dark, besides. But she had recognized the small tan Volkswagen of her tenant, Mia, its headlights shining. The passenger door opened and a slender figure emerged, leaving the door ajar: Mia's teenage daughter, Pearl. The dome light lit the inside of the car like a shadow box, but the car was packed with bags nearly to the ceiling and Mrs. Richardson could only just make out the faint silhouette of Mia's head, the messy topknot perched at the crown of her head. Pearl bent over the mailbox, and Mrs. Richardson imagined the faint squeak as the mailbox door opened, then shut. Then Pearl hopped back into the car and closed the door. The brake lights flared red, then winked out, and the car puttered off into the growing night. With a sense of relief, Mrs. Richardson had gone down to the mailbox and found a set of keys on a plain ring, with no note. She had planned to go over in the morning and check the rental house on Winslow Road, even though she already knew that they would be gone.

It was because of this that she had allowed herself to sleep in, and now it was half past twelve and she was standing on the tree lawn in her robe and a pair of her son Trip's tennis shoes, watching their house burn to the ground. When she had awoken to the shrill scream of the smoke detector, she ran from room to room looking for him, for Lexie, for Moody. It struck her that she had not looked for Izzy, as if she had known already that Izzy was to blame. Every bedroom was empty except for the smell of gasoline and a small crackling fire set directly in the middle of each bed, as if a demented Girl Scout had been camping there. By the time she checked the living room, the family room, the rec room, and the kitchen, the smoke had begun to spread, and she ran outside at last to hear the sirens, alerted by their home security system, already approaching. Out in the driveway, she saw that Trip's Jeep was gone, as was Lexie's Explorer, and Moody's bike, and, of course, her husband's sedan. He usually went into the office to play catch-up on Saturday mornings. Someone would have to call him at work. She remembered then that Lexie, thank god, had stayed over at Serena Wong's house last night. She wondered where Izzy had gotten to. She wondered where her sons were, and how she would find them to tell them what had happened.

><

By the time the fire was put out the house had not, despite Mrs. Richardson's fears, quite burned to the ground. The windows were all gone but the brick shell of the house remained, damp and blackened and steaming, and most of the roof, the dark slate shingles gleaming like fish scales from their recent soaking. The Richardsons would not be allowed inside for another few days, until the fire department's engineers had tested each of the beams still standing, but even from the tree lawn—the closest the yellow CAUTION tape would allow them to come—they could see there was little inside to be saved.

"Jesus Christ," Lexie said. She was perched on the roof of her car, which was now parked across the street, on the grass bordering the duck pond. She and Serena had still been asleep, curled up back-to-back in Serena's queen size, when Dr. Wong shook her shoulder just after one, whispering, "Lexie. Lexie, honey. Wake up. Your mom just called." They had stayed up past two A.M., talking—as they had been all spring—about little Mirabelle McCullough, arguing about whether the judge had decided right or wrong, about whether her new parents should've gotten custody or if she should've been given back to her own mother. "Her name isn't even really Mirabelle McCullough, for god's sake," Serena had said at last, and they'd lapsed into sullen, troubled silence until they both fell asleep.

Now Lexie watched the smoke billow from her bedroom window, the front one that looked over the lawn, and thought of everything inside that was gone. Every T-shirt in her dresser, every pair of jeans in her closet. All the notes Serena had written her since the sixth grade, still folded in paper footballs, which she'd kept in a shoebox under her bed; the bed itself, the very sheets and comforter charred to a crisp. The rose corsage her boyfriend, Brian, had given her at homecoming, hung to dry on her vanity, the petals darkened from ruby to dried-blood red. Now it was nothing but ashes. In the change of clothes she had brought to Serena's, Lexie realized suddenly, she was better off than the rest of her family: in the backseat she had a duffel bag, a pair of jeans, a toothbrush. Pajamas. She glanced at her brothers, at her mother, still in her bathrobe on their tree lawn, and thought, *They have literally nothing but the clothes on their backs. Literally* was one of Lexie's favorite words, which she deployed even when the situation was anything but literal. In this case, for once, it was more or less true.

Trip, from his spot beside her, absentmindedly ran one hand through his hair. The sun was high overhead now and the sweat made his curls stand up rather rakishly. He had been playing basketball at the community center when he heard fire trucks wailing, but had thought nothing of it. (This morning he had been particularly preoccupied, but in truth he likely would not have noticed anyway.) Then, at one, when everyone got hungry and decided to call it a game, he had driven home. True to form, even with the windows down he had not noticed the huge cloud of smoke wafting toward him, and he only began to realize something was wrong when he found his street blocked off by a police car. After ten minutes of explaining, he had finally been allowed to park his Jeep across from the house, where Lexie and Moody were already waiting. The three of them sat on the car's roof in order, as they had in all the family portraits that had once hung in the stairwell and were now reduced to ash. Lexie, Trip, Moody: senior, junior, sophomore. Beside them they felt the hole that Izzy, the freshman, the black sheep, the wild card, had left behind—though they were still certain, all of them, that this hole would be temporary.

"What was she thinking?" Moody muttered, and Lexie said, "Even *she* knows she's gone too far this time, that's why she ran off. When she comes back, Mom is going to murder her."

"Where are we going to stay?" Trip asked. A moment of silence unreeled as they contemplated their situation.

"We'll get a hotel room or something," said Lexie finally. "I think that's what Josh Trammell's family did." Everyone knew this story: how a few years ago Josh Trammell, a sophomore, had fallen asleep with a candle lit and burned his parents' house down. The long-standing rumor at the high school was that it wasn't a candle, it was a joint, but the house had been so thoroughly gutted there was no way to tell, and Josh had stuck to his candle story. Everyone still thought of him as *that dumbass jock who burned the house down*, even though that had been ages ago, and Josh had recently graduated from Ohio State with honors. Now, of course,

Josh Trammell's fire would no longer be the most famous fire in Shaker Heights.

"One hotel room? For all of us?"

"Whatever. Two rooms. Or we'll stay at the Embassy Suites. I don't know." Lexie tapped her fingers against her knee. She wanted a cigarette, but after what had just happened—and in full view of her mother and ten firemen—she didn't dare light one. "Mom and Dad will figure it out. And the insurance will pay for it." Although she had only a vague sense of how insurance worked, this seemed plausible. In any case, this was a problem for the adults, not for them.

The last of the firemen were emerging from the house, pulling the masks from their faces. Most of the smoke had gone, but a mugginess still hung everywhere, like the air in the bathroom after a long, hot shower. The roof of the car was getting hot, and Trip stretched his legs down the windshield, poking the wipers with the toe of his flip-flop. Then he started to laugh.

"What's so funny?" Lexie said.

"Just picturing Izzy running around striking matches everywhere." He snorted. "The nutcase."

Moody drummed a finger on the roof rack. "Why is everybody so sure she did it?"

"Come on." Trip jumped down off the car. "It's *Izzy*. And we're all here. Mom's here. Dad's on his way. Who's missing?"

"So Izzy's not here. She's the only one who could be responsible?"

"*Responsible?*" put in Lexie. "Izzy?"

"Dad was at work," Trip said. "Lexie was at Serena's. I was over at Sussex playing ball. You?"

Moody hesitated. "I biked over to the library."

"There. You see?" To Trip, the answer was obvious. "The only ones here were Izzy and Mom. And Mom was asleep."

"Maybe the wiring in the house shorted. Or maybe someone left the stove on."

"The firemen said there were little fires everywhere," Lexie said. "Multiple points of origin. Possible use of accelerant. Not an accident."

"We all know she's always been mental." Trip leaned back against the car door.

"You're all always picking on her," Moody said. "Maybe that's why she acts *mental*."

Across the street, the fire trucks began to reel in their hoses. The three remaining Richardson children watched the firemen set down their axes and peel away their smoky yellow coats.

"Someone should go over and stay with Mom," Lexie said, but no one moved.

After a minute, Trip said, "When Mom and Dad find Iz, they are going to lock her up in a psych ward for the rest of her life."

No one thought about the recent departure of Mia and Pearl from the house on Winslow Road. Mrs. Richardson, watching the fire chief meticulously taking notes on his clipboard, had completely forgotten about her former tenants. She had not yet mentioned it to her husband or her children; Moody had discovered their absence only earlier that morning, and was still unsure what to make of it. Far down Parkland Drive the small blue dot of their father's BMW began to approach.

"What makes you so sure they'll find her?" Moody asked.

2

The previous June, when Mia and Pearl had moved into the little rental house on Winslow Road, neither Mrs. Richardson (who technically owned the house) nor Mr. Richardson (who handed over the keys) had given them much thought. They knew there was no Mr. Warren, and that Mia was thirty-six, according to the Michigan driver's license she had provided. They noticed that she wore no ring on her left hand, though she wore plenty of other rings: a big amethyst on her first finger, one made from a silver spoon handle on her pinkie, and one on her thumb that to Mrs. Richardson looked suspiciously like a mood ring. But she seemed nice enough, and so did her daughter, Pearl, a quiet fifteen-year-old with a long dark braid. Mia paid the first and last months' rent, and the deposit, in a stack of twenty-dollar bills, and the tan VW Rabbit—already battered, even then—puttered away down Parkland Drive, toward the south end of Shaker, where the houses were closer together and the yards smaller.

Winslow Road was one long line of duplexes, but standing on the curb you would not have known it. From the outside you saw only one front door, one front-door light, one mailbox, one house number. You might, perhaps, spot the two electrical meters, but those—per city ordinance—were concealed at the back of the house, along with the garage. Only if you came into the entryway would you see the two inner doors, one leading to the upstairs apartment, one to the downstairs, and their shared basement beneath. Every house on Winslow Road held two families, but outside appeared to hold only one. They had been designed that way on purpose. It allowed residents to avoid the stigma of living in a duplex house—of renting, instead of owning—and allowed the city planners to preserve the appearance of the street, as everyone knew neighborhoods with rentals were less desirable.

Shaker Heights was like that. There were rules, many rules, about what you could and could not do, as Mia and Pearl began to learn as they settled into their new home. They learned to write their new address: 18434 Winslow Road *Up*, those two little letters ensuring that their mail ended up in their apartment, and not with Mr. Yang downstairs. They learned that the little strip of grass between sidewalk and street was called a *tree lawn*— because of the young Norway maple, one per house, that graced it—and that garbage cans were not dragged there on Friday mornings but instead left at the rear of the house, to avoid the unsightly spectacle of trash cans cluttering the curb. Large motor scooters, each piloted by a man in an orange work suit, zipped down each driveway to collect the garbage in the privacy of the backyard, ferrying it to the larger truck idling out in the street, and for months Mia would remember their first Friday on Winslow Road, the fright she'd had when the scooter, like a revved-up flame-colored golf cart, shot past the kitchen window with engine roaring. They got used to it eventually, just as they got used to the detached garage—stationed well at the back of the house, again to preserve the view of the street—and learned to carry an umbrella to keep them dry as they ran from car to house on rainy days. Later, when Mr. Yang went away for two weeks in July, to visit his mother in Hong Kong, they learned that an unmowed lawn would result in a polite but stern letter from the city, noting that their grass was over six inches tall and that if the situation was not rectified, the city would mow the grass—and charge them a hundred dollars—in three days. There were many rules to be learned.

And there were many other rules that Mia and Pearl would not be aware of for a long time. The rules governing what colors a house could be painted, for example. A helpful chart from the city categorized every home as a Tudor, English, or French style and laid out the appropriate colors for architects and homeowners alike. "English-style" houses could be painted only slate blue, moss green, or a certain shade of tan, to ensure aesthetic harmony on each street; Tudor houses required a specific shade of cream on the plaster and a specific dark brown on the timbers. In Shaker Heights there was a plan for everything. When the city had been laid out in 1912—one of the first planned communities in the nation—schools had been situated so that all children could walk without crossing a major street; side streets fed into major boulevards, with strategically placed rapid-transit stops to ferry commuters into downtown

Cleveland. In fact, the city's motto was—*literally*, as Lexie would have said—"Most communities just happen; the best are planned": the underlying philosophy being that everything could—and should—be planned out, and that by doing so you could avoid the unseemly, the unpleasant, and the disastrous.

But there were other, more welcoming things to discover in those first few weeks as well. Between cleaning and repainting and unpacking, they learned the names of the streets around them: Winchell, Latimore, Lynnfield. They learned their way around the local grocery store, Heinen's, which Mia said treated you like aristocracy. Instead of wheeling your cart out to the parking lot, a cart boy in a pressed poplin shirt hung a number on it and handed you a matching red-and-white tag. Then you hooked the tag on the window of your car and drove up to the front of the store, where another cart boy would wheel your groceries out to you and pack them tidily into your trunk and refuse to accept a tip.

They learned where the cheapest gas station was—at the corner of Lomond and Lee Roads, always one cent less than anywhere else; where the drugstores were and which gave double coupons. They learned that in nearby Cleveland Heights and Warrensville and Beachwood, residents placed their discarded belongings at the curb like ordinary people, and they learned which days were garbage days on which streets. They learned where to buy a hammer, a screwdriver, a quart of new paint and a brush: all could be found at Shaker Hardware, but only between the hours of nine thirty and six P.M., when the owner sent his employees home for dinner.

And, for Pearl, there was the discovery of their land-lords, and of the Richardson children.

Moody was the first of the Richardsons to venture to the little house on Winslow. He had heard his mother describing their new tenants to his father. "She's some kind of artist," Mrs. Richardson had said, and when Mr. Richardson asked what kind, she answered jokingly, "A struggling one."

"It's all right," she reassured her husband. "She gave me a deposit right up front." "That doesn't mean she'll pay the rent," Mr. Richardson said, but they both knew it wasn't the rent that was important—only three hundred dollars a month for the upstairs—and they certainly didn't need it to get by. Mr. Richardson was a defense attorney and Mrs. Richardson worked for the local paper, the *Sun Press*. The Winslow house was theirs free and clear; Mrs. Richardson's parents had bought it as an investment property when she was a teenager. Its rent had helped put her through Denison, then had become a monthly "booster"—as her mother had put it—while she started off as a cub reporter. Then, after she'd married Bill Richardson and become Mrs. Richardson, it had helped make up the down payment on a beautiful Shaker house of their own, the same house on Parkland that she would later watch burn. When Mrs. Richardson's parents had died, five years ago and within months of each other, she had inherited the Winslow house. Her parents had been in an assisted-living home for some time by then, and the house she had grown up in had already been sold. But they had kept the Winslow house, its rent paying for their care, and now Mrs. Richardson kept it, too, as a sentimental memory.

No, it wasn't the money that mattered. The rent—all five hundred dollars of it in total—now went into the Richardsons' vacation fund each month, and last year it had paid for their trip to Martha's Vineyard, where Lexie had perfected her backstroke and Trip had bewitched all the local girls and Moody had sunburnt to a peeling crisp and Izzy, under great duress, had finally agreed to come down to the beach—fully clothed, in her Doc Martens, and glowering. But the truth was, there was plenty of money for a vacation even without it. Because they did not *need* the money from the house, it was the *kind* of tenant that mattered to Mrs. Richardson. She wanted to feel that she was doing good with it. Her parents had brought her up to do good; they had donated every year to the Humane Society and UNICEF and always attended local fund-raisers, once winning a three-foot-tall stuffed bear at the Rotary Club's silent auction. Mrs. Richardson looked at the house as a form of charity. She kept the rent low—real estate in Cleveland was cheap, but apartments in good neighborhoods like Shaker could be pricey—and she rented only to people she felt were deserving but who had, for one reason or another, not quite gotten a fair shot in life. It pleased her to make up the difference.

Mr. Yang had been the first tenant she'd taken after inheriting the house; he was an immigrant from Hong Kong who had come to the United States knowing no one and speaking only fragmentary, heavily accented

English. Over the years his accent had diminished only marginally, and when they spoke, Mrs. Richardson was sometimes reduced to nodding and smiling. But Mr. Yang was a good man, she felt; he worked very hard, driving a school bus to Laurel Academy, a nearby private girls' school, and working as a handyman. Living alone on such a meager income, he would never have been able to live in such a nice neighborhood. He would have ended up in a cramped, gray efficiency somewhere off Buckeye Road, or more likely in the gritty triangle of east Cleveland that passed for a Chinatown, where rent was suspiciously low, every other building was abandoned, and sirens wailed at least once a night. Plus, Mr. Yang kept the house in impeccable shape, repairing leaky faucets, patching the front concrete, and coaxing the stamp-sized backyard into a lush garden. Every summer he brought her Chinese melons he had grown, like a tithe, and although Mrs. Richardson had no idea what to do with them—they were jade green, wrinkled, and disconcertingly fuzzy—she appreciated his thoughtfulness anyway. Mr. Yang was exactly the kind of tenant Mrs. Richardson wanted: a kind person to whom she could do a kind turn, and who would appreciate her kindness.

With the upstairs apartment she had been less successful. The upstairs had had a new tenant every year or so: a cellist who had just been hired to teach at the Institute of Music; a divorcée in her forties; a young newlywed couple fresh out of Cleveland State. Each of them had deserved a little booster, as she'd begun to think of it. But none of them stayed long. The cellist, denied first chair in the Cleveland Orchestra, left the city in a cloud of bitterness. The divorcée remarried after a whirlwind four-month romance and moved with her new husband to a brand-new McMansion in Lakewood. And the young couple, who had seemed so sincere, so devoted, and so deeply in love, had quarreled irreparably and separated after a mere eighteen months, leaving a broken lease, some shattered vases, and three cracked spots in the wall, head-high, where those vases had shattered.

It was a lesson, Mrs. Richardson had decided. This time she would be more careful. She asked Mr. Yang to patch the plaster and took her time finding a new tenant, the right sort of tenant. 18434 Winslow Road *Up* sat empty for nearly six months until Mia Warren and her daughter came along. A single mother, well spoken, artistic, raising a daughter who was polite and fairly pretty and possibly brilliant.

"I heard Shaker schools are the best in Cleveland," Mia had said when Mrs. Richardson asked why they'd come to Shaker. "Pearl is working at the college level already. But I can't afford private school." She glanced over at Pearl, who stood quietly in the empty living room of the apartment, hands clasped in front of her, and the girl smiled shyly. Something about that look between mother and child caught Mrs. Richardson's heart in a butterfly net. She assured Mia that yes, Shaker schools were excellent—Pearl could enroll in AP classes in every subject; there were science labs, a planetarium, five languages she could learn.

"There's a wonderful theatre program, if she's interested in that," she added. "My daughter Lexie was Helena in *A Midsummer Night's Dream* last year." She quoted the Shaker schools' motto: *A community is known by the schools it keeps*. Real estate taxes in Shaker were higher than anywhere else, but residents certainly got their money's worth. "But you'll be renting, so of course you get all the benefits with none of the burden," she added with a laugh. She handed Mia an application, but she'd already decided. It gave her immense satisfaction to imagine this woman and her daughter settling into the apartment, Pearl doing her homework at the kitchen table, Mia perhaps working on a painting or a sculpture— for she had not mentioned her exact medium—in the enclosed porch overlooking the backyard.

Moody, listening to his mother describe their new tenants, was intrigued less by the artist than by the mention of the "brilliant" daughter just his age. A few days after Mia and Pearl moved in, his curiosity got the better of him. As always, he took his bike, an old fixed-gear Schwinn that had belonged to his father long ago in Indiana. Nobody biked in Shaker Heights, just as nobody took the bus: you either drove or somebody drove you; it was a town built for cars and for people who had cars. Moody biked. He wouldn't be sixteen until spring, and he never asked Lexie or Trip to drive him anywhere if he could help it.

He pushed off and followed the curve of Parkland Drive, past the duck pond, where he had never seen a duck in his life, only swarms of big, brash Canadian geese; across Van Aken Boulevard and the rapid-transit tracks to Winslow Road. He didn't come here often— none of the children had much to do with the rental house—but he knew where it was. A few times, when he was younger, he had sat in the idling car in the driveway, staring at the peach tree in the yard and skimming the radio stations while his mother ran in to drop something off or check on something. It didn't happen often; for the most part, except when his mother was looking for tenants, the house mostly ran itself. Now he realized, as his wheels bumped over the joints between the big sandstone slabs that made up the sidewalks, that he had never been inside. He wasn't sure any of the kids ever had.

In front of the house, Pearl was carefully arranging the pieces of a wooden bed on the front lawn. Moody, gliding to a stop across the street, saw a slender girl in a long, crinkly skirt and a loose T-shirt with a message he couldn't quite read. Her hair was long and curly and hung in a thick braid down her back and gave the impression of straining to burst free. She had laid the headboard down flat near the flowerbeds that bordered the house, with the side rails below it and the slats to either side in neat rows, like ribs. It was as if the bed had drawn a deep breath and then gracefully flattened itself into the grass. Moody watched, half hidden by a tree, as she picked her way around to the Rabbit, which sat in the driveway with its doors thrown wide, and extracted the footboard from the backseat. He wondered what kind of Tetris they had done to fit all the pieces of the bed into such a small car. Her feet were bare as she crossed the lawn to set the footboard into place. Then, to his bemusement, she stepped into the empty rectangle in the center, where the mattress belonged, and flopped down on her back.

On the second story of the house, a window rattled open and Mia's head peered out. "All there?"

"Two slats missing," Pearl called back.

"We'll replace them. No, wait, stay there. Don't move." Mia's head disappeared again. In a moment she reappeared holding a camera, a real camera, with a thick lens like a big tin can. Pearl stayed just as she was, staring up at the half-clouded sky, and Mia leaned out almost to the waist, angling for the right shot. Moody held his breath, afraid the camera might slip from her hands onto her daughter's trusting upturned face, that she might tumble over the sill herself and come crashing down into the grass. None of this happened. Mia's head tilted this way and that, framing the scene below in her viewfinder. The camera hid her face, hid everything but her hair, piled in a frizzy swirl atop her head like a dark halo. Later, when Moody saw the finished photos, he thought at first that Pearl looked like a delicate fossil, something caught for millennia in the skeleton belly of a prehistoric beast. Then he thought she looked like an angel resting with her wings spread out behind her. And then, after a moment, she looked simply like a girl asleep in a lush green bed, waiting for her lover to lie down beside her.

"All right," Mia called down. "Got it." She slid back inside, and Pearl sat up and looked across the street, directly at Moody, and his heart jumped.

"You want to help?" she said. "Or just stand there?"

Moody would never remember crossing the street, or propping his bike in the front walkway, or introducing himself. So it would feel to him that he had always known her name, and that she had always known his, that somehow, he and Pearl had known each other always.

Together they ferried the pieces of the bed frame up the narrow stairway. The living room was empty except for a stack of boxes in one corner and a large red cushion in the center of the floor.

"This way." Pearl tugged her armful of bed slats higher and led Moody into the larger bedroom, which held nothing except a faded but clean twin mattress leaning against one wall.

"Here," said Mia, depositing a steel toolbox at Pearl's feet. "You'll want these." She gave Moody a smile, as if he were an old friend. "Call me if you need another set of hands." Then she stepped back into the hallway, and in a moment they heard the snick of a box being slit open.

Pearl wielded the tools with expert hands, levering the side panels into place against the headboard, propping them up on one ankle while she bolted them into place. Moody sat beside the open toolbox and watched her with unfolding awe. In his house, if something broke, his mother called a repairman to fix it—the stove, the washer, the disposal—or, for almost anything else, it was discarded and replaced. Every three or four years, or when the springs began to sag, his mother picked a new living room set, the old set moved into the basement rec room, and the old-old set from the rec room was given away to the juvenile boys' home on the West Side, or to the women's shelter downtown. His father did not tinker with the car in the garage; when it rattled or squealed he brought it to the Lusty Wrench, where Luther had tended to every car the Richardsons had owned for the past twenty years. The only time he himself had handled any tools, Moody realized, was in eighth-grade shop: they'd been put in groups, one team measuring and one sawing and one sanding, and at the end of the term everyone dutifully screwed their pieces together to make a little box-shaped candy dispenser that gave you three Skittles every time you pulled the handle. Trip had made an identical one in shop the year before and Lexie had made an identical one the year before that and Izzy made yet another the following year, and despite the whole term of shop, despite the four identical candy dispensers stashed somewhere in their house, Moody was not sure that anyone in the Richardson household could do more than work a Phillips screwdriver.

"How'd you learn to do all that?" he asked, handing Pearl another bed slat.

Pearl shrugged. "From my mom," she said, pinning the slat in place with one hand and plucking a screw from the pile on the carpet.

The bed, when assembled, proved to be an old-fashioned twin with bed knobs, the kind Goldilocks might have slept in.

"Where'd you get it?" Moody set the mattress in place and gave it an experimental bounce.

Pearl replaced the screwdriver in the toolbox and latched it shut. "We found it."

She sat down on the bed, back propped against the footboard, legs stretched along the bed's length, gazing up at the ceiling, as if testing it out. Moody sat down at the head of the bed, near her feet. Wisps of grass stuck to her toes and her calves and the hem of her skirt. She smelled like fresh air and mint shampoo.

"This is *my room*," Pearl said suddenly, and Moody sprang up again. "Sorry," he said, a hot flush rising to his cheeks.

Pearl glanced up, as if for a moment she'd forgotten he was there. "Oh," she said. "That's not what I meant." She picked a sliver of grass from between her toes and flicked it away and they watched it settle on the carpet. When she began again, her tone was one of wonder. "I've never had my own room before."

Moody turned her words over in his mind. "You mean you always had to share?" He tried to imagine a world where this was possible. He tried to imagine sharing a room with Trip, who littered the floor with dirty socks and sports magazines, whose first action when he came home was to snap the radio on—always to "Jammin" 92.3—as if without that inane bass thumping, his heart might not beat. On vacation, the Richardsons always booked three rooms: one for Mr. and Mrs. Richardson, one for Lexie and Izzy, one for Trip and Moody—and at breakfast Trip would make fun of Moody for sometimes talking in his sleep. For Pearl and her mother to have had to share a room—Moody almost could not believe that people could be so poor.

Pearl shook her head. "We've never had a house of our own before," she said, and Moody stifled the urge to tell her that this wasn't a house, it was only half a house. She traced the dips of the mattress with her fingertip, circling the buttons in each dimple.

Watching her, Moody could not see all that she was remembering: the finicky stove in Urbana, which they'd had to light with a match; the fifth-floor walk-up in Middlebury and the weed-choked garden in Ocala and the smoky apartment in Muncie, where the previous tenant had let his pet rabbit roam the living room, leaving gnawed-in holes and several questionable stains. And the sublet in Ann Arbor, years ago now, that she'd most hated to leave, because the people who'd lived there had had a daughter just a year or two older than she was, and every day of the six months she and her mother had lived there she had played with that lucky girl's collection of horse figurines and sat in her child-sized armchair and lain in her white-frosted canopy bed to sleep, and sometimes, in the middle of the night when her mother was asleep, she would turn on the bedside light and open that girl's closet and try on her dresses and her shoes, even though they were all a little too big. There had been photos of that girl everywhere in the house—on the mantel, on the end tables in the living room, in the stairwell a big, beautiful studio portrait of her with chin in hand—and it had been so easy for Pearl to pretend that this was her house and that these were her things, her room, her life. When the couple and their daughter had returned from their sabbatical, Pearl had not even been able to look at the girl, tanned and wiry and too tall now for those dresses in the closet. She had cried all the way to Lafayette, where they would stay for the next eight months, and even the prancing china palomino she had stolen from the girl's collection gave her no comfort, for though she waited nervously, there was never any complaint about the loss, and what could be less satisfying than stealing from someone so endowed that they never even noticed what you'd taken? Her mother must have understood, for they didn't sublet again. Pearl hadn't complained either, knowing now that she preferred an empty apartment to one filled with someone else's things.

"We move around a lot. Whenever my mom gets the bug." She looked at him fiercely, almost a glare, and Moody saw that her eyes, which he'd thought were hazel, were a deep jade green. At that moment Moody had a sudden clear understanding of what had already happened that morning: his life had been divided into a before and an after, and he would always be comparing the two.

"What are you doing tomorrow?" he asked.

3

The next few weeks became a series of tomorrows for Moody. They went to Fernway, his old elementary school, where they clambered up the slide and shimmied up the pole and tumbled from the catwalk to the wood chips below. He took Pearl to Draeger's for hot fudge sundaes. At Horseshoe Lake, they climbed trees like children, throwing stale chunks of bread to the ducks bobbing below. In Yours Truly, the local diner, they sat in a high-backed wooden booth and ate fries smothered in cheese and bacon and fed quarters into the jukebox to play "Great Balls of Fire" and "Hey Jude."

"Take me to see the Shakers," Pearl suggested one day, and Moody laughed.

"There aren't any Shakers in Shaker Heights," he said. "They all died out. Didn't believe in sex. They just named the town after them."

Moody was half right, though neither he nor most of the kids in the town knew much about its history. The Shakers had indeed left the land that would become Shaker Heights long before, and by the summer of 1997 there were exactly twelve left in the world. But Shaker Heights had been founded, if not on Shaker principles, with the same idea of creating a utopia. Order—and regulation, the father of order—had been the Shakers' key to harmony. They had regulated everything: the proper time for rising in the morning, the proper color of window curtains, the proper length of a man's hair, the proper way to fold one's hands in prayer (right thumb over left). If they planned every detail, the Shakers had believed, they could create a patch of heaven on earth, a little refuge from the world, and the founders of Shaker Heights had thought the same. In advertisements they depicted Shaker Heights in the clouds, looking down upon the grimy city of Cleveland from a mountaintop at the end of a rainbow's arch. Perfection: that was the goal, and perhaps the Shakers had lived it so strongly it had seeped into the soil itself, feeding those who grew up there with a propensity to overachieve and a deep intolerance for flaws. Even the teens of Shaker Heights—whose main exposure to Shakers was singing "Simple Gifts" in music class—could feel that drive for perfection still in the air.

As Pearl learned more about her new hometown, Moody began to learn more about Mia's art, and the intricacies and vagaries of the Warren family finances.

Moody had never thought much about money, because he had never needed to. Lights went on when he flipped switches; water came out when he turned the tap. Groceries appeared in the refrigerator at regular intervals and reappeared as cooked meals on the table at mealtimes. He had had an allowance since he was ten, starting at five dollars per week and increasing steadily with inflation and age up to its current twenty dollars. Between that and birthday cards from aunts and relatives, each reliably containing a folded bill, he had enough for a used book from Mac's Backs, or the occasional CD, or new guitar strings, whatever he felt he needed.

Mia and Pearl got as much as they could used—or better yet, free. In just a few weeks, they'd learned the location of every Salvation Army store, St. Vincent de Paul's, and Goodwill in the greater Cleveland area. The week they'd arrived, Mia had gotten a job at Lucky Palace, a local Chinese restaurant; several afternoons and evenings a week, she took and packaged up takeout orders at the counter. They soon learned that for dining out, everyone in Shaker seemed to prefer Pearl of the Orient, just a few blocks away, but Lucky Palace did a good takeout business. In addition to Mia's hourly pay, the servers gave her a share of their tips, and when there was extra food, she took a few containers home— slightly stale rice, leftover sweet-and-sour pork, vegetables just past their prime—which sustained her and Pearl for most of the week. They had very little, but that wasn't immediately obvious: Mia was good at repurposing. Lo mein, without its sauce, was topped with Ragú from a jar one night, reheated and topped with orange beef another. Old bedsheets, purchased for a quarter each at the thrift store, turned into curtains, a tablecloth, pillow covers. Moody thought of math class: a practical application of combinatorics. How many different ways could you combine mu shu pancakes and fillings? How many different combinations could you make with rice, pork, and peppers?

"Why doesn't your mom get a real job?" Moody

asked Pearl one afternoon. "I bet she could get more hours a week. Or maybe even a full-time spot at Pearl of the Orient, or some other place." He had wondered this all week, ever since he'd learned about Mia's job. If she took on more hours, he reasoned, she would make enough for them to have a real sofa, real meals, perhaps a TV.

Pearl stared, brow furrowed, as if she simply did not understand the question.

"But she *has* a job," she said. "She's an artist."

They had lived this way for years, with Mia taking a part-time job that earned just enough for them to get by. For as long as she could remember, Pearl had understood the hierarchy: her mother's real work was her art, and whatever paid the bills existed only to make that art possible. Her mother spent several hours every day working—though at first Moody had not realized this was what she was doing. Sometimes she was downstairs in the makeshift darkroom she'd rigged up in the basement laundry room, developing rolls of film or making prints. Sometimes she seemed to spend all her time reading—things that weren't obviously relevant to Moody, like cooking magazines from the 1960s, or car manuals, or an immense hardcover biography of Eleanor Roosevelt from the library—or even staring out the living room window at the tree just outside it. One morning when he arrived, Mia was toying with a loop of string, playing cat's cradle, and when they returned she was still at it, weaving ever more complicated nets between her fingers and then suddenly unraveling them back into a single loop and beginning again. "Part of the process," Pearl informed him as they cut through the living room, with the nonchalant air of a native unfazed by the curious customs of the land.

Sometimes Mia went out with her camera, but more often she might spend days, or even weeks, preparing something to photograph, with the actual taking of the photographs lasting only a few hours. For Mia, Moody learned, did not consider herself a photographer. Photography, at its heart, was about documentation, and he soon understood that for Mia photography was simply a tool, which she used as a painter might use a brush or a knife.

A plain photograph might be doctored later: with embroidered carnival masks obscuring the faces of the people within, or the figures themselves might be clipped out, paper-doll style, and dressed in clothes cut from fashion magazines. In one set of photos, Mia rinsed the negatives before making prints that were oddly distorted—a photo of a clean kitchen speckled with spots from lemonade; a photo of laundry on the clothesline rendered ghostlike and warped by bleach. In another set, she carefully double-exposed each frame—layering a far-off skyscraper over the middle finger of her hand; superimposing a dead bird, wings akimbo on the pavement, over a blue sky, so that except for the closed eyes, it looked as if it were flying.

She worked unconventionally, keeping only photos she liked and tossing the rest. When the idea was exhausted, she kept a single print of each shot and destroyed the negatives. "I'm not interested in syndication," she said to Moody rather airily, when he asked why she didn't make multiples. She seldom photographed people—occasionally, she would take a picture of Pearl, as with the bed on the lawn, but she never used them in her work. She never used herself either: once, Pearl told Moody, she had done a series of self-portraits, wearing different objects as masks—a piece of black lace, five-fingered horse-chestnut leaves, a damp and pliant starfish—had spent a month on these photos, narrowing them down to a set of eight. They'd been beautiful and eerie, and even now Pearl could see them exactly: her mother's bright eye like a pearl peeking out between the legs of the starfish. But at the last moment Mia had burned the prints and negatives, for reasons even Pearl could not fathom. "You spent all that time," she'd said, "and just *pfft*"—she snapped her fingers—"like that?"

"They weren't working" was all Mia would say.

But the pictures she did keep, and sold, were startling.

In their luxurious sublet in Ann Arbor, Mia had taken various pieces of her hosts' furniture apart and arranged the components—bolts as thick as her finger, unvarnished crossbeams, disembodied feet—into animals. A bulky secretary desk from the nineteenth century transformed into a bull, the sides of the disassembled drawers forming muscled legs, the cast-iron knobs of its drawer pulls serving as the bull's nose and eyes and glinting balls, a handful of pens from inside the desk fanned out into the crescents of horns. With Pearl's help, she had laid the pieces out on the cream-colored Persian carpet, which as a backdrop looked like a field fogged with steam, and then she had climbed on top of a table to photograph it from above before they picked it back apart and reassembled it into a desk. An old Chinese birdcage, broken down into a web of arched wires, had become an eagle, its brassy skeletal wings spread as if about to take flight. An overstuffed sofa had become an elephant, trunk raised in trumpet song. The series of photos that emerged from this project were both intriguing and unsettling, the animals incredibly intricate and lifelike, and then you looked closer and realized what they had been made of. She had sold quite a few of these, through her friend Anita, a gallery owner in New York—a person Pearl had never met in a place she'd never been. Mia hated New York, would never go even to promote her own work. "Anita," Mia had said into the phone once, "I love you dearly but I cannot come to New York for a show. No, not even if it meant I'd sell a hundred pieces." A pause. "I know it does, but you know I can't. All right. You do what you can, and that's good enough for me." Still, Anita had managed to sell a half dozen of the series, which meant instead of cleaning houses Mia had been able to spend the next six months working on a new project.

That was how her mother worked: one project for four or six months, then on to the next. She'd work and work and come up with a group of photos and Anita would usually be able to sell at least a few of them in her gallery. At first the prices had been so modest—a few hundred dollars per piece—that Mia sometimes had to take on two jobs, or even three. But as time went on, her work became regarded well enough in the art world that Anita could sell more pieces, for more money: enough to pay for what Mia and Pearl needed—food, rent, gas for the Rabbit—even after Anita's fifty-percent cut. "Two or three thousand dollars, sometimes," Pearl told him with pride, and Moody did quick mental math: if Mia sold ten pictures a year . . .

Sometimes the photos did not sell—a project Mia did with skeletal leaves sold only one, and for several months she took up a series of odd jobs: housecleaning, flower arranging, cake decorating. She was good at anything that involved her hands, and she preferred the jobs where she did not have to work with customers, where she could be alone and thinking, to waitressing, secretary-ing, salesclerking. "I was a salesgirl once, before you were born," she told Pearl. "I lasted one day. One. The manager kept telling me how to put the dresses on hang-ers. Customers would pull the beads off clothes and de-mand discounts. I'd rather mop a floor, alone in the house, than deal with that."

But other projects did sell, and got attention. One series—which Mia began after she'd been doing some seamstress work—supported them for nearly a year. She would go to thrift stores and buy old stuffed animals—faded teddy bears, ratty plush dogs, threadbare rabbits—the cheaper the better. At home, she took them apart at the seams, washed their pelts, fluffed their filling, repol-ished their eyes. Then she stitched them back together, inside out, and the results were eerily beautiful. The ragged fur, in reverse, took on the look of shorn velvet. The whole animal, resewn and restuffed, had the same shape but a different bearing, the backs and necks straighter, the ears perkier; the eyes shone now with a knowing glint. It was as if the animal had been reincarnated, older and bolder and wiser. Pearl had loved watching her mother at work, bent over the kitchen table, laboring with the precision of a surgeon—scalpel, needle, pins—to transform these toys into art. Anita had sold every photo in this series; one had even, she reported, made its way to MoMA. She'd begged Mia to take another round, or to reprint the series, but Mia had refused. "The idea is done," she said. "I'm working on something else now." And she always was, always something a bit different, always something that had struck her fancy. She would be famous someday, Pearl was certain; someday her adored mother would be one of those artists, like de Kooning or Warhol or O'Keeffe, whose name everyone knew. It was why part of her, at least, didn't mind the life they'd always lived, their thrift-store clothes, their salvaged beds and chairs, the shifting precariousness of it all. One day everyone would see her mother's brilliance.

To Moody, this kind of existence was all but unfathomable. Watching the Warrens live was like watching a magic trick, as miraculous as transforming an empty soda can into a silver pitcher, or pulling a steaming pie from a silk top hat. No, he thought: it was like watching Robinson Crusoe conjure up a living out of nothingness. The more time he spent with Mia and Pearl, the more fascinated he became with them.

Through his afternoons with Pearl, Moody slowly learned some of what their life on the road was like. They traveled lightly: two plates and two cups and a handful of mismatched silverware; a duffel of clothes each; and, of course, Mia's cameras. In the summer, they drove with the windows down, for the Rabbit had no air-conditioning; in the winter, they drove by night, the heat cranked up, and in the daytime would park in a sunny spot, sleeping in the snug greenhouse of the car before starting again as the sun set. At night, Mia pushed the bags into the footwells and laid a folded army blanket across them and the backseat, forming a bed that could just hold them both. For privacy, they draped a sheet from the hatchback over the headrests of the front seats to make a little tent. At mealtimes they stopped by the side of the road, feeding themselves from the paper bag of groceries behind the driver's seat: bread and peanut butter, fruit, sometimes salami or a stick of pepperoni, if Mia found it on sale. Sometimes they drove for just a few days, sometimes for a week, until Mia found a spot that felt right, and they would stop.

They would find an apartment for rent: usually a studio, sometimes an efficiency, whatever they could afford and wherever they could go month to month, for Mia did not like to be tied down. They would set up their new apartment as they had in Shaker, with castoffs and thrift-store finds made fresh, or at least tolerable; Mia would enroll Pearl in the local school and find work enough to support them. And then Mia would begin her next project, working, worrying the idea like a bone, for three months or four or six months, until she had a set of photographs to dispatch to Anita in New York City.

She would set up a darkroom in the bathroom, after Pearl had fallen asleep. After the first few moves, she'd gotten it down to a science: trays for washing prints in the bathtub, a clothesline for drying strung from the shower rod, a rolled-up towel across the bottom of the door to block out any extra light. When she was finished, she stacked her trays, folded her enlarger into its case, hid her jugs of chemicals under the sink, and scrubbed the bathtub so that it was sparkling for Pearl's shower the next morning. She would crack the bathroom window and go to bed, and by the time Pearl woke, the sour smell of developer would be gone. Once Mia mailed her photographs, Pearl always knew, they would pack up the car again and the entire process would repeat. One town, one project, and then it was time to move on.

This time, though, was to be different. "We're staying put," Pearl told him, and Moody felt suddenly, giddily buoyant, like an overfilled balloon. "My mom promised. This time we're staying for good."

Their itinerant, artistic lifestyle appealed to him: Moody was a romantic at heart. He made the honor roll every semester, but unburdened by practicalities, he had daydreams about leaving school, traveling the country à la Jack Kerouac—only writing songs instead of poems. Mac's Backs supplied him with well-worn copies of *On the Road* and *Dharma Bums*, the poems of Frank O'Hara and Rainer Maria Rilke and Pablo Neruda, and to his delight he found in Pearl another poetic soul. She hadn't read as much as he had, of course, because they had moved so often, but she had spent most of her childhood in libraries, taking refuge among the shelves as a new girl bouncing from school to school, absorbing books as if they were air—and, in fact, she told him shyly, she wanted to be a poet. She copied her favorite poems into a beat-up spiral notebook that she kept with her at all times. "So they'll always be with me," she said, and when she finally allowed Moody to read some of them, he was speechless. He wanted to twine himself in the tiny curlicues of her handwriting. "Beautiful," he sighed, and Pearl's face lit up like a lantern, and the next day Moody brought his guitar, taught her to play three chords, and bashfully sang one of his songs for her, which he'd never sung for anyone else.

Pearl, he soon discovered, had a fantastic memory. She could remember passages after reading them through just once, could recall the dates of the Magna Carta and the names of the kings of England and every one of the presidents in order. Moody's grades came from meticulous studying and plenty of flash cards, but everything seemed to come easily to Pearl: she could glance at a math problem and intuit the answer while Moody dutifully worked line after line of algebra down the page; she could read an essay and put her finger, at once, on the most salient point or the biggest logical flaw. It was as if she had glanced at a pile of jigsaw puzzle pieces and saw the whole picture without even consulting the box. Pearl's mind, it became clear, was an extraordinary thing, and Moody could not help but admire how fast her brain worked, how effortlessly. It was a pure pleasure, watching her click everything into place.

The more time they spent together, the more Moody began to feel he was in two places at once. At any given moment—every moment he could arrange, in fact—he was there with Pearl, in the booth at the diner, in the fork of a tree, watching her big eyes drink in everything around them as if she were ferociously thirsty. He would crack dumb jokes and tell stories and dredge up bits of trivia, anything to make her smile. And at the same time, in his mind, he was roaming the city, searching desperately for the next place he could take her, the next wonder of suburban Cleveland he could display, because when he ran out of places to show her, he was sure, she would disappear. Already he thought he saw her growing silent over their fries, prodding the last congealed lump of cheese on the plate; already he was sure her eyes were drifting across the lake to the far shore.

This was how Moody made a decision he would question for the rest of his life. Until now he had said nothing about Pearl or her mother to his family, guarding their friendship like a dragon guards treasure: silently, greedily. Deep down he had the feeling that somehow it would change everything, the way in fairy tales magic was spoiled if you shared the secret. If he had kept her to himself, perhaps the future might have been quite different. Pearl might never have met his mother or his father, or Lexie or Trip or Izzy, or if she had, they might have been people she only greeted but didn't know. She and her mother might have stayed in Shaker forever, as they'd planned; eleven months later, the Richardson house might still have been standing. But Moody did not think of himself as interesting enough to hold her attention in his own right. Had he been a different Richardson, it might have been different; his brother and sisters never worried whether other people would like them. Lexie had her golden smile and her easy laugh,

Trip had his looks and his dimples: why wouldn't people like them, why would they ever even ask such a thing? For Izzy, it was even simpler: she didn't care what people thought of her. But Moody did not possess Lexie's warmth, Trip's roguish charm, Izzy's self-confidence. All he had to offer her, he felt, was what his family had to offer, his family itself, and it was this that led him to say, one afternoon in late July, "Come over. You can meet my family."

When Pearl entered the Richardsons' house for the first time, she paused with one foot on the threshold. It was just a house, she told herself. Moody lived here. But even that thought struck her as slightly surreal. From the sidewalk, Moody had nodded at it almost bashfully. "That's it," he'd said, and she had said, "You live *here*?" It wasn't the size—true, it was large, but so was every house on the street, and in just three weeks in Shaker she'd seen even larger. No: it was the greenness of the lawn, the sharp lines of white mortar between the bricks, the rustle of the maple leaves in the gentle breeze, the very breeze itself. It was the soft smells of detergent and cooking and grass that mingled in the entryway, the one corner of the throw rug that flipped up like a cowlick, as if someone had mussed it and forgotten to smooth it out. It was as if instead of entering a house she was entering the *idea* of a house, some archetype brought to life here before her. Something she'd only heard about but never seen. She could hear signs of life in far-off rooms—the low mumble of a TV commercial, the beep of a microwave running down its count—but distantly, as if in a dream.

"Come on in," Moody said, and she stepped inside.

Later it would seem to Pearl that the Richardsons must have arranged themselves into a tableau for her enjoyment, for surely they could not always exist in this state of domestic perfection. There was Mrs. Richardson in the kitchen making cookies, of all things—something her own mother never did, though if Pearl begged hard she would sometimes buy a log of shrink-wrapped dough for them to slice into rounds. There was Mr. Richardson, a miniature out on the wide green lawn, deftly shaking charcoal into a shining silver grill. There was Trip, lounging on the long wraparound sectional, impossibly handsome, one arm slung along the back as if waiting for some lucky girl to come and sit beside him. And there was Lexie, across from him in a pool of sunlight, turning her luminous eyes from the television toward Pearl as she came into the room, saying, "Well now, and who do we have here?"

4

The only member of the Richardson family that Pearl did not see much of in those giddy early days was Izzy—but at first she didn't notice. How could she, when the other Richardsons greeted her with their long, enveloping arms? They dazzled her, these Richardsons: with their easy confidence, their clear sense of purpose, no matter the time of day. At Moody's invitation, she spent hours at their house, coming over just after breakfast, staying until dinner.

Mornings, Mrs. Richardson sailed into the kitchen in high-heeled pumps, car keys and stainless-steel travel mug in hand, saying, "Pearl, so nice to see you again." Then she click-clacked down the back hall, and in a moment the garage door rumbled open and her Lexus glided down the wide driveway, a golden pocket of coolness in the hot summer air. Mr. Richardson, in his jacket and tie, had left long before, but he loomed in the background, solid and impressive and important, like a mountain range on the horizon. When Pearl asked what his parents did all day, Moody had shrugged. "You know. They go to work." *Work!* When her mother said it, it reeked of drudgery: waiting tables, washing dishes, cleaning floors. But for the Richardsons, it seemed noble: they did important things. Every Thursday the paperboy deposited a copy of the *Sun Press* on Mia and Pearl's doorstep—it was free to all residents—and when they unfolded it they saw Mrs. Richardson's name on the front page under the headlines: CITY DEBATES NEW TAX LEVY; RESIDENTS REACT TO PRESIDENT CLINTON'S BUDGET; "VERY SQUARE AFFAIR" PREPARATIONS UNDERWAY IN SHAKER SQUARE. Tangible, black-and-white proof of her industriousness.

("It's not really a big deal," Moody said. "The *Plain Dealer* is the real paper. The *Sun Press* is just local stuff: city council meetings and zoning boards and who won the science fair." But Pearl, eyeing the printed byline—*Elena Richardson*—did not believe or care.)

They knew important people, the Richardsons: the mayor, the director of the Cleveland Clinic, the owner of the Indians. They had season tickets at Jacobs Field and the Gund. ("The Cavs suck," Moody put it succinctly. "Indians might win the pennant, though," countered Trip.) Sometimes Mr. Richardson's cell phone—a cell phone!—would ring and he would extend the antenna as he stepped out into the hallway. "Bill Richardson," he would answer, the simple statement of his name greeting enough.

Even the younger Richardsons had it, this sureness in themselves. Sunday mornings Pearl and Moody would be sitting in the kitchen when Trip drifted in from a run, lounging against the island to pour a glass of juice, tall and tan and lean in gym shorts, utterly at ease, his sudden grin throwing her into disarray. Lexie perched at the counter, inelegant in sweatpants and a tee, hair clipped in an untidy bun, picking sesame seeds off a bagel. They did not care if Pearl saw them this way. They were so artlessly beautiful, even right out of bed. Where did this ease come from? How could they be so at home, so sure of themselves, even in pajamas? When Lexie ordered from a menu, she never said, "Could I have . . . ?" She said, "I'll have . . ." confidently, as if she had only to say it to make it so. It unsettled Pearl and it fascinated her. Lexie would slide down off her stool and walk across the kitchen with the elegance of a dancer, barefoot on the Italian tiles. Trip swigged the last of his orange juice and headed for the stairs and the shower, and Pearl watched him, her nostrils quivering as she breathed in the scent of his wake: sweat and sun and heat.

At the Richardson house were overstuffed sofas so deep you could sink into them as if into a bubble bath. Credenzas. Heavy sleigh beds. Once you owned an enormous chair like this, Pearl thought, you would simply have to stay put. You would have to plant roots and make the place that held this chair your home. There were ottomans and framed photographs and curio cabinets full of souvenirs, their very frivolousness reassuring. You did not bring home a carved seashell from Key West or a miniature of the CN Tower or a finger-sized bottle of sand from Martha's Vineyard unless you intended to stay. Mrs. Richardson's family, in fact, had lived in Shaker for three generations now—almost, Pearl learned, since the city had been founded. To have such a deep taproot in a single place, to be immersed in it so thoroughly that it had steeped into every fiber of your being: she couldn't imagine it.

Mrs. Richardson herself was another source of fascination. If she had been on a television screen, she would have felt as unreal as a Mrs. Brady or a Mrs. Keaton. But there she was right in front of Pearl, always saying kind things. "What a pretty skirt, Pearl," she would say. "That color suits you. All honors classes? How smart you are. Your hair looks so nice today. Oh, don't be silly, call me Elena, I insist"—and then, when Pearl continued to call her Mrs. Richardson, she was secretly proud of Pearl's respectfulness, Pearl was sure of it. Mrs. Richardson was quick to hug her—her, Pearl, a virtual stranger—simply because she was one of Moody's friends. Mia was affectionate but never effusive; Pearl had never seen her mother embrace anyone other than her. And yet there was Mrs. Richardson coming home for dinner, pecking each of her children atop the head and not even pausing when she got to Pearl, dropping a kiss onto her hair without a moment of hesitation. As if she were just one more chick in the brood.

Mia could not help but notice her daughter's infatuation with the Richardsons. Some days Pearl spent the entire day at the Richardson house. She had been pleased at first, watching Moody and her lonely daughter, who had been uprooted so many times, who had never really been close to anyone. For so long, she could see now, she had made her daughter live by her whim: moving on anytime she needed new ideas; anytime she had felt stuck or uneasy. *That's over now*, Mia had promised her as they drove toward Shaker. *From now on, we are staying put.* She could see the similarities between these two lonely children, even more clearly than they could: the same sensitive personalities lurking inside both of them, the same bookish wisdom layered over a deep naïveté. Moody would come by early each morning, before Pearl had even finished breakfast, and on waking Mia would draw the curtains to see Moody's bike sprawled on the front lawn, and come into the kitchen to find him and Pearl at the table, dregs of raisin bran in the mismatched bowls before them. They would be gone all day, Moody pushing his bike by the handlebars alongside them. Mia, rinsing the bowls in the sink, made a mental note to look for a bike for Pearl. Perhaps the bike shop on Lee Road had a used one.

But as the weeks went on, it worried Mia a little, the influence the Richardsons seemed to have over Pearl, the way they seemed to have absorbed her into their lives—or vice versa. At dinner Pearl talked about the Richardsons as if they were a TV show she was fanatical about. "Mrs. Richardson's going to interview Janet Reno when she comes to town next week," she might say one day. Or, "Lexie says her boyfriend, Brian, is going to be the first black president." Or—with a faint blush— "Trip's going to be starting forward on the soccer team in the fall. He just found out." Mia nodded and mm-hmmed, and wondered every evening if this was wise, if it was right for her daughter to fall under the spell of a family so entirely. Then she thought about the previous spring, when Pearl had gotten a cough so bad Mia had finally taken her to the hospital, where they learned it had turned into pneumonia. Sitting by her daughter's bedside in the dark, watching her sleep, waiting for the antibiotics the doctor had given her to take effect, Mia had allowed herself to imagine: if the worst had happened, what kind of life would Pearl have lived? Nomadic, isolated. Lonely. *That's done with,* she had told herself, and when Pearl had recovered they'd ended up in Shaker Heights, where Mia had promised they would stay. So she said nothing, and the next day another afternoon would pass with Pearl over at the Richardsons' again, becoming more bewitched.

Pearl had started at new schools often enough, sometimes two or three times a year, to have lost her fear about it, but this time she was deeply apprehensive. To start a school knowing you'd be leaving was one thing; you didn't need to worry what other people thought of you, because soon you'd be gone. She had drifted through every grade like that, never bothering to get to know anyone. To start a school knowing you'd see these people all year, and next year, and the year after that, was quite different.

But as it turned out, she and Moody shared nearly all their classes, from biology to Honors English to health. The first two weeks of school, he guided her through the hallways with the confidence only a sophomore could have, telling her which water fountains were the coldest, where to sit in the cafeteria, which teachers would give you a tardy slip if they caught you in the halls after the late bell, and which would wave you on with an indulgent smile. She began to navigate the school with the help of the murals, painted by students over the years: the exploding Hindenburg marked the science wing; Jim Morrison brooded by the auditorium balcony; a girl blowing pink bubbles led the way to the mysteriously named Egress, a cavernous hallway that doubled as overflow lunchtime seating. A trompe l'oeil row of lockers marked the hallway down to the Social Room, a lounge designated for the seniors, where there was a microwave for making popcorn during free periods, and a Coke machine that cost only fifty cents instead of seventy-five like the ones in the cafeteria, and a chunky black cube of a jukebox left over from the seventies and now loaded with Sir Mix-a-Lot and Smashing Pumpkins and the Spice Girls. The year before, one student had painted himself and three friends, peeking down Kilroy-style, in the domed ceiling near the main entrance; one of them was winking, and every time Pearl passed beneath the dome she felt they were welcoming her in.

After school she went to the Richardsons' house and sprawled on the sectional in the family room with the older children and watched Jerry Springer. It was a little ritual the Richardson kids had developed over the past few years, one of the few times they agreed on anything. It had never been planned and it was never discussed, but every afternoon, if Trip didn't have practice and Lexie didn't have a meeting, they gathered in the family room and turned to Channel 3. To Moody, it was a fascinating psychological study, every episode another example of just how strange humanity could be. To Lexie, it was akin to anthropology, the stripper moms and polygamous wives and drug-dealing kids a window into a world so far from hers it was like something out of Margaret Mead. And to Trip, the whole thing was pure comedy: a glorious slapstick spectacle, complete with bleeped-out tirades and plenty of chair throwing. His favorite moments were when guests' wigs were pulled off. Izzy found the whole thing unspeakably idiotic and barricaded herself upstairs, practicing her violin. "The only thing Izzy actually takes seriously," Lexie explained. "No," Trip countered, "Izzy takes everything too seriously. That's her problem."

"The ironic thing," Lexie said one afternoon, "is that in ten years we're going to see Izzy on *Springer*."

"Seven," Trip said. "Eight at most. 'Jerry, Get Me Out of Jail!'"

"Or 'My Family Wants to Commit Me,'" Lexie agreed.

Moody shifted uncomfortably in his seat. Lexie and Trip treated Izzy as if she were a dog that might go rabid at any minute, but the two of them had always gotten along. "She's just a little impulsive, that's all," he said to Pearl.

"A little impulsive?" Lexie laughed. "You don't really know her yet, Pearl. You'll see." And the stories began to pour out, Jerry Springer temporarily forgotten.

Izzy, at ten, had been apprehended sneaking into the Humane Society in an attempt to free all the stray cats. "They're like prisoners on death row," she'd said. At eleven, her mother—convinced that Izzy was overly clumsy—had enrolled her in dance classes to improve her coordination. Her father insisted she try it for one term before she could quit. Every class, Izzy sat down on the floor and refused to move. For the recital—with the aid of a mirror and a Sharpie—Izzy had written NOT YOUR PUPPET across her forehead and cheeks just before taking the stage, where she stood stock-still while the others, disconcerted, danced around her.

"I thought Mom was going to die of embarrassment," Lexie said. "And then last year? Mom thought she wore too much black and bought her all these cute dresses. And Izzy just rolled them up in a grocery bag and took the bus downtown and gave them to some person on the street. Mom grounded her for a month."

"She's not crazy," Moody protested. "She just doesn't think."

Lexie snorted, and Trip hit unmute on the remote, and Jerry Springer roared to life again.

The sectional seated eight, but even with only three Richardson children, there was always a fair amount of jockeying to get the spots with the best view. Now, with the addition of Pearl, there were even more complicated maneuverings. Whenever she could manage it, Pearl would drop—unobtrusively, nonchalantly, she hoped—into the seat next to Trip. All her life, her crushes had been from afar; she'd never had the courage to speak to any of the boys who caught her fancy. But now that they'd settled in Shaker Heights for good, now that Trip was here, in this house, sitting on the very same couch—well, it was perfectly natural, she told herself, that she might sit next to him now and then; no one could read into that, surely, least of all Trip. Moody, meanwhile, felt he deserved the seat beside Pearl: he was the one who had introduced her to the fold, and of all the Richardsons he felt his claim—as the one who'd known her longest—was paramount. The end result was that Pearl would settle beside Trip, Moody would plop down beside her, sandwiching her between them, Lexie would stretch out on the corner, smirking at the three of them, and turn on the television, and all four of them turned their attention to the screen while remaining keenly aware of everything happening in the room.

The Richardson children, Pearl soon learned, had their most heated discussions about Jerry Springer. "Thank god we live in Shaker," Lexie said one day during a provocative episode entitled "Stop Bringing White Girls Home to Dinner!" "I mean, we're lucky. No one sees race here."

"Everyone sees race, Lex," said Moody. "The only difference is who pretends not to."

"Look at me and Brian," said Lexie. "We've been together since junior year and no one gives a crap that I'm white and he's black."

"You don't think his parents would rather he was dating somebody black?" said Moody.

"I honestly don't think they care." Lexie popped the tab on another Diet Coke. "Skin color doesn't say anything about who you are."

"Shhh," said Trip. "It's back."

It was during one of those afternoons—during "I'm Having Your Husband's Baby!"—that Lexie suddenly turned to Pearl and asked, "Do you ever think about trying to find your father?" Pearl gave her a calculated blank stare, but Lexie continued anyway. "I mean, like where he is. Don't you ever want to meet him?"

Pearl turned her eyes to the TV screen, where burly security guards were wrestling an orange-haired woman built like a BarcaLounger back into her seat. "I'd have to start by finding out *who* he is," she said. "And, I mean, look at how well *this* is going. Why wouldn't I want to?"

Sarcasm didn't come naturally to her, and even to herself she sounded more plaintive than ironic.

"He could be anybody," Lexie mused. "An old boyfriend. Maybe he split when your mom got pregnant. Or maybe he got killed in an accident before you were born." She tapped one finger on her lip, brainstorming possibilities. "He could have left her for another woman. Or—" She sat up, titillated. "Maybe he *raped* her. And she got pregnant and kept the baby."

"Lexie," Trip said suddenly. He slid across the sofa and slung an arm over Pearl's shoulders. "Shut the fuck up." For Trip to pay attention to a conversation that wasn't about sports, let alone tune in on someone else's feelings, was nothing short of unusual, and they all knew it.

Lexie rolled her eyes. "I was just *kidding*," she said. "Pearl knows that. Don't you, Pearl?"

"Sure," Pearl said. She forced herself to smile. "Duh." She felt a sudden rush of dampness beneath her arms, her heart pounding, and she wasn't sure if it was Trip's arm around her shoulders, or Lexie's comments, or both. Above them, somewhere overhead, Izzy practiced Lalo on her violin. On the screen, the two women leapt from their seats again and began to claw at each other's hair.

But Lexie's comment rankled. It was nothing Pearl hadn't thought about herself over the years, but hearing it spoken aloud, from someone else's mouth, made it feel more urgent. She had wondered these things, now and again, but when she'd asked as a child, her mother had given her flippant answers. "Oh, I found you in the bargain bin at the Goodwill," Mia had said once. Another time: "I picked you from a cabbage patch. Didn't you know?" As a teen, she'd finally stopped asking. This afternoon, the question still churning in her mind, she got home and found her mother in the living room, applying paint to a photograph of a stripped-down bicycle.

"Mom," she began, then found she could not repeat Lexie's blunt words. Instead she asked the question that ran below all the other questions like a deep underground river. "Was I wanted?"

"Wanted where?" With one careful lick of the brush Mia supplied a Prussian-blue tire in the empty fork of the bike.

"Here. I mean, did you want me. When I was a baby."

Mia said nothing for such a long time that Pearl wasn't sure if she'd heard. But after a long pause, Mia turned around, paintbrush in hand, and to Pearl's amazement, her mother's eyes were wet. Could her mother be crying? Her unflappable, redoubtable, indomitable mother, whom she had never seen cry, not when the Rabbit had broken down by the side of the road and a man in a blue pickup had stopped as if to help, taken Mia's purse, and driven away; not when she'd dropped a heavy bedstead—salvaged from the side of the road—on her baby toe, smashing it so hard the nail eventually turned a deep eggplant and fell away. But there it was: an unfamiliar shimmer over her mother's eyes, as if she were looking into rippled water.

"Were you wanted?" Mia said. "Oh, yes. You were wanted. Very, very much."

She set the paintbrush down in the tray and walked rapidly out of the room without looking at her daughter again, leaving Pearl to contemplate the half-finished bicycle, the question she'd asked, the puddle of paint slowly forming a skin over the bristles of the brush.

5

As if the Jerry Springer episode had awakened her to Pearl's presence, Lexie began to take a new interest in her little brother's friend—Little Orphan Pearl, she said to Serena Wong one evening on the phone. "She's so quiet," Lexie marveled. "Like she's afraid to speak. And when you look at her, she turns bright red—red-red, like a tomato. A literal tomato."

"She's super shy," Serena said. She'd met Pearl a few times, at the Richardsons', but hadn't yet heard her say a word. "She probably just doesn't know how to make friends."

"It's more than that," Lexie mused. "It's like she's trying not to be seen. Like she wants to hide in plain sight."

Pearl, so timid and quiet, so unsure of herself, fascinated Lexie. And being Lexie, she began with the surface. "She's cute," she said to Serena. "She'd look so adorable out of those baggy T-shirts."

This was how, one afternoon, Pearl came home with a bagful of new clothes. Not new, precisely, as Mia found when she put them to wash: patched jeans from the seventies with a ribbon down the side, a flowered cotton blouse just as old, a cream-colored T-shirt with

Neil Young's face on the front. "Lexie and I went to the thrift store," Pearl explained when Mia came back upstairs from the laundry room. "She wanted to go shopping."

In fact, Lexie had first taken Pearl to the mall. It was natural, she had felt, that Pearl would turn to her for advice; Lexie was used to people wanting her opinion, to the point where she often assumed they did and just hadn't quite said so. And Pearl was a little sweetheart, that was clear: those big dark eyes, somehow made to look even bigger and darker with no makeup at all; that long dark frizzy hair that, when turned loose from its braid, as she one afternoon convinced Pearl to do, looked as if it might swallow her up. The way she looked at everything in their house—everything everywhere, really—as if she'd never seen it before. The second time Pearl had come over, Moody had left her in the sunroom and gone to get drinks, and Pearl, instead of sitting down, had turned in a slow circle, as if she were in Oz instead of the Richardsons' house. Lexie, who had been coming down the hall with the latest *Cosmo* and a Diet Coke in hand, had stopped outside the doorway, just out of view, and watched her. Then Pearl had reached out one timid finger and traced a vine in the wallpaper, and Lexie had felt a warm gush of pity for her, the sad little mouse. Just then Moody came out of the kitchen with two cans of Vernors. "Didn't know you were here," he'd said. "We were going to watch a movie." "I don't mind," Lexie had said, and she found she didn't. She settled herself into the big chair in the corner, one eye on Pearl, who sat down at last and popped the tab of her soda. Moody pushed a tape into the VCR, and Lexie flicked open her magazine. Something occurred to her, a good deed she might do. "Hey, Pearl, you can have this when I'm done," she said, and felt the fuzzy internal glow of teenage generosity.

So that afternoon in early October, she decided to take Pearl on a shopping trip. "Come on, Pearl," she said. "We're going to the mall."

When Lexie said *the mall*, she did not for a moment consider Randall Park Mall, off busy Warrensville Road, past a tire place, a rent-to-own store, and an all-night day care—*Randall Dark Mall*, some kids called it. Living in Shaker, she thought only of where she did all her shopping: Beachwood Place, a manicured little mall set off from the street on its own little oval, anchored by a Dillard's and a Saks and a new Nordstrom. She had never heard the term *Bleach-White Place* and would have been horrified if she had. But despite a trip to the Gap and Express and the Body Shop, Pearl bought nothing but a pretzel and a pot of kiwi-flavored lip balm.

"Didn't you see anything you liked?" Lexie asked. Pearl, who had only seventeen dollars and knew Lexie's weekly allowance was twenty, paused.

"It's all the same stuff, you know?" she said at last. She waved a hand in the general direction of the Chick-fil-A and the mall beyond it. "Everyone shows up at school looking like clones." She shrugged and glanced at Lexie out of the corner of her eye, wondering if she sounded convincing. "I just like to shop at places that are a little different. Where I can get something no one else will have."

Pearl stopped, eyeing the blue-and-white Gap bag dangling from Lexie's arm by its drawstrings, wondering suddenly if she would be offended. But Lexie was seldom, if ever, offended: subtle implications and subtexts tended to bounce off the fine mesh of her brain. She tipped her head to one side. "Like where?" she asked.

So Pearl had directed Lexie down Northfield Road, past the racetrack, to the thrift store, where women on break from the Taco Bell down the street, or getting ready for the night shift, browsed alongside them. She had been in dozens of thrift stores in dozens of cities in her life and somehow every single one had the exact same smell—dusty and sweet—and she had always been sure that the other kids could smell it on her clothes, even after double washings, as if the scent had soaked right into her skin. This one, where she and her mother had rummaged through the bins for old sheets to use as curtains, was no different. But now, hearing Lexie's delighted squeal, she saw the store through new eyes: a place where you could find cocktail dresses from the sixties for Homecoming, surgical scrubs for lounging on sleepy days, a wide assortment of old concert tees, and, if you were lucky, bells, *real* bell-bottoms, not the back-again retro ones from the Delia's catalog but the actual thing, with wide flares, the denim tissue-thin at the knees from decades of wear.

"Vintage." Lexie sighed and set upon the rack with reverence. Instead of the blouses and hippie skirts Mia always selected for her, Pearl found herself with an armful of quirky T-shirts, a skirt made from an old pair of Levi's, a navy zip-up hoodie. She showed Lexie how to read the price tags—on Tuesdays anything with a green tag was half off, on Wednesdays, it was yellow—and, when Lexie found a pair of jeans that fit, Pearl expertly pried off the orange price tag and replaced it with a green one from an ugly eighties polyester blazer. Under Pearl's guidance, the jeans came to $4, Pearl's entire bag to $13.75, and Lexie was so pleased that she pulled into the Wendy's drive-through and treated them to a Frosty apiece. "Those jeans fit you like they were *made* for you," Pearl told her in return. "You were destined to have them."

Lexie let a spoonful of chocolate melt against her tongue. "You know what?" she said, half closing her eyes, as if to put Pearl in sharper focus. "That skirt would go great with a striped button-down. I've got an old one you can have." When they got back to her house, she pulled a half dozen shirts from the closet. "See?" she said, smoothing the collar around Pearl's neck, carefully buttoning a single button between her breasts for the minimum of modesty, the way all the senior girls were wearing them that year. She swiveled Pearl toward the mirror and nodded approvingly. "You can take those," she said. "They look cute on you. I've got too many clothes as it is."

Pearl had bundled the shirts into her bag. If her mother noticed, she decided, she would say she got them at the thrift store with everything else. She wasn't sure why but she felt sure her mother would not approve of her taking Lexie's old things, even if Lexie didn't want them. Mia, putting the clothes to wash, noticed that the shirts smelled of Tide and perfume rather than dust, that they were crisp, as if they'd been ironed. But she said nothing, and the following evening all of Pearl's new clothes appeared in a neat pile at the foot of her bed, and Pearl breathed a sigh of relief.

A few days later, in the Richardsons' kitchen and clad in one of Lexie's shirts, she noticed Trip looking at her again and again out of the corner of his eye and adjusted her collar with a smug little smile. Trip himself was not even aware of why he was glancing at her, but he could not help noticing the little hourglass of skin her shirt revealed: the bare triangle framed by her collarbones; the bare triangle of midriff, with the delicate indent of her navel; the intermittent flash of navy blue bra above and below that single fastened button.

"You look nice today," he said, as if he were noticing her for the first time, and Pearl turned a deep pink, right down to the roots of her hair. He seemed embarrassed, too, as if he had just revealed a fondness for a very uncool TV show.

Moody could not let this pass. "She always looks nice," he said. "Shut up, Trip."

As usual, however, Trip did not notice his brother's irritation. "I mean extra nice," he said. "That shirt suits you. Brings out the color of your eyes."

"It's Lexie's," Pearl blurted out, and Trip grinned. "Looks better on you," he said, almost shyly, and headed outside.

The next day, Moody raided his savings and presented Pearl with a notebook, a slim black Moleskine held shut with an elastic garter. "Hemingway used this exact same kind," he told her, and Pearl thanked him and zipped it into her bookbag. She would copy her poems into it, he thought, instead of that ratty old spiral notebook, and it gave him some comfort—when she smiled at Trip or blushed at his compliments—to know that he'd given her the notebook that was holding her favorite words and thoughts.

The following week, Mrs. Richardson decided to have the carpet steamed, and all the children were told to stay out of the house until dinnertime. "If I see one boot print—Izzy—or one cleat mark—Trip—on those carpets, you will lose your allowance for a year. Understood?" Trip had an away soccer game, and Izzy had a violin lesson, but Lexie, it happened, had nothing to do. Serena Wong had cross-country practice and all her other friends were occupied one way or another. After tenth period, she tracked Pearl down at her locker.

"Whatcha up to?" Lexie asked, popping a white tablet of gum into Pearl's hand. "Nothing? Let's go to your place."

In all her previous years, Pearl had been reluctant to invite friends to her home: their apartments had always been crowded and cluttered, often in run-down sections of town, and odds were high that on any given day Mia might be working on one of her projects—which, to an outsider's eye, meant doing something odd and inexplicable. But Lexie appearing at her elbow, Lexie asking to come over to her house, Lexie asking to spend time with her—she felt like Cinderella looking up to see the prince's outstretched hand.

"Sure," she said.

To Pearl's delight—and Moody's great irritation—the three of them climbed into Lexie's Explorer and they headed down Parkland Drive toward the house on Winslow, TLC blasting from the rolled-down windows. When they pulled up in front of the house, Mia, who was outside watering the azaleas, fought the sudden but overpowering urge to drop the hose and run inside and lock the door behind her. Just as Pearl had never asked friends over, Mia never invited outsiders either. *Don't be ridiculous,* she told herself. *This is what you wanted, wasn't it? For Pearl to have friends.* By the time the doors of the Explorer opened and the three teenagers piled out, she had turned off the water and greeted them with a smile.

As Mia made a batch of popcorn—Pearl's favorite, and the only snack in the cupboard—she wondered if the conversation would be hobbled by her presence. Perhaps they would sit there in awkward silence, and Lexie would never want to come over again. But by the time the first kernels pinged against the pot lid, the three teens had already discussed Anthony Brecker's new car, an old VW bug painted purple; how Meg Kaufman had come to school drunk the week before; how much better Anna Lamont looked now that she was straightening her hair; and whether the Indians should change their logo ("Chief Wahoo," Lexie said, "is so blatantly racist"). Only when the subject of college applications came up did the conversation stall. Mia, shaking the pot so the popcorn wouldn't scorch, heard Lexie groan and a thunk that might have been her forehead hitting the table.

College applications had been increasingly on Lexie's mind. Shaker took college seriously: the district had a ninety-nine percent graduation rate and virtually all the kids went on to college of some kind. Everyone Lexie knew was applying early and, as a result, all anyone could talk about in the Social Room was who was applying where. Serena Wong was applying to Harvard. Brian, Lexie said, had his heart set on Princeton. "Like Cliff and Clair would let me go anywhere else," he'd said. His parents were really named John and Deborah Avery, but his father was a doctor and his mother was a lawyer and, truth be told, they did exude a certain Cosbyish vibe, his father sweatered and affable and his mother wittily competent and no-nonsense. They'd met at Princeton as undergraduates, and Brian had pictures of himself as a baby in a Princeton onesie.

For Lexie, the precedent was not quite so clear: her mother had grown up in Shaker and had never gone far—just down to Denison for her undergrad before boomeranging back. Her father had come from a small town in Indiana and, once he'd met her mother at college, simply stayed, moving back with her to her hometown, finishing a JD at Case Western, working his way up from a junior associate to partner at one of the biggest firms in the city. But Lexie, like most of her classmates, had no desire to stay anywhere near Cleveland. It huddled on the edge of a dead, dirty lake, fed by a river best known for burning; it was built on a river whose very name meant sadness: Chagrin. Which then gave its name to everything, pockets of agony scattered throughout the city, buried like veins of dismay: Chagrin Falls, Chagrin Boulevard, Chagrin Reservation. Chagrin Real Estate. Chagrin Auto Body. Chagrin reproducing and proliferating, as if they would ever run short. The Mistake on the Lake, people called it sometimes, and to Lexie, as to her siblings and friends, Cleveland was something to be escaped.

As the deadline for early applications approached, Lexie had decided to apply early to Yale. It had a good drama program, and Lexie had been the lead in the musical last year, even though she'd only been a junior. Despite her air of frivolity, she was near the top of her class—officially, Shaker did not rank its students, to reduce competitive feelings, but she knew she was somewhere in the top twenty. She was taking four AP classes and served as secretary of the French Club. "Don't let the shallowness fool you," Moody had told Pearl. "You know why she watches TV all afternoon? Because she can finish her homework in half an hour before bed. Like that." He snapped his fingers. "Lexie's got a good brain. She just doesn't always use it in real life." Yale seemed a stretch but a distinctly possible one, her guidance counselor had said. "Plus," Mrs. Lieberman had added, "they know kids from Shaker always go on to do well. They'll give you an edge."

Lexie and Brian had been together since junior year, and she liked the idea of being just a train ride away. "We can visit each other all the time," Lexie pointed out to him as she printed the Yale early application. "And we can even meet up in New York." It was this last that finally swayed her: New York, which had exuded a glamorous pull on her imagination ever since she'd read *Eloise* as a child. She didn't want to go to school *in* New York; her guidance counselor had floated the idea of Columbia, but Lexie had heard the area was *sketchy*. Still, she liked the idea of being able to jaunt in for a day—a morning at the Met looking at art, maybe a splurge at Macy's or even a weekend away with Brian—and then zip away from the crowds and the grime and the noise.

Before any of that could happen, though, she had to write her essay. A good essay, Mrs. Lieberman had insisted, was what she needed to set herself apart from the pack.

"Listen to this dumbass question," she groaned that afternoon in Pearl's kitchen, fishing the printed-out application from her bag. "'Rewrite a famous story from a different perspective. For example, retell *The Wizard of Oz* from the point of view of the Wicked Witch.' This is a college app, not creative writing. I'm taking AP English. At least ask me to write a real essay."

"How about a fairy tale," Moody suggested. He looked up from his notebook and the open algebra textbook before him. "'Cinderella' from the point of view of the stepsisters. Maybe they weren't so wicked after all. Maybe she was actually a bitch to *them*."

"'Little Red Riding Hood' as told by the wolf," Pearl suggested.

"Or 'Rumpelstiltskin,'" Lexie mused. "I mean, that miller's daughter cheated him. He did all that spinning for her and she said she'd give him her baby and then she reneged on their deal. Maybe she's the villain here." With one maroon fingernail she tapped the top of the Diet Coke she'd bought just after school, then popped the tab. "I mean, she shouldn't have agreed to give up her baby in the first place, if she didn't want to."

"Well," Mia put in suddenly. She turned around, the

bowl of popcorn in her hands, and all three of them jumped, as if a piece of furniture had begun to speak. "Maybe she didn't know what she was giving up until afterward. Maybe once she saw the baby she changed her mind." She set the bowl down in the center of the table. "Don't be too quick to judge, Lexie."

Lexie looked chastened for an instant, then rolled her eyes. Moody darted a look at Pearl: *See how shallow?* But Pearl didn't notice. After Mia had gone back into the living room—embarrassed at her outburst—she turned to Lexie. "I could help you," she said, quietly enough that she thought Mia could not hear. Then, a moment later, because this did not seem like enough, "I'm good at stories. I could even write it for you."

"Really?" Lexie beamed. "Oh my god, Pearl, I'll owe you forever." She threw her arms around Pearl. Across the table, Moody gave up on his homework and slammed his math book shut, and in the living room, Mia jammed her paintbrush into a jar of water, lips pursed, paint scrubbing from the bristles in a dirt-colored swirl.

6

Pearl, true to her word, handed Lexie a typed-up essay the next week—the story of the frog prince, from the point of view of the frog. Neither Mia, who did not want to admit she'd been eavesdropping, nor Moody, who did not want to be labeled a goody two-shoes, said a word about it. But both were growing increasingly uneasy.

When Moody arrived in the morning so they could walk to school together, Pearl would emerge from her room wearing one of Lexie's button-downs, or a spaghetti-strap tank, or dark red lipstick. "Lexie gave it to me," she explained, half to her mother and half to Moody, both of whom were staring at her in dismay. "She said it was too dark for her, but that it looked good on me. Because my hair's darker." Under the smudge of lipstick, her lips looked like a bruise, tender and raw.

"Wash that off," Mia said, for the first time ever. But the next morning Pearl came out wearing one of Lexie's chokers, which looked like a gash of black lace around her neck.

"See you at dinner," she said. "Lexie and I are going shopping after school."

By late October, as one by one applications were sent

in, a spirit of celebration set in among the seniors. Lexie's application had been submitted, and she was in a benevolent mood. Her essay—thanks to Pearl—was good, her SAT scores were strong, her GPA was over 4.0 thanks to her AP classes, and she could already picture herself on Yale's campus. She felt she should reward Pearl in some way for her assistance and, after some thought, came up with the perfect idea: something she was sure Pearl would love, but would never get invited to on her own. "Stacie Perry's having a party this weekend," she said. "Want to come?"

Pearl hesitated. She had heard about Stacie Perry's parties, and the chance to go to one was tantalizing. "I don't know if my mom will let me."

"Come on, Pearl," Trip said, leaning over the arm of the couch. "I'm going. I'm gonna need someone to dance with." After that, Pearl needed no further persuasion.

At Shaker Heights High School, Stacie Perry's parties were things of legend. Mr. and Mrs. Perry had a big house and took frequent trips, and Stacie took full advantage. With the tension of early applications released, and weeks yet until finals, the seniors were ready for fun. All week the Halloween party was the hot topic of discussion: who was going, and who wasn't?

Moody and Izzy, of course, had not been invited; they knew Stacie Perry only by reputation, and the invite list had mostly been seniors. Pearl, despite Lexie's involvement, still knew almost no one besides the Richardsons, and Moody was often the only person she spoke with during school. Lexie and Serena Wong, though, had both been invited by Stacie herself, and thus had dispensation to bring a guest—even a sopho-more that no one really knew.

"I thought we were going to rent *Carrie*," Moody grumbled. "You said you'd never seen it."

"Next weekend," Pearl promised. "That's actually Halloween anyway. Unless you want to go trick-or-treating."

"We're too old," Moody said. Shaker Heights, as with everything, had regulations about trick-or-treating: si-rens wailed at six and eight to mark the start and end, and although there were no official age restrictions, people tended to look askance at teens who showed up at their doors. The last time he had gone trick-or-treating, he'd been eleven, and he'd gone as an M&M.

For Stacie's party, though, a costume was de rigueur. Brian was not going—he had put off his early applica-tion to Princeton and, along with a handful of other pro-crastinators, was scrambling to finish by the deadline—so he did not factor into the calculations. "Let's be Char-lie's Angels," Lexie cried in a burst of inspiration, so she and Serena and Pearl donned bell-bottoms and polyes-ter shirts and teased their hair as high as they could. Hairdos fully inflated, they posed, back-to-back, fin-gers pointed like guns, and surveyed themselves in the mirror in a haze of hairspray.

"Perfect," Lexie said. "Blond, brunette, and black." She aimed her finger at Pearl's nose. "You ready for this party, Pearl?"

The answer, of course, was no. It was the most surreal night Pearl had ever experienced. All evening, cars driven by skateboarders and animals and Freddy Kruegers pulled up to park at the edges of Stacie's huge lawn. At least four boys wore *Scream* masks; a couple donned football jerseys and helmets; a creative few wore long jackets and fedoras and sunglasses and feather boas. ("Pimps," Lexie explained.) Most of the girls wore skimpy dresses and hats or animal ears, though one had transformed herself into Princess Leia; another, dressed as a fembot, hung on the arms of an Austin Powers. Stacie herself was dressed as an angel, in a silvery spaghetti-strapped minidress, glittery wings and fishnets, and a halo on a headband.

By the time Lexie and Serena and Pearl arrived at nine thirty, everyone was already drunk. The air was thick with sweat and the sharp sour smell of beer, and couples dry humped in darkened corners. The kitchen floor was sticky with spilled drinks, and some girl was lying flat on her back on the table among the half-empty liquor bottles, smoking a joint and giggling as a boy licked rum from her navel. Lexie and Serena poured themselves drinks and wriggled into the makeshift dance floor in the living room. Pearl, left alone, stood in the corner of the kitchen, nursing a red Solo cup full of Stoli and Coke and looking for Trip.

Half an hour later, she caught a glimpse of him, out on the patio, dressed as a devil in a red blazer from the thrift store and a pair of devil horns. "I didn't think he even knew Stacie," she shouted into Serena's ear when Serena came back to refill her drink. Serena shrugged. "Stacie said she saw him with his shirt off after soccer practice one day and thought he was *fine*. She said—and I quote—he was the bomb diggity." She took a swig and giggled. Her face, Pearl noticed, was flushed. "Don't tell Lexie, okay? She'd barf." She headed back toward the living room, wobbling slightly on her wedge heels, and through the sliding-glass door Pearl watched Trip poke a redheaded girl between the shoulder blades with his plastic pitchfork. She fluffed her hair and made a plan. In a little while Trip's cup would be empty. He would come inside and he would see her. *What's up, Pearl,* he would say. And then she would say something clever to him. She tried to think of something. What would Lexie say to a boy she liked?

But as she racked her brain for something sultry and witty, she noticed that Trip had disappeared from the patio. Had he come inside, or had he left already? She wriggled her way into the living room, cup held aloft, but it was impossible to see anyone. Puff Daddy and Mase poured from the stereo, the bass thumping so loud she could feel it in her throat, then faded back to make way for Notorious B.I.G. The only light came from a few candles, and all she could make out were silhouettes writhing and grinding in decidedly unchaste ways. She wormed her way out into the backyard, where a knot of boys were chugging beer and arguing about the football team's chances of the playoffs. "If we beat Ignatius," one of them shouted, "and U.S. beats Mentor—"

Lexie, meanwhile, was having a momentous night. She loved dancing; she and Serena and their friends went downtown any time clubs had a teen night—or any time they thought their fake IDs, identifying them as college juniors, would get them past a bouncer. Once they'd snuck into a rave in a disused warehouse down in the Flats and danced until three, glow necklaces ringing their wrists and their throats. They often danced together, with the ease of two girls who had known each other for more than half their lives, hip to hip or pelvis to pelvis, Lexie backing up to twitch her rear against Serena. Tonight they were dancing together when Lexie felt someone press up against her from behind. It was Brian, and Serena gave her a knowing smirk before turning away.

"You're not even in costume," Lexie protested, smacking him on the shoulder.

"I am in costume," Brian insisted. "I'm a guy who just mailed his application to Princeton." He wrapped his arms around her waist and put his mouth to her neck.

Half an hour later, the dancing and the liquor and the sweet, heady rush of being eighteen had filled them both with a feverish flush. In the time they'd been dating, they'd done some stuff, as Lexie had coyly put it to Serena, but *it*, the big *it*, had sat between them for a while, like a deep pool of water in which they only dipped their toes. Now, pressed against Brian, mellowed by rum and Coke, music pounding through both their bodies like a shared heartbeat, she was filled with the sudden longing to plunge into that pool and dive straight to the bottom. When she had been younger and less experienced, Lexie had had visions about her first time. She'd planned it out: candles, flowers, Boyz II Men on the CD player. At the very least, a bedroom and a bed. Not the backseat of a car, the way some of her friends had; definitely not in the stairwell of the high school, as rumor had it Kendra Solomon had. But now she found that she didn't care about that anymore. "Want to go for a drive?" she asked. Both of them knew what she was suggesting.

Without speaking, they hurried out to the curb, where Lexie's car was waiting.

By the time Lexie and Brian had gone, Pearl was back in her corner of the kitchen, waiting for Trip to reappear. But he didn't, not by ten thirty, not by eleven. With each hour that passed, and each bottle that emptied, things got louder and looser. At just past midnight Stacie Perry herself, trying to pour a glass of water, vomited into the Brita pitcher, and Pearl decided it was time to head home. But there was no sign of Lexie, even when she fought her way through the pulsating mass of bodies in the living room. Peeking outside, she couldn't tell whether Lexie's Explorer was still parked in the uneven row of cars.

"Have you seen Lexie?" she asked anyone who seemed remotely sober. "Or Serena?" Most people stared at her as if trying to place her. "Lexie?" they said. "Oh, Lexie Richardson? You came with her?" At last one girl, splayed in the lap of a football player in the big armchair, said, "I think she took off with her boyfriend. Isn't that right, Kev?" In response Kev put his meaty hands to her face and pulled her mouth toward his, and Pearl turned away.

She wasn't entirely sure where she was, and the vodka blurred the already sketchy map of Shaker in her mind. Could she walk home from here? How long would it take? What street did Stacie even live on? For a minute Pearl allowed herself to fantasize. Maybe Trip would come through the sliding-glass door, a crisp waft of cool air following him into the kitchen. *You need a ride home?* he'd say.

But of course this didn't happen, and at last, Pearl snuck the cordless phone from the kitchen counter, ducked outside by the garage, where it was quieter, and called Moody.

Twenty minutes later a car pulled up in front of Stacie's house. The passenger window rolled down, and from her perch on the front steps, Pearl saw Moody's scowling face.

"Get in" was all he said.

The inside of the car was all buttery leather, soft as skin under her thighs.

"Whose car is this?" she asked stupidly, as they pulled away from the curb.

"My mom's," Moody said. "And before you ask, she's asleep, so let's not waste time here."

"But you don't have a license yet."

"Being allowed to do something and knowing how to do it are not the same thing." Moody wheeled the car around the corner and turned onto Shaker Boulevard. "So how drunk are you?"

"I had one drink. I'm not drunk." Even as she said this, Pearl wasn't sure it was true—there had been a lot of vodka in that cup. Her head spun and she closed her eyes. "I just didn't know how to get home."

"Trip's car was still there, you know. We passed it on the way out. Why didn't you ask him?"

"I couldn't find him. I couldn't find anyone."

"Probably upstairs with some girl."

They rode in silence for a while, those words churning in Pearl's mind: *upstairs with some girl*. She tried to picture it, what happened up in those darkened rooms, imagined Trip's body against hers, and a hot flush crept over her. According to the clock on the dashboard, it was nearly one o'clock.

"You see now," Moody said. "What they're like." As they approached Mia and Pearl's block, he clicked the lights off and pulled up to the curb. "Your mom is going to be pissed."

"I told her I was going out with Lexie and she said I could stay out until twelve. I'm only a little late." Pearl glanced up at the lighted kitchen window. "Do I stink?"

Moody leaned in close. "You smell a little like smoke. But not like booze. Here." He pulled a pack of Trident from his pocket.

The Halloween party would, by all accounts, last until three fifteen A.M., and end with a number of kids passed out on the Perrys' Oriental living room carpet. Lexie would creep home at two thirty, Trip at three, and the next day they would still be asleep past noon. Later Lexie would apologize to Pearl in a whispered confession: she and Brian had been thinking about it for a while and tonight seemed like the night and—she didn't know, she just wanted to tell someone, she hadn't even told Serena yet, did she look any different? She *would* look different, to Pearl—thinner, sharper, her hair pulled back in a drooping ponytail, traces of mascara and glitter still streaked at the corners of her eyes; she could see in the faint crease just between Lexie's eyebrows what she would look like twenty years from now: something like her mother. From then on, it would seem to Pearl that everything Lexie did was tinged with sex, a kind of knowingness in her laugh and her sideways glances, in the casual way she touched everyone, on the shoulder, on the hand, on the knee. It loosened you, she would think; it lightened you. "And how about you?" Lexie would say at last, squeezing Pearl's arm. "You found your way home okay? Did you have fun?" And Pearl, with the caution of the recently singed, would simply nod.

For now, she peeled the wrapper from the gum and put it between her lips and felt the mint bloom on her tongue. "Thanks."

><

Despite Pearl's insistence that her mother wouldn't mind, Mia minded her lateness very much. When Pearl finally came upstairs—smelling of smoke and alcohol and something Mia was fairly certain was weed—she had not known what to say. "Go to bed," she had finally managed. "We'll talk about it in the morning." Morning had come, Pearl had slept in, and even when she finally emerged near noon, disheveled and sandy eyed, Mia still hadn't known what to say. You wanted Pearl to have a more normal life, she reminded herself; well, this is what teens do. Part of her felt she should be more involved—that she needed to know what Pearl was up to, what Lexie was up to, what all of them were up to— but what was she to do? Tag along to their parties and hockey games? Forbid Pearl to go out at all? She'd ended up saying nothing, and Pearl had consumed a bowl of cereal in silence and returned to bed.

Soon, however, an opportunity presented itself. The Tuesday after the Halloween party, Mrs. Richardson stopped by the duplex on Winslow Road. "To see if you need anything now that you're all settled in," she said, but Mia watched her gaze roam around the kitchen and into the living room. She was familiar with these visits, despite what leases said about *limited rights of entry*, and she stepped back to let Mrs. Richardson get a better view. After nearly four months, there was still little furniture. In the kitchen, two mismatched chairs and a gateleg table missing one leaf, all salvaged from the curbside; in Pearl's room, the twin bed and a three-drawer dresser; in Mia's room still only a mattress on the floor and stacks of clothing in the closet. A row of cushions on the living room floor, draped in a bright flowered tablecloth. But the kitchen linoleum was scrubbed and the stove and fridge were clean, the carpet was spotless, Mia's mattress bed was made with crisp striped sheets. Despite the lack of furniture, the apartment did not feel empty. "May we paint?" Mia had asked when they'd moved in, and Mrs. Richardson hesitated before saying, "As long as it's not too dark." She had meant, at the time, no black, no navy, no oxblood, though the next day it had occurred to her that perhaps Mia had meant a mural—she was an artist, after all—and you might end up with Diego Rivera, or you might end up with glorified graffiti. But there were no murals. Each room had been painted a different color—the kitchen a sunny yellow, the living room a deep cantaloupe, the bedrooms a warm peach—and the overall effect was of stepping into a box of sunlight, even on a cloudy day. All over the apartment hung photographs, unframed and tacked up with poster gum, but striking nonetheless.

There were studies of shadows against a faded brick wall, photographs of feathers clotting the shoreline of Shaker Lake, experiments Mia was conducting with printing photographs on different surfaces: vellum, aluminum foil, newspapers. One series stretched across an entire wall, photographs taken week by week of a nearby construction site. At first, there was nothing but a brown hill in front of a brown expanse. Slowly, frame by frame, the mound turned green with weeds, covered in brushy grass and scrub and, eventually, a small shrub clinging to its peak. Behind it, a three-story tan house slowly arose, like a great beast climbing out of the earth. Front loaders and trucks flitted in and out of the scene like ghosts caught unawares. In the last photograph, a bulldozer razed the dirt to even the terrain, flattening the landscape like a popped bubble.

"My goodness," Mrs. Richardson said. "Are these all yours?"

"Sometimes I need to see them up on the wall for a while, before I know whether I've got something. Before I know which ones I like." Mia looked around at the photographs, as if they were old friends and she was reminding herself of their faces.

Mrs. Richardson peered closely at a photo of a sullen young girl in a cowgirl outfit. Mia had snapped it at a parade they'd passed on the way into Ohio. "You have such a gift for portraiture," she said. "Look at the way you've captured this little girl. You can almost see right down into her soul."

Mia said nothing but nodded in a way Mrs. Richardson decided was modesty.

"You should consider taking portraits professionally," Mrs. Richardson suggested. She paused. "Not that you're not a professional already, of course. But in a studio, maybe. Or for weddings and engagements. You'd be very highly sought after." She waved a hand at the photographs on the wall, as if they could articulate what she meant. "In fact, perhaps you could take portraits of our family. I'd pay you, of course."

"Perhaps," Mia said. "But the thing about portraits is, you need to show people the way they want to be seen. And I prefer to show people as *I* see them. So in the end I'd probably just frustrate us both." She smiled placidly, and Mrs. Richardson fumbled for a response.

"Is any of your work for sale?" she asked.

"I have a friend in New York who runs a gallery, and she's sold some of my prints." Mia ran a finger along one photograph, tracing the curve of a rusted bridge.

"Well, I'd love to buy one," Mrs. Richardson said. "In fact, I insist. If we don't support our artists, how can they create great work?"

"That's very generous of you." Mia's eyes slid toward the window briefly, and Mrs. Richardson felt a twinge of irritation at this lukewarm response to her philanthropy.

"Do you sell enough to get by?" she asked.

Mia correctly interpreted this as a question about rent and her ability to pay it. "We've always gotten by," she said, "one way or another."

"But surely there must be times when photographs

don't sell. Through no fault of your own, of course. And how much does a photograph typically sell for?"

"We've always gotten by," Mia said again. "I take side jobs when I need to. Housecleaning, or cooking. Things like that. I'm working part time at Lucky Palace now, that Chinese restaurant over on Warrensville. I've never had a debt I didn't pay."

"Oh, of course I wasn't implying that," Mrs. Richardson protested. She turned her attention to the largest print, which had been stuck up alone over the mantelpiece. It was a photograph of a woman, back to the camera, in mid-dance. The film caught her in blurred motion—arms everywhere, stretched high, to her sides, curved to her waist—a tangle of limbs that, Mrs. Richardson realized with a shock, made her resemble an enormous spider, surrounded by a haze of web. It perturbed and perplexed her, but she could not turn away. "I never thought of making a woman into a spider," she said truthfully. Artists, she reminded herself, didn't think like normal people, and at last she turned to Mia with curiosity. She had never before met anyone like her.

Mrs. Richardson had, her entire existence, lived an orderly and regimented life. She weighed herself once per week, and although her weight did not fluctuate more than the three pounds her doctor assured her was normal, she took pains to maintain herself. Each morning she measured exactly one half cup of Cheerios, the serving size indicated on the box, using the flowered plastic measuring cup she'd gotten from Higbee's as a new bride. Each evening, at dinner, she allowed herself one glass of wine—red, which the news said was most beneficial for your heart—a faint scratch in the wine-glass marking the right level to pour. Three times weekly she took an aerobics class, checking her watch through-out to be sure her heart rate had exceeded one hundred and twenty beats per minute. She had been brought up to follow rules, to believe that the proper functioning of the world depended upon her compliance, and follow them—and believe—she did. She had had a plan, from girlhood on, and had followed it scrupulously: high school, college, boyfriend, marriage, job, mortgage, children. A sedan with air bags and automatic seat belts. A lawn mower and a snowblower. A matching washer and dryer. She had, in short, done everything right and she had built a good life, the kind of life she wanted, the kind of life everyone wanted. Now here was this Mia, a completely different kind of woman leading a completely different life, who seemed to make her own rules with no apologies. Like the photograph of the spider-dancer, Mrs. Richardson found this perturbing but strangely compelling. A part of her wanted to study Mia like an anthropologist, to understand why—and how—she did what she did. Another part of her—though she was only vaguely aware of it at the moment—was uneasy, wanted to keep an eye on Mia, as you might keep your eye on a dangerous beast.

"You keep everything so clean," she said at last, run-ning a finger along the mantelpiece. "I should hire you to come to our house." She laughed and Mia echoed it po-litely, but she could see the seed of an idea cracking and sprouting in Mrs. Richardson's mind. "Wouldn't that be perfect," Mrs. Richardson said. "You could come just for a few hours a day and do a little light housekeeping. I'd pay you for your time, of course. And then you'd have all the rest of your day to take pictures." Mia began searching for the right, delicate words to uproot this idea, but it was too late. Mrs. Richardson had already latched on to it with vigor. "Now, really. Why don't you come and work for us? We had a woman who came to clean and do some dinner prep before, but she went back home to Atlanta in the spring, and I could certainly use the help. You'd be doing me a favor, really." She turned around to face Mia squarely. "In fact, I insist. You must have time for your art."

Mia could see there was no point in protesting, that protesting, in fact, would only make things worse and lead to ill will. She had learned that when people were bent on doing something they believed was a good deed, it was usually impossible to dissuade them. She thought with dismay of the Richardsons, of the vast and gleaming Richardson house, of Pearl's face when her mother dared set foot on this precious soil. And then she imagined herself safely installed in the Richardsons' kingdom, half obscured in the background, keeping watch over her daughter. Reasserting her presence in her daughter's life.

"Thank you," she said. "That's so very generous of you to offer. How could I refuse?" And Mrs. Richardson beamed.

7

The arrangements were soon settled: in exchange for three hundred dollars a month, Mia would vacuum, dust, and tidy the Richardson house three times a week and prepare dinner nightly. It seemed an excellent deal—just a few hours of work per day for the equivalent of their rent—but Pearl was displeased. "Why did she ask *you*?" she demanded with a groan, and Mia bit her tongue and reminded herself that her daughter was, after all, fifteen. "Because she's trying to be nice to us," she retorted, and thankfully, Pearl let the subject drop. But inside she was furious at the thought of Mia invading what she thought of as *her* space—the Richardson house. Her mother would be just a few yards away in the kitchen, hearing everything, observing everything. The afternoons on the couch, the joking she'd come to feel a part of, even the ridiculous ritual of watching Jerry Springer—everything would be ruined. Just days before, she'd worked up the courage to swat Trip's hand when he'd made a joke about her pants—*Why so many pockets*, he'd demanded, *what are you hiding in there?* First he'd patted the pockets at the sides of her knees, then those at her hips, then, when he'd reached for the ones on her rear, she'd smacked him, and to her smitten delight he'd said, "Don't be mad, you know I love you," and put his arm around her shoulder. With her mother there, though, she would never dare such a thing, and neither, she suspected, would Trip.

Mr. Richardson, too, found the new arrangements awkward. It was one thing, he thought, to hire a housekeeper; it was another to hire someone they already knew, the mother of one of their children's friends. But Mrs. Richardson, he could see, felt it was a generous gesture, so instead of arguing, he made a point of speaking to Mia on her first morning in the house.

"We're very grateful for your help," he told her, as she pulled the bucket of cleaning supplies from under the sink. "It's a huge, huge help to us." Mia smiled and reached for a bottle of Windex and said nothing, and Mr. Richardson cast about for something else to say. "How do you like Shaker?"

"It's quite a place." Mia sprayed the counter and swept the sponge across it, corralling crumbs into the sink. "Did you grow up in Shaker, too?"

"No, just Elena." Mr. Richardson shook his head. "I'd never even heard of Shaker Heights before I met her." Their first week at Denison, he had fallen for the ardent young woman collecting signatures around campus to end the draft. By the time they graduated, he had fallen for Shaker Heights as well, the way Elena described it: the first planned community, the most progressive community, the perfect place for young idealists. In his own little hometown, they'd been suspicious of ideas: he'd grown up surrounded by a kind of resigned cynicism, though he'd been sure the world could be better. It was why he'd been so eager to leave, and why he'd been smitten as soon as they'd met. Northwestern had been his first choice; he'd been turned down, had settled for the only school that let him leave the state, but once he'd met Elena it had seemed, to him, like fate intervening. Elena was determined to return to her hometown after school, and the more she told him about it, the more willing he was. It seemed only natural to him that such a place would have formed his principled fiancée, who always strove for perfection, and he gladly followed her back to Shaker Heights after graduation.

Now, almost two decades later, well settled in their careers and their family and their lives, as he filled up his BMW with premium gas, or cleaned his golf clubs, or signed a permission form for his children to go skiing, those college days seemed fuzzy and distant as old Polaroids. Elena, too, had mellowed: of course she still donated to charity and voted Democrat, but so many years of comfortable suburban living had changed both of them. Neither of them had ever been radical—even at a time of protests, sit-ins, marches, riots—but now they owned two houses, four cars, a small boat they docked at the marina downtown. They had someone to plow the snow in the winter and mow the lawn in the summer. And of course they'd had a housekeeper for years, a long string of them, and now here was the newest, this young woman in his kitchen, waiting for him to leave so she could clean his house.

He recollected himself, smiled bashfully, picked up his briefcase. At the doorway to the garage, he paused.

"If working here ever stops suiting your needs, please let me know. There will be no hard feelings, I promise."

Mia soon settled into a schedule: she arrived in the morning at eight thirty, soon after everyone had gone off to work or school, and would be finished by ten. Then she would go home to her camera, returning at five o'clock to cook. "There's no need to make two trips," Mrs. Richardson had pointed out, but Mia had insisted midday was the best time for her photography. The truth was that she wanted to study the Richardsons both when they were there and when they weren't. Every day, it seemed, Pearl absorbed something new from the Richardson family: a turn of phrase ("I was *literally* dying"), a gesture (a flick of the hair, an eye roll). She was a teen, Mia told herself over and over; she was trying on new skins, like all teenagers did, but privately she stayed wary of the changes she saw. Now, every afternoon, she would be there to check on Pearl, to observe these Richardsons who fascinated her daughter so. Every morning she would be free to investigate on her own.

In the course of her cleaning, Mia began to observe carefully. She knew when Trip had failed a math test by the shredded scraps in his trash bin, when Moody had been writing songs by the crumpled wads of paper in his. She knew that no one in the Richardson family ate the crust of the pizza or brown-spotted bananas, that Lexie had a weakness for gossip magazines and—based on her bookshelf—Charles Dickens, that Mr. Richardson liked to eat those cream-filled caramel bull's-eyes by the bagful while he worked in his study at night. By the time she finished an hour and a half later, the house tidy, she had a very good sense of what each member of the family was doing.

This was how, a week into her new duties, Mia came to be in the Richardson kitchen when Izzy wandered downstairs at nine thirty in the morning.

The day before, Izzy had startled, but not surprised, her family by being suspended from school. In the middle of orchestra, she had, according to the freshmen vice principal, broken the teacher's bow over her knee and thrown the pieces in the teacher's face. Despite repeated questionings and stern talking-tos both at school and at home, she had refused to say anything about what had caused this outburst. It was, as Lexie put it, vintage Izzy: freak out for no reason, do something crazy, learn nothing from it. Consequently, after a hasty meeting with her mother, the principal, and the aggrieved orchestra teacher, she had been suspended from school for three days. Mia was cleaning the stove when Izzy stomped in—somehow clomping in bare feet as loudly as she did in her Doc Martens—and stopped.

"Oh," she said. "It's you. The indentured servant. I mean, the tenant-slash-cleaning lady."

Mia had heard a thirdhand version of events from Pearl the day before. "I'm Mia," she said. "I'm guessing you're Izzy."

Izzy settled herself onto a bar stool. "The crazy one."

Mia wiped the counter carefully. "No one's said anything like that to me." She rinsed the sponge and set it in its holder to dry.

Izzy lapsed into silence and Mia began to scour the

sink. When she had finished, she turned on the broiler. Then she took a piece of bread from the loaf in the bread box, spread it with butter and sprinkled it thickly with sugar, and set it in the oven until the sugar had melted to a bubbling, golden caramel. She set another piece of bread on top, cut the sandwich in two, and set it in front of Izzy—a suggestion, not a command. It was something she did sometimes for Pearl, when she was having what Mia called "a low day." Izzy, who had been watching silently but with interest, said nothing but pulled the plate toward her. In her experience, when someone tried to do something for her, it came from either pity or distrust, but this simple gesture felt like what it was: a small kindness, with no strings attached. When she had finished the last bite of sandwich, she licked butter from her fingers and looked up.

"So you want to hear what happened?" she asked, and the whole story emerged.

><

The orchestra teacher, Mrs. Peters, was widely disliked by everyone. She was a tall, painfully thin woman with hair dyed an unnatural flaxen and cropped in a manner reminiscent of Dorothy Hamill. According to Izzy, she was *useless as a conductor* and everyone knew to just watch Kerri Schulman, the first-chair violin, for the tempo. A persistent rumor—after some years, calcified as fact—insisted that Mrs. Peters had a drinking problem. Izzy hadn't entirely believed it, until Mrs. Peters had borrowed her violin one morning to demonstrate a bowing; when she'd handed it back, the chin rest damp with sweat, it had smelled unmistakably of whiskey. When she brought her big camping thermos of coffee, people said, you knew Mrs. Peters had been on a bender the night before. Moreover, she was often bitingly sarcastic, especially to the second violins, *especially* the ones who—as one of the cellos put it drily—were "pigmentally blessed." Stories about her had filtered down to Izzy even in middle school.

Izzy, who had been playing violin since she was four, and had been assigned second chair even though she was a freshman, should have had nothing to fear. "You'll be fine," the cello had told her, eyeing Izzy's frizzy golden hair—the dandelion fro, Lexie liked to call it. Had Izzy kept her head down, Mrs. Peters would likely have ignored her. But Izzy was not the type to keep her head down.

The morning of her suspension, Izzy had been in her seat, practicing a tricky fingering on the E string for the Saint-Saëns piece she'd been working on in her private lessons. Around her the hum of violas and cellos tuning up grew quiet as Mrs. Peters stormed in, thermos in hand. It was clear from the start that she was in an extraordinarily foul mood. She snapped at Shanita Grimes to spit out her gum. She barked at Jessie Leibovitz, who had just broken her A string and was fishing in her case for a replacement. "Hangover," Kerri Schulman mouthed to Izzy, who nodded gravely. She had only a general sense of what this meant—a few times Trip had come home from hockey parties and had seemed, she thought, extra dense and groggy in the morning, even for Trip—but she knew it involved headaches and ill temper. She tapped the tip of her bow against her boots.

At the podium, Mrs. Peters took a long swig from her mug of coffee. "Offenbach," she barked, raising her right hand. Around the room students riffled through their sheet music.

Twelve bars into *Orpheus*, Mrs. Peters waved her arms. "Someone's off." She pointed her bow at Deja Johnson, who was at the back of the second violins. "Deja. Play from measure six."

Deja, who everyone knew was painfully shy, glanced up with the look of a frightened rabbit. She began to play, and everyone could hear the slight tremor from her shaking hand. Mrs. Peters shook her head and rapped her bow on her stand. "Wrong bowing. Down, up-up, down, up. Again." Deja stumbled through the piece again. The room simmered with resentment, but no one said anything.

Mrs. Peters took a long slurp of coffee. "Stand up, Deja. Nice and loud now, so everyone can hear what they're *not* supposed to be doing." The edges of Deja's mouth wobbled, as if she were going to cry, but she set her bow to string and began once more. Mrs. Peters shook her head again, her voice shrill over the single violin. "Deja. Down, up-up, down, up. Did you not understand me? You need me to speak in Ebonics?"

It was at this point that Izzy had jumped from her seat and grabbed Mrs. Peters's bow.

She could not say, even when telling Mia the story, why she had reacted so strongly. It was partly that Deja

Johnson always had the anxious face of someone expecting the worst. Everyone knew that her mother was an RN; in fact, she worked with Serena Wong's mother down at the Cleveland Clinic, and her father managed a warehouse on the West Side. There weren't many black kids in the orchestra, though, and when her parents showed up for concerts, they sat in the last row, by themselves; they never chitchatted with the other parents about skiing or remodeling or plans for spring break. They had lived all of Deja's life in a comfortable little house at the south end of Shaker, and she had gone from kindergarten all the way up to high school without—as people joked—saying more than ten words a year.

But unlike many of the other violinists—who resented Izzy for making second chair her first year—Deja never joined in the snide comments, or called her "the freshman." In the first week of school, Deja, as they'd filed out of the orchestra room, had leaned over to zip an unfastened pocket on Izzy's bookbag, concealing her exposed gym clothes. A few weeks later, Izzy had been digging through her bag, desperately looking for a tampon, when Deja had discreetly leaned across the aisle and extended a folded hand. "Here," she'd said, and Izzy had known what it was before she even felt the crinkle of the plastic wrapper in her palm.

Watching Mrs. Peters pick on Deja, in front of everyone, had been like watching someone drag a kitten into the street and club it with a brick, and something inside Izzy had snapped. Before she knew it, she had cracked Mrs. Peters's bow over her knee and flung the broken pieces at her. There had been a sudden squawk from Mrs. Peters as the jagged halves of the bow—still joined by the horsehair—had whipped across her face and a shrill squeal as the mug of steaming coffee in her hand tipped down her front. The practice room had erupted in a babble of laughter and shrieking and hooting, and Mrs. Peters, coffee dripping down the tendons of her neck, had grabbed Izzy by the elbow and dragged her from the room. In the principal's office, waiting for her mother to arrive, Izzy had wondered if Deja had been pleased or embarrassed, and she wished she'd had a chance to see Deja's face.

Although Izzy was sure, now, that Mia would understand all of this, she did not know how to put everything she felt into words. She said only, "Mrs. Peters is a total bitch. She had no right to say that to Deja."

"Well?" said Mia. "What are you going to do about it?"

It was not a question Izzy had been asked before. Until now her life had been one of mute, futile fury. In the first week of school, after reading T. S. Eliot, she had tacked up signs on all the bulletin boards: I HAVE MEASURED OUT MY LIFE WITH COFFEE SPOONS and DO I DARE TO EAT A PEACH? and *DO I DARE DISTURB THE UNIVERSE?* The poem made her think of her mother, doling out her creamer in a precise teaspoon, flipping out about pesticides if Izzy bit into an apple without washing it, rigidly drawing restrictions around her every move—and made her think of her older siblings, too, of Lexie and Trip and everyone like them, which to Izzy felt like everyone. So concerned about wearing the right things, saying the right things, being friends with the right people. She had fantasies of students whispering in the halls—*Those signs? Who put them up? What did they mean?*—noticing them, thinking about them, *waking up,* for God's sake. But in the rush before first period everyone funneled past them up and down the stairwells, too busy passing notes and cramming for quizzes to even glance up at the bulletin boards, and after second period she found that some dour security guard had torn the signs down, no doubt perplexed by these missives, leaving only flyers for Youth Ending Hunger, Model UN, and French Club. The second week of school, when Ms. Bellamy had asked them to memorize a poem and recite it in front of the class, Izzy had selected "This Be The Verse," a poem she felt—based on her fourteen and a half years—summed up life quite accurately. She had gotten no further than "They fuck you up, your mum and dad—" before Ms. Bellamy had peremptorily told her to sit down and given her a zero.

What was she going to do about it? The very idea that she *could* do something stunned her.

At that moment Lexie's car pulled into the driveway and Lexie came in, bookbag slung over one shoulder, smelling of cigarette smoke and ck one. "Thank God, there it is," she said, plucking her wallet off the edge of the counter. Lexie, Mrs. Richardson liked to say, would leave her head at home if it weren't attached. "Having fun on your vacation day?" she said to Izzy, and Mia saw a light in Izzy switch off.

"Thanks for the sandwich," she said, and slid down from her stool and went upstairs.

"Jesus," Lexie said, rolling her eyes. "I will never

understand that girl." She looked at Mia, waiting for a sympathetic nod, but it didn't come. "Drive carefully" was all Mia said, and Lexie bounced out, wallet in hand, and in a moment her Explorer revved outside.

Izzy had the heart of a radical, but she had the experience of a fourteen-year-old living in the suburban Midwest. Which was to say: she cast about for ideas for exacting revenge—egged windows, flaming bags of dog shit—and chose the best thing in her limited repertoire.

Three afternoons later, Pearl and Moody were in the living room watching Ricki Lake when they saw Izzy stride calmly down the hallway, a six-pack of toilet paper under each arm. They exchanged a single, hasty glance and then, without discussion, chased after her.

"You are a freaking idiot," Moody said, when they had intercepted Izzy in the foyer and safely barricaded her in the kitchen. Over the years he had saved Izzy from her own stupidity—as he thought of it—a number of times, but this, for him, was a new record. "TP-ing her house?"

"It's a bitch to clean up," Izzy said. "It'll piss her off. And she deserves to be pissed off."

"And she'll know it was you. The girl she just suspended." Moody kicked the toilet paper under the table. "If you don't get caught in the act. Which you probably would have."

Izzy scowled. "You have a better idea?"

"You can't just target Mrs. Peters," Mia said. All three children looked up in astonishment. They had forgotten, for a moment, that Mia was there, yet there she was, chopping a pepper for dinner and sounding like no parent they'd ever encountered. Pearl flushed and shot a glance at her mother. What was she thinking, butting in like this, let alone butting into *this* conversation, of all things? What Mia was thinking about, however, was her own teenage years, memories she'd packed away long ago for safekeeping but now unfolded and dusted clean.

"Someone I knew once glued the lock on the history teacher's door," she said. "He'd been late and she'd given him detention and he missed playing in a big football game. The next day he squirted a whole tube of Krazy Glue into the lock. They had to break down the door." A faraway smile crept over her mouth. "But he only did hers, so they knew it was him right away. He got grounded for a month."

"Mom." Pearl's entire face was aflame. "Thanks. We've got this." Hastily, she nudged Izzy and Moody out of the kitchen and out of Mia's earshot. Now they would think her mother was a total nutcase, she thought, unable to even look at them. Had she glanced at their faces, though, she would have seen not derision but admiration. From the gleam in Mia's eye both Moody and Izzy could see she was far savvier—and far more interesting—than they'd imagined. It was their first clue, they would realize later, that there was another side to her.

All evening Izzy turned over Mia's story, her question from before: *What are you going to do about it?* In those words she heard a permission to do what she'd always been told not to: to take matters into her own hands, to make trouble. By this point, Izzy's anger had ballooned to cover not only Mrs. Peters but the principal who'd hired her, the vice principal who had handed out the suspension, every teacher—every adult—who'd ever cudgeled a student with arbitrary, unearned power. The next day, she cornered Moody and Pearl and outlined her plan.

"It's going to piss her off," said Izzy. "It's going to piss everyone off."

"You're going to get in trouble," Moody protested, but Izzy shook her head.

"I'm doing this," she said. "I'm only going to get in trouble if you *don't* help me."

$$\ggg\lll$$

A toothpick, inserted into a standard keyhole and snapped off flush, is a marvelous thing. It causes no damage to the lock, yet it prevents the key from entering, so the door cannot be opened. It is not easily removed without a pair of needle-nosed tweezers, which are often not handy and take some time to procure. The more impatient the key wielder, the more firmly and insistently the key is jammed into the keyhole, the more tenaciously the toothpick will cling to the innards of the lock, and the longer it will take to extract it even with the right equipment. A reasonably adept teenager, working quickly, can insert a toothpick into a lock, snap it off, and walk away in approximately three seconds. Three teenagers, working in unison, can therefore immobilize an entire high school containing one hundred and twenty-six doors in less than ten minutes, quickly enough to avoid notice and settle into their usual spots in the hallway to watch what ensues.

By the time the first teachers noticed their doors were

jammed, it was already 7:27. By 7:40, when most of the teachers arrived at their classrooms and found themselves stymied, Mr. Wrigley, the custodian, was upstairs in the science wing attempting to pry the first sliver of toothpick out of the chemistry lab's lock with the tip of his penknife. By 7:45, when Mr. Wrigley returned to his office in search of his toolbox and the tweezers inside it, he found a large crowd of teachers clustered in his doorway, clamoring about the jammed locks. In the confusion someone dislodged the doorstop that had been holding Mr. Wrigley's door open and let it slam shut, and Mr. Wrigley finally discovered the toothpick that Izzy herself had carefully placed in his keyhole much earlier, when he had stepped out for a mug of coffee.

All this time students had been trickling in, first the early birds, who came at 7:15 to secure a parking spot on the oval that surrounded the school, then the students who got dropped off by parents or walked. By the time the late arrivals straggled in at 7:52 and the bell for first period was ringing, the hallways were crammed with gleeful students, bewildered secretaries, and furious teachers.

It would be another twenty minutes before Mr. Wrigley returned from his truck, having rummaged in the toolbox in the trunk and finally, to his immense relief, found a second pair of tweezers. It would be another ten minutes after that when he managed to extract the first toothpick from the first classroom door and the chemistry teacher could at last get to his desk. Morning announcements were postponed, replaced by stern instructions over the P.A. system—that all students were to line up outside their first-period classes—which no one heard. The atmosphere in every hallway was like that of a surprise party, with no host in evidence but everyone, somehow, as the surprised and delighted guest. From a locker someone produced a boom box, complete with batteries. Andre Williams, the kicker of the football team, extended the antenna, hoisted it onto his shoulder, and clicked the dial to WMMS—"Buzzard Radio"—and an impromptu dance party to the Mighty Mighty Bosstones erupted before Mrs. Allerton, the U.S. history teacher, reached him and told him to shut it off. Mr. Wrigley continued to work his way down the hallway, one door at a time, prying splinters of wood from the Yale locks and gathering them in his calloused palm.

Down in the arts wing, Mrs. Peters, nursing her extra-large thermos and a splitting headache, began to fidget. The orchestra room was far from the science wing, where Mr. Wrigley was slowly progressing. At this rate hers would be one of the last, if not the last, door to be unjammed. She had asked Mr. Wrigley several times if he couldn't go faster, if he couldn't take a moment and open her door first, and by the third time, he turned to her, brandishing a scrap of wood in his upturned tweezers. "I'm going as fast as I can, Mrs. Peters," he'd said. "Going as fast as I can. Everybody's gotta wait their turn." He turned back to the keyhole before him, where Mr. Desanti, the ninth-grade math teacher, had tried to force his key into the lock and splintered the toothpick deep into the cylinders. "Everybody gotta be first," he muttered, loud enough to be sure Mrs. Peters would hear. "Everybody gotta be important. Well. The man with the tweezers says, everybody gotta wait their turn." He thrust the tweezers into the lock again, and Mrs. Peters turned away.

That had been an hour and a half ago, and she suspected, accurately, that Mr. Wrigley was holding her room for last, to punish her. Fine, she thought. But couldn't he at least open up the faculty lounge? She had checked three times now, and the door was still locked. With every minute that passed, she became more aware of the full thermos of coffee—almost an entire potful— she'd emptied while waiting. The girls' bathrooms had swinging doors, unlockable. Surely she would not have to go in there with the students, she thought; surely he would open the faculty lounge soon and she could use the unisex restroom there, the one reserved for teachers. As each minute ticked by, her impatience with Mr. Wrigley grew and spread to the principal, to the entire world. Couldn't anyone think ahead? Couldn't anyone prioritize? Couldn't anyone take basic human needs into account? She gave up her post by the orchestra room and took up a new waiting spot outside the faculty lounge, her handbag clutched across her abdomen like a shield. Five cups of coffee trickled their slow way through her innards. For a few moments she considered simply getting into her car and driving away. She could be home in twenty-five minutes. But the longer she stood, the longer twenty-five minutes seemed, and the more certain it seemed to her that sitting, in any context, would bring disaster.

"Dr. Schwab," she said as the principal walked by.

"Can't you ask Mr. Wrigley to open the faculty lounge, please?"

Dr. Schwab had had a difficult morning. It was 9:40 and half of the classrooms were still locked; although he'd asked teachers to bring their students into the classrooms and keep them there until all the doors had been opened, eight hundred students were still loose in the hallways. Some of them had spilled out onto the steps; groups of them had formed circles on the lawn, laughing and kicking hacky sacks and, in some cases, even smoking right there on school property. He rubbed his temple with one knuckle. Beneath his collar his neck began to chafe, and he wiggled a finger beneath his tie.

"Helen," he said with as much patience as he could muster, "Mr. Wrigley is going as fast as he can. In the meantime, the girls' bathroom is right down the hall. I'm sure you can use it just this one time." He headed off, doing quick mental calculations. If everyone was back in the classrooms by 10:30—which seemed optimistic— they could run an abbreviated schedule, with each period running thirty-four minutes instead of fifty—

Mrs. Peters waited another fifteen minutes and then could wait no more. She squeezed the handles of her purse tighter, as if that would somehow help, and trotted down the hallway to the girls' bathroom. It was the main restroom, positioned right where the main hallway met the main staircase, and even on a normal day it was crowded. Today it was mobbed. A group of boys stood in a ring outside, smashing the apples from their lunches against their foreheads and egging each other on with guttural roars. A group of girls clustered around the water fountain, half of them pretending not to notice the boys, the other half of them flirting with the boys outright. Above them, a mural of a shark looked down with a gaping mouth. Mrs. Peters felt a brief pang of irritation at their youth, their frivolity, their ease. On a normal day she would have told them to move along, or demanded hall passes from each one, but today she was in no condition to care.

She elbowed her way through the crowd. "Excuse me. Excuse me. Boys. Girls. A teacher needs to get through."

Inside, the bathroom was crammed with girls. Girls gossiping, girls fixing their hair, girls primping. Mrs. Peters nudged her way past with increasing urgency. "Excuse me. Girls. Excuse me, girls." Every girl in the bathroom looked up, wide-eyed, at the intrusion.

"Hi, Mrs. Peters," said Lexie. "I didn't know teachers ever used this bathroom."

"The faculty lounge is still locked," Mrs. Peters said in what she hoped was a dignified tone. Around her she noticed that all the girls had gone silent. In ordinary circumstances she would have approved of this sign of respect, but today she would have preferred to be ignored. She turned and headed for the farthest stall, by the window, but when she reached it she found that it had no door.

"What happened to the door?" she asked stupidly.

"It's been broken forever," Lexie said. "Since the first week of school. They really ought to fix it. You come in here and there's only three stalls you can use and you end up being late for class."

Mrs. Peters didn't bother to listen to the rest of Lexie's speech. She yanked the door of the next stall open and slammed it behind her. With trembling hands she slid the latch into place and fumbled with her skirt. But at the sight of the white porcelain bowl her body—which had been waiting for nearly two and a half hours—could resist no longer. With a tremendous gush her bladder gave way, and Mrs. Peters felt a warm rush flood down her legs, and a spreading puddle snaked its way across the tiles and out of the stall.

From behind the flimsy partition Mrs. Peters heard someone say, "Oh. My. God." Then a shocked, utter silence. She held completely still, as if—she thought irrationally—the girls outside might simply forget about her. The silence seemed to stretch itself out like taffy. The damp patch on her skirt, and her soaked pantyhose, turned chilly. And then the giggling began, the kind of giggles that grew all the more obvious for being stifled. Bags were quickly zipped. Footsteps scurried into the hallway. Mrs. Peters heard the door swing open, then shut, and a few moments later she heard roars of laughter from the hallway. She stayed in the stall a long time, until she heard Dr. Schwab on the P.A. system informing everyone that all doors were now unlocked and all students should be in class or risk detention. When she came out into the bathroom again, it was empty, and she left concealing her stained skirt with her pocketbook, refusing to look at the puddle, which was slowly trickling past the sinks toward the drain in the corner.

If anyone in second-period orchestra rehearsal noticed that Mrs. Peters was wearing different clothing when class began at last, no one said a word. They practiced the Offenbach and the Barber and Mozart's Twenty-fifth with blank faces. But the word had already spread. It would be days before, pausing outside the classroom, she heard someone refer to her as "Mrs. Pissers," and it would be years—well past her retirement—before the nickname and story, passed down from class to class, faded away.

The toothpick incident would have a lasting effect on the school as well. There were no cameras in the hallways, and no one seemed to have spotted the vandals, whoever they'd been. There was some talk of instituting better security—several teachers mentioned nearby Euclid, which had recently made news for installing metal detectors at each entrance—but the general feeling was that Shaker Heights, unlike Euclid, should not *need* such security, and the administration decided to downplay the incident as a minor prank. In the minds of Shaker students, however, Toothpick Day would acquire the status of legend, and in future years, during Senior Prank Week, toothpicks were banned from the school by threat of detention.

The day after Toothpick Day, Izzy caught Deja Johnson's eye and smiled, and Deja—though she had no idea that this entire event had been on her behalf, and even less of an idea that Izzy Richardson was behind it—smiled back. They wouldn't become friends exactly, but Izzy would feel there was a bond between them, and every day in orchestra she made a point of smiling at Deja Johnson, and noted with satisfaction that Mrs. Peters now left Deja alone.

The toothpicks' most lasting effect, however, turned out to be on Izzy herself. She kept thinking of Mia's smile that day in the kitchen, the capability she saw there to delight in mischief, in breaking the rules. Her own mother would have been horrified. She recognized a kindred spirit, a similar subversive spark to the one she often felt flaring inside her. Instead of shutting herself up in her room all afternoon, she began to come down when Mia arrived and linger in the kitchen while she cooked—much to her siblings' amusement. Izzy ignored them. She was too fascinated by Mia to care. And then, a few days later, Mia answered the door of the little Winslow house to find Izzy outside.

"I want to be your assistant," Izzy blurted out.

"I don't need an assistant," Mia told her. "And I'm not sure your mother would like it."

"I don't care." Izzy put her hand on the doorframe, as if afraid Mia might slam the door in her face. "I just want to learn about what you're doing. I could mix up your chemicals or file your papers or whatever. Anything."

Mia hesitated. "I can't afford an assistant."

"You don't have to pay me. I'll do it for free. Please." Izzy was not used to asking favors, but something in her voice told Mia that this was a need, not a want. "Whatever needs doing, I'll do it. Please."

Mia looked down at Izzy, this wayward, wild, fiery girl suddenly gone timid and dampened and desperate. She reminded Mia, oddly, of herself at around that age, traipsing through the neighborhood, climbing over fences and walls in search of the right photograph, defiantly spending her mother's money on film. Single-minded almost to excess. Something inside Izzy reached out to something in her and caught fire.

"All right," Mia said, and opened the door wider to let Izzy inside.

zzy's newfound fascination with Mia proved lasting. Instead of sequestering herself in her bedroom with her violin, she would walk the mile and a half to the house on Winslow right after school, where Mia would be hard at work. She would watch Mia, learning to frame a shot, develop film, make a print. Pearl, meanwhile, did the exact reverse, walking with Moody to his house, lounging in the sunroom with the three oldest Richardson children. Deep down she was grateful to Izzy for diverting her mother's attention: for so many years, it had been only the two of them, and now, on the Richardsons' big sofa, she stretched her legs out in luxurious satisfaction. At five o'clock, Izzy would hop into the passenger seat of the Rabbit and Mia would drive them both to the Richardsons', where Izzy would perch at the end of the kitchen counter and Mia would prepare dinner, listening intently to her daughter and the others in the next room. Only when Mia headed home—with Pearl in the passenger seat this time—would Izzy join her siblings and slump onto the couch beside them. "Someone's got a little crush on Mia," Lexie singsonged, and Izzy rolled her eyes and went upstairs.

But *crush* was, perhaps, the right term. Izzy hung on

Mia's every word, sought and trusted her opinion on everything. Along with the basics of photography, she began to absorb Mia's aesthetics and sensibilities. When she asked Mia how she knew which images to put together, Mia shook her head. "I don't," she said. "This— this is how I figure out what I think." She waved a hand at the X-Acto knife on the table, the photograph she was carefully cutting apart: a line of cars speeding across the Lorain-Carnegie Bridge, beneath the watchful eyes of the two huge statues carved into the bridge's pillars. She had meticulously excised each car, leaving only its shadow. "I don't have a plan, I'm afraid," she said, lifting the knife again. "But then, no one really does, no matter what they say."

"My mother does. She thinks she has a plan for everything."

"I'm sure that makes her feel better."

"She hates me."

"Oh, Izzy. I'm sure that's not true."

"No, she does. She hates me. That's why she picks on me and not any of the others."

Mia had, since starting to work at the Richardsons', noted the peculiar dynamic between Izzy and the rest of her family, especially her mother. Truth be told, her mother *was* harsher on Izzy: always criticizing her behavior, always less patient with her mistakes and her shortcomings. She seemed to hold Izzy to a higher standard than her other children, to demand more from her, yet at the same time to overlook her successes in favor of her faults. Izzy, Mia noticed, tended to respond by needling her mother even more, pushing her buttons with the expertise only a child could.

"Izzy," she said now, "I'll tell you a secret. A lot of times, parents are not the best at seeing their children clearly. There's so much wonderful about you." She gave Izzy's elbow a little squeeze and swept a handful of scraps into the garbage, and Izzy beamed. During those afternoons, when it was just the two of them, it was easy for Izzy to pretend that Mia was her mother, that the bedroom down the hallway was hers, and that when night fell she would go into it and sleep and wake in the morning. That Pearl—a mile and a half away, watching television with her own brothers and sister—did not exist, that this life belonged to her, Izzy, and her alone. In the evenings, back at home, with jazz screeching from Moody's room and Alanis Morissette wailing from Lexie's and Trip's stereo providing a thumping undercurrent of bass, Izzy would imagine herself in the house on Winslow: lying in bed reading, perhaps, or maybe writing a poem, Mia out in the living room working late into the night. There were many convoluted routes into this fantasy: she and Pearl had been accidentally switched at birth years ago; she had been taken home by her parents, who were therefore not her parents, and this was why no one in her family seemed to understand her, why she seemed so different from them all. Now, in her carefully spun dreams, she was reunited with her true mother. *I knew I'd find you someday,* Mia would say.

Everyone in the Richardson family noticed Izzy's improved demeanor. "She's almost *pleasant* around you,"

Lexie told Mia one day. Izzy's adoration for Mia, like everything she did, did not come by halves: there was nothing Izzy wouldn't do for her. And she soon found something, she was sure, that Mia really wanted.

In mid-November, Pearl and Moody, along with the rest of their modern European history class, had gone to the art museum to look at paintings. The docent giving the class a tour was elderly and thin and looked as if all the juice had been sucked out of him through a straw via his pursed mouth. He disliked high school groups: teens didn't listen. Teens could pay attention to nothing but the sexuality billowing off each other like steam. Velázquez, he thought; some still lifes, maybe some Caravaggio. Definitely no nudes. He led them the long way around to the Italian wing, through the main hall with its tapestries and suits of armor in glass cases.

The students themselves, however, paid little attention to the art, as students on field trips generally do. Andy Keen poked Jessica Kleinman between the shoulder blades and pretended, each time, it wasn't him. Clayton Booth and David Shearn talked about football, the Raiders' chances against St. Ignatius in the upcoming game. Jennie Levi and Tanisha McDowell studiously ignored Jason Graham and Dante Samuels, who were tallying and evaluating the naked breasts in the paintings the docent hurried them past. Moody, who loved art, was watching Pearl and wishing—not for the first time— that he were a photographer, so that he could capture the way the light from the frosted-glass gallery ceiling hit her upturned face and made it glow.

Pearl herself, though she tried to focus on the docent's

withered lecture, found her mind drifting. She stepped, sideways, into the next gallery over, a special curated exhibit on the theme of Madonna and Child. From across the room, Moody, dutifully taking notes on a Caravaggio, watched her go. When she didn't return after three, four, five minutes, he slid his pencil into the spiral of his notebook and followed.

It was a small room, with only a few dozen pieces on the wall, all showing the Virgin with Jesus on her lap. Some were medieval paintings in gilt frames hardly bigger than CD jewel cases; some were rough pencil sketches of Renaissance statues; some were larger-than-life oil paintings. One was a postmodern collage of photos from celebrity gossip mags, the Virgin had the head of Julia Roberts, Jesus the head of Brad Pitt. But the piece that had transfixed Pearl was a photograph: a black-and-white print, eight by ten, of a woman on a sofa, beaming down at the newborn in her arms. It was unmistakably Mia.

"But how——" Moody began.

"I don't know."

They stared at the photo for some time in silence. Moody, ever practical, began gathering information. The title of the piece, according to the card beside it, was *Virgin and Child #1* (1982); the artist was Pauline Hawthorne. He jotted these down in his notebook beneath his abandoned Caravaggio notes. There were no curator comments, other than a note that the photo had been lent for the exhibit by the Ellsworth Gallery in Los Angeles.

Pearl, on the other hand, focused on the photograph itself. There was her mother, looking a bit younger, a bit thinner, but with the same waifish build, the same high cheekbones and pointed chin. There was the tiny mole just underneath her eye, the scar that slashed like a white thread through her left eyebrow. There were her mother's slender arms, which looked so fragile and birdlike, as if they might snap under too great a weight, but which could carry more than any woman Pearl had ever seen. Even her hair was the same: piled in the same careless bundle right at the crown of her head. Beauty rolled off her in waves, like heat; the very image of her in the photograph seemed to glow. She wasn't looking at the camera; she was focused, totally and utterly absorbed, on the infant before her. *On me,* Pearl thought. She was sure it was her in the photo. What other baby would her mother be holding? There were no photos of herself as an infant, but she recognized herself in this child, in the bridge of the nose and the corners of the eyes, in the tight balled fists she had continued to make into toddlerhood and childhood, which in her concentration, without realizing it, she was making even now. Where had this photo come from? The gray-scale sofa on which her mother sat might be tan, or pale blue, or even canary; the window behind her looked out onto a blurred view of tall buildings. The person who'd taken it had been mere feet away, as if seated on an armchair just beside the couch. Who had it been?

"Miss Warren," Mrs. Jacoby said behind her. "Mr. Richardson." Pearl and Moody spun around, their faces prickling with heat. "If you are both ready to move on, the entire class is waiting for you."

And indeed, the entire class was gathered outside,

notebooks closed now, dutifully chaperoned by the docent, giggling and whispering as Moody and Pearl emerged.

On the bus ride back home, jokes began to circulate about what Moody and Pearl had been doing. Moody turned a deep crimson and slouched down in his seat, pretending not to hear. Pearl gazed out the window, oblivious. She said nothing at all until the bus reached the oval around the school and the students began to file out. "I want to go back," she said to Moody as they stepped off the bus.

And they did, that afternoon after school, persuading Lexie to drive them because there was no good way to get there otherwise, and letting Izzy tag along because the moment she heard *Mia* and *photograph,* she insisted on coming with them. Moody, who had done the persuading, hadn't told Lexie what they wanted to see, and when they stepped into the gallery her mouth fell open.

"Wow," she said. "Pearl—that's your mom."

The four of them surveyed the photograph: Lexie from the middle of the room, as if she needed distance for a better view; Moody nearly smudging it with his nose, as if he might find the answer between the pixels, and leaning so close that he set off a warning alarm. Pearl simply stared. And Izzy stood transfixed by the image of Mia. In the photo, she was as luminous as the full moon on a clear night. *Virgin and Child #1,* she read on the placard, and she allowed herself to imagine for a moment that the child in Mia's arms was her.

"That's so crazy," Lexie said at last. "God, that's so crazy. What's your mom doing in a photo in an *art museum*? Is she secretly famous?"

"The people in photos aren't famous," Moody put in. "The people who take them are."

"Maybe she was some famous artist's muse. Like Patti Smith and Robert Mapplethorpe. Or Edie Sedgwick and Andy Warhol." Lexie had taken an art history class at the museum the previous summer. She straightened up. "Well, let's ask her," she said. "We'll just ask her."

And they did as soon as they got home, trooping into the Richardson kitchen, where Mia had just finished dressing a chicken for dinner.

"Where have you all been?" she said as they came in. "I got here at five and no one was home."

"We went to the art museum," Pearl began, and then hesitated. Something about this didn't feel right to her, the same uneasy feeling you had when you set your foot on a wobbly step, just before it dipped beneath you. Moody and Izzy and Lexie clustered around her, and she saw how they must look to her mother, flushed and wide-eyed and curious.

Lexie nudged her in the back. "Ask her."

"Ask me what?" Mia set the chicken into a casserole dish and went to the sink to wash her hands, and Pearl, with the feeling of stepping off a very high diving board, plunged ahead.

"There's a photo of you," she blurted out. "At the art museum. A photo of you on a couch holding a baby."

Mia's back was still to them, the water rushing over

her hands, but all four of the children saw it: a slight stiffening of her posture, as if a string had been tightened. She did not turn around but kept on scrubbing at the gaps between her fingers.

"A photo of me, Pearl? In an art museum?" she said. "You just mean someone who looks like me."

"It was you," Lexie said. "It was definitely you. With that little dot under your eye and the scar on your eyebrow and everything."

Mia touched a knuckle to her brow, as if she'd forgotten the scar existed, and a drop of warm sudsy water ran down her temple. Then she rinsed her hands and shut off the faucet.

"I suppose it *could* have been me," she said. She turned around and began to dry her hands briskly on the dish towel, and to Pearl's chagrin her mother's face was suddenly stiff and closed in. It was disorienting, like seeing a door that had always been open suddenly shut. For a moment, Mia did not look like her mother at all. "You know, photographers are always looking for models. Lots of the art students did it."

"But you'd remember," Lexie insisted. "You were sitting on a couch in a nice apartment. And Pearl was on your lap. The photographer was—" She turned to Moody. "What's her name?"

"Hawthorne. Pauline Hawthorne."

"Pauline Hawthorne," Lexie repeated, as if Mia might not have heard. "You must remember it."

Mia shook the dish towel out with a quick snap of her wrist. "Lexie, I really can't remember all the odd jobs I've done," she said. "You know, when you're hard up, you do a lot of things just to try and make ends meet. I wonder if you can imagine what that's like."

She turned back to the sink and hung the towel to dry, and Pearl realized she'd gone about this all wrong. She should never have asked her mother like this, in the Richardson kitchen with its granite countertops and its stainless-steel fridge and its Italian terra-cotta tiles, in front of the Richardson kids in their bright, buoyant North Face jackets, especially in front of Lexie, who still had the keys to her Explorer dangling from one hand. If she'd waited until they were alone, back at home in the dim little kitchen in their half a house on Winslow Road, perched on their mismatched chairs at the one remaining leaf of their salvaged table, perhaps her mother would have told her. Already she saw her mistake: this was a private thing, something that should have been kept between them, and by including the Richardsons she had breached a barrier that should not have been broken. Now, looking at her mother's set jaw and flat eyes, she knew there was no sense in asking any more questions.

Lexie, for her part, was satisfied with Mia's explanation. "Ironic, isn't it," she said as they left the kitchen, shrugging, and Pearl let it go without even bothering to tell her that that wasn't what *ironic* meant. She was happy to let the matter drop. On the drive home, and for the rest of the evening, her mother was strangely silent, and she regretted ever bringing it up. Pearl had always been aware of money—in their circumstances, how could she not?—but she had never before contemplated what it must have been like for her mother with an infant, trying to scrape by. She wondered what else her mother had done to survive—so that they both could survive—those early years. She had never in her life gone to bed without Mia coming to kiss her good night, but that night she did, and Mia sat in the living room in a puddle of light, her face still shut, lost in thought.

The following morning, Pearl was relieved when she came into the kitchen and Mia was there, making toast as usual, and carrying on as if the previous day had not happened. But the matter of the photograph lingered in the air like a bad smell, and Pearl tucked her questions into the back corner of her mind and resolved to say nothing more about it, at least for now.

"Should I make some tea?" she asked.

><

Izzy, however, was determined to find answers. It was clear this photograph held some secret about Mia, and she promised herself that she would unravel it. As a freshman, she had no free periods, but she devoted several lunch periods to research in the library. She looked up Pauline Hawthorne in the card catalog and found a few books on art history. Apparently she had been quite well known. "A pioneer of modern American photography," one book called her. Another called her "Cindy Sherman before Cindy Sherman was Cindy Sherman." (At this point Izzy took a brief detour to look up Cindy Sherman, and spent so long perusing her photographs she was nearly late to class.)

Pauline Hawthorne's work, she learned, was known for its immediacy and its intimacy, for interrogating images of femininity and identity. "Pauline Hawthorne paved the way for me and other women photographers," Cindy Sherman herself said in one profile. Izzy pored over the reproductions of her photographs: her favorite was a shot of a housewife and her daughter on a swing, the child kicking her legs so hard the chains bent in an arc, defying gravity, the woman's arms outstretched as if to push her child away or desperate to pull her back. The photos stirred feelings she couldn't quite frame in words, and this, she decided, must mean they were true works of art.

She combed every entry for Pauline Hawthorne she'd found in the card catalog until she had accumulated the basic facts of her life: born in 1947 in New Jersey, attended Garden State College, exhibited her first works in New York City in 1970, had her first solo show in 1972. Her photographs, Izzy learned, had been some of the most sought after in the 1970s. The encyclopedia entry had a photograph of Pauline Hawthorne herself, a slender woman with large dark eyes and silvery hair in a no-nonsense bob. She looked like someone's math teacher.

Pauline Hawthorne, she learned, had died of brain cancer in 1982. Izzy settled herself at one of the two computers in the library, waited for the modem to connect, and typed Pauline's name into AltaVista. She found more photographs—the Getty had one, MoMA had three; a few articles analyzing her work; an obituary from the New York Times. Nothing else. She tried the public library, both branches, found a few more photography books and several articles on microfiche, but they added nothing new. What was the connection between Pauline Hawthorne and Mia? Perhaps Mia had simply been a model, like she said; maybe she'd just happened to sit for Pauline Hawthorne. This did not satisfy Izzy, who felt this was an improbable coincidence.

At last she turned to the only source she could think of: her mother. Her mother was a journalist, at least in name. True, her mother mostly covered small stories, but journalists found things out. They had connections, they had ways of researching that weren't accessible to just anyone. From early childhood, Izzy had been fiercely, stubbornly independent; she refused to ask for help with anything. Only the deep hunger to unravel this mysterious photograph could have convinced her to approach her mother.

"Mom," she said one evening, after several days of fruitless research. "Can you help me with something?"

Mrs. Richardson listened, as usual with Izzy, with only half her attention. A pressing deadline was looming, for a story on the Nature Center's annual plant sale.

"Izzy, this photo probably isn't even of Pearl's mother. It could be anyone. Someone who looks like her. I'm sure it's just a coincidence."

"It's not," Izzy insisted. "Pearl knew it was her mother and I saw it, too. Would you just look into it? Call the museum or something. See what you can find out. Please." She had never been good at wheedling—she'd always felt flattery was a form of lying—but she wanted this so badly. "I'm sure you can figure it out. You're a *reporter*."

Mrs. Richardson gave in. "All right," she said. "I'll see what I can find out. But it'll have to wait until after this deadline. I have to file this story by tomorrow.

"It'll probably be nothing, you know," she added, as Izzy danced toward the door with barely suppressed glee.

Izzy's words—*You're a reporter*—had touched her mother's pride like a finger pressed into an old bruise. Mrs. Richardson had wanted to be a journalist her entire life, long before the aptitude tests their guidance counselor had administered in high school. "Journalists," she explained in a civics speech about dream careers, "chronicle our everyday lives. They reveal truths and information that the public deserves to know, and they provide a record for posterity, so that future generations can learn from our mistakes and improve upon our achievements." For as long as she could remember, her own mother had always been busy with some committee or other, advocating for more school funding, more equity, more fairness, and bringing her young daughter along. "Change doesn't just happen," her mother had always said, echoing the Shaker motto. "It has to be planned." In history class, when young Elena had learned the term *noblesse oblige*, she'd understood it at once. Journalism, to Mrs. Richardson, seemed such a noble calling, one where you could do good from within the system, and in her mind she envisioned a mix of Nellie Bly and Lois Lane. After working on the school paper for four years—and working her way up to coeditor in chief by senior year—this seemed not only possible, but inevitable.

She graduated second in her class and had had her choice of colleges: a full ride at Oberlin, a partial scholarship at Denison, acceptances all over the state, from

Kenyon to Kent State to Wooster. Her mother had been in favor of Oberlin, had urged her to apply in the first place, but when Elena visited the campus, she'd felt immediately out of place. The coed dorms unsettled her, all the men in their skivvies, the girls in their robes, the knowledge that at any moment a boy might saunter into her room—or worse, the bathroom. On the steps of one building, three long-haired students in dashikis sat playing slide whistles; across the green, students held up posters in silent protest: DROP ACID, NOT BOMBS. I DON'T GIVE A DAMN ABOUT THE PRESIDENT. BOMBING FOR PEACE IS LIKE FUCKING FOR VIRGINITY. It felt, to Elena, like a foreign country where rules did not reach. She fought the urge to fidget, as if the campus were an itchy sweater.

So she'd headed to Denison the following fall instead, with an ambitious and illustrious future plotted out for herself. On the second day of classes she met Billy Richardson, tall and handsome in the Clark Kent vein, and by the end of the month they were going steady. Chastely they made plans for the future: after graduation, a white wedding in Cleveland, a house in Shaker, lots of children, law school for him, a cub reportership for her—a plan they followed meticulously. Soon after they married and settled into a rented duplex in Shaker, Mr. Richardson started law school and Mrs. Richardson was offered a position as a junior reporter at the *Sun Press*. It was a small paper, focused on local news, and the pay was commensurately low. Still, she decided, it was a promising enough place to start. In time, perhaps, she'd be able to make the jump over to the

Plain Dealer, Cleveland's "real" newspaper—though of course she'd never want to leave Shaker, could not imagine raising a family anywhere else.

She dutifully covered all the local news conferences, city politics, the regional effects of new regulations on everything from bridges to tree planting, sharing responsibilities with the other junior reporter, Dwight, who was a year younger. It was a good workplace, allowing her to take six weeks of maternity leave after Lexie's birth, then Trip's, then Moody's. By the time Izzy came around, however, Mrs. Richardson found herself still at the *Sun Press*—senior reporter, now, but still relegated to covering the small stories, the small news. Dwight, meanwhile, had moved to Chicago to take a job at the *Tribune.* Was it because of the time she'd taken off, or the fact—as she was starting to realize—that she had no desire to tunnel into hard stories and bitter tragedies? She would never be quite certain, but the more time passed, the less probable it seemed that she could move elsewhere, and it became a question of chickens and eggs. No one at the *Plain Dealer,* or anywhere else for that matter, seemed to be interested in taking on a reporter nearing forty, with four children and all the attendant obligations, who had never covered a big story, and it didn't matter whether that was the chicken or the egg.

And so she stayed. She focused on the feel-good stories, the complimentary write-ups of progress: the new recycling initiative, the remodeling of the library, the ribbon-cutting ceremony at the new playground behind it. She covered the swearing-in of the new city manager ("solemn") and the Halloween parade ("spirited"), the opening of Half Price Books at Van Aken Center ("a much-needed addition to Shaker's commercial district"), the debate on spraying for gypsy moths ("heated, on both sides"). She reviewed the production of *Grease* at the Unitarian Church and *Guys and Dolls* at the high school: "Rollicking," she wrote of one; "Sit Down; They're Rocking the Boat!" she wrote of the other. She became known as reliable and for turning in clean copy, if—though no one said it out loud—routine and rather pedestrian and terribly *nice*. Shaker Heights was dependably safe and thus the news, such as it was, was correspondingly dull. Outside in the world, volcanoes erupted, governments rose and collapsed and bartered for hostages, rockets exploded, walls fell. But in Shaker Heights, things were peaceful, and riots and bombs and earthquakes were quiet thumps, muffled by distance. Her house was large; her children safe and happy and well educated. This was, she told herself, the broad strokes of what she had planned out all those years ago.

Izzy's request, however, brought something new. Something intriguing, or at very least interesting. Something perhaps worth investigating at last.

>≫<

True to her word, Mrs. Richardson filed her story and turned to the mysterious photograph. On a lunch break the next day, she stopped by the museum to see it for herself. Until then, she'd been sure Izzy was just imagining things, but she had been right: it was definitely Mia. In a Pauline Hawthorne photograph! She had heard of Pauline Hawthorne, of course. What was the story here? Mrs. Richardson puzzled over this as she dropped a folded five into the museum's donation box and headed out to her car, genuinely intrigued.

Her first step was to call the art gallery that had lent the photograph to the exhibit. Yes, the owner told her, they'd purchased the photograph in 1982, from a dealer in New York. It had been shortly after Pauline's death, and there had been much excitement in the art world when this previously unknown photograph had been put up for sale. There had been a fierce auction and they'd been thrilled to walk away with it for fifty thousand—really a bargain. Yes, the photograph had been conclusively attributed to Pauline Hawthorne: the dealer had sold many of Pauline's works over the years, and the photograph—the only print, they'd been told—had been signed by Pauline herself on the back. No, the owner of the photograph had been anonymous, but they would be happy to give Mrs. Richardson the name of the art dealer.

Mrs. Richardson took it down—an Anita Rees—and, after a quick call to New York City's public information, obtained the phone number of the Rees Gallery in Manhattan. Anita Rees, when reached on the telephone, proved to be a true New Yorker: brisk, fast-talking, and unflappable.

"A Pauline Hawthorne? Yes, I'm sure I did. I represented Pauline Hawthorne for years." Through the phone Mrs. Richardson heard the faint blare of a siren passing by and then receding into the distance. In her mind that was always what New York sounded like:

honking, trucks, sirens. She had been to New York only once, in college, in the days when you had to hold your purse tight with both hands and didn't dare touch anything on the subway, even the poles. It had been cemented in her memory that way.

"But this photo," Mrs. Richardson said, "was sold after Pauline's death. By someone else. It was a photo of a woman holding a baby. *Virgin and Child #1*, it was called."

The phone line suddenly went so quiet that Mrs. Richardson thought they'd been disconnected. But after a moment, Anita Rees spoke again. "Yes, I remember that one."

"I'm just wondering," said Mrs. Richardson, "if you could give me the name of the person who sold the photograph."

Something new flared in Anita's voice: suspicion. "Where did you say you were calling from again?"

"My name is Elena Richardson." Mrs. Richardson hesitated for a moment. "I work as a reporter for the *Sun Press*, in Cleveland, Ohio. It's related to a story I'm researching."

"I see." Another pause. "I'm sorry, but the original owner of that photograph wished to remain anonymous. For personal reasons. I'm not at liberty to give the seller's name."

Mrs. Richardson crimped the corner of her notepad in annoyance. "I understand. Well, what I'm actually interested in is the subject of the photograph. Would you happen to have any information on who she is?"

This time there was no mistaking it: definite wary

silence, and when Anita Rees spoke again, it was with a touch of frost. "I'm afraid I don't have anything I can share about that. Good luck with your story." The line went dead with a soft click.

Mrs. Richardson set the phone down. As a journalist, she was no stranger to being hung up on, but this time irritated her more than most. Maybe there was something here, some strange mystery waiting to be unraveled. She glanced at her monitor, where a half-drafted piece—"Should Gore Run for President? Locals Weigh In"—sat waiting.

Art collectors were often reclusive, she thought. Especially where money was involved. This Anita Rees might not even know anything about the photo, other than whatever her commission was. And who had started her down this garden path anyway? Izzy. Her harebrained live wire of a daughter, the perpetual overreactor, prone to fits of furious indignation about nothing at all.

That alone, she thought, was a sign she was headed down a rabbit hole. She turned her notebook back to the page on the vice president and began to type.

9

Mrs. Richardson remained annoyed with Izzy all week, though truth be told, she was usually annoyed with Izzy for some reason or another. The roots of her irritation were long and many branched and deep. It was not—as Izzy herself suspected, and as Lexie, in moments of meanness, teased her—because she had been an accident, or unwanted. In fact, it was quite the opposite.

Mrs. Richardson had always wanted a large family. Having been an only child herself, she had grown up longing for brothers and sisters, envying her friends like Maureen O'Shaughnessy who never came home to an empty house and who always seemed to have someone to talk to. "It's not so great," Maureen assured her, "especially if you get brothers." Maureen was the oldest at fifteen and her sister Katie was the youngest at two and in between came six boys, but Mrs. Richardson was convinced that even six brothers would be better than growing up alone. "Lots of kids," she had said to Mr. Richardson when they'd gotten married, "at least three or four. And close together," she'd added, thinking of the O'Shaughnessys again, how it was an off year that didn't have an O'Shaughnessy in the grade. Everyone knew them; they were a dynasty in Shaker Heights, a huge and boisterous and exceedingly handsome clan that always seemed to be suntanned and windswept, like the Kennedys. Mr. Richardson, who had two brothers himself, agreed.

So they'd had Lexie first, in 1980, then Trip the next year and Moody the year after that, and Mrs. Richardson had secretly been proud of how fertile her body had proved, how resilient. She would push Moody in his stroller, with Lexie and Trip tagging along behind her, each clutching a handful of her skirt like baby elephants trailing their mother, and people on the street did a double take: this slender young woman couldn't possibly have borne three children, could she? "Just one more," she'd said to her husband. They had agreed to have the children early, so that afterward Mrs. Richardson could go back to work. A part of her wanted to stay home, to simply be with her children, but her own mother had always scorned those women who didn't work. "Wasting their potential," she had sniffed. "You've got a good brain, Elena. You're not just going to sit home and knit, are you?" A modern woman, she always implied, was capable—nay, required—to *have it all*. So after each birth, Mrs. Richardson had returned to her job, crafted the pleasant, wholesome stories her editor demanded, come home to fawn over her little ones, waited for the next baby to arrive.

It wasn't until Izzy that the charmed row of children came to an end. For starters, Mrs. Richardson had had terrible morning sickness, bouts of dizziness and vomiting that didn't end with the first trimester but continued on unabated—if anything, more vigorously—as the weeks went on. Lexie was nearly three, Trip two, Moody just one, and with three very young children at home and Mrs. Richardson incapacitated, the Richardsons found it necessary to engage a housekeeper—a luxury they would become accustomed to, and which they would continue all the way into the children's teenage years, all the way up to Mia. "It's a sign of a strong pregnancy," the doctors assured Mrs. Richardson, but a few weeks after hiring the housekeeper, she had begun to bleed and was placed on bed rest. Despite these precautions, Izzy had arrived precipitously soon thereafter, making her appearance—eleven weeks early—an hour after her mother arrived at the hospital.

Mrs. Richardson would remember the next few months only as a vague, terrifying haze. Of the logistical details, she remembered only a little. She remembered Izzy curled in a glass box, a net of purple veins under salmon-colored skin. She remembered watching her youngest through the portholes in the incubator, nearly pressing her nose to the glass to be sure Izzy was still breathing. She remembered shuttling back and forth between home and the hospital, whenever she could leave her oldest three in the capable hands of the housekeeper—naptime, lunchtime, an hour here and there—and, when the nurses allowed it, cradling Izzy against her: first in her two cupped hands, then in the hollow between her breasts, and finally—as Izzy grew stronger and filled out and began to look more like a baby—in her arms.

For Izzy did grow: despite her early start, she displayed

a tenacity of will that even the doctors remarked upon. She tugged at her IV; she uprooted her feeding tube. When the nurses came to change her, she kicked her thumb-sized feet and hollered so loudly the babies in nearby incubators woke and joined in. "Nothing wrong with her lungs," the doctors told the Richardsons, though they warned of a host of other problems that might arise: jaundice, anemia, vision issues, hearing loss. Mental retardation. Heart defects. Seizures. Cerebral palsy. When Izzy finally came home—two weeks after her scheduled due date—this list would be one of the few things Mrs. Richardson would recall about her time in the hospital. A list of things she would scan Izzy for over the next decade: Did Izzy simply not notice things, or was she going blind? Was she ignoring her mother out of stubbornness, or was she going deaf? Was her skin looking a bit yellow? Was she looking a bit pale? If Izzy's hand, reaching to add a stacking ring to her toy, fumbled, Mrs. Richardson found herself clutching the arms of her chair. Was it a tremor, or just a child learning the complicated business of managing her own fingers?

Everything Mrs. Richardson had put out of her mind from the hospital stay—everything she thought she'd forgotten—her body remembered on a cellular level: the rush of anxiety, the fear that permeated her thoughts of Izzy. The microscopic focus on each thing Izzy did, turning it this way and that, scrutinizing it for signs of weakness or disaster. Was she just a poor speller, or was this a sign of mental impairment? Was her handwriting just messy, was she just bad at arithmetic, were her temper tantrums normal, or was it something worse? As time went on, the concern unhooked itself from the fear and took on a life of its own. She had learned, with Izzy's birth, how your life could trundle along on its safe little track and then, with no warning, skid spectacularly off course. Every time Mrs. Richardson looked at Izzy, that feeling of things spiraling out of control coiled around her again, like a muscle she didn't know how to unclench.

"Izzy, sit up straight," she would say at the dinner table, thinking: *Scoliosis. Cerebral palsy.* "Izzy, calm down." Though she would never quite articulate it this way, resentment began to sheathe concern. ANGER IS FEAR'S BODYGUARD, a poster in the hospital had read, but Mrs. Richardson had never noticed it; she was too busy thinking, *It wasn't supposed to happen this way.* "After all the trouble you've caused——" she would begin sometimes, when Izzy misbehaved. She never finished the sentence, even in her mind, but the old anxiety snaked through her veins. Izzy herself would remember only her mother saying, *No, no, Izzy, why can't you listen to me, Izzy, behave yourself, Izzy, for god's sakes, no, are you insane?* Drawing the boundaries over which Izzy dared to step.

Had Izzy been a different kind of child, this might have led her to be cautious, or neurasthenic, or paranoid. Izzy, however, had been born to push buttons, and as she grew—with excellent vision and hearing, no sign of seizures or palsy, and a clearly agile mind—the more closely her mother watched her and the more she chafed at the attention. When they went to the pool, Lexie and Trip and Moody were allowed to splash in the shallow end, but Izzy—then age four—had to sit on a towel, coated in sunscreen and shaded by an umbrella. After a week of this, she jumped headfirst into the deep end and had to be rescued by the lifeguard. The following winter, when they went sledding, Lexie and Trip and Moody slid shrieking down the hill, backward and belly first and three at a time and once—in Trip's case—standing up like a surfer. Mrs. Richardson, perched atop the hill, applauded and cheered. Then Izzy went down once, tipped over halfway down, and Mrs. Richardson refused to let her get into the sled again. That evening, after everyone had gone to bed, Izzy dragged Moody's sled across the street and slid down the bank of the duck pond and out onto the frozen water four times before a neighbor noticed and called her parents. At ten, when her mother fretted about her picky eating, wondering if she might be anemic, Izzy declared herself a vegetarian. After being grounded from sleepovers—"If you can't behave at home, Izzy, we can't trust you to behave in someone else's house"—Izzy took to sneaking outside at night and returning with pinecones or a handful of crab apples or a buckeye to leave on the kitchen island. "I have no idea where that could have come from," she would say in the morning, as her mother eyed her latest offering. The sense all the children had—including Izzy—was that she was a particular disappointment to their mother, that for reasons unclear to them, their mother resented her. Of course, the more Izzy pushed, the more anger stepped in to shield her mother's old anxiety, like a shell covering a snail. "My god, Izzy," Mrs. Richardson said, over and over again, "what is *wrong* with you?"

Mr. Richardson was more tolerant of Izzy. It had been Mrs. Richardson who had held her, Mrs. Richardson who had heard all the doctors' prognoses, the dire warnings about what might be in store for her. Mr. Richardson, newly graduated from law school, was busy building his practice, working long hours in an attempt to make partner. To him, Izzy seemed a trifle willful, but he was glad to see her undaunted after such a terrifying start. He delighted in her intelligence, in her spirit. In fact, she reminded him of her mother, when she'd been younger: he'd been drawn to that spark, that certainty of purpose, how she always knew her mind and had a plan, how deeply concerned she was with right versus wrong—the fiery side of her that seemed, after so many safe years in the suburbs, to have cooled down to embers. "It's okay, Elena," he would say to Mrs. Richardson. "She's fine. Let her be." Mrs. Richardson, however, could not let Izzy be, and the feeling coalesced in all of them: Izzy pushing, her mother restraining, and after a time no one could remember how the dynamic had started, only that it had existed always.

⋙⋘

The weekend after Thanksgiving, while Mrs. Richardson was still irked at Izzy, the Richardsons were due to attend a birthday party thrown by old family friends.

"Can Pearl come, too?" Moody asked. "The Mc-Culloughs won't mind. They've invited everyone they know to this thing."

"Plus she'll be one more person to gush over the baby," Izzy said. "Which you know is the whole point of this entire party."

Mrs. Richardson sighed. "Izzy, there are times when it's appropriate to invite one of your friends, and times when events are just for family," she said. "This is a family event. Pearl is not part of the family." She snapped her purse shut and slung it over her shoulder. "You need to learn the distinction. Come on, we're late."

So only the Richardsons went to the McCulloughs' that weekend, arriving in two cars—Lexie and Trip and Moody in one, Mr. and Mrs. Richardson in another, with a glowering Izzy in the backseat. No one could have missed the house. Vehicles filled both sides of the street—the McCulloughs had cleared the parking restrictions with the Shaker Heights Police in advance—and spilled over onto nearby South Woodland Boulevard, and an enormous bundle of pink and white balloons bobbed over the mailbox.

Inside, the house was already full to overflowing. There were mimosas and an omelet station. There were caterers offering bite-sized quiches and poached eggs in puddles of velvety hollandaise. There was a three-tiered pink-and-white cake, draped in fondant and topped with a sugar figurine of a baby holding the number 1 in its chubby hands. And everywhere pink and white streamers unfurling their triumphant way toward the kitchen table, where Mirabelle McCullough, the birthday girl, nestled in Mrs. McCullough's arms.

Mrs. Richardson had met Mirabelle before, of course, months earlier, when she'd first arrived at the McCullough household. She and Linda McCullough had grown up together—Shaker class of 1971, old friends since meeting in second grade—and there had been a lovely symmetry to their paths as they'd both gone away to school and come back and settled in Shaker into careers of their own. Only where the Richardsons had right away had Lexie, then Trip and Moody and Izzy in quick succession, Mrs. McCullough had undergone over a decade of trying before she and her husband had decided on adoption.

"It's just *providential*, as my mother used to say," Mrs. Richardson had told her husband on hearing the news. "There's simply no other word for it. You know what Mark and Linda have been through, all that waiting. I mean, I bet they'd have taken a crack baby, for goodness sakes. And then out of the blue the social worker calls them at ten thirty in the morning, saying there's been a little Asian baby left at a fire station, and by four o'clock in the afternoon there she is in their house."

She had gone over the very next day to meet the baby and in between cooing over the child heard Linda recount the story—how she'd gotten the call and had driven directly to Babies "R" Us, buying everything from a complete wardrobe to a crib to six months' supply of diapers. "Maxed out the Visa," Linda McCullough had said with a laugh. "Mark was still putting the crib together when the social worker pulled up with her. But look at her. Just look at her. Can you believe this?" She had bent over the infant cradled against her, with a look of pure astonishment.

That had been ten months earlier, and the adoption process was well underway now. They hoped to have it finalized in a month or two, Mrs. McCullough told Mrs. Richardson as she handed her a mimosa. Little Mirabelle was a darling thing: a fuzz of dark hair topped by a pink ribbon headband, a round pert face with two enormous brown eyes staring out at the crowd, Mrs. McCullough's beaded necklace clenched in her fingers.

"Oh, she looks like a little doll," gasped Lexie. Mirabelle turned her face away and buried it in Mrs. McCullough's sweater.

"This is the first big party we've had since she came to us," Mrs. McCullough said, running a hand over the girl's dark head. "She's not used to having so many people around. Are you, Mimi?" She kissed the baby's palm. "But we couldn't let her first birthday go by without a celebration."

"How can you know it's her birthday?" Izzy asked. "If she was abandoned and all."

"She wasn't abandoned, Izzy," Mrs. Richardson said. "She was left at a fire station where someone would find her safely. It's a very different thing. It's brought her to this very good home."

"But you don't know her real birthday, then, do you?" Izzy said. "Did you just pick some random day?"

Mrs. McCullough adjusted the baby in her arms. "The social workers estimated she was two months old when she came to us, give or take a couple of weeks. That was January thirtieth. So we decided we'd celebrate November thirtieth as her birthday." She gave Izzy a tight smile. "We think we're very lucky, to be able to give her a birthday. It's the same as Winston Churchill's. And Mark Twain's."

"Is her name really Mirabelle?" Izzy asked.

Mrs. McCullough stiffened. "Her full name will be Mirabelle Rose McCullough, once the paperwork goes through," she said.

"But she must have had a name before," Izzy said. "Don't you know what it is?"

As a matter of fact, Mrs. McCullough did know. The baby had been tucked in a cardboard box, wearing several sets of clothing and cocooned in blankets against the January cold. There had been a note in the box, too, which Mrs. McCullough had eventually convinced the social worker to let her read: *This baby name May Ling. Please take this baby and give her a better life.* That first night, when the baby had finally fallen asleep in their laps, Mr. and Mrs. McCullough spent two hours flipping through the name dictionary. It had not occurred to them, then or at any point until now, to regret the loss of her old name.

"We felt it was more appropriate to give her a new name to celebrate the start of her new life," she said. "Mirabelle means 'wonderful beauty.' Isn't that lovely?" Indeed, staring down that night at the baby's long lashes, the little rosebud mouth half open in deep and contented slumber, she and her husband had felt nothing could be more appropriate.

"When we got our cat from the shelter, we kept her name," said Izzy. She turned to her mother. "Remember? Miss Purrty? Lexie said it was lame but you said we couldn't change it, it would be too confusing to her."

"Izzy," Mrs. Richardson said. "Behave yourself." She turned to Mrs. McCullough. "Mirabelle has grown *so* much over the past few months. I wouldn't recognize her. So skinny before, and now look at her, she's chubby and glowing. Oh, Lexie, look at those little cheeks."

"Can I hold her?" Lexie asked. With Mrs. McCullough's help, she settled the baby against her shoulder. "Oh, look at her skin. Just like café au lait." Mirabelle reached out and laced her fingers into Lexie's long hair, and Izzy drifted sullenly away.

"I do *not* get the obsession," Moody murmured to Trip, in the corner behind the kitchen island, where they had retreated with paper plates of quiche and pastries. "They eat. They sleep. They poop. They cry. I'd rather have a dog."

"But girls love them," said Trip. "I bet if Pearl were here she'd be all over that baby."

Moody could not tell whether Trip was mocking him or simply thinking about Pearl himself. He wasn't sure which possibility bothered him more.

"You were listening in health class when they talked about precautions, right?" he asked. "Otherwise there are going to be dozens of girls running around with baby Trips. Horrific thought."

"Ha ha." Trip forked a piece of egg into his mouth. "You just worry about yourself. Oh wait, in order to knock someone up, someone has to actually sleep with you." He tossed his empty plate into the garbage can and went off in search of a drink, leaving Moody alone with the last few bites of his quiche, now gone cold.

At Lexie's request, Mrs. McCullough took her for a tour of Mirabelle's room: decorated in pink and pale green, with a hand-stitched banner above the crib spelling out her name. "She loves this rug," Mrs. McCullough said, patting the sheepskin on the floor. "We put her down after her bath and she rolls around and just laughs and laughs." Then there was Mirabelle's playroom, a whole enormous bedroom devoted to her toys: wooden blocks in all colors of the rainbow, a rocking elephant made from velvet, an entire shelf of dolls. "The room at the front of the house is bigger," explained Mrs. McCullough. "But this room gets the best sun—all morning and most of the afternoon. So we made the other into the guest room and kept this one as a place for Mirabelle to play."

When they returned downstairs, even more guests had arrived, and Lexie reluctantly relinquished Mirabelle to the newcomers. By cake-cutting time, the birthday girl, worn out from all the socializing, had to be whisked away for a bottle and put down for a nap, and to Lexie's great disappointment she was still asleep at the end of the party, when the Richardsons headed home.

"I wanted to hold her again," she complained as they made their way back to their cars.

"She's a baby, not a toy, Lex," Moody put in.

"I'm sure Mrs. McCullough would love it if you'd offer to babysit," Mrs. Richardson said. "Drive carefully, Lexie. We'll see you at home." She nudged Izzy toward the other car by one shoulder. "And *you* need to be less rude next time we go to a party, or you can just stay home. Linda McCullough babysat *you* when you were little, you know. She changed your diapers and took you to the park. You think about that the next time you see her."

"I will," said Izzy, and slammed her car door.

><

Lexie could talk of nothing else but Mirabelle McCullough for the next few days. "Baby fever," Trip said, and nudged Brian. "Watch out, dude." Brian laughed uneasily. Trip was right, though: Lexie was suddenly, furiously interested in all things baby, even going to Dillard's to buy a frilly and thoroughly impractical lavender dress as a present for Mirabelle.

"My god, Lexie, I don't remember you being so excited about babies when Moody and Izzy were little," her mother said. "Or dolls for that matter. In fact—" Mrs. Richardson cast her mind back. "Once you actually shut Moody in the pots and pans cupboard."

Lexie rolled her eyes. "I was *three*," she said. She was still talking about the baby on Monday, and when Mia arrived in the kitchen that afternoon, Lexie was delighted to have a fresh audience.

"Her hair is so gorgeous," she gushed. "I've never seen so much hair on a little baby. So silky. And she has the biggest eyes—they just take everything in. She's so alert. They found her at a fire station, can you believe that? Someone literally just left her there."

Across the room, Mia, who had been wiping the countertops, froze.

"A fire station?" she said. "A fire station where?"

Lexie waved a hand. "I don't know. Somewhere in East Cleveland, I think." The details had been less important to her than the tragic romance of it all.

"And when did this happen?"

"January. Something like that. Mrs. McCullough said that one of the firemen came out for a smoke and found her there in a cardboard box." Lexie shook her head. "Like she was a puppy someone didn't want."

"And now the McCulloughs plan to keep her?"

"I think so." Lexie opened the cupboard and helped herself to a Nutri-Grain bar. "They've wanted a baby forever and then Mirabelle appeared. Like a miracle. And they've been trying to adopt for so long. They'll be such devoted parents." She peeled the wrapper from the granola bar and popped it into the garbage can and went upstairs, leaving Mia deep in thought.

Mia's arrangement with Mrs. Richardson paid for their rent, but she and Pearl still needed money for groceries and the power bill and gas, so she had kept a few shifts per week at Lucky Palace, which between wages and leftover food was just enough to keep them supplied. Lucky Palace had a cook, a prep cook, a busboy, and one full-time waitress, Bebe, who had started a few months before Mia. Bebe had come over from Canton two years earlier, and although her English was rather choppy, she liked to talk with Mia, finding her a sympathetic listener who never corrected her grammar or seemed to have trouble understanding her. While they rolled plastic silverware in napkins for the dinner takeout orders, Bebe had told Mia quite a lot about her life. Mia shared very little in return, but she'd learned over the years that people seldom noticed this, if you were a good listener—which meant you kept the other person talking about herself. Over the course of the past six months she'd learned nearly all of Bebe's life story, and it was because of this that Lexie's account of the party had caught her attention.

For Bebe, a year earlier, had had a baby. "I so scared then," she told Mia, fingers working the soft paper of the napkin. "I have nobody to help me. I cannot go to work. I cannot sleep. All day long I just hold the baby and cry."

"Where was the baby's father?" Mia had asked, and Bebe had said, gone. "I tell him I having a baby, two weeks later he disappear. Somebody told me he move back to Guangdong. I move here for him, you know that? Before that we living in San Francisco, I am work in dentist's office as a receptionist, I get good money, really nice boss. He get a job here in the car plant, he say, Cleveland is nice, Cleveland is cheap, San Francisco so expensive, we move to Cleveland, we can buy a house, have a yard. So I follow him here and then—"

She was silent for a moment, then dropped a neat rolled-up napkin onto the pile, chopsticks, fork, and knife all swaddled together inside. "Here nobody speak Chinese," she said. "I interview for receptionist, they tell me my English not good enough. Nowhere I can find work. Nobody to watch the baby." She had probably had postpartum depression at the very least, Mia realized, perhaps even a postpartum psychotic break. The baby wouldn't nurse, and her milk had dried up. She had lost her job—a minimum-wage post packing Styrofoam cups into cartons—when she'd gone into the hospital to have the baby, and had no money for formula. At last—and this was the part that Mia felt could not be a coincidence—she had, in desperation, gone to a fire station and left her baby on the doorstep.

Two policemen had found Bebe several days later, lying under a park bench, unconscious from dehydration and hunger. They'd brought her to a shelter, where she'd been showered, fed, prescribed antidepressants, and released three weeks later. But by then no one could tell her what had happened to her baby. A fire station, she had insisted, she'd left the baby at a fire station. No, she couldn't remember which. She had walked with the baby in her arms, round and round the city, trying to figure out what to do, and at last she'd passed a station, the windows glowing warm against the dark night, and she'd made up her mind. How many fire stations could there be? But no one would help her. When you left her, you terminated your rights, the police told her. Sorry. We can't give you any more information.

Bebe, Mia knew, was desperate to find her daughter again, had been searching for her for many months now, ever since she'd gotten herself back together. She had a job now, a steady if low-paying one; she'd found a new apartment; her mood had stabilized. But she hadn't been able to find out where her baby had gone. It was as if her child had simply disappeared. "Sometimes," she told Mia, "I wonder if I am dreaming. But which one is the dream?" She dabbed her eyes with the back of her cuff. "That I can't find my baby? Or that I have the baby at all?"

In all her years of itinerant living, Mia had developed one rule: Don't get attached. To any place, to any apartment, to anything. To anyone. Since Pearl had been born they'd lived, by Mia's count, in forty-six different towns, keeping their possessions to what would fit in a Volkswagen—in other words, to a bare minimum. They seldom stayed long enough to make friends anywhere, and in the few cases where they had, they'd moved on with no forwarding address and lost contact. At each move, they discarded everything they could leave behind, and sent off Mia's art to Anita to be sold, which meant they'd never see it again.

So Mia had always avoided getting involved in the affairs of others. It made everything simpler; it made it easier when their lease was up or she'd grown tired of the town or she'd felt, uneasily, that she wanted to be elsewhere. But this, with Bebe—this was different. The idea that someone might take a mother's child away: it horrified her. It was as if someone had slid a blade into her and with one quick twist hollowed her out, leaving nothing inside but a cold rush of air. At that moment Pearl came into the kitchen in search of a drink and Mia wrapped her arms around her daughter quickly, as if she were on the edge of a precipice, and held her so long and so tightly that Pearl finally said, "Mom. Are you okay?"

These McCulloughs, Mia was sure, were good people. But that wasn't the point. She thought suddenly of those moments at the restaurant, after the dinner rush had ended and things were quiet, when Bebe sometimes rested her elbows on the counter and drifted away. Mia understood exactly where she drifted to. To a parent, your child wasn't just a person: your child was a *place*, a kind of Narnia, a vast eternal place where the present you were living and the past you remembered and the future you longed for all existed at once. You could see it every time you looked at her: layered in her face was the baby she'd been and the child she'd become and the adult she would grow up to be, and you saw them all simultaneously, like a 3-D image. It made your head spin. It was a place you could take refuge, if you knew how to get in. And each time you left it, each time your child passed out of your sight, you feared you might never be able to return to that place again.

Early, early on, the very first night she and Pearl had begun their travels, Mia had curled up on their makeshift bed in the backseat of the Rabbit, with baby Pearl snuggled in the curve of her belly, and watched her daughter sleep. There, so close that she could feel Pearl's warm, milky breath on her cheek, she had marveled at this little creature. *Bone of my bones and flesh of my flesh*, she had thought. Her mother had made her go to Sunday school every week until she was thirteen, and as if the words were a spell she suddenly saw hints of her mother's face in Pearl's: the set of the jaw, the faint wrinkle between the eyebrows that appeared as Pearl drifted into a puzzling dream. She had not thought about her mother in some time, and a sharp bolt of longing flashed through her chest. As if it had disturbed her, Pearl yawned and stretched and Mia had cuddled her closer, stroked her hair, pressed her lips to that unbelievably soft cheek. *Bone of my bones and flesh of my flesh,* she had thought again as Pearl's eyes fluttered closed once more, and she was certain that no one could ever love this child as she did.

"I'm fine," she said to Pearl now, and with a wrenching effort she let her daughter go. "All finished here. Let's go home, okay?"

Even then Mia had a sense of what she was starting; a hot smell pricked her nostrils, like the first wisp of smoke from a far-off blaze. She did not know if Bebe would get her baby back. All she knew was that the thought of someone else claiming her child was unbearable. How could these people, she thought, how could these people take a child from its mother? She told herself this all night and into the next morning, as she dialed, as she waited for the phone to ring. It wasn't right. A mother should never have to give up her child.

"Bebe," she said, when a voice picked up on the other end. "It's Mia, from work. There's something I think you should know."

10

This was why, while Pearl and Mia were eating dinner Tuesday evening, the doorbell rang followed
by a frantic knocking. Mia ran down to the side
door, and Pearl heard a murmur of voices and crying,
and then her mother came into the kitchen followed by a
young Chinese woman, who was sobbing.

"I knock and knock," Bebe was saying. "I ring the
doorbell and they don't answer so I knock and knock. I
can see that woman inside. Peeking out from behind the
curtain to check if I go away."

Mia guided her to a chair—her own, with a plate of
half-finished noodles still in front of it. "Pearl, get Bebe
some water. And maybe make some tea." She sat down
in the other chair and leaned across the table to take
Bebe's hand. "You shouldn't have just gone over there
like that. You couldn't expect them to just let you come
right in."

"I call her first!" Bebe wiped her face on the back of
her hand, and Mia took a napkin from the table and
nudged it toward her. It was actually an old flowered
handkerchief from the thrift store, and Bebe scrubbed
at her eyes. "I look them up in the phone book and call
them, right after I hang up with you. Nobody answer. I

just get the machine. What kind of message I am going to leave? So I try them again, and again, all morning, until finally somebody answer at two o'clock. *She* answer."

Across the kitchen, Pearl set the kettle on the stove and clicked on the burner. She had never met Bebe before, though her mother had mentioned her once or twice. Her mother hadn't said how pretty Bebe was—big eyes, high cheekbones, thick black hair swept up into a ponytail—or how young. To Pearl, anyone over about twenty seemed impossibly adult, but she guessed that Bebe might be twenty-five or so. Definitely younger than her mother, but there was something almost childish in the way she spoke, in the way she sat with her feet primly together and her hands clasped, in the way she glanced up at Mia helplessly, as if she were Mia's daughter, too, that made her think of Bebe as if she were another teenager. Pearl did not realize, nor would she for a while yet, how unusually self-possessed her mother was for someone her age, how savvy and seasoned.

"I tell her who I am," Bebe was saying. "I say, 'This is Linda McCullough?' And she say yes, and I tell her, 'My name is Bebe Chow, I am May Ling's mother.' Just like that, she hang up on me." Mia shook her head.

"I call her back and she pick up the phone and hang it up again. And then I call her again and I get just a busy signal." Bebe wiped her nose with the napkin and crumpled it into a ball. "So I go over there. Two buses and I have to ask the driver where to change, and then I walk another mile to their house. Those huge houses—everybody over there drive, no one wants take a bus to work. I ring the front doorbell, and nobody answer, but she watching from upstairs, just looking down at me. I ring the bell again and again and I calling, 'Mrs. McCullough, it's me, Bebe, I just want to talk to you,' and then the curtain closed. But she still in there, just waiting for me to go away. Like I am going to go away when my baby is in there.

"So I keep on knocking and ringing. Sooner or later she have to come out and then I can talk to her." She glanced at Mia. "I just want to see my baby again. I think, I can talk with these McCulloughs and get them to understand. But she will not come out."

Bebe fell silent for a long time and looked down at her hands, and Pearl saw the skin, reddened and raw, along the sides of her fists. She must have been banging on the door for a long, long time, she realized, and she thought simultaneously of how much pain Bebe must have been in, must still be in, and how terrified Mrs. McCullough, locked inside the house, must have felt.

The rest of the story poured out haltingly, as if Bebe were only now piecing the scene together herself. Sometime later a Lexus had pulled up, with a police car right behind it, and Mr. McCullough had emerged. He had told Bebe to leave the property, two police officers flanking him like bodyguards. Bebe had tried to tell them she only wanted to see her baby, but wasn't sure now what she had said, if she had argued or threatened or raged or begged. All she could remember was the line Mr. McCullough kept repeating—"You have no right to be here. You have no right to be here"—and finally one of the officers took her by the arm and pulled her away.

Go, they had said, or they would take her down to the station and charge her with trespassing. This she recalled clearly: as the policemen pulled her away from the house, she could hear her child crying from behind the locked front door.

"Oh, Bebe," Mia said, and Pearl could not tell if she was disappointed or proud.

"What else I can do? I walk all the way here. Forty-five minutes. Who else I can ask for help but you?" She glared at Pearl and Mia fiercely, as if she thought they might contradict her. "I am her *mother*."

"They know that," Mia said. "They know that very well. Or they wouldn't have run you off like that." She nudged the mug of tea—lukewarm now—toward Bebe.

"What I can do now? If I go over there again, they call the police and arrest me."

"You could get a lawyer," Pearl suggested, and Bebe gave her a gentle pitying glance.

"Where I am going to get money for a lawyer?" she asked. She glanced down at her clothing—black pants and a thin white button-down—and Pearl understood suddenly: this was her work uniform; she'd left work without even bothering to change. "In the bank I have six hundred and eleven dollars. You think a lawyer help me for six hundred and eleven dollars?"

"Okay," said Mia. She pushed the remains of Pearl's dinner—glazed now with a white sheen of fat—to one side. All this time she had been thinking; in fact, she'd been thinking about this ever since Lexie had mentioned the baby: about what she would do if she were in Bebe's position, about what it was possible for anyone in

Bebe's position to do. "Listen to me. You want to fight this fight? Here's what you do."

$$\rightarrowtail\!\!\!\leftarrowtail$$

Wednesday afternoon, had any of the Richardson children been paying attention to the commercials during Jerry Springer, they might have noticed the teasers for the Channel 3 evening news, with a photo of the McCulloughs' house. If they had, they might have notified their mother, who was hammering out a story on a proposed school levy and would not be home to watch the news—or to alert Mrs. McCullough.

But as it happened, Lexie and Trip were so involved in a spirited argument over which guest had better hair, the drag queen or his embittered ex-wife, that no one heard the commercials. Pearl and Moody, looking on in bemusement, didn't even glance at the screen, and Lexie had interrupted before Trip was halfway through his case for the drag queen. Izzy, meanwhile, was at Mia's in the darkroom, watching her pull a new print from the developer and hang it to dry. So no one saw the teasers for the nightly news or watched the news that evening. Mrs. McCullough was also not a news watcher, and thus, when she answered her doorbell early Thursday morning with Mirabelle on her hip, expecting a parcel from her sister, she was alarmed to find Barbra Pierce— Channel 9's bouffanted local investigative journalist— standing on her front steps with a microphone in hand.

"Mrs. McCullough!" Barbra cried, as if they'd run into each other at a party and it was all a delightful coincidence. Behind her loomed a burly cameraman in a parka, though all Mrs. McCullough registered was the barrel of a lens and a blinking red light like one glowing eye. Mirabelle began to cry. "We understand that you're in the process of adopting a little girl. Are you aware her mother is fighting to regain custody?"

Mrs. McCullough slammed the door shut, but the news crew had gotten what they'd come for. Only two and a half seconds of footage, but it was enough: the slender white woman at the door of her imposing brick Shaker house, looking angry and afraid, clutching the screaming Asian baby in her arms.

With a vague sense of foreboding, Mrs. McCullough checked the clock. Her husband was en route to work downtown and would not be there for another thirty-five minutes at least. She called one friend after another, but none of them had seen the news story the night before either, and they could offer only moral support, not enlightenment. "Don't worry," each said in turn. "It'll be okay. Just Barbra Pierce stirring up trouble."

Mr. McCullough, meanwhile, arrived at work and took the elevator up to the seventh floor, where Rayburn Financial Services had their offices. He had just extricated one arm from his overcoat when Ted Rayburn appeared in his doorway.

"Listen, Mark," he said. "I don't know if you saw the news last night on Channel Three, but there's something you should know about." He shut the door behind him, and Mr. McCullough listened, still clutching his overcoat against himself, as if it were a towel. Ted Rayburn, in the same measured, slightly concerned tones he used with clients, described the news segment: the outside shot of the McCulloughs' house, shaded in the evening light, but still familiar to him from their years of hosting cocktail parties, brunches, summer barbecues. The anchor's lead-in: *Adoptions are about giving new homes to children who don't have families. But what if the child already has a family?* And the interview with the mother—Bee-something, Ted hadn't caught the full name—who had begged for her baby on camera. "I make a mistake," she said, every syllable carefully enunciated. "Now I have a good job. I have my life together now. I want my baby back. These McCulloughs have no right adopt a baby when her own mother wants her. A child belong with her mother."

Ted Rayburn had nearly finished when the phone on the desk rang, and Mr. McCullough, seeing the number, knew that it was his wife, and what was happening, and what he would now have to explain to her. He picked up the receiver.

"I'm coming home," he said, and set it down again and picked up his keys.

><

Mia, who did not own a television, had not seen the news segment either. But Wednesday afternoon, just before it aired, Bebe dropped by to tell her how the interview had gone. "They think this is a good story," she said. She was wearing her black pants and a white shirt with a faded soy-sauce stain on the cuff, and from this Mia knew she was headed in to work. "They talk to me for almost an hour. They have very many questions for me."

She broke off at the sound of footsteps on the stairs. It was Izzy, just arrived from school, and both of them fell silent at the sight of a stranger. "I better go," Bebe said after a moment. "The bus coming soon." On the way out the door, she leaned close to Mia. "They say people really going to get behind me," she whispered.

"Who was that?" Izzy asked, when Bebe had gone.

"Just a friend," Mia had answered. "A friend from work."

The producers at Channel 3, as it turned out, had good instincts. In the hours after the segment aired, the station had been flooded with calls about the story— enough to warrant a follow-up, and enough for Channel 9, ever competitive, to deploy Barbra Pierce first thing the next morning.

"Barbra Pierce," Linda McCullough said to Mrs. Richardson Thursday evening. "Barbra Pierce with her stilettos and her Dolly Parton hair. Showed up on my doorstep and shoved a microphone in my face." The two women had just watched Barbra Pierce's segment, each on her own couch in front of the television holding the cordless phone to her ear, and Mrs. Richardson had the sudden eerie feeling that they were fourteen again, Princess phones in their laps, watching *Green Acres* in tandem so that they could hear each other laugh.

"That's what Barbra Pierce does," Mrs. Richardson said. "Ms. Sensational Action News in a skirt suit. She's a bully with a cameraman."

"The lawyer says we're on solid footing," Mrs. Mc-Cullough said. "He says that by leaving the baby, she gave up custody to the state and the state gave it to us, so her grievance is really with the state and not us. He says the process is eighty percent complete and it'll only take another month or two for Mirabelle to be ours permanently, and then this woman will have no claim on her at all."

They had tried so long, she and her husband, for a baby. After their wedding, she'd gotten pregnant right away. And then, a few weeks later, she'd begun bleeding, and she knew even before they consulted the doctor that the baby was gone. "Very common," the doctor had reassured her. "Half of all pregnancies end in the first few weeks. Most women don't even know they'd conceived." But Mrs. McCullough had known, and three months later, when it happened again, and again four months after that, and again five months after *that*, she had been painfully aware each time that something alive had sparked in her, and that somehow that little spark had gone out.

The doctors prescribed patience, vitamins, iron supplements. Another pregnancy came; this time it was nearly ten weeks before the bleeding began. Mrs. Mc-Cullough cried at night, and after she fell asleep, her husband cried beside her. After three years of trying, she had been pregnant five times, and there was still no baby. Wait six months, the obstetrician recommended; let your body recover. When the waiting period was up, they tried again. Two months later she was pregnant; a month later, she was not. Each time she told no one, hoping that if she sealed the knowledge tight inside her, it would stay and grow. Nothing changed. By then her old friend Elena had a girl and a boy and was pregnant with a third, and though Elena called often, though she would happily have taken Linda into her arms and let her cry—as they'd done so often for each other growing up, over big things and small—Mrs. McCullough found this was something she could not share. She never told Elena when she was pregnant, so how could she tell her the pregnancy had ended? She did not even know how to begin. *I lost another one. It happened again.* Whenever they had lunch, Mrs. McCullough could not keep herself from staring at Mrs. Richardson's rounding belly. She felt like a pervert, she so badly wanted to touch it, to stroke it, to caress it. In the background, Lexie and Trip babbled and tottered, and it became easier, after a while, to simply avoid it all. Mrs. Richardson, for her part, noticed that her dear friend Linda called her less, that when she herself called, she often got the machine—Mrs. McCullough's cheery voice singing, "Leave a message for Linda and Mark, and we'll call you back!" But no one ever did.

The year after Izzy was born, Mrs. McCullough became pregnant again. By then it was exhausting: the plotting of her cycle, the waiting, the calls to the doctor. Even the sex—carefully scheduled for her most fertile days—had begun to feel like a chore. Who'd ever have believed it, she thought, remembering high school, when she and Mark had fumbled frantically against each other in the backseat of his car. The doctors put her on strict bed rest: no more than forty minutes a day on her feet, including trips to the bathroom; no exertions. She made it to almost five months before she woke at two A.M. with a terrible stillness in her belly, like the silence after a bell has stopped ringing. At the hospital, while she lay in a drugged fog, the doctors coaxed the baby from her womb. "Do you want to see her?" one asked when it was over, and a nurse held out the baby, swaddled in a white cloth, in her cupped palms. To Mrs. McCullough, she looked impossibly tiny, impossibly rose colored, impossibly glossy and smooth, like something blown from pink glass. Impossibly still. She nodded vaguely, shut her eyes again, spread her legs to let the doctors stitch her up.

She began to walk the long way around to the store to avoid the playground, the elementary school, the bus stop. She began to hate pregnant women. She wanted to slap them, to throw things at them, to grab them by the shoulders and bite them. On their tenth wedding anniversary, Mr. McCullough took her to Giovanni's, her favorite restaurant, and as they entered, a vastly pregnant woman waddled up behind them. Mrs. McCullough pushed the door open and then, as the pregnant woman came up behind, let it shut in the woman's face, and Mr. McCullough, turning back to take his wife's arm, for a moment could not recognize this woman, so callous, so different from the endlessly maternal woman he'd always known.

Finally, after one last doctor's appointment full of heartrending phrases—*low-motility sperm; inhospitable womb; conception likely impossible*—they'd decided to adopt. Even IVF would likely fail, the doctors had advised them. Adoption was their best chance for a baby. They'd put their names on every waiting list they could find, and from time to time an adoption agent would call with a possible match. But something always fell through: the mother changed her mind; a father or a cousin or a grandmother showed up out of the blue; the agency decided another, often younger couple was a better fit. A year passed, then two, then three. Everyone, it seemed, wanted a baby, and demand far exceeded supply. That January morning, when the social worker had called to say that she'd gotten their name from one of the adoption agencies, that she had a baby who was theirs if they wanted her: it had felt like a miracle. If they wanted her! All that pain, all that guilt, those seven little ghosts—for Mrs. McCullough never forgot a single one—had, to her amazement, packed themselves into a box and whisked themselves away at the sight of baby Mirabelle: so concrete, so vivid, so inescapably present. Now, at the thought that Mirabelle might be taken as well, Mrs. McCullough realized that the box and its contents had never disappeared, that they had simply been stored away, waiting for someone to open the lid.

The news had cut to commercial, and through the line Mrs. Richardson could hear the tinny jingle of the Cedar Point ad on the McCulloughs' set, a fraction of a second behind her own. She watched an elderly woman stumble, fall, fumble for the transmitter around her neck, and Barbra Pierce's voice-over echoed in her mind. *This couple wants to adopt her child. But she won't let her baby go without a fight.*

"It'll blow over," Mrs. Richardson said to Mrs. McCullough now. "People will forget about it. It'll pass."

But it did not pass. Improbable as it seemed, something about the story had touched a nerve in the community. The news was slow: a woman had had septuplets; bears, the *New York Times* reported with a straight face, were the main cause of car break-ins at Yosemite. The most pressing political question—for a few more weeks, at least—was what President Clinton would name his new dog. The city of Cleveland was safe and bored, and eager for a sensation a bit closer to home.

On Friday morning there were two more camera crews at the McCulloughs' door, and three segments that evening, on Channels 5, 19, and 43. Footage of Bebe Chow holding a picture of May Ling at one month old, pleading for her baby back. Shots of the McCulloughs' house with its curtains drawn and front-door light off; a photo of Mr. and Mrs. McCullough, dressed in black tie at a benefit for leukemia, that had run in the glossy society pages of *Shaker* magazine the year before; footage of Mr. McCullough's BMW backing out of the garage and driving away as a reporter jogged alongside holding a microphone up to the window.

By Saturday all the camera crews were back, Mrs. McCullough had locked herself in the house with Mirabelle, and the secretaries at Mr. McCullough's investment firm had been instructed to decline any calls from news sources with "No comment." Every night Mirabelle McCullough—or May Ling Chow, as some pointedly chose to call her—was a featured story on the evening news, always accompanied by photographs. At first there was only Bebe's snapshot of May Ling as a newborn, but then—on the advice of the McCulloughs' lawyer, who wanted to provide a counterpoint—came more recent portraits from the McCulloughs, taken at the Dillard's photo studio, showing Mirabelle in a frilly yellow Easter dress with bunny ears, or in a pink romper standing beside an old-fashioned rocking horse. Supporters were emerging on both sides, and by Saturday afternoon, a local lawyer, Ed Lim, had offered to represent Bebe Chow, gratis, and sue the state for custody of her daughter.

><

Saturday evening, at dinner, Mr. Richardson announced, "Mark and Linda McCullough called this afternoon to ask if I'd work with their lawyer. Seems he doesn't have a lot of court experience, and they thought I might be a good backup."

Lexie nibbled at her salad. "So will you?"

"None of this is their fault, you know." Mr. Richardson sawed off a bite of chicken. "They just want to do right by the baby. And the suit isn't directed at them. It's at the state. But they'll be dragged into it, and they're the ones who'll be affected by it most."

"Except for Mirabelle," Izzy said. Mrs. Richardson opened her mouth for a sharp remark, but Mr. Richardson quieted her with a glance.

"This whole thing is about Mirabelle, Izzy," he said. "Everyone involved—we all just want what's best for her. We just have to figure out what that is."

We, Izzy thought. Her father had become part of this already. She thought of the image the newspaper kept running of Bebe Chow: the sadness in her eyes, the palm-sized photo of baby May Ling in her hand, one corner creased, as if it had been kept in a pocket (which it had). Right away she'd recognized the woman she'd seen in Mia's kitchen, who had fallen silent as soon as she'd come in, who'd stared at her as if she were afraid, almost hunted. "Just a friend," Mia had said when Izzy had asked who she was, and if Mia trusted Bebe, Izzy knew where her loyalties lay.

"Baby stealer," she said.

A shocked silence dropped over the table like a heavy cloth. Across the table, Lexie and Trip exchanged wary, unsurprised glances. Moody shot Izzy a look that said *shut up*, but she wasn't watching.

"Izzy, apologize to your father," said Mrs. Richardson.

"What for?" Izzy demanded. "They're practically kidnapping her. And everyone's just letting them. Daddy's even helping."

"Let's calm down," Mr. Richardson began, but it was too late. When it came to Izzy, Mrs. Richardson was seldom calm, and for that matter, Izzy herself never was.

"Izzy. Go to your room."

Izzy turned to her father. "Maybe they could just pay her off. How much is a baby worth in today's market? Ten thousand bucks?"

"Isabelle Marie Richardson—"

"Maybe they can bargain her down to five." Izzy dropped her fork onto her plate with a clatter and left the room. *Mia should hear about this,* she thought, running upstairs and into her bedroom. She would know what to do. She would know how to fix this. Lexie's laugh floated up the stairwell and down the hallway, and Izzy slammed the door shut.

Downstairs, Mrs. Richardson sank back into her seat, hands shaking. It would take her until the next morning to think of a suitable punishment for Izzy: confiscating her beloved Doc Martens and throwing them in the trash. If you dress like a thug, she would insist as she opened the trash barrel, of course you act like a thug. For now, she pressed her lips together tightly and set her knife and fork down in a neat X across her plate.

"Should we keep the news quiet?" she asked. "That you're working with the McCulloughs, I mean."

Mr. Richardson shook his head. "It'll be in the paper tomorrow," he said, and he was right.

On Sunday, the *Plain Dealer* ran the story on the front page, just below the fold: LOCAL MOTHER FIGHTS FOR DAUGHTER'S CUSTODY. It was a good article, Mrs. Richardson thought, sipping her coffee and skimming over it with a professional eye: an overview of the case; a quick mention that the McCulloughs would be represented by William Richardson of Kleinman, Richardson, and Fish; a statement from Bebe Chow's lawyer. *"We are confident,"* said Edward Lim, *"that the state will see fit to return custody of May Ling Chow to her biological mother."* The very fact that the paper had run it so prominently, however, suggested that the real coverage was only beginning.

At the bottom of the article, a single sentence caught Mrs. Richardson's eye: "Ms. Chow had been informed of her daughter's whereabouts by a coworker at Lucky Palace, a Chinese restaurant on Warrensville Road." Even so carefully and anonymously phrased, she realized with a jolt who that coworker must be. It could not be a coincidence. So it was her tenant, her quiet little eager-to-please tenant, who had started all of this. Who had, for reasons still unclear, decided to upend the poor McCulloughs' lives.

Mrs. Richardson folded the paper precisely and set it down on the table. She thought again of Mia's disaffection when she'd offered to buy one of Mia's photos, of Mia's reticence about her past. Of Mia's—well, *standoffishness*, even as she spent hours a day in Mrs. Richardson's own home, in this very kitchen. A woman whose wages she paid, whose rent she had subsidized, whose daughter spent hours and hours under this very roof every single day. She thought of the photograph at the art museum, which now, in her memory, took on a secretive, sly tinge. How hypocritical of Mia, with her stubborn privacy, to insert herself into places where she didn't belong. But that was Mia, wasn't it? A woman who took an almost perverse pleasure in flouting the normal order. It was unfairness itself, that this woman was causing such trouble for her dear friend Linda, that Linda should have to suffer for it.

On Monday, she sent the children to school and dawdled at home until Mia arrived to clean. She wasn't sure what she was looking for, but she needed to see Mia in person, to look her in the eyes. "Oh," Mia said as she came in the side door. "I didn't expect you to be home. Should I come back later?"

Mrs. Richardson tipped her head to one side and studied her tenant. Hair, as always, unkempt atop her head. A loose white button-down untucked over jeans. A smudge of paint on the back of one wrist. Mia stood there with one hand on the doorway, a half smile on her face, waiting for Mrs. Richardson to respond. A sweet face. A young face, but not an innocent face. She didn't care, Mrs. Richardson realized, what people thought of her. In a way, that made her dangerous. She thought suddenly of the photograph she'd seen at Mia's house that first day, when she'd invited Mia into her home. The woman turned arachnid, all silent, stealthy arms. What kind of person, she thought, would transform a woman into a spider? What kind of person, for that matter, saw a woman and even thought *spider*?

"I'm just leaving," she said, and lifted her bag from the counter.

Even years later, Mrs. Richardson would insist that that digging into Mia's past was nothing more than justified retribution for the trouble Mia had stirred up. It was purely for Linda's sake, she would insist—her oldest and dearest friend, a woman who'd only been trying to do right by this baby and now, because of Mia, was having her heart broken. Linda did not deserve that. How could she, Elena, stand by and let someone ruin her best friend's happiness? She would never admit even to herself that it hadn't been about the baby at all: it had been some complicated thing about Mia herself, the dark discomfort this woman stirred up that Mrs. Richardson would have much preferred to have kept in its box. For now, the newspaper still in her hand, she told herself that it was for Linda. She would make a few calls. She would see what she could find out.

11

Mrs. Richardson's first step was to read up on Pauline Hawthorne. She'd heard of Pauline Hawthorne before, of course. When she'd taken her art electives in college, Pauline Hawthorne had been *the* hot new thing, much talked about, much imitated by the photography students who wandered the campus with cameras strung around their necks like badges. Now that she saw the photographs again she remembered them. A woman seen in the mirror of a beauty parlor, half her hair wound neatly in curlers, the other half streaming loose in a tousled swirl. A woman touching up her makeup in the side mirror of a Chrysler, cigarette dangling from her lacquered lips. A woman in an emerald-green housecoat and heels, vacuuming her goldenrod carpet, the colors so saturated they seemed to bleed. Striking enough that even all these years later, she remembered seeing them flashed up on the projector screen in the darkened lecture hall, catching her breath as for a moment she was plunged into that vibrant Technicolor world.

Pauline, she learned now, had been born in rural Maine and moved to Manhattan at the age of eighteen, living for several years in Greenwich Village before bursting onto the art scene in the early 1970s. Every art book Mrs. Richardson consulted described her in glowing terms: a self-taught genius, a feminist photographic pioneer, a dynamic and generous intellect.

About her personal life Mrs. Richardson could find very little, only a brief mention that she had maintained an apartment on the Upper East Side. She did find one interesting tidbit, however: Pauline Hawthorne had taught at the New York School of Fine Arts—though apparently not out of need for money. A few years into Pauline Hawthorne's career, her photographs had been selling for tens of thousands—quite a lot for a photographer of that time, let alone a woman. After her death in 1982, their value skyrocketed, with MoMA paying nearly two million to add one to its permanent collection.

On a hunch, Mrs. Richardson looked up the number for the registrar at the New York School of Fine Arts. The registrar, when presented with Mrs. Richardson's credentials and told she was verifying some facts for a story, proved to be extremely helpful. Pauline Hawthorne had taught the advanced photography class at the school for many years, right up until the year she had died. No, there was no Mia Warren in any of Professor Hawthorne's classes in those last few years. But there had been a Mia Wright in the fall of 1980; might that be who Mrs. Richardson was looking for?

Mia Wright, it turned out, had enrolled that term in the School of Fine Arts as a freshman, but in the spring of 1981 had requested, and been granted, a leave of absence for the following academic year. She had never returned. Mrs. Richardson, doing some quick mental math, calculated that Mia—if this was even the same Mia—would not yet have been pregnant with Pearl that spring. So why would Mia have taken a leave from school, if not because she was pregnant?

The registrar balked at giving out student addresses, even fifteen-year-old ones. But Mrs. Richardson managed to learn, through some artful questioning, that the address on file for Mia Wright had been a local one, with no parents listed.

She would have to work the problem from the other end, then. And soon an opportunity presented itself, in the form of a much-anticipated letter. Since Thanksgiving, Lexie had checked the mail first thing when she came home, and at last, in mid-December, a fat envelope bearing the Yale logo in the corner finally landed in their mailbox. Mrs. Richardson had called all their relatives to share the good news; Mr. Richardson arrived home with a cake.

"Lexie, I'm taking you out for a fancy brunch this weekend to celebrate," Mrs. Richardson said at dinner. "After all, it's not every day you get into Yale. We'll have some fun girl time."

"What about me?" Moody said. "I just get to stay home and eat cereal?"

"She said *fun girl time*." Trip laughed, and Moody scowled. "You want in on fun girl time?"

"Now, Moody," Mrs. Richardson said. "It's like Trip said. This is just to celebrate Lexie. We're going to get dressed up and have a little girls' morning out. "

"Then what about me?" Izzy demanded. "Does that mean I get to come?"

Mrs. Richardson had not anticipated this. But Lexie's eyes were already alight, Lexie was already chattering about where she wanted to go, and it was too late to say no. And then, that evening, as she was washing her face before bed, an idea occurred to Mrs. Richardson, a way this luncheon might serve another purpose, too.

The next afternoon she came into the sunroom just before dinner. Under normal circumstances she left the kids alone, feeling that teens needed their space, that they were entitled to some degree of privacy. Today, though, she was looking for Pearl. As always, she was sprawled on the couch with Lexie and Trip and Moody, all of them half sunk into its overstuffed cushions. Izzy lay on her stomach on the armchair, chin propped on one armrest, feet in the air over the other.

"Pearl, there you are," Mrs. Richardson began. She settled herself gingerly on the arm of the sofa beside Pearl. "The girls and I are going out for brunch on Saturday, to celebrate Lexie's good news. Why don't you come, too?"

"Me?" Pearl threw a quick glance over her shoulder, as if Mrs. Richardson might be talking to someone else.

"You're practically part of the family, aren't you?" Mrs. Richardson laughed.

"Of course you should come," Lexie said. "I want you to."

"Go tell your mother," Mrs. Richardson said. "She's in the kitchen. I'm sure she'll say it's all right. Tell her it's my treat. Tell her," she added, "that I insist."

Across the room, Izzy slowly pushed herself up on her elbows, eyes narrowing. It had been over three weeks since her mother had promised to look into Mia's mysterious photograph, and when she'd asked about it, her mother had said only, "Oh, Izzy, you always make such a big deal out of nothing." Now her sudden interest in Pearl struck Izzy as strange.

"Why'd you invite *her*?" she demanded, once Pearl had skipped out of hearing.

"Izzy. How often does Pearl get to go out to brunch? You need to learn to be more generous." Mrs. Richardson rose and straightened her blouse. "Besides, I thought you liked Pearl."

><

This was how Pearl found herself at a wooden table in the corner next to Lexie, across from Mrs. Richardson and a sulky Izzy. Lexie had chosen the 100th Bomb Group, a restaurant out near the airport where the family went for very special occasions, the most recent being Mr. Richardson's forty-fourth birthday.

The 100th Bomb Group was crowded that morning, a dizzying swirl of activity and a bewildering buffet that stretched the length of the room. At a carving station, a burly man in a white apron sliced roast beef from an enormous rare haunch. At the omelet station, chefs poured a stream of frothy golden egg into a skillet and turned out a fluffy omelet filled with whatever you desired, even things it had never occurred to Pearl to put in an omelet: mushrooms, asparagus, coral-colored chunks of lobster. All over the walls hung memorabilia of the men from the bomb squadron: maps of major battles against the Nazis, their medals, their dog tags, their letters to sweethearts at home, photographs of their planes, photographs of the men themselves, dashing in uniforms and cadet hats and the occasional mustache.

"Look at him," Lexie said, tapping a photo just behind Pearl's ear. "Captain John C. Sinclair. Wouldn't you just love to meet him?"

"You realize," Izzy said, "that if he's still alive, he'd be about ninety-four now. Probably has a walker."

"I mean, wouldn't you have wanted to meet him, if you'd been alive back then. Way to split hairs, Izzy."

"He probably bombed cities, you know," Izzy said. "He probably killed lots of innocent people. All these guys probably did." She waved a hand at the expanse of photographs around them.

"Izzy," Mrs. Richardson said, "let's save the history lesson for another time. We're here to celebrate Lexie's achievement." She beamed across the table at Lexie, and by extension at Pearl, who sat beside her. "To Lexie," she said, raising her Bloody Mary, and Lexie and Pearl raised their goblets of orange juice, luminous in the sun.

"To Lexie," Izzy echoed. "I'm sure Yale will be all you've ever wanted." She took a swig from her water glass, as if wishing it were something stronger. At the table beside them, a baby slammed its chubby palms on the tablecloth and the silverware jumped with a clatter.

"Oh my god," Lexie mouthed. She leaned across the aisle toward the baby. "You are so cute. Yes, you are. You're the cutest baby in the entire world."

Izzy rolled her eyes and stood up. "Keep an eye on her," she said to the baby's parents. "You never know when someone might steal your baby." Before anyone could respond, she headed across the room toward the buffet.

"Please excuse my daughter," Mrs. Richardson said to the parents. "She's at a difficult age." She smiled at the baby, who was now trying to cram the fat end of a spoon into its mouth. "Lexie, Pearl, why don't you go ahead, too? I'll wait here."

When everyone was back at the table, Mrs. Richardson began the delicate work of turning the conversation by degrees. As it happened it was easier than she'd expected. She began with that trusty topic, the weather: she hoped it wouldn't be too cold for Lexie in New Haven; they would have to order her a warmer coat from L.L. Bean, a new pair of duck boots, a down duvet. Then she turned to Pearl.

"How about you, Pearl?" she said. "Have you ever been to New Haven?"

Pearl swallowed a forkful of omelet and shook her head. "No, I never have. My mom doesn't like the East Coast much."

"Really," Mrs. Richardson said. She slid the tip of her knife into a poached egg and the yolk ran out in a golden puddle. "It's a shame you've never been able to travel out there. So much to see. So much culture. We took a trip to Boston a few years ago, remember, girls? The Freedom Trail, and the Tea Party ship, and Paul Revere's house. And, of course, there's New York, so much to do there." She gave Pearl a benevolent smile. "I hope you'll be able to see it someday. I truly believe there's nothing like travel to broaden a young person's perspective."

Pearl felt stung, as Mrs. Richardson had known she would. "Oh, we've traveled a lot," she said. "We've been all over the place. Illinois, Iowa, Kansas, Nebraska—" She paused, casting about for something more glamorous. "We've even been out to California. A few times."

"How wonderful!" Mrs. Richardson refilled Pearl's glass from the carafe of juice on the table. "You really *have* been all over. Quite the traveler, actually. And do you like it, moving around so much?"

"It's okay." Pearl stabbed a piece of egg with her fork. "I mean, we move whenever my mom finishes a project. New places give her new ideas."

"You're growing up to be a real citizen of the world," Mrs. Richardson said, and Pearl, despite herself, blushed. "You probably know more about this country than any other teenager. Even Lexie and Izzy—and we travel quite a bit—even Lexie and Izzy have only been to a handful of states." Then, casually, "Where have you spent the most time? Where you were born, I imagine?"

"Well." Pearl swallowed the egg. "I was born in San Francisco. But we left when I was just a baby. I don't remember it at all. We never stay in any place too long."

Mrs. Richardson filed this piece of information away in her brain. "You'll have to go back someday," she said. "I believe in knowing where your roots lie. That kind of thing shapes your identity so much. I was born right here in Shaker, did you know that?"

"Mom," Izzy said. "Pearl doesn't want to hear all of that. No one wants to hear all of that."

Mrs. Richardson ignored her. "My grandparents were one of the first families to move out here," she said. "This used to be considered the country, can you believe it? They'd have stables and carriage houses and go riding on the weekends." She turned to Lexie and Izzy. "You girls won't remember my grandparents. Lexie was only a baby when they passed. Anyway, they moved here and stayed. They really believed in what Shaker stood for."

"Weren't the Shakers celibate and communist?" Izzy asked, sipping her water.

Mrs. Richardson shot her a look. "Thoughtful planning, a belief in equality and diversity. Truly seeing everyone as an equal. They passed that on to my mother, and she passed it on to me." She turned back to Pearl. "Where did your mother grow up?"

Pearl fidgeted. "I'm not really sure. California, maybe?" She poked her omelet, now gone rubbery. "She doesn't talk about it much. I don't think she has any family left anymore." In truth, Pearl had never had the courage to ask Mia directly about her origins, and Mia had deflected her roundabout questions with ease. "We're nomads," she would say to Pearl. "Modern-day gypsies, that's us. Never set foot in the same place twice." Or: "We're descended from circus folk," she'd said another time. "Wandering is in our blood."

"You should find out," Lexie put in. "I did it last year, for my History Day project. There's a huge database at Ellis Island—passenger arrival lists and ship manifests and all that stuff. If you know the date your ancestors immigrated, you can research family history from there with census records. I traced ours back to just before the Civil War." She set down her orange juice. "Do you think your mom would know when her ancestors came over?"

Mrs. Richardson felt the conversation skating toward thin ice. "Lexie, you sound like a budding reporter," she said, rather sharply. "Maybe you should look into journalism when you start at Yale."

Lexie snorted. "No thanks."

"Lexie," Izzy interrupted before their mother could speak, "wants to be the next Julia Roberts. Today, Miss Adelaide; tomorrow, America's Sweetheart."

"Shut up," Lexie said. "Julia Roberts probably started off doing high school plays, too."

"I'd like it," Pearl said. Everyone stared.

"Like what?" Lexie asked.

"Being a reporter," Pearl said. "I mean, being a journalist. You get to find out everything. You get to tell people's stories and figure out the truth and write about it." She spoke with the earnestness that only a teenager could truly have. "You use words to change the world. I'd love to do that." She glanced up at Mrs. Richardson, who for the first time realized how very big and sincere Pearl's eyes were. "Like you do. I'd love to do what you do."

"Really," Mrs. Richardson said. She was genuinely touched. For a moment it felt as if Pearl were simply one of Lexie's friends, there to celebrate her marvelous daughter: a promising young woman Mrs. Richardson might mentor, and nurture, purely on potential. "That's wonderful. You should try to write for the *Shakerite*—a school paper's a great way to learn the basics. And then, when you're ready, maybe I can help you find an internship." She stopped, suddenly remembering why she'd invited Pearl to this brunch in the first place. "Something to think about anyway," she finished, and gave her drink a fierce stir with its celery stick. "Izzy, is that all you're eating? Toast and jelly? Honestly, you could have just eaten that at home."

><

It took several calls to find the San Francisco Office of Vital Records, but once Mrs. Richardson had them on the phone, there were no more hitches. Within ten minutes, the clerk had faxed over a birth certificate request form with no questions asked. Mrs. Richardson ticked off the box for an "informational" copy and filled in Pearl's name and birth date, along with Mia's name. The space for father's name, of course, was left blank, but the clerk had assured her that they'd be able to find the correct document even without it, that the certificates were public record. "Two to four weeks—if we've got it, we'll send it over," she'd promised, and Mrs. Richardson filled out her own address, attached a check for eighteen dollars, and dropped the envelope into the mail.

It took five weeks, but when the birth certificate arrived in the Richardson mailbox, it was a bit of a disappointment. Under "Father" the word *NONE* had been neatly typed. Mrs. Richardson pursed her lips in disappointment. She felt it should be unlawful, allowing someone to conceal the name of a parent. There was something unseemly about it, this unwillingness to be forthcoming, to state your origins plainly. Mia had already proved herself to be a liar and capable of more lies. What else might she be hiding? It was, she thought, like refusing to hand over maintenance records at the sale of a secondhand car. Didn't you have the right to know where something came from, so that you knew what malfunctions might be in store? Didn't she—as this woman's employer, as well as her landlady—have a right to know the same?

><

At least, she thought, she had one new piece of information: Mia's birthplace, listed as Bethel Park, Pennsylvania, on the birth certificate next to *Mia Warren*.

Directory assistance in Bethel Park informed her that there were fifty-four entries for "Warren" in the township. Mrs. Richardson, after some thought, called the city's department of records, which was not quite as accommodating as the one in San Francisco had been. There was no Mia Warren in the records, the woman on the phone insisted.

"What about Mia Wright?" Mrs. Richardson asked on an impulse, and after a brief pause and the clacking of a keyboard, the woman replied that yes, a Mia Wright had been born in Bethel Park in 1962. Oh, and there was also a Warren Wright born in 1964; was it possible Mrs. Richardson had her names mixed up?

Mrs. Richardson thanked her and hung up.

It took several days, but by dint of careful reporting skills and copious phone calls, Mrs. Richardson finally found the key she had been looking for. It came in the form of an obituary in the *Pittsburgh Post*, dated February 17, 1982.

SERVICES FOR HIGH SCHOOL SENIOR
TO BE HELD FRIDAY

Funeral services for Warren Wright, 17, will be held Friday, February 19, at 11 a.m. at the Walter E. Griffith Funeral Home, 5636 Brownsville Road. Mr. Wright is survived by his parents, Mr. and Mrs. George Wright, longtime residents of Bethel Park, and an older sister, Mia Wright, who graduated from the district in 1980. In lieu of flowers, the family suggests donations to the Bethel Park High Football Team, of which Mr. Wright was a starting running back.

It could not be a coincidence, Mrs. Richardson decided. Mia Wright. Warren Wright. Mia Warren. She called Bethel Park directory services again and when she hung up she looked down at the note she had jotted on a slip of paper. George and Regina Wright, 175 North Ridge Road. A zip code. A phone number.

It was so easy, she thought with some disdain, to find out about people. It was all out there, everything about them. You just had to look. You could figure out anything about a person if you just tried hard enough.

><

By the time Mrs. Richardson had found Mia's parents, the case of little May Ling/Mirabelle was still in the news—if anything, even more so. True, the country was now titillated by the president's tawdry indiscretions, but scandalous as it was, the whole affair felt faintly comic. Across the city, opinions ranged from *It has nothing to do with how he runs the country* to *All presidents have affairs* to the more succinct *Who cares?* But the public—and especially the public in Shaker Heights—was deeply invested in the Mirabelle McCullough case now, and this, unlike the intern scandal, felt deadly serious.

Nearly every evening there was at least an update on the case—which, as of yet, had only recently been assigned a hearing date for March and entered into the docket as *Chow v. Cuyahoga County*. The fact that the case involved Shaker—a community that liked to hold itself up as the standard-bearer—caught everyone's interest, and everyone in the city had an opinion. A mother deserved to raise her child. A mother who abandoned her child did not deserve a second chance. A white family would separate a Chinese child from her culture. A loving family should matter more than the color of the parents. May Ling had a right to know her own mother. The McCulloughs were the only family Mirabelle had ever known.

The McCulloughs were rescuing Mirabelle, their

supporters insisted. They were giving an unwanted child a better life. They were heroes, breaking down racism through cross-cultural adoption. "I think it's wonderful, what they're doing," one woman told reporters during an on-the-street segment. "I mean, that's the future, isn't it? In the future we'll all be able to look past race." "You can just see what a wonderful mother she is," one of the McCulloughs' neighbors said a few minutes later. "You can tell that when she looks down at that baby in her arms, she doesn't see a Chinese baby. All she sees is a *baby*, plain and simple."

That was exactly the problem, Bebe's supporters insisted. "She's not just a baby," protested one woman, when Channel 5 sent a reporter to Asia Plaza, Cleveland's Chinese shopping center, in search of the Asian perspective. "She's a *Chinese* baby. She's going to grow up not knowing anything about her heritage. How is she going to know who she is?" Serena Wong's own mother happened to be shopping at the Asian grocery that morning and—to Serena's simultaneous pride and mortification—had spoken quite forcefully on the subject. "To pretend that this baby is just *a baby*—to pretend like there's no race issue here—is disingenuous," Dr. Wong had snapped, while Serena fidgeted at the edge of the shot. "And no, I'm not 'playing the race card.' Ask yourself: would we be having such a heated discussion if this baby were blond?"

The McCulloughs themselves, after much discussion with their lawyers, granted an exclusive interview to Channel 3. Positive publicity, Mr. Richardson had agreed, so Channel 3 sent a camera crew and a producer to the McCulloughs' living room and filmed them sitting on the sectional with Mirabelle in front of a roaring fire, while he sat just offscreen. "Of course we understand why Miss Chow feels the way she does," Mrs. McCullough said. "But we've had Mirabelle for most of her life and we're all that she remembers. I feel that Mirabelle is truly my child, that she came to me this way for a reason."

"There's no one out there," Mr. McCullough added, "who can honestly say Mirabelle isn't better off in a steady home with two parents."

"Some people have suggested that Mirabelle will lose touch with her birth culture," the producer said. "How do you respond to those concerns?"

Mrs. McCullough nodded. "We're trying to be very sensitive to that," she said. "You'll notice that we're adding more and more Asian art to our walls." She waved a hand at the scrolls with ink-brushed mountains that hung by the fireplace, the glazed pottery horse on the mantel. "We're committed, as she gets older, to teaching her about her birth culture. And of course she already loves the rice. Actually, it was her first solid food."

"At the same time," Mr. McCullough said, "we want Mirabelle to grow up like a typical American girl. We want her to know she's exactly the same as everyone else." The news segment ended with a shot of the McCulloughs standing over Mirabelle's crib as she cooed at her mobile.

Even the Richardson children found themselves divided on this thorny subject. Mrs. Richardson, of course, was firmly on the side of the McCulloughs, as was Lexie. "Look at the life Mirabelle has now," Lexie cried at dinner one evening in mid-February. "A big house to play in. A yard. Two rooms full of toys. Her mom can't give her that kind of life." Mrs. Richardson agreed: "They love her so much. They've been waiting so long. And they've raised her since she was a newborn. She doesn't remember her mother now. Mark and Linda are the only parents she's known. It would be cruel to everyone to take her away now, when they've been nothing but the ideal parents."

Moody and Izzy, on the other hand, were inclined to take Bebe's side. "She made one mistake," Moody insisted. Pearl had told him most of Bebe's story, and Moody, as in all things, was on Pearl's side. "She thought she couldn't take care of the baby and then things changed and she could. It shouldn't mean her kid gets taken away forever." Izzy was more succinct: "She's the mom. They're not." Something about the case had lit a spark in her, though she could not yet put her finger on it, and would not be able to articulate it for a long while.

"Cliff and Clair were fighting about it last night," Brian told Lexie one afternoon. They were lying in his bed, half dressed, having skipped lacrosse and field hockey practice for a different kind of exercise. "Cliff and Clair *never* fight." It had started over dinner, and by the time he'd gone to bed his parents had lapsed into a stony, stubborn silence. "My dad thinks she's better off with the McCulloughs. He thinks she has no future with a mother like Bebe. He said moms like Bebe are the kind of parents who keep the cycle of poverty going."

"But what do *you* think?" Lexie persisted. Brian hesitated. His mother had interrupted his father's tirade—something she did often, but never with such vehemence. "And what about all those black babies going to white homes?" she had said. "You think that breaks the cycle of poverty?" She dropped a pot into the sink with a clatter and turned on the water. Steam rose up in a hissing cloud. "If they want to help the black community, why don't they make some changes to the system first instead?" His father's reasoning made all logical sense to Brian—the baby safe and cared for and adored, with every possible opportunity. And yet there was something about the little brown body wrapped in Mrs. McCullough's long, pale arms that discomfited him as it had his mother. He felt a flare of annoyance—no, anger—at Bebe for putting him in this position.

"I think if she'd been more careful this whole thing could've been avoided," he said stiffly. "I mean, use a condom. How hard is that? A buck at the drugstore and this whole thing would never have happened."

"Way to miss the point, Bry," Lexie said, and fished her jeans up from the floor.

Brian tugged them out of her hands. "Forget about it. Not our problem, right?" He put his arms around her, and Lexie forgot all about little Mirabelle, the McCulloughs, everything except his lips on her ear.

With Ed Lim's help, Bebe had formally filed papers and had been granted visitation rights in the interim, once per week for two hours. Mr. and Mrs. McCullough were to maintain custody of the baby for the time being.

No one was satisfied with this arrangement.

"Only in the library or 'public place,'" Bebe complained to Mia. "She cannot even come to my home. I have to hold my baby in the library. And the social worker sitting right there, watching me all the time. Like I am some criminal. Like I might hurt my own baby. Those McCulloughs, they say I can come to their house, visit her there. They think I am going to sit there and smile while they steal my baby? They think I am going to sit there by the fireplace and look at pictures of some other woman holding my child?"

Meanwhile, Mrs. McCullough had her own complaints.

"You have no idea what it's like," she told Mrs. Richardson over the phone. "Handing your baby over to a stranger. Watching some woman you don't even know walk away carrying your child. I break out in hives every time the doorbell rings, Elena. After they leave, I literally get down on my knees and pray she'll come back like she's supposed to. The night before I can't even sleep. I've had to take sleeping pills." Mrs. Richardson gave a sympathetic cluck. "And it's never the same day. Every week I say, please, can we just pick a set time. Please, let's just settle on one day. At least that way I would know it was coming. I'd have time to prepare myself. But no, she never tells the social worker until the day before. Says she doesn't know her work schedule until then. I get a call in the afternoon—*Oh, we'll be by tomorrow at ten*. Less than half a day's notice. I'm completely on edge."

"It's only for a while, Linda," Mrs. Richardson said

soothingly. "The court date is just at the end of March and, of course, the state will decide the baby belongs with you."

"I hope you're right," Mrs. McCullough said. "But what if they decide—" She stopped, her throat tightening, and took a deep breath. "I don't want to think about it. They can't possibly. They wouldn't." Her tone sharpened. "If she can't even arrange her work schedule, how can she possibly expect to be stable enough to raise a child?"

"This too shall pass," Mrs. Richardson said.

Mrs. Richardson's calm, however, belied her true feelings. The more she thought about Mia, the angrier she became, and the more she could not stop thinking about her.

She had spent her whole life in Shaker Heights, and it had infused her to the core. Her memories of childhood were a broad expanse of green—wide lawns, tall trees, the plush greenness that comes with affluence—and resembled the marketing brochures the city had published for decades to woo the right sort of residents. This made a certain amount of sense: Mrs. Richardson's grandparents had been in Shaker Heights almost from the beginning. They had arrived in 1927, back when it was still technically a village—though it was already being called the finest residential district in the world. Her grandfather had grown up in downtown Cleveland on what they called Millionaires' Row, his family's crenellated wedding cake of a house tucked beside the Rockefellers and the telegraph magnate and President McKinley's secretary of state. However, by the time

Mrs. Richardson's grandfather—by then a successful lawyer—was preparing to bring his bride home, downtown had grown noisy and congested. Soot clogged the air and dirtied the ladies' dresses. A move to the country, he decided, would be just the thing. It was madness to move so far from the city, friends insisted, but he was an outdoorsman and his bride-to-be an avid equestrienne, and Shaker Heights offered three bridle paths, streams for fishing, plenty of fresh air. Besides, a new train line whisked businessmen straight from Shaker to the heart of the city: nothing could be more modern. The couple bought a house on Sedgewick Road, hired a maid, joined the country club; Mrs. Richardson's grandmother found a stable for her horse, Jackson, and became a member of the Flowerpot Garden Club.

By the time Mrs. Richardson's mother, Caroline, was born in 1931, things were less rural but no less idyllic. Shaker Heights was officially a city; there were nine elementary schools and a new redbrick senior high had just been completed. New and regal houses were springing up all over town, each following strict style regulations and a color code, and bound by a ninety-nine-year covenant forbidding resale to anyone not approved by the neighborhood. Rules and regulation and order were necessary, the residents assured each other, in order to keep their community both unified and beautiful.

For Shaker Heights was indeed beautiful. Everywhere lawns and gardens flourished—residents promised to keep weeds pulled, to grow only flowers, never vegetables. Those who were lucky enough to live in Shaker were certain theirs was the best community in

America. It was the kind of place where—as one resident discovered—if you lost your thousand-dollar diamond wedding ring shoveling the driveway, the service department would remove the entire snowbank, carry it to the city garage, and melt it under heat lamps in order to retrieve your treasure. Caroline grew up picnicking by the Shaker lakes in the summer, skating on city-flooded rinks in the winter, caroling at Christmas. She saw matinees of *Song of the South* and *Anna and the King of Siam* at the cinema at Shaker Square and on special occasions—such as her birthday—her father took her to Stouffer's Restaurant for a lobster luncheon. As a teenager, Caroline became the drum majorette for the school's marching band, went parking down by the Canoe Club with the boy who would become her husband a few years later.

It was, as far as she could imagine, a perfect life in a perfect place. Everyone in Shaker Heights felt this. So when it became obvious that the outside world was less perfect—as *Brown v. Board* caused an uproar and riders in Montgomery boycotted buses and the Little Rock Nine made their way into school through a storm of slurs and spit—Shaker residents, including Caroline, took it upon themselves to be better than that. After all, were they not smarter, wiser, more thoughtful and forethoughtful, the wealthiest, the most enlightened? Was it not their duty to enlighten others? Didn't the elite have a responsibility to share their well-being with those less fortunate? Caroline's own mother had always raised her to think of those in need: she had organized Christmastime toy drives, had been a member of the local Children's Guild, had even overseen the compilation of a Guild cookbook, with all proceeds benefiting charities, and contributed her own personal recipe for molasses cookies. When the troubles of the outside world made their presence felt in Shaker Heights—a bomb at the home of a black lawyer—the community felt obliged to show that this was not the Shaker way. A neighborhood association sprang up to encourage integration in a particularly Shaker Heights manner: loans to encourage white families to move into black neighborhoods, loans to encourage black families to move into white neighborhoods, regulations forbidding FOR SALE signs in order to prevent white flight—a law that would remain in effect for decades. Caroline, by then a homeowner herself with a one-year-old—a young Mrs. Richardson—joined the integration association immediately. Some years later, she would drive five and a half hours, daughter in tow, to the great March on Washington, and Mrs. Richardson would forever remember that day, the sun forcing her eyes into a squint, the scrum of people pressed thigh to thigh, the hot fug of sweat rising from the crowd, the Washington Monument rising far off in the distance, like a spike stretching to pierce the clouds. She clamped her mother's hand in hers, terrified that her mother might be swept away. "Isn't this incredible," her mother said, without looking down at her. "Remember this moment, Elena." And Elena would remember that look on her mother's face, that longing to bring the world closer to perfection—like turning the peg of a violin and bringing the string into tune. Her conviction that it was possible if you only tried hard enough, that no work could be too messy.

But three generations of Shaker reverence for order and rules and decorum would stay with Elena, too, and she would never quite be able to bring those two ideas into balance. In 1968, at fifteen, she turned on the television and watched chaos flaring up across the country like brush fires. Martin Luther King, Jr., then Bobby Kennedy. Students in revolt at Columbia. Riots in Chicago, Memphis, Baltimore, D.C.—everywhere, everywhere, things were falling apart. Deep inside her a spark kindled, a spark that would flare in Izzy years later. Of course she understood why this was happening: they were fighting to right injustices. But part of her shuddered at the scenes on the television screen. Grainy scenes, but no less terrifying: grocery stores ablaze, smoke billowing from their rooftops, walls gnawed to studs by flame. The jagged edges of smashed windows like fangs in the night. Soldiers marching with rifles past drugstores and Laundromats. Jeeps blocking intersections under dead traffic lights. Did you have to burn down the old to make way for the new? The carpet at her feet was soft. The sofa beneath her was patterned with roses. Outside, a mourning dove cooed from the bird feeder and a Cadillac glided to a dignified stop at the corner. She wondered which was the real world.

The following spring, when antiwar protests broke out, she did not get in her car and drive to join them. She wrote impassioned letters to the editor; she signed petitions to end the draft. She stitched a peace sign onto her knapsack. She wove flowers into her hair.

It was not that she was afraid. It was simply that Shaker Heights, despite its idealism, was a pragmatic

place, and she did not know how to be anything else. A
lifetime of practical and comfortable considerations settled atop the spark inside her like a thick, heavy blanket.
If she ran off to Washington to join the protests, where
would she sleep? How would she stay safe? What would
become of her classes, would she be expelled, could she
still graduate and go to college? The spring of their senior year, Jamie Reynolds had pulled her aside after history class one day. "I'm dropping out," he said. "Going
to California. Come with me." She had adored Jamie
since the seventh grade, when he had admired a sonnet
she'd written for English. Now, at almost eighteen, he
had long hair and a shaggy beard, a dislike for authority, a VW van in which, he said, they could live. "Like
camping out," he'd said, "except we can go anywhere,"
and she had wanted so badly to go with him, anywhere,
to kiss that crooked, bashful smile. But how would they
pay for food, where would they do their laundry, where
would they bathe? What would her parents say? The
neighbors, her teachers, her friends? She'd kissed Jamie
on the cheek and cried when, at last, he was out of sight.

Months later, off at Denison, she sat with classmates
and watched the draft lottery live on the grainy common-
room television. Jamie's birthday—March 7—had come
up on the second pick. So he would be among the first
to be called to fight, she thought, and she wondered
where he had gone, if he knew what awaited him, if
he would report, or if he would run. Beside her, Billy
Richardson squeezed her hand. His birthday was one of
the last drawn, and anyway, as an undergraduate, he
had been granted a deferral. He was safe. By the time

they graduated, the war would be over and they would marry, buy a house, settle down. She had no regrets, she told herself. She'd been crazy to have considered it even for a moment. What she had felt for Jamie back then had been just a tiny, passing flame.

All her life, she had learned that passion, like fire, was a dangerous thing. It so easily went out of control. It scaled walls and jumped over trenches. Sparks leapt like fleas and spread as rapidly; a breeze could carry embers for miles. Better to control that spark and pass it carefully from one generation to the next, like an Olympic torch. Or, perhaps, to tend it carefully like an eternal flame: a reminder of light and goodness that would never—could never—set anything ablaze. Carefully controlled. Domesticated. Happy in captivity. The key, she thought, was to avoid conflagration.

This philosophy had carried her through life and, she had always felt, had served her quite well. Of course she'd had to give up a few things here and there. But she had a beautiful house, a steady job, a loving husband, a brood of healthy and happy children; surely that was worth the trade. Rules existed for a reason: if you followed them, you would succeed; if you didn't, you might burn the world to the ground.

And yet here was Mia, causing poor Linda such trauma, as if she hadn't been through enough, as if Mia were any kind of example of how to mother. Dragging her fatherless child from place to place, scraping by on menial jobs, justifying it by insisting to herself—by insisting to everyone—she was making *Art*. Probing other people's business with her grimy hands. Stirring up trouble. Heedlessly throwing sparks. Mrs. Richardson seethed, and deep inside her, the hot speck of fury that had been carefully banked within her burst into flame. Mia did whatever she wanted, Mrs. Richardson thought, and what would result? Heartbreak for her oldest friend. Chaos for everyone. *You can't just do what you want,* she thought. Why should Mia get to, when no one else did?

It was only this loyalty to the McCulloughs, she would tell herself, the desire to see justice for her oldest friend, that led her to step over the line at last: as soon as she could get away, she would take a trip to Pennsylvania and visit Mia's parents. She would find out, once and for all, who this woman was.

12

T hose days, it seemed to Pearl that everything was saturated with sex; everywhere it oozed out, like dirty honey. Even the news was full of it. On *The Today Show,* a host discussed the rumors about the president and a stained blue dress; even more salacious stories circulated about a cigar and where it might have been placed. Schools across the country dispatched social workers to "help young people cope with what they're hearing," but in the hallways of Shaker Heights High School, the mood was hilarity rather than trauma. *What's the difference between Bill Clinton and a screwdriver? A screwdriver turns in screws, and . . .* She wondered, sometimes, if the whole country had fallen into a Jerry Springer episode. *What do you get when you cross Ted Kaczynski with Monica Lewinsky? A dynamite blowjob!*

Between math and biology and English, people traded jokes as gleefully as children with baseball cards, and every day the jokes became more explicit. *Did you hear about the Oval Office Cigars? They're ribbed and lubricated.* Or: *Monica, whispering to her dry cleaner: Can you get this stain out for me? Dry cleaner: Come again? Monica: No, it's mustard.* Pearl blushed, but pretended she'd heard it before. Everyone seemed so blasé about saying words she'd never even dared to whisper. Everyone, it seemed, was fluent in innuendo. It confirmed what she'd always thought: everyone knew more about sex than it appeared, everyone except her.

It was in this mood that Pearl, in mid-February, found herself walking to the Richardson house alone. Izzy would be at Mia's, poring over a contact sheet, trimming prints, absorbing Mia's attention, making space for Pearl to be elsewhere. Moody had failed a pop quiz on *Jane Eyre* and had stayed after to retake it. Mr. and Mrs. Richardson were at work. And Lexie, of course, was otherwise occupied. When Pearl had passed her at her locker, Lexie had said, "See you later, Brian and I are—hanging out," and in Pearl's mind all the nebulous things that were swirling in the air rushed in to fill that pause. She was still thinking about it when she got to the Richardsons' and found only Trip at home, stretched out across the couch in the sunroom, long and lean, math book spread on the cushion beside him. He had kicked off his tennis shoes but still had on his white tube socks, and she found this oddly endearing.

A month ago, Pearl would have backed out quickly and left him alone, but any other girl, she was sure, would have told Trip to move over, plopped down on the couch beside him. So she stayed, teetering on the edge of a decision. They were alone in the house: anything could happen, she realized, and the thought was intoxicating. "Hey," she said. Trip looked up and grinned.

"Hey, nerd," he said. "C'mere, help a guy out." He sat up and moved over to make room and nudged his notebook toward her. Pearl took it and examined the problem, keenly aware that their knees were touching.

"Okay, this is easy," she said. "So to find x—" She bent over the notebook, correcting his work, and Trip watched her. She had always struck him as a mousy little thing, cute even, but not a girl he'd thought much about, beyond the baseline of teenage hormones that made anything female worth looking at. But today there was something different about Pearl, something about the way she held herself. Her eyes were quick and bright— had they always been that way? She flicked a lock of hair out of her face and he wondered what it might feel like to touch it, gently, as you might stroke a bird. With three quick strokes she sketched the problem on the page— across, down, and then a sinuous line that made him think suddenly of lips and hips and other curves.

"Do you get it?" Pearl was saying, and Trip found, to his amazement, that he did.

"Hey," he said. "You're pretty good at this."

"I'm good at lots of things," she said, and then he kissed her.

It was Trip who tipped her backward onto the couch, knocking his book to the floor, who put his hands on, then under, her shirt. But it was Pearl who, some time later, wriggled out from beneath him, took him by the hand, and led him to his room.

In Trip's half-made bed, in Trip's room with yesterday's shirt on the floor, with the lights off and the shade half closed, striping both their bodies with sunlight, she let instinct take over. It was as if, for the first time in her life, her thoughts had turned off and her body was moving on its own. Trip was the hesitant one, fumbling over the clasp of her bra, though surely he'd unhooked many before. She interpreted this—rightly—as a sign that he was nervous, that this moment meant something to him, and found it sweet.

"Tell me when to stop," he said, and she said, "Don't."

The moment, when it came, was a flash of pain, the sudden physicality of both their bodies, of his weight on her, of her knees levered against his hips. It was quick. The pleasure—this time, at least—for her came afterward, when he gave a huge shudder and collapsed against her, his face pressed against her neck. Clinging to her, as if driven by an intense, unshakable need. It thrilled her, the thought of what they'd just done, the effect she could have on him. She kissed him on the side of his ear, and without opening his eyes he gave her a sleepy smile, and she wondered briefly what it might be like to fall asleep beside him, to wake up next to him every morning.

"Wake up," she said. "Someone will be home soon."

They put on their clothes quickly, in silence, and only then did Pearl begin to feel embarrassed. Would her mother know? she wondered. Would she look different somehow? Would everyone see her and read it in her face, what she'd done? Trip tossed her her T-shirt and she tugged it over her head, suddenly shy at the thought of his eyes on her body. "I better go," she said.

"Wait," Trip said, and gently untangled her hair from her collar. "That's better." They grinned at each other shyly, then both looked away. "See you tomorrow," he said, and Pearl nodded and slipped out the door.

><

That evening, Pearl watched her mother with a wary eye. She had checked her reflection in the bathroom mirror again and again and was fairly sure there was nothing different about her to the naked eye. Whatever had changed in her—and she felt both exactly the same and completely different—was on the inside. Still, every time Mia looked at her, she tensed. As soon as dinner was over, she retreated to her bedroom, claiming she had a lot of homework, to mull over what had happened. Were she and Trip dating now? she wondered. Had he used her? Or—and this was the perplexing thought—had she used him? She wondered if, when she saw him next, she would still be as drawn to him as before. If, when he saw her, he would pretend nothing had happened—or worse, laugh in her face. She tried to replay every moment of that afternoon: every movement of their hands, every word they'd said and breath they'd taken. Should she talk to him, or avoid him until he sought her out? These questions spun through her head all night, and in the morning, when Moody arrived to walk to school, she did not look him in the eye.

All day long, Pearl did her best impression of normal. She kept her head bent over her notes; she did not raise her hand. As each class drew to an end, she braced herself in case she ran into Trip in the hall, rehearsed what she'd say. She never did, and each time she made it to her next class without seeing him, she breathed a sigh of relief. Beside her, Moody noticed only that she was quiet and wondered if something was upsetting her. Around her, the buzz of high school life continued unchanged, and after school she went home, saying she didn't feel well. Whatever happened the next time she saw Trip, she didn't want it to be in front of Lexie and Moody. Mia noticed her quietness, too, wondered if she was coming down with something, and sent her to bed early, but Pearl lay awake until late, and in the morning, when she went to wash her face, she saw dark circles under her eyes and was sure Trip would never look at her again.

But at the end of the day, Trip appeared at her locker. "What're you up to," he asked, almost shyly, and she flushed and knew exactly what he was asking.

"Just hanging out," she said. "With Moody." She toyed with the dial of her combination lock, twisting it this way and that, and decided to be bold again. "Unless you've got a better idea?"

Trip traced his fingers along the blue painted edge of the locker door. "Is your mom home?"

Pearl nodded. "Izzy'll be over there, too." Separately each ran through a mental list of places: none where they could be alone. After a moment, Trip said, "I might know somewhere." He pulled his pager from his pocket and fished a quarter from his bookbag. Pagers were strictly forbidden at the high school, which meant that all the cool kids now had them. "Meet me at the pay phone when you're done, okay?" He sprinted off, and Pearl gathered her books and shut her locker.

Her heart was pounding as if she were a child playing tag—though she wasn't sure if she was being chased or doing the chasing. She cut through the Egress and toward the front of the school, where the pay phone hung outside the auditorium. Trip was just hanging up.

"Who did you call?" Pearl asked, and Trip suddenly looked abashed.

"You know Tim Michaels?" he said. "We've been on soccer together since we were ten. His parents don't get home till eight, and sometimes he brings a date down to the rec room in the basement." He stopped, and Pearl understood.

"Or sometimes he lets you bring one?" she said.

Trip flushed and stepped closer, so she was nearly in his arms. "A long time ago," he said. "You're the only girl I want to bring down there now." With one finger he traced her collarbone. It was so out of character, and so earnest, that she nearly kissed him right there. At that moment, the pager in his hand buzzed. All Pearl could see was a string of numbers, but it meant something to Trip. The kids who carried pagers communicated in code, spelling out their messages with digits. *CAN I USE YOUR PLACE*, Trip had tapped into the pay phone, and Tim, changing in the locker room before basketball practice, glanced at his buzzing pager and raised an eyebrow. He hadn't noticed Trip with anyone new lately. *K WHO IS SHE*, he'd sent back, but Trip chose not to answer and dropped the pager back into his pocket.

"He says it's fine." He tugged at one of the straps of Pearl's bookbag. "So?"

Pearl found, suddenly, that she didn't care about whatever girls had come before. "Are you driving?" she asked.

They were at the back door of Tim Michaels's house before she remembered Moody. He would be wondering where she was, why she hadn't met him at the science wing as usual so they could walk together. He would wait awhile and then head home and he wouldn't find her there either. She would have to tell him something, she realized, and then Trip had retrieved the spare key from under the back doormat, Trip had opened the back door and was taking her hand, and she forgot about Moody and followed him inside.

"Are we dating?" she asked afterward, as they lay together on the couch in Tim Michaels's rec room. "Or is this just a thing?"

"What, do you want my letter jacket or something?"

Pearl laughed. "No." Then she grew serious. "I just want to know what I'm getting into."

Trip's eyes met hers, level and clear and deep brown. "I'm not planning on seeing anyone else. Is that what you wanted to know?"

She had never seen him so sincere. "Okay. Me either." After a moment, she said, "Moody is going to freak out. So's Lexie. So will everyone."

Trip considered. "Well," he said, "we don't have to tell anyone." He bent his head to hers so that their foreheads touched. In a few moments, Pearl knew, they would have to get up; they would have to dress and go back outside into the world where there were so many other people besides them.

"I don't mind being a secret," she said, and kissed him.

><><

Trip kept his word: although Tim Michaels pestered him repeatedly, he refused to divulge the name of his new mystery girl, and when his other friends asked where he was headed after school, he made excuses. Pearl, too, told no one. What could she have said? Part of her wanted to tell Lexie, to reveal her membership in this exclusive club of the experienced, to which they both now belonged. But Lexie would demand every intimate detail, would tell Serena Wong and everyone in the school would know within a week. Izzy, of course, would be disgusted. Moody—well, there was no question of her telling Moody. For some time, Pearl had been increasingly aware that Moody's feelings toward her were different, in quality and quantity, than hers toward him. A month before, as they fought through the crowd at a movie theater—they'd gone to see *Titanic* at last, and the lobby was mobbed—he'd reached back and seized her hand so they wouldn't be separated, and though she was glad to have someone ferrying her through the mass of people, she had felt something in the way he'd clasped her hand, so firmly, so proprietarily, and she'd known. She'd let him keep her hand until they broke through to the door of the theater, and then gently disentangled it under the guise of reaching into her purse for some lip balm. During the movie—as Leonardo DiCaprio sketched Kate Winslet in the nude, as the camera zoomed in on a hand smudging a fogged car window—she felt Moody stiffen and glance over at her, and she dug her hand into the bag of popcorn, as if bored by the tragic spectacle onscreen. Afterward, when Moody suggested they stop off at Arabica for some coffee, she'd told him she had to get home. The next morning, at school, everything seemed back to normal, but she knew something had changed, and she held this knowledge inside her like a splinter, something she was careful not to touch.

So she learned to lie. Every few days, when she and Trip snuck away together—Tim Michaels's schedule permitting—she left a note in Moody's locker. *Have to stay after. See you at your house, 4:30?* Later, when Moody asked, Pearl always had an excuse that was plausibly vague. She'd been making posters for the annual spaghetti dinner fund-raiser. She'd been talking to their English teacher about their upcoming paper. In reality, after their trysts, Trip would drop her off a block away and head off to practice, and she would turn up at the Richardson house on foot as usual while he went off to hockey practice, or to a friend's house, or circled the block for a few minutes until coming home himself.

They were observed only once. Mr. Yang, on his way home from bus-driving duty, steered his light blue Saturn down Parkland Drive and saw a Jeep Cherokee pulled to the side of the road, two teens inside pressed against each other. As he passed, they finally pulled apart and the girl opened her door and stepped out and he recognized his young upstairs neighbor, Mia's quiet, pretty daughter. It was none of his business, he thought to himself, though for the rest of the afternoon he found himself daydreaming back to his own teenage years in Hong Kong, sneaking into the botanical gardens with

Betsy Choy, those dreamlike afternoons he had never told anyone about, and had not remembered to relive, for many years. The young are the same, always and everywhere, he thought, and he shifted the car into gear and drove on.

><

Since the Halloween party, Lexie and Brian had also been sneaking away together as often as they could—after practice, at the end and sometimes the start of their weekend dates, and once, during finals week, in the middle of the day between Lexie's physics exam and Brian's Spanish exam. "You're an addict," Serena had teased her. To Lexie's great annoyance, someone always seemed to be at the Richardson house whenever she and Brian most wanted to be alone. But between Brian's father being on call and his mother working late, the Avery house was often empty, and in a pinch they made do with Lexie's car, pulling off to a deserted parking lot and clambering into the backseat under the old quilt she'd begun to keep there for just this purpose.

To Lexie, the world seemed nearly perfect, and her fantasies were her real life with all the colors dialed up. After their dates, when she and Brian had reluctantly disentangled themselves and gone home, she would snuggle down in bed, still imagining his warmth, and picture the future, when they would live together. It would be like heaven, she thought, falling asleep in his arms, waking up beside him. She could not imagine anything more satisfying: the very thought filled her with a warm, almost postcoital glow. Of course they would have a little house. A yard in back where she could sunbathe; a basketball hoop just above the garage door for Brian. She would have lilacs in a vase on the dresser and striped linen sheets on the bed. Money, rent, jobs were not a concern; she did not think about these things in her real life, so they did not appear in her fantasy life either. And someday—here the fantasy began to twirl and sparkle like a firework against the night sky—there would be a baby. It would look just like the photo Brian's mother kept on the mantel, of Brian at one: curly headed, chubby cheeked, with brown eyes so big and soft that when you looked into them you felt like you were melting. Brian would bounce the baby on his hip, toss the baby in the air. They would picnic in the park and the baby would roll in the grass and laugh when the blades tickled his feet. At night they would sleep with the baby between them in a warm, soft, milk-scented lump.

In Shaker Heights, every student had sex ed not just once, but five times: in the fifth and sixth grade, considered "early intervention" by the school board; in the "danger years" of seventh and eighth grade; and again in tenth grade, the last hurrah, in which sex ed was combined with nutrition basics, self-esteem discussions, and job-application advice. But Lexie and Brian were also teenagers, poor at calculating odds and even poorer at assessing risks. They were young and sure they loved each other. They were dazzled and dizzied by the vision of the future they planned to share, which Lexie wanted so badly, sometimes, that she lay awake at night thinking about it. Which meant that more than once, when

Lexie reached into her purse and found no condoms, they were not deterred. "It'll be fine," she whispered to Brian. "Let's just—"

And so it was that in the first week of March, Lexie found herself in the drugstore, contemplating the shelf of pregnancy tests.

She took a two-pack of EPTs off the bottom shelf and, tucking them under her purse, brought them to the register. The woman working there was young, maybe only thirty or thirty-five, but she had wrinkles all around her lips that made her mouth look permanently puckered. *Please don't ask any questions*, Lexie prayed. *Please just pretend you don't notice what I'm buying*.

"I remember when I found out I was pregnant with my first," the woman said suddenly. "Took the test at work. I was so nervous I puked." She put the tests into a plastic bag and handed it to Lexie. "Good luck, honey." This moment of unexpected kindness nearly made Lexie cry—whether at the shame of being noticed, or the fear her test would say the same, she wasn't sure—and she grabbed the bag and turned away quickly without even saying good-bye.

At home, Lexie locked the bathroom door and opened the box. The instructions were simple. One line meant no, two lines meant yes. Like a Magic 8 Ball, she thought, only with much bigger consequences. She set the damp stick on the counter and bent over it. Already she could see the lines forming. Two of them, bright pink.

Someone knocked on the bathroom door. "Just a second," she called. Quickly she swaddled the test in toilet paper, using almost half the roll, and shoved it down to the bottom of the garbage can. Izzy was still standing outside in the hallway by the time she'd flushed and washed her hands and opened the door at last.

"Admiring yourself in the mirror?" Izzy peered around her sister into the bathroom, as if someone else might be hiding there.

"Some of us," Lexie said, "like to take a minute to brush our hair. You should try it sometime." She swept past Izzy and into her bedroom, where, as soon as the door was shut, she huddled in bed and tried to think about what to do.

><

For a little while, Lexie believed, truly, that they could keep the baby. They could work something out. They could fix this, as everything had always been fixed for her before. She would be due—she counted on her fingers—in November. Perhaps she could defer at Yale for a semester and start late. Or perhaps the baby could live with her parents while she was away at college. Of course she would come home every break to see it. Or maybe—and this was the best dream of all—maybe Brian would transfer to Yale, or she could transfer to Princeton. They could rent a little house. Maybe they could get married. She pressed her hand to her stomach—still as flat as ever—and imagined a single cell pulsing and dividing deep inside, like in the videos in biology class. Inside her there was a speck of Brian, a spark of him turning over and over within her, transforming itself. The thought was precious. It felt like a promise, a present someone had shown her, then stowed away on a high closet shelf for later. Something she was going to have anyway, so why not now?

She began, circumspectly, by talking about Mirabelle, as she had been for months. "You wouldn't believe how teeny her fingers are, Bry," she said. "The teeniest little nails. Like a doll, you wouldn't believe it. The way she just melts into you when you hold her." Then she progressed to other babies she'd recently seen, with the help of *People* magazine. Using Brian's shoulder as a pillow, fanning the glossy pages, she ranked them in order of cuteness, occasionally soliciting his opinion.

"You know who'd have the cutest babies, though?" she said. Her heart began to pound. "Us. That's who. We'd have the most adorable kids. Don't you think? Mixed kids always come out so beautiful. Maybe it's because our genes are so different." She flipped through the magazine. "God, I mean, even Michael Jackson's kid is cute. And *he's* frickin' terrifying. There's the power of mixed kids."

Brian dog-eared a page in his book. "Michael Jackson is barely black. Take it from me. And that is one white-looking baby."

She leaned into Brian's arm, nudging the photo spread closer. In it, Michael Jackson lounged on a golden throne, holding an infant in his arms. "But look how cute." She paused. "Don't you kind of wish *we* had one right now?"

Brian sat up, so abruptly Lexie nearly fell over. "You're crazy," he said. "That's the craziest shit I've ever heard." He shook his head. "Don't even say shit like that."

"I'm just *imagining*, Bry. God." Lexie felt her throat tighten.

"You're imagining a baby. I'm imagining Cliff and Clair killing me. They wouldn't even have to touch me. They'd just give me that look and I'd be dead. Instant. Instant death." He ran his hand over his hair. "You know what they'd say? *We raised you to be better than that.*"

"It really sounds that awful to you? Us together, a little baby?" She crimped the edge of the magazine with her fingernails. "I thought you wanted us to stay together forever."

"I do. Maybe. Lex, we're eighteen. You know what people would say? Everybody would say, oh look, another black kid, knocked a girl up before he even graduated from high school. More teen parents. Probably going to drop out now. That's what everybody would say." He shut his book and tossed it onto the table. "No way am I going to be that guy. No. Way."

"Okay." Lexie shut her eyes and hoped Brian wouldn't notice. "I didn't say let's have kids right now, you know. I'm just *imagining*. Just trying to picture what the future might be like, is all."

Hard as it was to admit, she knew he was right. In Shaker, high schoolers did not have babies. They took AP classes; they went to college. In eighth grade everyone had said Carrie Wilson was pregnant: her boyfriend, it was well known, was seventeen and a dropout from Cleveland Heights, and Tiana Jones, Carrie's best friend, had confirmed to several people that it was true. Carrie spent several weeks looking smug and mysterious, rubbing her hand on her belly, before Mr. Avengard, the vice principal, called an assembly to address the entire grade. "I understand there are rumors flying," he said, glaring out at the crowd. The faces looked so young to him: braces, acne, retainers, the very first bristles of a beard. *These children*, he thought, *they think it's all a joke*. "No one is pregnant," he told them. "I know that none of you young ladies and gentlemen would be that irresponsible." And indeed, as weeks passed, Carrie Wilson's stomach remained as flat as ever, and people eventually forgot all about it. In Shaker Heights, either teens did not get pregnant or they did an exceptionally good job of hiding it. Because what would people say? *Slut*, that's what the kids at school would say. *Ho*, even though she and Brian were eighteen and therefore legally adults, even though they had been together for so long. The neighbors? Probably nothing, not when she walked by with her belly swollen or pushing a stroller—but when she'd gone inside, they'd all talk. Her mother would be mortified. There would be shame and there would be pity, and Lexie knew she was not equipped to withstand either one.

There was only one thing to do, then. She curled up on the bed, feeling small and pink and tender as a cocktail shrimp, and let her fantasy go, like a balloon soaring into the sky until it burst.

><

At dinner that night Mrs. Richardson announced her plan to visit Pittsburgh—"For research," she told everyone. "A story on zebra mussels in Lake Erie, and you know Pittsburgh has had its own problems with invasive wildlife." She had thought carefully about a plausible excuse and, after much thought, had come up with a topic that no one would have questions about. As she'd expected, no one paid much attention—except Lexie, who briefly closed her eyes and whispered a silent thanks to whatever deity had made this happen. The next morning, Lexie pretended to be running late, but once everyone had gone, she checked to be sure the house was empty before dialing the number to a local clinic, which she had looked up the night before. "The eleventh," she told them. "It has to be the eleventh."

The evening before her mother left for Pittsburgh, Lexie called Pearl. "I need a favor," she said, her voice dropped halfway to a whisper, even though they were on the line only she and Trip shared, and Trip was out.

Pearl, still wary after the Halloween party, sighed. "What," she said. In her mind she ran through the list of things Lexie, of all people, might want. None of the usual things applied. To borrow a top? To borrow a lipstick? Pearl had nothing that Lexie Richardson would ever need to use. To ask her advice? Lexie never asked anyone's advice. Lexie was the one who dispensed advice, whether it had been asked for or not.

"I need you," Lexie said, "to come with me to this clinic tomorrow. I'm getting an abortion."

There was a long moment of silence while Pearl struggled to process this information. Lexie was pregnant? A flash of selfish panic shot through her—she and Trip had been at Tim Michaels's just that afternoon. Had they been careful enough? What about the last time? She tried to reconcile what Lexie was saying with the Lexie she knew. Lexie wanted an abortion? Baby-crazy Lexie, quick-to-judge-others Lexie, Lexie who'd been so unforgiving about Bebe's *mistakes*?

"How come you're not asking Serena?" she said at last.

Lexie hesitated. "I don't want Serena," she said. "I want you." She sighed. "I don't know. I thought you'd understand more. I thought you wouldn't judge."

Pearl, despite everything, felt a tingle of pride. "I'm not judging," she said.

"Look," said Lexie. "I need you. Are you going to help me or not?"

At seven thirty A.M., Lexie pulled up in front of the house on Winslow. True to her promise, Pearl was waiting at the curb. She'd told her mother that Lexie was giving her a ride to school.

"Are you sure about this?" she asked. She had spent the night imagining what she would do in Lexie's situation, every time feeling that flash of panic surge through her again from her scalp to the soles of her feet. It would stay with her until the following week, when she would feel cramps beginning and sigh in relief.

Lexie did not look away from the windshield. "I'm sure."

"It's a big decision, you know." Pearl tried to think of an analogy she was sure Lexie would understand. "You can't take it back. It's not like buying a sweater."

"I *know*."

Lexie slowed as they approached a traffic light and Pearl noticed dark rings beneath her eyes. She had never seen Lexie look so tired, or so serious.

"You didn't tell anyone, did you?" Lexie asked, as the car eased into motion again.

"Of course not."

"Not even Moody?"

Pearl thought of the lie she'd told Moody last night—that she couldn't walk to school with him as usual because she had a dentist appointment that morning. He hadn't seemed suspicious; it had never occurred to him that Pearl might lie. She'd been relieved, but also a little hurt: that over and over again, he believed her so easily, that he didn't think her capable of anything but the truth.

"I haven't told him anything," she said.

The clinic was an unassuming beige building with clean, shiny windows, flowering shrubs in front, a parking lot. You could be there to have your eyes checked, to meet your insurance agent, to have your taxes done. Lexie pulled into a spot at the edge of the lot and handed the keys to Pearl. "Here," she said. "You'll need to drive back. You have your temp on you?"

Pearl nodded and refrained from reminding her that technically, the temporary permit allowed her to drive only with a licensed adult over twenty-one. Lexie's fingers on the keys were white and cold, and on a sudden impulse Pearl took Lexie's hand in hers.

"It'll all be fine," she said, and together they went into the clinic, where the doors slid open as if they were expected.

The nurse at the desk was a stout woman with copper-colored hair, who looked at the two girls with benign sympathy. She must see this every day, Pearl thought, girls coming in terrified at what's about to happen, terrified about what will happen if they don't.

"Do you have an appointment, honey?" the woman asked. She looked from Pearl to Lexie pleasantly.

"I do," Lexie said. "Eight o'clock."

The woman tapped at her keyboard. "And your name?"

Quietly, as if she were ashamed, as if it were really her name, Lexie said, "Pearl Warren."

It was all Pearl could do to keep her mouth from dropping open. Lexie studiously avoided her eyes as the woman consulted her screen. "Do you have someone to drive you home?"

"I do," Lexie said. She tipped her head toward Pearl, again without meeting her eyes. "My sister's here. She'll drive me home."

Sisters, Pearl thought. They looked nothing alike, she and Lexie. No one would ever believe that she—small, frizzy haired—was related to willowy, sleek Lexie. It would be like saying a Scottish terrier and a greyhound were littermates. The woman glanced at them quickly. After a moment, she either seemed to find this plausible or decided to pretend she did.

"Go ahead and fill these out," she said, handing Lexie a clipboard of pink forms. "They'll be ready for you in a few minutes."

When they were safely settled into the chairs farthest from the desk, Pearl leaned over the clipboard.

"I cannot *believe* you are using *my name*," she hissed.

Lexie slumped in her chair. "I panicked," she said. "When I called, they asked for my name and I remembered that my mom knows the director here. And you know—my dad's been in the news, the whole case with the McCulloughs. I didn't want them to recognize my name. I just said the first name that came into my head. Which was yours."

Pearl was unappeased. "Now they all think *I'm* the one who's pregnant."

"It's just a name," Lexie said. "I'm the one in trouble. Even if they don't know my real name." She took a deep breath but seemed to deflate further. Even her hair, Pearl noticed, seemed lank, falling in front of her face so it half covered her eyes. "You—you could be anyone."

"Oh, for god's sake." Pearl took the clipboard from Lexie's lap. "Give me those." She began to fill out the forms, starting with her own name. *Pearl Warren.*

She had almost finished when the door at the end of the waiting room opened and a nurse dressed in white stepped out. "Pearl?" she said, checking the file folder in her hands. "We're ready for you."

On the line for "Emergency contact," Pearl quickly jotted down her own mother's name and their home phone number. "Here," she said, thrusting the clipboard into Lexie's hands. "Done."

Lexie stood slowly, like a person in a dream. For a moment they stood there, each clasping an end of the clipboard, and Pearl was sure she could feel Lexie's heart pounding all the way down her fingertips and into the wood of the clipboard's back.

"Good luck," she said softly to Lexie. Lexie nodded and took the forms, but at the doorway stopped to look back, as if to make sure Pearl were still there. The look in her eyes said: *Please. Please, I don't know what I'm doing. Please, be here when I get back.* Pearl fought the urge to run up and take her hand, to follow her down the hallway, as if they really were sisters, the kind of girls who would see each other through this kind of ordeal, the kind of girls who, years later, would hold each other's hands during childbirth. The kind of girls unfazed by each other's nakedness and pain, who had nothing in particular to hide from one another.

"Good luck," she said again, louder this time, and Lexie nodded and followed the nurse through the door.

>≪×≫<

At the same time that her daughter was changing into her hospital gown, Mrs. Richardson was ringing the doorbell of Mr. and Mrs. George Wright. She had driven the three hours to Pittsburgh in one swoop, without even stopping to use the restroom or stretch her legs. Was she really doing this? she wondered. She was not completely certain what she would say to these Wrights, nor what information, precisely, she hoped to obtain from them. But there was a mystery here, she knew, and she was equally sure the Wrights held the key to it. She had traveled for stories a few times in the past—down to Columbus, to investigate state budgeting cuts; up to Ann Arbor, when a former Shaker student had started at quarterback in the Michigan-OSU game. It was no different, she told herself. It was justified. She had to find out, in person.

If Mrs. Richardson had had any doubts about whether she'd found the right family, they were dispelled as soon as the door opened. Mrs. Wright looked strikingly like Mia—her hair was a bit lighter, and she wore it cut short, but her eyes and face resembled Mia's enough that Mrs. Richardson glimpsed what Mia would look like in thirty years.

"Mrs. Wright?" she began. "I'm Elena Richardson. I'm a reporter for a newspaper in Cleveland."

Mrs. Wright's eyes were narrow and wary. "Yes?"

"I'm writing a feature about promising teen athletes whose careers were cut short. I'd like to talk to you about your son."

"About Warren?" Surprise and suspicion flashed across Mrs. Wright's face, and Mrs. Richardson could see the two emotions wrestling there. "Why?"

"I came across his name while I was researching," she said carefully. "Several stories said he was the most promising teen running back they'd seen in decades. That he had a shot at going pro."

"Some scouts came to watch their games," Mrs. Wright said. "They said a lot of nice things about him, after he died." A long, quiet moment passed, and when she looked up again, the suspicion had faded away, and was replaced by a look of weathered pride. "Well, I guess you can come in."

Mrs. Richardson had planned out this beginning and trusted her instincts to lead the conversation in the direction she wanted it to go. Getting information out of interviewees, she had learned over the years, was sometimes like walking a large, reluctant cow: you had to turn the cow onto the right path while letting the cow believe it was doing the steering. But the Wrights, it turned out, were unexpectedly easy subjects. Over mugs of coffee and a plate of Pepperidge Farm cookies, the Wrights seemed almost eager to talk about Warren. "I'm just interested in keeping his memory alive," she said, and as soon as she began to ask questions, the gush of information that poured out of them was almost more than she could write down.

Yes, Warren had been the starting running back on the football team; yes, he'd been a forward on the hockey team as well. He'd started with peewee when he was seven or eight; would Mrs. Richardson like to see some photos? He'd just had a natural gift for sports, they hadn't trained him; no, Mr. Wright had never been much good at sports himself. More of a watcher, he would say, than a player. But Warren had been different—he just had a talent for it; his coach had said he might make a Division I school, if he trained hard enough. If the accident hadn't happened—

Here Mr. and Mrs. Wright both fell silent for a moment, and Mrs. Richardson, curious as she was to learn more, felt a pang of true pity. She looked down at the photograph of Warren Wright in his football uniform, which Mrs. Wright had pulled from the mantel to show her. He must have been seventeen then, just the same age as Trip. They didn't look much alike, the two boys, but something in the pose reminded her of her son, the tilt of the head, the mischievous trace of a smirk at the corners of the lips. "He was quite a heartbreaker," she murmured, and Mrs. Wright nodded.

"I've got children myself," Mrs. Richardson found herself saying. "And a boy around that age. I'm so sorry."

"Thank you." Mrs. Wright gave the photo one last long look, then set it back on the mantel and angled it carefully, wiped a speck of dust from the glass. This woman, Mrs. Richardson thought, had endured so much. Part of her wanted to close her notebook and cap her pen and thank her for her time. But she hesitated, remembering why she'd come. If it had been *her* daughter who had run off and lied about who she was, she told herself, if it had been *her* daughter who'd stirred up trouble for well-meaning people—well, she wouldn't blame anyone for asking questions. Mrs. Richardson took a deep breath.

"I was hoping to speak to Warren's sister as well," she said, and pretended to consult her notes. "Mia. Would you be willing to give me her current phone number?"

Mr. and Mrs. Wright exchanged uneasy looks, as she had known they would.

"I'm afraid we've been out of contact with our daughter for some time," Mrs. Wright said.

"Oh dear, I'm so sorry." Mrs. Richardson glanced from one parent to the other. "I hope I haven't broached a taboo subject." She waited, letting the uneasy silence grow. No one, she had learned from experience, could stand such silence for long. If you waited long enough, someone would start talking, and more often than not they would give you a chance to press further, to crack the conversation open and scoop out what you needed to know.

"Not exactly," Mr. Wright said after a moment. "But we haven't spoken with her since shortly after Warren died."

"How sad," Mrs. Richardson said. "That happens

quite a lot, one family member taking a loss very hard. Dropping out of contact."

"But what happened with Mia had nothing to do with what happened to Warren," Mrs. Wright broke in. "What happened with Warren was an accident. Teenage boys being reckless. Or maybe just the snow. Mia—well, that's a different story. She was an adult. She made her own choices. George and I—" Mrs. Wright's eyes welled up.

"We didn't part on the best terms," put in Mr. Wright.

"That's terrible." Mrs. Richardson leaned closer. "That must have been so hard for you both. To lose both of your children at once, in a way."

"What choice did she give us?" Mrs. Wright burst out. "Showing up in that state."

"Regina," Mr. Wright said, but Mrs. Wright did not stop.

"I told her, I didn't care how nice these Ryan people were, I didn't approve of it. I didn't think it was right to sell your own child."

Mrs. Richardson's pencil froze in midair. "Pardon?"

Mrs. Wright shook her head. "She thought she could just give it up and go on with her life. Like nothing had happened. I had two children, you know. I knew what I was talking about. Even before we lost Warren." She pinched the bridge of her nose, as if there were a mark there that she wanted to rub out. "You don't ever get over that, saying good-bye to a child. No matter how it happens. That's your flesh and blood."

Mrs. Richardson's head was spinning. She set her

pencil down. "Let me see if I have this right," she said. "Mia was pregnant and was planning to let this couple—the Ryans—adopt her baby?"

Mr. and Mrs. Wright exchanged looks again, but this time the look between them said: in for a penny. It was clear, to Mrs. Richardson's practiced eye, that they wanted to talk about it, that perhaps they had been waiting to talk to someone about it for a long, long time.

"Not exactly," Mr. Wright said. There was a long pause. Then: "It was their baby, too. They couldn't have their own. She was carrying it for them."

n the fall of 1980, Mia Wright, just turned eighteen, left the little yellow house in Bethel Park for the New York School of Fine Arts. She had never been outside of Pennsylvania before, and she left home with two suitcases and her brother's love and without her parents' blessing.

She had not told her parents she was applying to art school until the acceptance letter had arrived. It was not wholly unexpected, or should not have been. As a child she had been fascinated by things that, to her bemusement, no one else seemed to even notice. "You were such a woolgatherer," her mother would say. "You sat in your stroller just staring out at the lawn. You'd sit in the tub and pour water back and forth from one cup to another for an hour if I'd let you." What Mia remembered of those moments was watching the blades of grass in the breeze, changing color as they went, from dark to light, like the nap of velvet when you brushed your hand over it; the way the stream of water broke itself into droplets as it splashed against the cup's rim. Everything, she noticed, seemed capable of transmogrification. Even the two boulders in the backyard sometimes turned to silver in the early morning sunlight. In the books she read, every stream might be a river god, every tree a dryad in disguise, every old woman a powerful fairy, every pebble an enchanted soul. Anything had the potential to transform, and this, to her, seemed the true meaning of art.

Only her brother, Warren, seemed to understand the hidden layer she saw in things, but then they had always had an understanding, since before he had been born. "My baby," Mia would say to anyone who would listen, tapping her mother's belly with a finger, and infallibly Warren would kick in reply. "My baby. In there," she informed strangers in the grocery store, pointing. When they'd brought him home from the hospital, she had immediately claimed him as her own.

"My Wren," she'd called him, not only because Warren had been too long to pronounce, but because it suited him. Even in those early days, he'd looked like a vigilant chick, head tipped to one side, two impossibly bright and focused eyes, searching the room for her. When he cried, she knew which toy would calm him. When he wouldn't nap, Mia lay next to him in the center of their parents' bed, blankets heaped around them in a chenille nest, singing him songs and patting his cheek until he dozed. When he fell skinning the cat on the monkey bars, it was Mia he ran crying for, and Mia who dabbed the gash on his temple with iodine and stuck a bandage across it.

"You'd think she was the mother," their mother had said once, half in tones of complaint, half in admiration.

They had their own words for things, a jargon of obscure origin: for reasons even they had forgotten, they referred to butter as *cheese*; they called the grackles that perched in the treetops *icklebirds*. It was a circle they drew around the two of them like a canopy. "Don't tell anyone from France," Mia would begin, before whispering a secret, and Warren's reply was always, "Wild giraffes couldn't drag it out of me."

And then, at eleven—almost twelve—Mia discovered photography.

Warren, just turned ten, had himself discovered not only sports but that he was good at them. Baseball in the summer, football in the fall, hockey in the winter, basketball in all the spaces in between. He and Mia were still close, but there were long afternoons at the baseball diamond in the park, long hours practicing passes and practicing layups. So it was natural that Mia, too, would find a passion of her own.

At the junk shop in town she spotted an old Brownie Starflex sitting in the corner of the front window. The camera had lost its flash and neck strap, but the shop owner assured her it would work, and as soon as Mia flipped up the little silver hood and saw the junk shop reflected in blurry miniature in the lens, she wanted it immensely. She dipped into the cat-shaped bank where she saved her allowance and began to carry the camera everywhere. She ignored the manual's suggestion that she write the Kodak Company for its helpful book *How to Make Good Pictures* and went by instinct alone. With the camera dangling from two of her mother's old silk scarves knotted together, she began to take photos— odd photos, to her parents' eyes: run-down houses, rusted-out cars, objects discarded on the side of the road. "Funny thing to be taking a picture of," the clerk at the Fotomat remarked as he handed over an envelope of prints. That set had contained three images, taken over successive days, of a bird's corpse on the sidewalk, and he wondered briefly, not for the first time, if the Wright girl was a little touched in the head.

For Mia, however, the photographs were only a vague approximation of what she wanted to express, and she soon found herself not only altering the prints—with everything from ballpoint pen to splashes of laundry detergent—but experimenting with the camera itself, bending its limited range to her desires. The Starflex, like all Brownies, allowed no focusing. The shutter cocked automatically to avoid double exposures—which the manual billed as a convenience for the amateur. All you had to do was all that you could do: peek into the view-finder and press the shutter. Instead of holding the camera level against her chest, per the instructions, Mia tipped it at different angles, knotted her makeshift straps higher or lower. She draped silk scarves and wax paper over the lens; she tried shooting in fog, in heavy rain, in the smoke-filled lounge of the bowling alley.

"Waste of money," her mother sniffed, when Mia brought home yet another envelope of blurred and grainy photos.

With each roll of film, however, she began to under-stand more and more how a photograph was put to-gether, what it could do and what it could not, just how far you could stretch and twist it. Though she did not know it at the time, all of this was training her to be the photographer she would become. With only twelve exposures on a roll, she learned to be careful in composing her shots. And with no controls—no aperture control, no focus—she learned to be creative in the ways she manipulated her camera and her scene.

At this moment, fortuitously, their neighbor Mr. Wilkinson intervened. He lived up the hill from them, and for some time he'd seen Mia with her Brownie wandering the neighborhood, snapping pictures of this and that. Mia and Warren know only one thing about Mr. Wilkinson: he was a toy buyer and spent most of his time traveling to toy shows, perusing merchandise, sending reports to headquarters on which toys to stock. Every few months, Mrs. Wilkinson would round up the neighborhood children and distribute the sample toys Mr. Wilkinson had accumulated. Marvelous toys they were: a set of molds that you filled with plaster to cast Christmas ornaments; a Saturn-shaped ball on which you could bounce, pogo-style; a giant doll's head with hair of gold to coif; a box of perfumes to blend and pinkie-sized vials to hold your concoctions. "I need my basement back," she'd said, laughing, making sure each child got something, even if only a yo-yo. The Wilkinsons' son was grown by then, living somewhere in Maryland, and no longer needed toys.

For a long time, this was the only image Mia had of Mr. Wilkinson, a mysterious cross between Marco Polo and Santa Claus who filled his home with treasures. But one afternoon, just after her thirteenth birthday, Mr. Wilkinson had called to her sternly from his front porch.

"I've been seeing you traipsing around for a year now," he'd said. "I want to see what you've been up to."

Mia, terrified, collected a stack of her photographs and brought them to the Wilkinsons' the next morning. She had never shown her photos to anyone but Warren before, and Warren, of course, had oohed and aahed. But Mr. Wilkinson was an adult, a man, a man she barely knew. He would have no incentive to be kind.

When she rang the Wilkinsons' doorbell, Mrs. Wilkinson led her into the den, where Mr. Wilkinson sat at a large desk typing something on a cream-colored typewriter. But when Mia entered, he swiveled around in his chair and swung the typewriter shelf down and under, where it folded into a cabinet in the desk as neatly as if it had been swallowed.

"Now then," he said. He unfolded a pair of half-moon glasses that hung around his neck and placed them on his nose, and Mia's knees trembled. "Let's have a look."

Mr. Wilkinson, it turned out, was a photographer himself—though he preferred landscapes. "Don't like shots with people in them," he told her. "I'll take a tree over a person any day." When he went on a trip, he took his camera with him and always scheduled himself half a day to go exploring. From a file he pulled a stack of photographs: a redwood forest at dawn, a river snaking through a field shot with dew, a lake reflecting the sun in a glittering triangle that pointed to the woods beyond. The photographs all over the hallway, Mia realized, were his as well.

"You've got a good eye," Mr. Wilkinson said at last. "Good eye and good instincts. See this one here?" He tapped the top picture, a photo of Warren perched in the low branches of a sycamore, back to the camera, silhouetted against the sky. "That's a fine shot. How'd you know how to frame that?"

"I don't know," Mia admitted. "It just looked right."

Mr. Wilkinson squinted at another. "Hold on to that. Trust your eyes. They see well." He plucked out another photo. "But see this? You wanted that squirrel, didn't you?" Mia nodded. It had been running along the ridge of the fence and she'd been mesmerized by the undulating arc its body and tail had traced as it ran. Like watching a ball bounce, she'd thought as she clicked the shutter. But the photo had come out blurry, focused on the fence instead of the squirrel, the squirrel itself simply a smudge. She wondered how Mr. Wilkinson knew.

"Thought so. You need a better camera. That one's fine for a starter, or for birthday parties and Christmas. Not for you." He went to the closet and rummaged in the back, the old overcoats and bagged dresses inside muffling his voice. "You—you want to take real pictures." In a moment he returned and held out a compact box. "You need a real camera, not a toy."

It was a Nikon F, a little silver-and-black thing, heavy and solid in her hands. Mia ran her fingers over the pebbled casing. "But I can't take this."

"I'm not giving it, I'm lending it. You want it or not?" Without waiting for her to answer, Mr. Wilkinson opened a drawer in his desk. "I'm not using that one anymore. Someone might as well." He removed a black canister of film and tossed it to Mia. "Besides," he said, "I'm looking forward to seeing what you do with it."

By the time Mia went home that afternoon, she had learned how to wind the film onto the spool inside the camera, how to focus it, how to adjust the lens. Strange and beguiling new words swirled in her head: *f-stop, aperture*. Over and over again she lifted the camera to her eye to peer through the viewfinder. Under the hairline cross at its center, everything was transformed.

Mr. Wilkinson taught her how to extract the film from its roll and develop it, and Mia came to love the sharp bite of the developer, how to watch for the sheen of silver on the film's surface that told her it was ready. Like a pilot dipping the plane into a tailspin to practice pulling back out, she would deliberately take photos out of focus, with the wrong shutter speed or the wrong ISO, to see what happened. She learned how to control the light and the camera to get the effects she wanted, like a musician learning the intricacies of an instrument.

"But how can you—?" she would ask, watching the print form on the paper and comparing it to the image she'd had in her mind. At first Mr. Wilkinson would know the answer. "Dodging." "Use a diffused bright fill." "Let's try freelensing." But soon her questions became more advanced, sending him to the copy of *Photographic Techniques* he kept on the bookshelf.

"The young lady wants a greater depth of field," he mused one afternoon. By now Mia was fifteen. "What the young lady needs is a view camera."

Mia had never heard of such a thing. But soon all her

earnings, from clerking at Dickson's Pharmacy to wait-ressing at the Eat'n Park, were earmarked for a camera, and she spent hours poring over Mr. Wilkinson's cam-era catalogs and photography magazines.

"You spend more time reading those things than you do taking pictures," Mr. Wilkinson teased her, but she eventually settled on one—the Graphic View II—and even Mr. Wilkinson couldn't dispute her choice.

"That's a solid camera," he said. "Good value for your money. You take care of that, it'll be with you your whole life." And when the Graphic View II arrived, procured secondhand from a classified ad, well loved and packed into its own case like an expensive violin, Mia knew this would be true.

To her parents the camera was less impressive. "You spent how much on that?" her mother asked, while her father shook his head. It looked, to them, like some-thing from the Victorian era, balanced on a spindly tri-pod, with a pleated belly like a bellows and a dark cloth that Mia ducked underneath. She tried to explain to them how it worked, but at the first mention of *shifts* and *tilts* their attention began to wander. Even her be-loved Warren gave up at that point—"I don't need to know how it works, Mi," he told her at last, "I just want to see the pictures"—and Mia realized that she was crossing into a place she would have to go alone.

She took pictures of the jungle gym at the local park, of streetlights at night, of city workers chopping down an oak that had been struck by lightning. She lugged the view camera downtown to photograph a rusty bridge stretching over the spot where the three rivers collided.

By toying with the settings, she took a picture of Warren's football game, from up in the bleachers, where the players looked like miniatures, the kind you'd see on a train set. "That's me?" Warren had said, peering at one of the figures, the one long in the end zone, waiting for the pass. "That's you, Wren," Mia said. She had a sudden image of herself as a sorceress, waving her hand over the field and transforming the boys below into pea-sized plastic dolls.

She took that print to Mr. Wilkinson's the next day, only to find a strange woman at the door. Mr. Wilkinson's daughter-in-law, it turned out. "Della passed in her sleep," the daughter-in-law told her, eyeing Mia, the camera around her neck, the photograph in her hand. "What did you say you needed?" After the funeral, the daughter-in-law and her husband convinced Mr. Wilkinson to move into a retirement home in Silver Spring, nearer to them. It happened so quickly Mia did not even have the chance to say good-bye, let alone show him the photograph, and she and her camera were alone again.

><

In the fall of 1979, her senior year of high school, Mia applied to the New York School of Fine Arts with a series of photographs she'd taken of abandoned buildings around town. She'd dabbed the prints with a damp cloth and, while the emulsion was wet, used the tip of a needle to scrape away the image, leaving a pin-thin white line. The results were a kind of reverse scrimshaw: a spectral worker slumped on the steps outside a shuttered factory;

the outline of a sedan atop the empty hydraulic lift of Jamison's Auto Repair; a pair of phantom children scrambling hand in hand up a hill of slag. At the sight of those children, Warren had squinted and peered closer. The two children could have been anyone, but they weren't anyone: there was the little cowlick at the crown of Warren's head, there was the knotted silk scarf around Mia's neck, the weight of the camera pulling her slightly askew. There were no pictures of the two of them doing such a thing but it seemed to them they'd spent their childhoods playing on the slag heaps that butted up against the park, and looking at his sister's photograph, Warren felt as if Mia had taken a photo of the ghosts of their past selves, about to fade into the ether. "When you get it back, can I have it?" he'd asked.

To her parents, the photos—and Mia's work in general—were less enchanting. They did not even call what she did "work," or "art," which in their minds would have been just as bad. They were middle-class people, had lived all their married lives in a butter-colored middle-class ranch house in a stolid, middle-class town. To them, work was fixing something or making something useful; if it didn't have a use, they couldn't quite make out why you'd do it. "Art" was something that people with too much time and money on their hands did. And could you blame them? Her father was a handy-man, founder and sole proprietor of Wright's Repair, one day working at the church repairing the eaves where a board had broken and a family of squirrels had wriggled their way into the nave, another day at a neighbor's house snaking the drains or replacing a U-bend under the sink that had rusted away. Her mother was a nurse at the hospital, counting pills, drawing blood, changing bedpans, no stranger to night and double shifts. They worked with their hands, they worked long hours, they saved all they could and put it into a paid-off house and two Buicks and their two children, whom they were proud to say—accurately—lacked for nothing but were never spoiled.

But there was Mia, sprawled on the floor for hours, taking a perfectly good picture of Warren and cutting him out like a paper doll, setting up her cutout brother in a diorama of leaves in an old shoebox—all for one photograph, in which Warren looked like an elf surrounded by giant acorns: clever, but it hardly seemed worth the time she'd put in. There was Mia the second her father got home, his shoes barely off and the grease not yet washed from his hands, begging for two dollars for more film, promising *I'll pay it back, I promise*, though truth be told, she seldom did. There was Mia who, when her mother gave her money for new school clothes, patched the holes in her old jeans instead and spent the money on yet more film, running around in skirts that were inches too short, shirts that were faded and worn, taking yet more pictures. There was Mia who, when she went out and got a job as a waitress at the Eat'n Park, instead of using her earnings to buy her own clothes or a used car, saved them and spent everything on a camera, of all things. It wasn't even a camera the rest of them could use—she'd tried to explain to them once about movement and lens distance and they'd all lost interest almost at once—though she did take a family portrait of the four of them, her senior year of high school, that her mother had framed and hung on the living room wall. The camera folded down into a valise the size of a briefcase and somehow this made it even more disappointing to her parents: all that money packed away into such a small space.

How could you blame Mia's parents for not understanding? They had been born in the wartime years; they'd been raised by parents who'd come of age in the Depression, who threw nothing out, not even moldy food. They were old enough to remember when rags became felt for the war effort, when cans and scrap metal could become bullets and cans of grease explosives. Practicality was baked into their bones. They wasted nothing, especially not time.

So when it came to college, they had assumed she would go somewhere practical, like Pitt or perhaps Penn State, to study something like business or hotel management. They had assumed this photography thing was an adolescent phase, like boy chasing, or vegetarianism. What else had they worked so hard for all these years? For Mia to throw their money away on art school? No, if she wanted art school so badly, she would have to pay her own way. It wasn't mean, they insisted. It was sensible. They weren't forbidding her from going. They were not angry, they assured her; certainly not, definitely not. But they'd sat her down in the living room and put it bluntly: this art thing was a waste of time. They were disappointed in her. And they certainly wouldn't pay for it. "I thought we raised you to be smarter," her mother said, her voice laced with disapproval.

Mia had listened sadly, but it was what she'd expected. She had known all along her parents would not approve; all this time they had indulged her hobby but now that she was eighteen, she knew, things would be different. She was supposed to be an adult, when childish indulgences were supposed to be set aside, not dived into headfirst. She had already done a series of calculations, and if her parents had agreed to contribute at all she would have been taken aback. The school had been so impressed by her portfolio that they'd offered her a tuition scholarship. Her room and board and supplies, she estimated, she would pay for with a part-time job. Her parents glanced at each other, as if they'd known all along their threat wouldn't work, and absorbed this news in silence.

The week before Mia was to leave, Warren appeared in the doorway of her room.

"Mi, I've been thinking," he said, so seriously she almost giggled until he reached into his back pocket and pulled out a folded stack of bills. "I think you should take this. It won't pay for all the rest, but it'll be most of it."

"And the car, Wren?" she asked. Warren had been saving up to buy a car, had even, after much research, picked out the very car he planned to buy: a Volkswagen Rabbit. It was not the car she'd have expected from him: she'd have guessed a Trans Am, or a Thunderbird, something flashy and fun. But gas was running $1.10 a gallon, and not only was the Rabbit one of the few cars he could afford, the ads promised it would get 38 miles per gallon as well, and she was amused to see this practical side of Warren emerging here, of all places.

She folded his hand over the bills and pushed it gently away. "Go get that car, Wren," she said. "Get it and promise to pick me up at the bus station whenever I come home."

Mia had boarded a Greyhound to Philly, then New York, with one suitcase of clothing and one of cameras. From a bulletin board, she'd found an apartment in the Village, not far from campus, with two other girls. She'd gotten a job as a waitress at a little diner near Grand Central and another at the Dick Blick in SoHo. With the last of her savings she'd headed over to the photography store on West 17th, where a young man sold her film and paper as she tried not to stare at his yarmulke. Thus equipped, she'd begun her classes: Figure Drawing I, Light and Color I, Survey of Art I, Introduction to Critical Studies, and—with the most excitement—Introduction to Photography, taught by the renowned Pauline Hawthorne.

It turned out that despite their best intentions, her parents had prepared her exceptionally well for art school.

Each morning she got up at four thirty and went to work pouring coffee for businessmen about to catch their trains. The hot plates she carried from the kitchen seared the insides of her forearms with arc-shaped scars. Her mother had always managed, even on her double shifts, to make each patient more than a body in a bed— chatting with them about their daughter's dance recital or their brother's recent car trouble, asking after their pets—and watching her for years, Mia had learned this talent, too: remembering who took cream and sugar, who liked ketchup on their eggs, who always left the crust on the edge of the plate and was delighted to find, next time, that she'd had the crusts cut off in the kitchen. She learned to anticipate people's needs: just as her mother knew when to appear with the next dose of morphine or to empty the bedpan, she learned to appear with the coffeepot just as they were setting down their empty mugs, to watch her customers for the little fidgets and stretches that signaled they were in a hurry and ready for the check, or that they were relaxed and wanted to linger. Because of this, the businessmen and ad men liked to sit in her section, and they usually left an extra dollar—or sometimes a five—on the table. In the kitchen, when the manager wasn't looking, she ate the leftover wedges of toast and cold forkfuls of scrambled eggs from the plates instead of scraping them into the garbage. This was her breakfast.

When her shift was over, she changed in the little closet of an employee bathroom, rolling her work uniform and apron into a tight cylinder before tucking it in her knapsack, so they would not wrinkle. She did not own an iron and this way, if she was careful, she could wear the same uniform for a week or more before she had to brave the Laundromat. Then, in jeans and a T-shirt, she headed to class.

From her father she had learned to change the oil in a car, to wire a socket, to chisel, to saw—which meant she wielded her tools expertly: she knew how far you could flex a piece of wire or a sheet of metal before it broke, how to make clean lines and soft bulges and curves, how to coax a copper pipe into angles and bends. From her mother she had learned how to handle cloth—from drapey gauze to thick canvas—and how to make it behave, what its limits were, how much you could stretch it and how much it could hold. How to clean a tool, properly, so that no trace of what had touched it remained. Now, in class, when they were asked to make a chair from metal, she already knew how to weld and make things strong; when they were told to work with cloth, she knew—with a quick squeeze of the fabric—how to transform corduroy and linen into a tree, six feet tall, that even her teacher would admire. She knew how thin you needed to make paint so that it would flow and how thick you could make it so that it would clump on the canvas like clay, something to be sculpted. In figure drawing, when the model unbelted her robe and let it puddle at her feet, she alone wasted no time blushing but began, immediately, to sketch the model's long limbs and the curve of her breast: at the hospital, helping her mother, she had seen too many bodies to be shy about anything.

At three o'clock, after her classes ended, she went to work again. Twice a week she had shifts at the Dick Blick, selling art supplies to her fellow students, or restocking the back room. She talked art with the older students, and they told her what they were working on, why they preferred knife to brush or acrylic to oil, or Fujicolor to Kodachrome. In the back room, her boss—who had a daughter about Mia's age and thus had a soft spot for this girl, working multiple jobs to pay her rent—allowed her to keep the pencils and pastels that had snapped in transit, the paint tubes that had leaked, the brushes and canvases that had been dinged or come unstapled. Anything that could no longer be sold Mia took home and repaired, restretching the canvases or mending them on the back with tape, sanding the splintered handle of a brush, sharpening two half pencils to use in place of a whole. In this way she was able to acquire a good portion of her supplies for free.

Three evenings a week, Mia boarded the 1 and rode to 116th Street, where she put on a different uniform and waited tables at a bar near Columbia. The undergrads she served tended to be either haughty and obnoxious or leering and obnoxious, more so as the night wore on, but they tipped her, and at the end of a good night she might have thirty or forty dollars in her apron. She ate the last bites of their burgers and their forgotten fries and the stubs of their pickles for dinner and folded all the cash into her jeans pocket.

She scraped her way through the first year with some money saved even after her rent was paid. Now and then, when she called home—for she did call home, she and her parents all insisted there was no ill will between them; they asked politely how school was going and showed, or at least feigned, interest in her answers—Warren asked if it was worth it. He had always been the happy-go-lucky one, ready to take things as they came; she had been the driven one, the ambitious one, the planner.

"It's worth it," she assured him. And she would tell him about her classes, what paintings she'd studied that week, and her favorite, the real reason she woke at four thirty every morning and stayed up late every night: photography.

When she spoke of Pauline Hawthorne, her tone was half the adoration of a schoolgirl for a crush, half the adoration of a devotee for a saint. It had not been clear, at first, that it would turn out that way. On the first day of photography class, the students had sat upright at their desks, each with a 35mm camera and two notebooks— as specified by the supplies list—in hand. When class began, Pauline strode to the back of the room, flicked off the lights, and, without introducing herself, clicked on the slide projector. A Man Ray photograph burst onto the screen before them: a voluptuous woman, her back transformed into a cello by two painted f-holes. Complete silence filled the room. After five minutes, Pauline twitched her thumb, and the cello woman was replaced by an Ansel Adams landscape, Mount McKinley glowering over a lake of pure white. No one said anything. Another click: a Dorothea Lange portrait of a Dust Bowl woman, her dark hair in a deep part, the merest hint of a smile lifting the corners of her lips. For the entire two hours of the class this continued, a survey of photographs they all recognized but which—as Pauline must have realized—they had never spent much time looking at. Mia, from her reading at the library, recognized them all, but found that after she'd stared at them for long enough, they took on new contours, like faces of people she loved.

After the two hours had passed, Pauline clicked the slide projector off and the class sat blinking in the sudden brightness. "Next class, bring the photo you're proudest of," she said, and left the room. They were the first and only words she'd said.

The next class, after much thought, Mia had brought one of the photos she'd taken with her large-format camera. Introduction to Photography focused on handheld cameras, but Pauline had said *the photo you're proudest of*, and this was hers: a shot of her brother playing street hockey in their backyard, their house and the rest of their neighborhood spread out behind him like miniatures. She had climbed all the way to the top of the hill behind their house to take it. On entering, they found index cards with each student's name pinned up on the walls around the classroom, with clips fastened below them. At two minutes past the hour, Pauline entered— again, without introducing herself—and the class gathered beside each photo in turn, Pauline commenting on the composition or the technique of the picture, students timidly answering her questions about point of view or tone. Some were carefully constructed scenes; one or two had attempted something artistic: a silhouette of a girl backlit by an enormous movie screen; a close-up of a tangled telephone cord wrapped around a receiver.

Mia and the rest of her classmates had braced themselves against Pauline's questioning. After that first class, they'd been sure she was one of the dragons, as the harsher teachers were known: the ones who delighted in making their students uncomfortable, who thought the best way to push students out of their comfort zones was to bulldoze them into rubble during critiques. But

Pauline, it turned out, was no dragon. Despite her no-nonsense air, she found something in each photograph to highlight and praise. It was why—despite being well established—she chose to teach the beginning students. "Look at how the little sister is laughing here," she said, tapping one of the family portraits. "She's the only one not looking at the camera—which gives you a sense that there's something outside the frame. Is she a rebel? Or does this hint at the whole family's spirit?" Or: "Notice how the skyscraper here looks like it's about to pierce the moon. That's a thoughtful choice of perspective." Even her criticisms—which were as common as her praise—were not what Mia had expected. "Water is hard," she said simply, when someone pointed out that a photo of a waterfall was badly blurred. "Let's suppose this was done on purpose. What effect does it have?"

Mia's photograph had been last, and when the class gathered before it, Pauline had paused for a moment, as if taken aback. She had studied it carefully, for two min-utes, three, five, and in the silence the class grew un-easy. "Who's Mia Wright?" she asked finally, and Mia stepped forward. Everyone else took a half step back, as if whatever lightning were about to strike might hit them, too. Then Pauline began to ask questions. Why did you have this line run from right to left? Why did you shift the camera this way? Why did you focus on the hockey stick, and not the net? Mia answered as best she could: she had wanted to capture how small the house and the lawn were in comparison to the hills be-hind it; she had wanted to show the texture of the grass and the way the blades crushed under her brother's shoes. But at a certain point, as Pauline's questions became more technical, she had become flustered and inarticulate. The line had just looked right that way. The shift had just looked right that way. The depth of field had just looked right that way. At last, just as the class session ended, Pauline stepped away with a nod.

"Bring your cameras next time," she said. "We'll start to take some photos." She picked up her bag and left the room, leaving Mia unsure if she'd just passed or failed utterly.

Over the next few classes Pauline treated Mia just like any other student. They learned to wind film into the camera, how to compose a photo, how to calculate the proper aperture and width. All of this Mia knew already, from Mr. Wilkinson's tutelage and her own experimentations over the years. As Pauline explained it, however, her intuitive feelings about how to shape her shots became more conscious. She learned to articulate her reasons for choosing a specific f-stop, to not only find the settings that made it *look right* but to explain why it looked right that specific way. Two weeks into the semester, as the class began making their first prints, Pauline stopped by Mia's station in the darkroom. In the glare of the red light she looked as if she had been carved from a giant ruby.

"How long have you been working with the view camera?" she asked, and when Mia told her, she said, "Would you like to show me some more of your photos?"

The following Saturday, Mia found herself in the

lobby of Pauline's apartment, an envelope of photos clutched in her hand. The building had a doorman, and Mia, having never encountered one before, was so awe-struck she did not listen when he told her which floor, and resorted to pressing each button in the elevator in turn and checking the names on each door before duck-ing back inside and pressing the next. When she at last came out on the sixth floor, she found Pauline standing in the open doorway.

"There you are," she said. "The doorman called up to say you were here ten minutes ago. I was starting to won-der." She was barefoot but otherwise looked exactly the same as she did in class: a black T-shirt and a long black skirt and long beaded earrings that jingled like chimes as she walked. Mia, blushing, followed her into a large, white-walled, sunlit room where everything seemed to glow. She had expected a photographer's apartment to be covered in photographs, but the walls were bare. Later she would learn that Pauline's studio was upstairs, that she never hung anything because when she wasn't work-ing, she wanted the white space. Palate cleanser, Pauline would explain. But at this moment, Mia simply sat down beside her on the nubbly gray couch, where they laid photograph after photograph across the coffee table. Pau-line was full of questions, as she had been that second day of class: Why did you set the camera so low in this one? Why so close in that one? Did you think about adjusting tilt here? What were you thinking about when you took this shot? In the photographs Mia lost her shyness. They were so engrossed that when a woman entered and set two cups of coffee down on the end table, one beside each of them, she jumped.

"Mal," said Pauline, with an offhand wave. "Mal, this is Mia Wright, one of my students."

Mal was slender with long, wavy brown hair. She wore jeans and a green blouse and, like Pauline, she was barefoot.

"Thought you'd like some coffee," Mal said. "Lovely to meet you, Mia." She kissed Pauline on the cheek and went away.

Mia spent all afternoon there, until it was time for her shift at the bar. Pauline and Mal pressed her to stay for dinner, until she finally admitted she had to go to work. "Then next week," Pauline suggested, "when you have a day off." Over the following months she would visit Pauline and Mal often, talking photography with Pauline, watching her at work in her studio, listening to Pauline think aloud about whatever she was working on at the time. "I've been reading about ancient Egypt," Pauline might begin, flipping a book open. "Tell me what you think of this." At their dinner table Mia tried foods she'd never tasted: artichokes, olives, Brie. Mal, she learned, was a poet, had published several collections of poems. "But no one cares about poetry," Mal said with a rueful laugh. She lent Mia books by the stack: Elizabeth Bishop, Anne Sexton, Adrienne Rich.

By the time winter came, Mia would bring her newest photographs to show Pauline nearly every week, and they would talk them over, Pauline pressing her to articulate what she'd done and why. Before, Mia had taken photographs by feel, relying on instinct to tell her what was right and what was wrong. Pauline challenged her to be intentional, to plan her work, to make a statement in each photograph, no matter how straightforward the photo might seem. "Nothing is an accident," Pauline would say, again and again. It was her favorite mantra, Mia had learned, in both photography and in real life. In Pauline and Mal's house, nothing was simple. In her parents' house, things had been good or bad, right or wrong, useful or wasteful. There had been nothing in between. Here, she found, everything had nuance; everything had an unrevealed side or unexplored depths. Everything was worth looking at more closely.

After these sessions, Pauline and Mal would always press Mia to stay for dinner. They knew, by now, about the three jobs, and Mal would urge extra servings on her, would send her home with Tupperware full of leftovers, which she would return on the next visit. They would, in fact, have encouraged her to stay the night, to settle into one of their guest rooms and stay for good, if either of them could have thought of a way to suggest it.

Because Mia was proud: this was quite obvious. Although she accepted their hospitality gratefully, after that first visit she made a point of never arriving empty-handed. She brought them little things she had made: bunches of leaves gathered in Central Park and bound with a ribbon into a ruddy bouquet; a thumb-size basket woven from grass; once, a little sketch of the two of them she'd drawn in ink, even a handful of pure-white pebbles after Pauline mentioned she'd begun a new project with stones. It was clear to both Pauline and Mal that these gifts eased Mia's guilt over all they offered her—their food, their knowledge, their affection—and that otherwise Mia's pride would prevent her from coming back.

And they very much wanted her to come back. By Christmastime it had become clear to all of them—Pauline, Mal, and Mia's other teachers and fellow classmates—that Mia was immensely talented.

"You're going to be famous, you know that, right?" Warren said to his sister one evening. She had come home for Christmas, and true to his word, he'd come to pick her up at the bus station in the little tan VW Rabbit he'd bought that fall. Now, four days after Christmas, he was bringing her back. Without discussing it they had agreed to take the long route, along the winding back roads, in order to stretch out these last few minutes together. Warren was now a junior in high school, and it seemed to Mia that he'd grown in the time she was away: not taller, but that something about him had deepened. His voice had lowered and he'd begun to grow into his hands and fingers and feet, which for the past few years had been too large for him, like a puppy's paws. In the fading afternoon light the stubble on his throat looked like only a shadow, but she knew it for what it was.

"We'll see" was all she said. Then: "And you? What are you going to be when you grow up?" In kindergarten, when the teacher had asked this question, Warren had answered with his plans for that afternoon—the afternoon being as far into the future as his five-year-old mind could imagine. Since then, "What are you going to be when you grow up" had been their way of asking about plans for the day, and even now, Mia teased him, Warren never seemed to be able to look more than a week or two ahead.

"Tommy Flaherty and I are going hunting Friday," he said now. "Getting in one more trip before school starts." Mia made a face. She had never approved of hunting, though everyone in their neighborhood had a deer head or two somewhere in their houses.

"I'll call you when I get back," she said, and kissed him on the cheek. She was struck again by how he'd grown, how he seemed leaner and stronger and more solid than she'd remembered. She wondered if there was a girl in his life. What would he look like the next time she came home, she thought—and when would that be? Summer, perhaps, unless she got a job to save up for next year. There was so much to do. Already, in the few months since she'd come to New York, her work had developed: from her time with Pauline, from studying the work of her classmates, even from the long hours she put in at her many jobs and the constant rotation of strangers she encountered there. It had become smarter and more deliberate, more technically advanced and adventurous, riskier and edgier, and everyone—including Mia herself, and Warren, waving to her through the passenger window before leaning over to crank it closed—was certain she would go far. Nothing was going to distract her from her work, she promised herself. The work was the only thing that mattered. She would not allow herself to think about anything else.

She was so focused on her work that, on the afternoon in March when the man with the briefcase began staring at her, she did not notice right away. It was midafternoon when she got on at Houston Street, heading up to her job near Columbia, and the 1 was quiet, with only a handful of passengers. Mia was thinking about her project for Pauline—*Document a transformation over time*—when she felt the sudden prickle on her skin that meant she was being watched. Mia was used to stares—this was New York, after all—and like all women she had learned to ignore them, as well as the catcalls that sometimes accompanied them. But this man she couldn't quite read. He seemed respectable enough: neat striped suit, dark hair, briefcase between his feet. Wall Street, she guessed. The look in his eyes wasn't lust, or even playfulness. It was something else—a strange mix of recognition and hunger—and it unsettled her. After three stops, when the man had not stopped staring, she bundled up her things and stepped off at Columbus Circle.

At first she thought she had lost him. The train pulled away and she settled herself onto a grimy bench to await the next one and then, as the handful of passengers cleared the station, she saw him again: briefcase in hand now, scanning the platform. Looking for her, she was sure. Before he spotted her she turned and made for the staircase at the far end of the platform and followed the tunnel, walking as briskly as she could without attracting attention, to the platform for the C. She would be late for work now, but it didn't matter. She would get off in a stop or two and walk over to Broadway and catch the right train, once she had gotten away, even if it meant paying another fare.

When the C came, Mia stepped onto a middle car and scanned the seats. The car was half full, enough people that she could call for help if she needed, but not so full that the crowd would hide anything untoward. She settled herself into an empty seat in the center. At 72nd Street there was no sign of him. But at 81st, just as Mia rose to leave, the door at the end of the car opened and in came the man with the briefcase. He was slightly disheveled now, a few locks of his hair falling into his face, as if he had been hurrying through the cars looking for her. Her eyes met his and there was no way to pretend she hadn't seen him. Mia's roommate had been mugged twice walking home late at night, and her classmate Becca had told her a man had pulled her into an alley off Christopher Street by her ponytail—she'd managed to fight him off, but he had pulled out a hank of her hair. Mia had seen the bald spot. Whatever was going to happen would happen now, whether she stayed on the train or off.

She stepped off the train and he followed her, and when the doors closed they stood frozen on the platform for a moment. There was no conductor or policeman in sight, only an old lady with a walker slowly trudging toward the stairs and, at the far end of the platform, a sleeping bum in tattered sneakers. If she ran, she thought, perhaps she could make it to the stairs before he caught her.

"Wait," the man called as the train began to pull away. "I just want to talk to you. Please." He stopped and held up his hands. Now she could see that he was younger than she'd thought, perhaps only in his thirties, and thinner, too. His suit, she could see, was expensive, fine silver thread running through the wool, and his shoes were, too: cordovan with tassels and smooth leather soles. Not the shoes of a man who ran.

"Please," the man went on. "I'm sorry I followed you. I'm sorry I was staring at you. You must have thought—" He shook his head. "I don't like my wife riding the subway because I worry she'll get followed by someone just like that."

"What do you want?" Mia croaked. She had not realized how dry her throat was. Behind her back, she tightened her grip on her keys, points out. *It doesn't look like much, but it'll hurt,* Becca had told her.

"Let me explain," the man said. "I'll stand right here. I won't come any closer. I just needed to talk to you." He put his briefcase down at his feet, between them, and Mia relaxed an infinitesimal amount. If he tried to lunge at her now, it would trip him.

His name was Joseph Ryan—"Joey," he'd corrected himself—and he worked, as she'd guessed, on Wall Street: he'd rattled off a string of names that she recognized as one of the big trading firms. He and his wife lived over on Riverside Drive; he was headed home now; they'd been married for nine years; they'd met as high school sweethearts; they didn't have any children. "We can't," Joseph Ryan explained. "She can't have children. And—" He stopped and looked at Mia beseechingly, ran a hand through his hair and took a deep breath, with the air of a man who knows he is about to utter something preposterous. "We've been looking for someone to carry a baby for us. The right person." And then: "We would pay her. Generously."

Mia's head spun. She dug the points of her keys into the heel of her hand—not for protection now, but to convince her that what she was hearing was real. "You want—" she managed at last. "Why me?"

Joseph Ryan fumbled in his pocket and produced a business card, and after a brief hesitation, Mia took a single step forward and stretched her arm to take it. "Please. Will you just come and talk with us? Tomorrow? At lunch? Our treat, of course."

Mia shook her head. "I have to work," she said. "I can't—"

"Dinner, then. My wife and I can explain everything to you. Look—the Four Seasons. Seven o'clock? At the very least, I promise you'll get a good meal." He bobbed his head like a shy schoolboy and picked up his briefcase. "If you don't show up, I'll understand," he said. "I can't imagine—having someone suggest this to you. On a subway platform." He shook his head. "But please—just think about it. You would help us so much. You would change our lives." And then he turned away and went up the staircase, leaving Mia standing on the platform, holding the card in her fingertips.

><

For the rest of her life Mia would wonder what her life would have been like if she had not gone to the restaurant that day. At the time it seemed like a lark: just a way to satisfy her curiosity, and get a nice meal in the bargain. Later, of course, she would realize it had changed everything forever.

That evening she stepped from 52nd Street into the lobby of the Four Seasons, in the only nice dress she owned: one she'd worn to her cousin Debbie's wedding the year before. She'd grown since then, so the dress was a bit too short and a bit too tight, and even if it had fit it would have been worlds of style away from this plush lobby, with its huge chandelier and its dense carpet and its jungle of potted plants. Even the air seemed lush and thick here, like velvet, swallowing up the click-click of ladies' heels and the chatter of men in suits, so that they passed as silently as gliding ships. Joseph Ryan had not told her where to meet them, so she stood awkwardly to one side, pretending to admire the painting that covered one of the lobby's enormous walls, trying to avoid the attention of the maître d', who floated around the entrance of the dining room like a solicitous specter.

Five minutes, she thought, and if they didn't come, she would go home. She had forgotten to wear a watch, so she began to count slowly, as she and Warren had as children playing hide-and-seek. She would count to three hundred, and then she would go home and forget this crazy thing had ever happened. And then, just as she reached a hundred and ninety-eight, Joseph Ryan appeared at her elbow, like a waiter.

"Picasso," he said.

"What?"

"The tapestry." Here in the lobby he seemed almost

bashful, and she had almost forgotten the menace she'd felt the day before. "Well, not a tapestry per se, I guess. He painted it on a curtain. They asked him for a painting, but he didn't have time to make one, so he gave them this instead. I've always admired it."

"I thought you were bringing your wife," Mia said.

"She's at the table." He made as if to take her arm, then thought better of it and put his hands into his jacket pockets instead. It was almost comical, his gentlemanliness, she thought as she followed him down the hallway.

A huge white room with—she blinked—a jade-green pool in the center. Trees inside, studded with pink blossoms and starred with lights. Like a fairy forest hidden in the center of a New York office building. All around the soft hum of conversation. A scrim of fine chains lacing the window, rippling like waves though there was no breeze. And then the strange thing happened. As they came into the dining room and Joseph Ryan approached the table in the corner, Mia saw herself somehow already sitting at the table, in a neat navy dress, a cocktail in her hand. For a moment Mia thought she was approaching a mirror, and she paused, confused. And then the woman at the table stood up and reached across to take Mia's hand.

"I'm Madeline," she said, and Mia had the uncanny sensation, as their hands met, of touching her reflection in a pool.

><

The rest of the evening unfolded as if some kind of dream. Every time she looked at Madeline Ryan she saw herself; they shared not just the curly dark hair and similar features but some of the same mannerisms: the same tendency to bite their bottom lips, the same absent habit of pulling one curl down, like a spring, to their earlobes and letting it bounce back up. They were not identical—Madeline's chin was a bit more pointed, her nose a little thinner, her voice deeper, richer, almost throaty—but they looked so similar they could have been mistaken for sisters. Late that night, long after the taxi the Ryans had summoned had dropped her back at home, Mia sat awake, thinking over all she'd heard.

How Madeline, at seventeen, had still not gotten her period, and how the doctor had then examined her and discovered that she had no uterus. One in five thousand women, Madeline had explained—there was a long German name for it, Mayer-something syndrome, which Mia had not fully caught. How the only way for them to have a child was a surrogate. This was 1981, and three years before headlines had trumpeted the arrival of Louise Brown, the world's first test-tube baby, but the odds of such a birth were still poor, and most people still viewed brewing babies in petri dishes as suspicious. "Not for us," Madeline had said, twisting the stem of the wineglass between her elegant fingers. "No Frankenbabies, no thank you." Instead, the Ryans had decided to take a more old-fashioned route: as old, Joseph pointed out, as the Bible. Sperm from the father, egg from—and carried by—a woman who seemed a suitable match. They had been advertising for months—discreetly, Madeline added—for a surrogate with the right characteristics, and had found no one. And then Joseph Ryan, riding the subway from a lunch meeting, had spotted an eerily familiar face at the other end of the car, and it had felt like fate.

"We see it," he said, "as an opportunity for us to do each other some mutual good." He and Madeline glanced at each other, and Madeline gave him the merest nod of the head, and they both sat up a little straighter and turned to Mia, who set her fork down.

"Don't think that we're entering into this lightly," Madeline said. "We've been thinking about this for a long time. And we've been looking for just the right woman." She tipped the carafe of water and refilled Mia's glass. "We think that woman is you."

In her room now, Mia did calculations. Ten thousand dollars, they had offered, to carry a healthy baby for them. They had said this to her as if outlining the terms of a job offer, laying out the benefits package in the most attractive way. "And of course we'd pay for all your medical expenses," Joseph had added.

At the end of dinner, Joseph had slid a folded sheet of paper across the table. "Our home number," he said. "Think it over. We'll draw up a contract for you to look over. We hope you'll call us." He had already paid the bill, which Mia had not seen but knew must be appallingly high: they'd had oysters and wine; a tuxedoed man had prepared steak tartare at their table, deftly folding the golden yolk into the ruby-red meat. Joseph hailed Mia a taxi. "We hope you'll call," he said again. Behind him, behind the glass window of the lobby,

Madeline buttoned the fur collar of her coat. Only after he had shut the door, and the taxi was on its way back downtown to Mia's cramped apartment, did she unfold the paper to see that astonishing figure again: *$10,000*. And below it, a single word: *please*.

The next morning, she'd thought it was a bizarre dream until she saw that creased note still lying on her dresser. Insane, she thought. Her womb was not an apartment for rent. She could barely imagine having a baby, let alone giving one away. In the gray and steely morning light, the evening before now looked like a childish fantasy. She shook her head, dropped the note into her dresser drawer, pulled out her uniform for work.

And then, a few weeks later, Mia learned her scholarship would not be renewed. Pauline and Mal opened the door and without speaking she handed them a letter, slit jaggedly open by a finger.

Dear Miss Wright: We trust that you have been benefiting from your first year at the New York School of Fine Arts. However, we are sorry to inform you that due to funding restrictions, we are unable to continue your financial aid for the 1981–1982 academic year. We of course hope that you will nevertheless continue your studies with us next year and—

"They're idiots," Pauline said, tossing the letter onto the coffee table. "They have no idea what they're losing out on."

"It's the state," Mal said. She retrieved the letter and slid it back into its envelope. "They cut funding so the school has to cover more, and scholarships suffer."

"It's no big deal," Mia said. "I'll get another job. I'll save up over the summer."

As she rode the elevator back downstairs that evening, however, she rested her head against the mirrored wall and bit back tears. She could not take on more hours than she was already working or she would have no time for her classes, and as it was she was barely making ends meet. If she worked full time all summer . . . She ran her mental calculations again. Unless she found a job that paid twice as much, she could not afford to stay.

"Are you all right, miss?" The elevator doors had opened and there she was, back in the lobby, the kindly doorman peering down at her through his glasses. Behind him a wine-colored carpet rolled all the way to the thick glass doors that sealed out Fifth Avenue. The lobby was hushed as a library, but beyond those doors, she knew, were the cracked concrete sidewalks and the rush and clamor and ruthlessness of the city.

"Fine," she said. They knew each other a bit now, as people in New York often do: his name was Martin and he grew up in Queens and rooted for the Mets—not the Yankees, he'd told her, *never* the Yankees—and had a dachshund at home named Rosie. For his part, Martin knew Mia's name and that she was the protégée of the Lady Artists upstairs—as he fondly referred to Pauline and Mal—and though Mia had told him little else about her life, his seasoned eye could divine quite a bit from the secondhand camera slung around her neck, the black-and-white uniform she sometimes still wore when she arrived, the containers of food she often carried home at Mal's insistence. He resisted the urge to pat her on the shoulder and pushed the front door open with one gloved hand.

"Have a good night," he said, and Mia stepped out onto Fifth Avenue and let the city swallow her up.

14

Mia did not consult her parents, or her roommates, or even Pauline and Mal. Looking back, she would realize this was proof that she had already made up her mind. The day after receiving the letter from the college, Mia broached the prospect of a raise with the manager of the diner. "Wish I could, honey," he told her, "but I can't pay you girls more without raising prices and losing customers." The manager of the Dick Blick said the same, and after that she didn't even bother to ask the bar owner. For a week, she dodged Pauline's repeated invitations to come for dinner; Mal, and probably Pauline as well, would sense her preoccupation right away. She sent a note to their apartment in lieu of her usual Sunday visit, claiming she had the stomach flu and had to stay home. For a week she thought only about her tuition—and the Ryans. She ruined an entire roll of film by pulling it out of the canister with the light on, something she'd never done before. She dropped a plate of eggs at the diner, sliced her finger on the jagged edge, watched a trickle of blood ooze onto the white china. Over and over during the day she passed her hand across the flat plain of her belly, as if inside she might feel something that could give her clarity.

One afternoon, on a break from work, she pulled Joseph Ryan's business card—the one he'd given her that first day—from her pocket and headed to the subway. Perhaps he was a con man. How did she know these Ryans would pay what they promised, that they were even named Ryan? But indeed, the address on the card brought her to the gleaming glass building of Dykman, Strauss & Tanner on Wall Street. Mia hesitated outside the glass lobby for a few minutes, watching the reflections of the people on the sidewalk glide over, and past, the shadows of the people within. Then she pushed through the revolving door and to the row of phone booths that lined the lobby. She fed a dime into the slot and dialed the phone number on the card. In a moment a female voice came on the line.

"Dykman, Strauss, and Tanner," the woman said. "Joseph Ryan's office. May I help you?"

Mia hung up and hoisted the phone book onto her lap. There were six Joseph Ryans listed in Manhattan, but none on Riverside Drive. She let the phone book swing back on its chain and fished in her pocket for another dime. This time she called directory assistance, which provided her with an address. It was almost time for her shift at the bar to begin, but she took the train uptown anyway, and found herself outside a redbrick prewar building with a black awning and a doorman. Whoever lived here could certainly pay ten thousand dollars for a child.

The next afternoon, when Madeline Ryan came out of the building, Mia followed her. For an hour she trailed her: all the way down 86th Street and around the neighborhood and back home. She saw how on the way out of the building, Madeline Ryan nodded to the doorman as he swept the door open for her, how she paused on the sidewalk, turning back to say something that made the doorman smile, patting him gently on the forearm before heading on her way. How Madeline slowed when she passed women pushing strollers, how she smiled at the babies in those strollers, whether they were cheerful or fretful or sleeping, how she smiled and said hello to the women, asked how they were, commented on the weather, even though—Mia could see it—there was a deep hunger in her eyes. She rushed to open doors for these women, even the nannies pushing fair-skinned children obviously not their own, holding the door open until woman and child were well into the bodega or the café or the bakery before letting it swing slowly shut after them with a wistful, almost mournful look. When a mother—harried, in heels—clip-clopped past her, Madeline Ryan scooped up a pacifier thrown out of the stroller and raced after them to hand it over. Mia had never noticed before how many babies there were: they were everywhere, the city was simply crawling with them, the streets swarming with unabashed fecundity, and she felt a deep pang of pity for Madeline Ryan. Madeline Ryan stopped at a flower stall, bought a bundle of peonies wrapped in green tissue, the buds still balled in tight hard fists. She headed toward home, and Mia let her go.

In the end, she told herself it was the math that decided her. The Ryans' offer was enough to pay for three more terms of school. It would buy her time to earn enough money to pay for the rest. If she did this, she could continue. If she did not, she could not. Put that way, the choice seemed obvious. And she would be doing them a good turn. They were kind, sincere people; she could see that. How badly, she thought, they must want to have a child. She could help them. She would help them. She repeated this to herself, over and over, then lifted the receiver to dial their number.

><

Three weeks later, she was leaving an obstetrician with a letter certifying her good health, her freedom from contagious diseases, and her properly configured anatomy. "Perfect baby-birthing hips," he had joked as she'd pulled her feet from the stirrups. "Everything in there looks fine. If you want to get pregnant, you shouldn't have any trouble." A week after that, she was applying for a one-year leave of absence from school. And then, just as April began and classes were winding down, she found herself in the guest room at the Ryans' elegant apartment. Madeline had purchased a beautiful pink terry robe for her. "Turkish cotton," she'd said, setting it on the bed with a pair of slippers. "We want to make sure you're comfortable." The bed had been made up with crisp white sheets, as if she were a cherished houseguest. Outside she could see the sun glint on the Hudson. Down the hall, she knew, Joseph would be busy in the Ryans' own bedroom, preparing.

There was a soft knock at the door, and Mia pulled the robe more tightly around herself. Her clothes sat folded neatly on the armchair in the corner. Madeline knocked again, then opened the door.

"Are you ready?" she asked. In her hands was a wooden breakfast tray with a covered teacup and a turkey baster with a bright yellow bulb. She set it down on the bedside table, then—awkwardly—knelt and put her arms around Mia. "Thank you," she whispered.

When Madeline had gone, Mia took a deep breath. Was she sure? She lifted the turkey baster from the tray: it was warm. Madeline must have rinsed it in hot water to take away the chill, she realized, and this small generous gesture made her eyes fill. She lifted the lid from the cup, loosened the belt on the bathrobe, and lay back on the bed.

A half an hour later—"You must keep your legs elevated for at least twenty minutes," Madeline had explained to her, "to increase the chances of conception"— Mia emerged from the guest room to find Madeline and Joseph in the living room, holding hands. She had put her own clothes back on, but as they looked up at her in unison—eyes wide, like nervous children—she had the sudden feeling of being naked.

"It's done," she said, and patted the waist of her jeans.

Madeline rose from the sofa in one fluid motion and clasped Mia's hand in hers. "We can't thank you enough," she said. "Here's hoping it takes." She set both of her palms on Mia's belly, as if offering a benediction, and Mia's muscles tensed and hardened.

"I'll call for the car—Joey can take you home,"

Madeline said, and then, "Of course we know it will take a few tries. This is going to take persistence, for all of us. We'll see you again day after tomorrow?"

Mia thought of the tray still sitting in the guest room, of Madeline rinsing the baster and the cup in the kitchen sink, readying them for their next use. "Of course," she said. "Of course." She was quiet all through the ride back to the Village, as Joseph Ryan chattered to her about how he and Madeline had met, where he'd grown up, the things they had planned for their child.

All summer this became the routine. The obstetrician had given her a chart to map out her most fertile periods, and during that week, she would visit the Ryans every other day. Then, the following week, she would wait, scanning her body for a sign. Each time she had backaches, headaches, cramps, and then—of course—no baby.

"It'll take a while," Madeline said as July came to a close. For four months now, no luck. "We always knew this. It doesn't happen right away." But Mia was worried. According to the contract they'd signed, the Ryans were free to call off the agreement after six months if no pregnancy resulted. She had kept her jobs at the diner and the bar and the art store—and had dodged questions from her fellow students, back from their summers off, buying supplies for the new term, wondering why she wasn't coming back. "I'm taking a year off to earn money," she'd said, which was true, and what she had told Pauline and Mal when, tactfully, they'd hinted at offering her a loan she was too proud to accept. But she knew, too, that if no baby arrived, she would get nothing, and she would have dropped the entire year for nothing, and her leave of absence would likely become permanent.

And then, in September, she waited and waited and nothing happened. No blood. No cramps. Just an intense feeling of fatigue, an overwhelming desire to crawl into bed and burrow beneath the comforter like a cat. Madeline nearly danced with delight when, two days later, Mia arrived at her apartment feeling the same way. She bundled Mia into her coat, as if Mia herself were a child, and herded her into the elevator, then into a taxi to a pharmacy on Broadway. From a bewildering array of boxes with confident names—Predictor, Fact, Accu-Test—she selected one and pressed it into Mia's hands.

The test, it turned out, was complicated. It involved a glass test tube in a special holder, suspended over an angled mirror. Mia was to add several drops of her urine and wait for an hour. If a dark ring formed, she was pregnant. She and Madeline sat in silence for forty-five minutes, side by side on the edge of the bathtub, and then Madeline suddenly took Mia's hand. "Look," she whispered, leaning toward the vanity, and Mia saw, in the little mirror, an iron-colored bull's-eye slowly appearing.

><

From then on things changed quickly. Mia's roommates did not notice anything until she began throwing up in the bathroom. "Sweet gig," one of them said. The other said, "I wouldn't go through all that, not for a million bucks." Weeks passed. The Ryans moved her to a little studio apartment they owned, a quiet walk-up just off West End Avenue. "We rent it out but the tenants just left," Madeline said to Mia. "Quieter for you. More space. Fewer people coming and going. And you'll be so much closer to us, for when things start happening." Mia quit her job at the art store—her belly was starting to show—but kept her other jobs, though she allowed the Ryans to linger under the impression that she had stopped working. After every doctor's appointment, she came by to give them the latest updates, and as her clothes began to tighten the Ryans presented her with new ones. "I saw this dress," Madeline would say, handing Mia a tissue-lined shopping bag with a flowered maternity dress inside it. "I thought it would look perfect on you." She was, Mia realized, buying Mia the maternity clothes she would have bought herself, and she smiled and accepted them, and wore the dress on her next visit.

She said nothing to her parents about any of this; she told them only, as Christmas approached, that she would not be coming home. Too expensive, she claimed, knowing they would never ask her about school if she didn't bring it up, and they didn't. But at the end of January, she finally told Warren the truth. "You never talk about class anymore," he said on the phone one evening. She was five months along by then, and though she could have kept it from him—how would he ever know?—she didn't like the thought of hiding it from him any longer.

"Wren, promise you won't tell Mom and Dad,"

she'd said, taking a deep breath. Afterward, there was a long silence on the phone.

"Mia," he'd said, and she knew he was serious, because he never used her full name. "I can't believe you would do something like this."

"I thought it through." Mia set one hand on her belly, where she had recently begun to feel faint flutterings. *The quickening*, Madeline had called it, as she laid her hands on Mia's skin—such an old-fashioned euphemism, one that made her think of quicksilver, a lithe little fish whipping about within her. "They're such good people. Kind people. I'm helping them out, Wren. They want this baby so much. And they're helping me, too. They've done so much for me."

"But don't you think it's going to be hard to give it up?" Warren asked. "I don't think I could do it."

"Well, you're not the one doing it, are you."

"Don't get pissy with me," Warren said. "If you'd asked me, I'd have told you not to."

"Just don't tell Mom and Dad," Mia said again.

"I won't," Warren said at last. "But I'll tell you this. I'm the baby's uncle, and I don't like it." There was an anger in his voice she had never heard before, at least not directed at her.

After that, she and Warren didn't speak for a while. Every week, when she thought about calling him, she decided not to. Why call and argue again, she reasoned. In a few months the baby would be born, she would go back to her old life, and things would be as they had been. "Don't get attached," she said to her belly when the baby nudged her with a foot. It was never clear to her, even then, whether she was speaking to the baby, or to her belly, or to herself.

She and Warren were still not speaking when her mother called, very early in the morning, to tell her about the accident.

><

It had been snowy, this much she knew. He and Tommy Flaherty had been coming home late at night—where they'd been, her mother hadn't said—and they'd taken a turn too fast and Tommy's Buick had skidded and then overturned. Mia would not remember the details: that the roof of the car had been crushed in, that the emergency workers had had to cut the Buick open like a tin can, that neither Warren nor Tommy had been wearing their seat belts. She would not remember, at least for a while, about Tommy Flaherty in his hospital bed, with a punctured lung, a concussion, and seven broken bones, even though he'd grown up just up the hill from them, even though he and Warren had been friends for years, even though he'd once had a crush on her. She would remember only that Warren had been driving, and that now he was dead.

A plane ticket was expensive, but she couldn't bear the thought of waiting, even an extra few hours. She wanted to be swallowed up by the house where she and Warren had grown up and played and argued and planned, where he no longer waited for her, which he would never enter again. She wanted to sink to her knees at the spot on the cold roadside where he had died. She wanted to see her parents, to not have to sit alone with the terrible numbness that threatened to swallow her up.

But when she stepped out of the taxi from the airport and came in the front door, her parents froze, staring at the bulge in her belly, which had grown too big for her to zip her coat. Mia's hand drifted down to her waist, as if one palm could hide what was growing there.

"Mom," she said. "Dad. It's not what you think."

A long silence unspooled in the kitchen, like gray ribbon. Hours and hours, it felt to Mia.

"Tell me," her mother said at last. "Tell us what we think."

"I mean." Mia looked down at her belly, as if she herself were bewildered to find it there. "It isn't my baby." Inside, the baby gave a fierce kick.

"What do you mean, it isn't *your* baby?" her mother said. "How can it not be your baby?"

"I'm a surrogate. I'm carrying it for this couple." Mia found herself trying to explain: about the Ryans, about how kind they were, how much they wanted a baby, how happy they would be. She tried to focus on how much she was helping them, as if this were a charitable deed, purely altruistic: like volunteering at a soup kitchen, or adopting a dog from a shelter. But her mother understood immediately.

"These Ryans," she said. "I suppose you're doing this for them just out of the goodness of your heart?"

"No," Mia admitted. "They're paying me. When the baby is born." She realized suddenly that she was still wearing her scarf and hat. A thin gray sludge trickled from her boot treads onto the cream-colored linoleum.

Her mother turned and headed for the doorway. "I can't cope with this now," she said, her voice fading as she stepped into the living room. "Not now." At the foot of the staircase she stopped and hissed, with a venom that shocked Mia: "Your brother is dead—*dead*, you realize that?—and you come home like this?" Footsteps pounded up the steps.

Mia glanced at her father. She felt exactly as she had as a child, when she'd broken something or ruined something or spent on film the money that her mother had meant for clothes: in those moments her mother would rage and scream and run to her room, leaving Mia with her father, who would squeeze her hand and let the quiet lap over them like milk, then say quietly, "Buy a new one," or "Give her an hour, and go apologize," or sometimes, simply, "Fix it." This was how they'd always fought. But this time her father did not take her hand. He did not say to her, *Fix it*. Instead he looked at her belly, as if he couldn't bear to look at her face. His eyes were wet and his jaw clenched.

"Dad?" she said at last. She would have preferred shouting to this protracted, knife-sharp silence.

"I can't believe you'd sell your own child," he said, and then he, too, left the room.

><

They didn't tell her to leave, but even after she hung her coat in the hall closet, set her bag down in her old bedroom, they didn't speak to her. At dinner she sat at her old place at the table and her mother set a plate and fork in front of her and her father passed the casserole that one of their neighbors had brought, but they said nothing to her, and when she asked questions—When was the funeral going to be? Had they seen Warren?—they answered as briefly as possible. Mia gave up eventually and wound noodles and tuna around her fork. There was a whole stack of casseroles in the fridge, a leaning tower of Pyrex baking dishes crimped in foil. As if no one knew what to do in the face of such tragedy except to make the heaviest, heartiest, most prosaic dish they could, to give the bereaved something solid to hold on to. None of them mentioned, or looked at, Warren's empty place by the window.

They decided everything without her, what the flowers would be, what the music would be, what color coffin Warren would be placed in: walnut with a blue silk lining. They suggested, tactfully, that Mia not go out; she must be tired, they said, they didn't want her to slip on the ice, but she understood: they didn't want the neighbors to see her. When Mia picked out a shirt and tie for Warren—the one he always chose when forced to dress up—her mother selected another, the white shirt and red-striped tie that she'd bought Warren when he entered high school, which he'd said made him look like a stockbroker, and which he never wore. At no point did they mention her interesting condition or her complicated situation. But when they said it would be best if she didn't attend the funeral—"We just don't want anyone getting the wrong idea," her mother had put it—Mia gave in. The night before the funeral, she packed her things. From the back of the closet, she pulled her old duffel bag and took the quilt from her bed, a few old blankets. Then she tiptoed across the hall into Warren's room.

His bed was still unmade; she wondered if her mother would ever make it again, or if she'd simply strip the sheets, strip the room, paint it white, and pretend nothing had ever happened there. What would they do with Warren's things? she wondered. Would they give them away? Would they pack them into crates in the attic, to grow musty and faded and old? On Warren's bulletin board she spotted the photo from her art school application: the etched-in image of the two of them, children, climbing up the mountain of slag. She unpinned it and added it to her bag. Then, on his desk, she found what she'd been looking for: the keys to Warren's car.

Her parents were asleep; her mother had been taking sleeping pills at night to calm her nerves, and the crack beneath their bedroom door was dark. The Rabbit started up with a throaty growl. "A Porsche purrs," Warren had told her once, "a VW kind of putts." She had to pull the front seat all the way forward to reach the clutch; his legs had always been longer than hers. Then she pressed down on the gearshift and, after a moment of hunting, fiddled her way into reverse, and the darkened house faded in her headlights as the car backed out of the driveway.

She drove all night and reached the Upper West Side as the sun was rising. She'd never had to park in Manhattan before and circled the neighborhood for ten minutes before squeezing into a spot on 72nd Street. In her apartment, she sank into her borrowed bed and wrapped herself in the quilt. It would be a long time, she knew, before she would sleep in a bed this comfortable again. When she woke, the late afternoon sun was already sinking over the Hudson, and she got to work. Only the things she'd brought with her, that were truly hers, went into her bag: her too-tight clothes, the handful of loose muumuus she'd bought herself at Goodwill, a few old quilts, some faded bedsheets, a handful of silverware. A file box of negatives, and her cameras. The fancy maternity dresses from the Ryans she folded neatly and placed in a paper grocery bag.

Once she'd finished, she sat down with a pen and a piece of paper. She'd been thinking about what to say all the long drive from Pittsburgh, and in the end, she'd decided to lie. "There is no easy way to say this," she wrote. "I lost the baby. I'm so ashamed and so sorry. You don't owe me anything from our agreement, but I feel I owe you. Here is money to pay you back for the medical appointments. I hope it's enough—it's all I can spare." She placed her note on top of a stack of bills— nine hundred dollars of her saved-up wages. Then she bundled them into the bag with the maternity dresses.

The regular doorman was off duty that night, and with Mia's coat nestled around her, the night doorman didn't seem to notice her belly. He accepted the parcel for the Ryans without once glancing at her face, and Mia headed back to the Rabbit, parked several blocks away. In her belly, the baby kicked once, then turned over, as if settling into sleep.

She drove all night, through New Jersey and Pennsylvania, miles of highway whipping by in the dark. As the sun began to rise, she turned off the highway just outside Erie and drove until she found a quiet rural road. Once she'd parked well off the roadside, she locked all the doors, climbed into the backseat, and wrapped herself in her old quilt. She'd expected it to smell like detergent, like home, and she braced herself for a whirl of nostalgia. But the quilt, having lain on her bed untouched for the past year, smelled like nothing— not clean, not dusty, no smell at all—and pulling it over her head to shield her eyes from the sun, Mia fell asleep.

All week she drove this way, as if in a fever: driving until exhaustion forced her to stop, sleeping until she was rested enough to drive again, ignoring the clock, the light and dark of each day. She stopped now and then, when she passed a town, to buy bread, peanut butter, apples, to refill the gallon jug in the passenger seat with water at a fountain. Throughout her belongings she had hidden two thousand dollars, saved up from her tips and wages since she'd come to New York: in the box of negatives, in the glove compartment, in the right cup of her bra. Ohio, Illinois, Nebraska. Nevada. And then, suddenly, the teeming swirl of San Francisco, the Pacific churning blue-gray and white before her, and she could go no further.

><

What else was there to know? Mia found an apartment, a room for rent in the Sunset in a house whose plaster was the color of sea salt, with a stern and elderly landlady who eyed her stomach and asked only, "There going to be an angry husband knocking on my door in a week?" For the last three months of her pregnancy, Mia walked the city, circling the lagoon in Golden Gate Park, climbing Coit Tower, one day crossing the Golden Gate Bridge in a fog so dense she could hear, but not see, the traffic rushing alongside her. The fog mirrored her state of mind so perfectly she felt as if she were walking through her own brain: a haze of formless, pervasive emotion, nothing she could grasp, but full of looming thoughts that appeared from nowhere, startling her, then receded into whiteness again before she was even sure what she had seen. Mrs. Delaney, her landlady, never smiled at her when they passed each other in the hallway, or when they happened to meet in the kitchen, but as the weeks went on, Mia would often come home to find a plate in the oven, a note on the counter that read *Had leftovers. Don't want to waste them.*

When Pearl was born—on an unseasonably warm May afternoon, at the hospital, after fourteen hours of labor—Mia took the birth record card from the nurse. She had been thinking for months now about what to name this child, mentally combing through all the people she'd known, the books she'd read in high school. Nothing had seemed right until she remembered *The Scarlet Letter*, and the right name came to her at once: *Pearl*. Round, simple, whole as the peal of a bell. And, of course, born into complicated circumstances. Beside it, on the line for "Mother's name," she wrote, in neat letters, *MIA WARREN*. Then she'd reached into the bassinet beside her bed and taken her daughter into her arms.

The first night back in the rented room, Pearl had cried and cried until Mia herself had begun to cry. She wondered if, in New York City, the Ryans would still be awake in their gleaming apartment, what they would say if she lifted the phone and said to them, I lied. The baby is here. Come and get her. They would take the next flight and arrive at her door, she knew, ready to spirit Pearl away. She could not tell if the thought was terrible or tempting or both, and she and Pearl both wailed. Then there was a soft knock at the door, and stern Mrs. Delaney appeared and held out her arms. "Give her here," she said, with such authority that Mia handed the soft bundle over without thinking. "Now you lie down and get some rest," Mrs. Delaney said, shutting the door behind her, and in the abrupt silence Mia flopped down on the bed and fell instantly asleep.

When she woke, she came bleary-eyed into the kitchen, then into the living room, where Mrs. Delaney sat in a pool of lamplight rocking a sleeping Pearl.

"Did you rest?" she asked Mia, and when Mia nodded, she said, "Good," and set the baby back into Mia's arms. "She's yours," Mrs. Delaney said. "You take care of her."

She spent the next few weeks in the same haze, but something had begun to shift. Mrs. Delaney never again came to take the baby away, no matter how hard Pearl cried, but in the evenings she would rap on the door with a bowl of soup, a cheese sandwich, a piece of meat loaf. Leftovers, she always claimed, but Mia understood the gift for what it was, and understood, too, when Mrs. Delaney followed these offerings with a gruff "Rent's due Thursday" or "Don't track mud into the hall," what she was trying to say.

Pearl was three weeks old—still old-mannish, squash-faced—and the fog was just beginning to lift, when Mal's phone call arrived.

Mia had sent Pauline and Mal a letter once she'd settled, with her new address and phone number. "I'm fine," she told them, "but I won't be coming back to New York. Here's where you can reach me if you need to." And now, Mal had needed to reach her. A few weeks ago, Pauline, it seemed, had started having headaches. Strange symptoms. "Auras," said Mal. "She said I looked like an angel, with a halo all around me." A scan had found a lump the size of a golf ball in her brain.

"I think," Mal said, after a long pause, "if you want to see her maybe you should come right away."

That evening, Mia booked a plane ticket, the second she'd ever bought. It took most of her savings, but a bus across the country would take days. Too long. She arrived at Pauline and Mal's apartment with a knapsack slung over her shoulder and Pearl in her arms. Pauline, twenty pounds thinner, looked like a more concentrated version of herself: whittled down, somehow, pared down to her essence.

They spent the afternoon together, Mal and Pauline cooing over the baby, and Mia spending the night, for the first and last time, in their guest room with Pearl beside her. In the morning she woke early to nurse Pearl on the couch in the living room and Pauline came in.

"Stay," Pauline said. Her eyes were almost feverishly bright, and Mia wanted to rise and fold Pauline into her arms. But Pauline waved her to sit and held up her camera. "Please," she said. "I want to take both of you."

She took a whole roll, one exposure after another, and then Mal came out with a pot of tea and a shawl for Pauline's shoulders, and Pauline put the camera away. By the time Mia boarded the plane back to San Francisco that evening, Pearl in her arms, she had forgotten all about it. "Do what it takes," Pauline had said to her as she had hugged her good-bye. For the first time, she had kissed Mia on the cheek. "I'm expecting great things from you." Her use of the present tense—as if this were just an ordinary good-bye, as if she, Pauline, had every expectation of watching Mia's career unfurl before her over decades—penned Mia's voice in her throat. She had pulled Pauline close and breathed her in, her particular scent of lavender and eucalyptus, and turned away again before Pauline could see her cry.

A week and a half later, Mal had called again, the call Mia had known was coming. Eleven days, she thought. She had known it would happen fast, but could not quite believe that eleven days ago Pauline had been alive. It was still warm, still June. The page on the calendar hadn't even changed. And then, a few weeks later, a package arrived in the mail. "She picked these to send to you," read the note, in Mal's angular handwriting. Inside were ten prints, eight by ten, black and white, each glowing as if lit from behind in that peculiar way of all of Pauline's work. Mia cradling Pearl in her arms. Mia lifting Pearl high above her head. Mia nursing Pearl, the fold of her blouse just concealing the pale globe of her breast. On the back of each, Pauline's unmistakable signature. And a note, clipped to a business card: *Anita will sell these for you when you need money.*

Send her your work, when you're ready. I've told her to expect you. P.

After that, Mia began to take pictures again, with a fervor that felt almost like relief. She walked the city again, for hours at a time, Pearl strapped to her back in a sling she'd fashioned from an old silk blouse. Most of her savings were gone by now, and every roll of film was precious, so she worked carefully, framing the image again and again in her mind before she took it. With each shutter click she thought of Pauline. By the time summer came, she had seven shots that she thought might have *something*, as Pauline had always put it.

Anita did not wholly agree. *Promising,* she wrote in response to the prints Mia sent. *But not yet. Take more risks.* In response Mia sent her the first of Pauline's photographs. *Then I need more time,* she wrote. *Get me as much time for this as you can. Don't give anyone my name.* Anita, after a heated auction, got Mia two years' worth of time, even after the fifty-percent commission. (She would make it count; it would be fifteen years before, faced with Pearl's hospital bill for pneumonia, she sold another.) Within a year, Mia had sent Anita another set of prints—each chronicling something's slow decay: a dead cottonwood, a condemned house, a rusting car— that she was ready to take on.

"Congratulations," she said to Mia, when she called her a month later. "I've sold one of them, the one with the car. Four hundred dollars. Not a lot, but a start."

Mia took it as a sign. For a while now she had been dreaming of deserts, of cactus and wide, red skies. New images were starting to form in her mind. "I'll call you in a week or two," she said, "and tell you where to wire the money."

Mrs. Delaney watched from the living room window as Mia packed the trunk of the Rabbit, set Pearl's bassinet snugly in the footwell of the front seat. To Mia's astonishment, when she pried the house key loose from the key ring and handed it back, Mrs. Delaney pulled her into an uncharacteristic hug.

"I never told you about my daughter, did I," she said, her voice thick, and then before Mia could speak, she took the key and hurried back up the front steps, the metal gate clanging shut behind her.

Mia thought about this all through the long drive, until outside of Provo, where she decided to stop—the first of the many stops she and Pearl would make over the years. All the long way, Pearl cooed from her bassinet beside her, as if she were sure, even at this early age, that they were headed for great and important things, as if she could somehow see all the way across the country and through time to everything that was coming their way.

15

M rs. Richardson, of course, could not know all of this. She could know only the basics of the story the Wrights had told her: that Mia had shown up, belly bulging, claiming to be a surrogate for some family named Ryan—the Wrights couldn't remember their first names. "Jamie, Johnny, something like that," Mr. Wright had said. "Someone on Wall Street, she said. Someone with a lot of money."

"I wasn't sure it was true," Mrs. Wright admitted. "I thought maybe she was just in trouble, that she was lying to us. But then that lawyer called." A few weeks after Mia had left, a lawyer had phoned the Wrights, asking if they had a way to get in touch with her. "He sent us a card," Mrs. Wright remembered. "In case she ever sent us her address. But we never heard from her again." She dabbed at the corner of her eye again with a tissue.

After some rummaging, Mrs. Wright found the lawyer's card and Mrs. Richardson copied down the address. *Thomas Riley, Riley & Schwartz, Partners at Law.* A 212 area code, an address on 53rd Street. She thanked the Wrights, and when Mrs. Wright pressed some extra cookies on her, she declined, embarrassed. The Wrights offered to lend her photos of Warren in his football uniform, too—maybe the paper would want to run them with the story, they'd suggested. "As long as we get them back," Mrs. Wright added. "They're the only copies we've got." Guilt clawed at the back of Mrs. Richardson's neck like a spider. They seemed like nice people, these Wrights—nice people who had been through a lot, nice people who could have been her neighbors in Shaker Heights. "If the paper wants photos, I'll get back in touch," she said. This, she told herself, was at least the truth.

"I'm so sorry about everything you've been through," she said at the door, and meant it. Then she hesitated. "If you ever managed to find out where your daughter is, would you want to get in touch with her again?"

"Maybe," Mrs. Wright said. "We've thought of hiring a detective to look for her, you know, see if we could get any leads. But it seems to us that if she wanted to be found, she'd have gotten in touch. She knows where we live. Our phone number's the same as it's been her whole life. She must think we're still angry at her."

"Are you?" Mrs. Richardson asked, on impulse, and neither Mr. Wright nor Mrs. Wright answered.

><

The number of the law firm was sixteen years old, but Mrs. Richardson decided it was worth a try. Back at her hotel, she dialed and, to her immense relief, a secretary picked up almost immediately.

"Riley, Schwartz, and Henderson," the woman said.

"Hello," Mrs. Richardson began. "I'm calling regarding a case Mr. Riley was working on quite some time ago." She paused, thinking quickly. "I have some information that my client thinks may be relevant. But before I pass along any information, I wanted to be sure Mr. Riley is still representing the Ryans. As you can imagine, this information is rather sensitive."

The secretary paused. "Which case did you say you were involved with?"

"The Ryans. The information I have regards a Mia Wright."

There was the sound of a drawer opening and a rustling of files. Mrs. Richardson held her breath. "Here we are. Joseph and Madeline Ryan. Yes, Mr. Riley is still on retainer for them, though"—she paused—"this file hasn't been active in quite some time. But Mr. Riley is in the office currently and I'd be happy to put you through to him. What did you say your name was?"

Mrs. Richardson hung up. Her heart was pounding. Then, after several minutes of careful thought, she flipped open her address book and dialed her friend Michael, who worked at the *New York Times*. They'd met in college, working on the *Denisonian*, and though Michael had jumped from there to the *Stamford Advocate* and then quickly to the news desk at the *Times*, while she had returned home and gone local, they had stayed in touch. He had once, she was quite sure, been in love with her, though he'd never said anything about it, and they'd both been married for years now. Recently he'd been nominated for a Pulitzer, though he'd lost out to someone from the AP reporting on the killings in Rwanda.

"Michael," she said. "Can you do me a favor?"

A week later, Michael would call back and confirm what she had already suspected: through journalistic sleight of hand known only to himself, he had managed to find hospital bills for a Mia Wright in 1981, at St. Elizabeth's in midtown Manhattan. They had been paid for by a Joseph Ryan, and they had stopped in February 1982, when Mia would have been six months pregnant, and if Mrs. Richardson had had any doubts about where Pearl had come from, they would vanish. She would have to think about what—if anything—to do with this information. The poor Ryans: wanting a baby so badly that they'd take such steps to get one. Yes, she knew something about that, she thought, thinking of Linda and Mark McCullough. But she felt a twinge of sympathy for Mia, too, one she hadn't felt before and had never expected to feel: how excruciating it must have been to think about giving her child away.

What would she have done if she'd been in that situation? Mrs. Richardson would ask herself this question over and over, before Michael's call and for weeks—and months—after. Each time, faced with this impossible choice, she came to the same conclusion. *I would never have let myself get into that situation*, she told herself. *I would have made better choices along the way.*

For now, Mrs. Richardson stacked her notes in her folder, which she had discreetly labeled M.W. Tomorrow she would drive back home.

><

On the way out of the clinic, Lexie was having trouble processing what was happening to her, what had just happened to her. Her legs and her body trotted confidently ahead while her head drifted along behind like a dawdling balloon. She had been pregnant and now she was not. There had been something alive inside her and now there was not. Deep in her belly she felt a vague cramping and a warm damp trickle into the thick sanitary pad the nurse had given her. The rest of the package was in her bag, along with a bottle of Advil. "You'll want this later on, when the anesthetic wears off," the nurse had told her.

Pearl took her arm. "You okay?"

Lexie nodded and the parking lot spun around and landed on its side. Pearl caught her as she began to tip. "Okay. Come on. Almost there."

The original plan had been to drive Lexie home. Her mother wasn't due back until tomorrow afternoon, and by then, Lexie had assumed, she would be back to normal, ready to pretend nothing had happened. But it was clear to Pearl, as she guided Lexie into the front seat of the Explorer, that Lexie was in no condition to go home. She was woozy from the anesthesia, and in the end, Pearl had to buckle the seat belt around her.

"Okay," she said. "We'll go to my house."

"What about your mom?" Lexie asked, and when Pearl said, "She can keep a secret," this seemed like the saddest thing Lexie had ever heard, and she burst into tears.

It was just past noon when they entered the house on Winslow, and Mia—cutting a maple tree out of a magazine ad with an X-Acto knife—looked up in alarm as they entered the kitchen. At the sight of the scalpel in Mia's hands, Lexie—who had calmed down by the end of the drive—began to cry again. To everyone's surprise, even her own, Mia pulled Lexie into her arms.

"You're all right," she said. "It's all going to be okay."

Lexie was never entirely sure, afterward, whether she had told Mia what had happened, or if Pearl had, or if Mia had simply intuited it on her own. All she would remember was Mia holding her tight, so tight that the world stopped spinning at last, Mia tucking her into a low soft bed that, it turned out later, was Mia's own.

Mia, in fact, had already had suspicions about Lexie's situation. Though Brian had cautiously flushed their condoms down the toilet, a few times when Mia emptied the garbage in Lexie's room she had found the condom wrappers balled into a wad of tissues. One afternoon, when she'd come back to the Richardson house to retrieve her purse, which she'd left behind that morning by mistake, she'd tripped over Brian's size 12 tennis shoes in the entryway right beside Lexie's platform sandals. There had been no sign of the two of them, but Mia had grabbed her bag from the kitchen island and hurried out, half afraid of what she might hear from upstairs, shutting the door quietly and hoping the noise wouldn't carry. Lexie, every time Mia saw her, struck her as terrifyingly young, and Mia did not want to think about what Lexie was certainly up to, nor what—by extension—Pearl might be up to as well.

So when Lexie had appeared in the doorway, half leaning on Pearl's arm, Mia took in her wan and grayish face, the pink discharge form from the clinic still clutched in her hand, the plastic bag full of pads dangling from Pearl's wrist, and understood immediately what had happened. If someone had asked her, a month or even a week before, to guess what she might have felt, she might have anticipated a sliver of gloating, or at least a moment of holier-than-thou. In the actual moment, however, she felt nothing but a flood of deep sympathy for Lexie, for the bind she had found herself in, for the pain—both physical and emotional—she would have to fight through to get out of that bind.

Lexie woke up nestled under a crisp white comforter. It was midafternoon, and the curtains were drawn, but a lamp in the corner had been left on, a towel draped over the shade to mute it, and the thoughtfulness of this pierced her. For the third time that day she found herself sobbing. And then Mia was there, sitting at her bedside, stroking her back.

"It's okay," she said to Lexie, and though she said nothing else, just this—*it's okay, it's okay*—Lexie found herself breathing easier. Mia settled herself cross-legged on the floor and handed Lexie a tissue, and Lexie realized that the bed wasn't simply low: it was a mattress set on the carpet. She blew her nose. There was no garbage can in sight, but Mia held out her hand, and after a moment of embarrassment Lexie handed over the damp wad of tissue.

"You slept a long time. That's good. Do you think you can eat something?" In the kitchen, Mia set a bowl of soup in front of her, and Lexie brought a spoonful to her lips: chicken noodle, salty, searingly hot. There was no sign of Pearl, but the clock on the stove read 3:15. School had let out a little while ago. She must have told her mother everything, Lexie thought.

"This wasn't supposed to happen," she blurted out. She felt an intense need to explain herself, to make sure Mia did not think ill of her. At that moment, Pearl came up into the apartment. She was flushed in the face and panting a little.

"I borrowed Moody's bike," she said. "Had to get home and see if you were doing okay."

"You didn't—" Lexie began, and Pearl shook her head.

"Of course I didn't tell him," she said. "I said I forgot I promised I'd get home early to help my mom with something." It unnerved her, how easy it had been to lie to Moody again, but she shook the feeling aside, as if she were brushing off cobwebs. "How are you doing?"

"She's going to be fine," Mia said, and patted Lexie's hand. "I'm sure of it."

Ten minutes later, as Mia was setting the soup bowl into the sink to soak, another set of footsteps came thumping up the stairs and Izzy arrived. Afternoons were her time with Mia, and she spent the last few periods of the day anticipating what Mia might be working on, thinking of things to share. At the sight of Lexie, she froze in the doorway.

"What are *you* doing here?"

Lexie scowled. "I came over to hang out with Pearl, obviously," she snapped. "You have a problem with that?"

Izzy glanced from Lexie to Pearl with deep suspicion. Her sister never came to the house on Winslow; she much preferred to spend her time in the comfort of the Richardsons' rec room, where there were comfortable chairs and a big TV and snacks and diet Cokes were plentiful. Here there was no TV, not even a couch. It was most unlike Lexie. Why would she and Pearl meet here rather than there? Yet there Lexie was, looking pale and uncertain and perhaps even a little red-eyed—all of which was most unlike Lexie, too.

"I'm helping Lexie with her English paper," Pearl said. "We thought we'd work better over here."

"It's okay, Izzy," Mia said. "But you know, since the girls are here, I'm not working today. Tomorrow, okay?" Then, when Izzy hesitated, she said, "Tomorrow, I promise. After school. Just like always." She gave Izzy's elbow a little squeeze as she turned her around in the doorway, and Izzy, with a glare at Lexie, clumped back down the stairs. In a moment they heard the door slam shut behind her.

"She is so pissed at me," Lexie murmured. "Well, what else is new." Now that Izzy was gone, she felt herself drained, and she slumped backward in her chair, letting her ponytail drape over the back.

Pearl eyed her. "You don't look so good."

"Back to bed," Mia said calmly. "You've been through a lot today." In the bedroom, she settled Lexie onto the mattress again and spread the comforter over her and patted her back gently, as if she were a child. It was oddly soothing.

"Shit," Lexie said. "The robocall. My parents will

know I cut." Shaker Heights took attendance seriously: at the start of each class, a teacher filled out a Scantron marking anyone absent. Back in the main office, a secretary ran the attendance sheets through a machine and a recorded call went out to the parents' home phone, alerting them about their truant children.

"I called you in," Mia said. "After you and Pearl got here. I said you weren't feeling well today and you'd be out all day and tomorrow."

Lexie felt as if her head were made of wood. "But you need a parent to excuse you," she mumbled, pushing herself up on her forearms. The room began to wobble.

"I told them I was your mother. How would they know the difference?" Mia put a hand on Lexie's shoulder and gently pushed her back down. Her voice, Lexie thought, was so calm. As if she knew how to get away with anything. "Rest," Lexie heard her say, and she was asleep almost at once.

When she woke again, it was late evening. She lay in the dimness, watching the sky darken, until Mia knocked on the door carrying a steaming mug of tea. "I thought you might be thirsty," she said, and Lexie accepted the cup and took a grateful sip. Peppermint. Under her fingers the mug was comfortingly solid, like a warm, strong shoulder.

"I called your father," Mia said. Her mother, Lexie remembered suddenly, was supposed to arrive home the next afternoon.

"Shit," she whispered. "Did you tell him?"

"I told him you were staying over here tonight. That Pearl had asked you to sleep over."

After a moment, Lexie said, "Thanks."

"You can stay as long as you need to. But I'm betting you'll be ready to go home tomorrow."

Lexie turned the mug around slowly between her palms. "And then?"

"Then it's up to you what you do. Who you tell."

Mia got up to leave, but Lexie, in a panic, grabbed her hand.

"Wait," she said. "Do you think I made a huge mistake?" She gulped. "Do you think I'm a terrible person?" She had never given much thought to Mia, but suddenly it felt crucial to know if Mia disapproved of her. In the face of Mia's kindness, she could not bear it if Mia disapproved of her.

"Oh, Lexie." Mia sat down again, still holding Lexie's hand. "You were in a very hard situation. A situation no one wants to be in."

"But what if I chose wrong?" Lexie paused, closing her eyes, trying to feel that spark of life that she'd been so certain was cartwheeling inside her before. "Maybe I should have kept it. Maybe I should have told Brian. We could have made it work."

"Would you have been ready to be a good mother?" Mia asked. "The kind of mother you'd have wanted to be? The kind of mother a child deserves?" They sat in silence for a few minutes, Mia's hand warm on Lexie's. Lexie felt an overwhelming urge to lean her head on Mia's shoulder, and after a moment, she did. For the first time, she wondered what it would have been like to grow up as Pearl, to have Mia as her mother, to have this life as her life. The thought made her a bit dizzy.

"You'll always be sad about this," Mia said softly. "But it doesn't mean you made the wrong choice. It's just something that you have to carry." She sat Lexie up gently and gave her a pat on the shoulder, then bent to pick up the empty mug.

"But do you think I made the wrong choice?" Lexie persisted. She felt sure Mia would know.

Mia paused, one hand on the doorknob. "I don't know, Lexie," she said. "I think you're the only one who can know that." The door closed softly behind her.

>×<

When Lexie opened her eyes, it was early morning. There was no sign of anyone, but someone had turned the lamp off, and someone had set a glass of water at her bedside.

Pearl was in the kitchen, eating a bowl of cereal.

"You look better," she said to Lexie. "You okay?"

"Getting there." Lexie settled herself gingerly onto the other mismatched chair opposite Pearl. "Where's your mom?"

"At your house. She went over to clean early. She's doing lunch shift at the restaurant today." Pearl suddenly remembered Lexie's views on the McCullough case and decided not to mention the reason for the unusual schedule: Bebe was meeting with her lawyer to prepare for the hearing, which was starting in less than two weeks, and had asked Mia to cover for her at work.

Instead she nudged the box of cereal toward Lexie, who tipped it toward her and took a handful.

"Did she sleep on the floor?"

"With me."

"Sorry."

Pearl shrugged. "It's okay. We're used to it. Sometimes we don't have space for two beds." She slid a bowl across the table. "Don't eat it out of the box, pour some out. Freak." Lexie seemed much younger somehow, and she couldn't tell if it was the morning light, soft and pale yellow, or Lexie herself—no makeup, hair loose around her face—or the strangeness of this moment, of Lexie breakfasting in her kitchen, of what they'd been through together the day before.

"Your mom was really nice to me last night." Lexie stirred the cereal in her bowl.

"My mom *is* nice," Pearl said, with a prickle of pride.

"I always thought she didn't like me."

"Well." Pearl considered. She, too, had had this feeling, but could sense now that something had shifted. "I don't think you knew each other."

"You think she likes me now?" Lexie asked at last.

"Maybe." Pearl grinned, and Lexie got up, slung an arm around her, and kissed her on the cheek.

The night before, as they lay side by side in Pearl's little twin bed, Mia had reached out to rub her daughter's back, something she hadn't done in years. When Pearl had been young, they had often shared a bed: it was easier to find one mattress than two, of course, but there had also been an intense comfort in being close together, like small animals sheltered deep in their den.

As Pearl had grown taller, sharing a bed became less and less feasible, and it had been a long time since they'd lain together this way.

"Poor Lexie," Mia murmured. "Such a hard place to be in." There was something she felt she needed to say, but she wasn't sure how, and after a moment she simply plunged in. "Are you—do you—" She paused. "We've never really had this talk before."

Pearl pulled away and flopped abruptly onto her back. "Oh my god, Mom. Let's not do this."

"I just want to make sure you know how to be careful." Mia rubbed a scratch on her thumbnail. She'd nicked it the day before, working on something. "I know you and Moody are very close."

Beside her she felt Pearl's whole body go very still, then, just as suddenly, relax again.

"Mom," Pearl said. "Moody and I are just friends."

"But maybe someday you'll want to be more. I know how it goes—" Mia stopped. She didn't, she realized suddenly; she didn't know how it went, not at all. As a teenager she'd had plenty of friends, some of them boys—but none as close as the friendship between her daughter and Moody seemed to be. They were together constantly, it seemed; they finished each other's sentences, they talked in a patois of inside jokes and shared references that sometimes she barely understood. More than once she'd seen Pearl lean over carelessly to fix Moody's collar; just the other day, she'd seen Moody reach out to pluck a wayward leaf from Pearl's hair with such tenderness that she could call it nothing other than love. But she herself had never felt that way about anyone, not as a teenager, not in art school, not since. It occurred to her that except for her brother, when they were children, she'd never seen a man naked. More than that: she'd never touched anyone and felt that warmth, that electric tension at the nearness of someone else. The only thing that had given her that feeling had been art—and then, of course, Pearl. She had nothing useful to say about this, she thought, and the silence billowed out between them.

"Mom." In the dark Mia couldn't tell if Pearl was serious or smiling. "You don't need to worry. I promise. There's nothing between Moody and me." She rolled over onto her side, away from Mia, the pillow now muffling her voice. "And I got an A in health class. I know all this stuff." It was the truth, she told herself; not a single word she'd said had been a lie. Omission, Pearl decided, was not the same as lying. She felt Mia begin to rub her back again, the same gentle caress that, as a child, had told her she was not alone, that her mother was there, which meant that everything was all right. As it had all those years ago, it put her to sleep almost at once.

After Pearl had begun to snore softly, Mia kept her hand in place, as if she were a sculptor shaping Pearl's shoulder blades. She could feel Pearl's heart, ever so faintly, beating under her palm. It had been a long time since her daughter had let her be so close. Parents, she thought, learned to survive touching their children less and less. As a baby Pearl had clung to her; she'd worn Pearl in a sling because whenever she'd set her down, Pearl would cry. There'd scarcely been a moment in the day when they had not been pressed together. As she got older, Pearl would still cling to her mother's leg, then her waist, then her hand, as if there were something in her mother she needed to absorb through the skin. Even when she had her own bed, she would often crawl into Mia's in the middle of the night and burrow under the old patchwork quilt, and in the morning they would wake up tangled, Mia's arm pinned beneath Pearl's head, or Pearl's legs thrown across Mia's belly. Now, as a teenager, Pearl's caresses had become rare—a peck on the cheek, a one-armed, half-hearted hug—and all the more precious because of that. It was the way of things, Mia thought to herself, but how hard it was. The occasional embrace, a head leaned for just a moment on your shoulder, when what you really wanted more than anything was to press them to you and hold them so tight you fused together and could never be taken apart. It was like training yourself to live on the smell of an apple alone, when what you really wanted was to devour it, to sink your teeth into it and consume it, seeds, core, and all.

><

After Pearl went to school, Lexie stayed at the house on Winslow all morning. She lay across the bed and drifted off to sleep, and was still asleep when Mia came home from the restaurant with two foam containers of leftover noodles and a new idea. When the phone rang at two o'clock, waking Lexie at last, Mia was back at the table sketching with a pencil on a scratch piece of paper.

"I know, Bebe," Mia was saying into the receiver as

Lexie came into the living room. "But you can't let it get to you. The hearing is going to be even worse. This is only the tip of the iceberg." She glanced at Lexie, then turned back to the phone. "It's going to be okay. Take a deep breath. I'll call you later."

"Was that—Mirabelle's mother?" Lexie asked, when Mia had hung up the phone. To her embarrassment, she could not remember the baby's birth name.

"She's a friend of mine." Mia settled herself back at the table and Lexie pulled up a chair alongside her. "There was an article today in the paper that said some unkind things about her. It suggested she was an unfit mother." She glanced at Lexie. "Maybe you knew that already. With your father representing the McCulloughs, of course."

Lexie flushed. Her father had been very busy lately—staying late at his office in preparation for the hearing, which was fast approaching—but she had been too preoccupied with Brian, with college, with the visit to the clinic and everything leading up to it, to pay much attention. "I didn't know anything," she said stiffly. Then: "Is she? An unfit mother, I mean."

Mia picked up her pencil and turned to her sketch again. A net, Lexie thought—no, perhaps it was a cage. "Was she before? Maybe. She was in a bad situation."

"But she abandoned her baby." This was something Lexie had heard her mother say enough times—into the telephone to Mrs. McCullough, anytime the case came up—to engrave it in her mind as fact.

"I think she was trying to do what was best for the baby. She knew she couldn't handle things." Mia scribbled a hasty note in the corner of her drawing. "The question is whether things are still the same. Whether she should get another chance."

"And you think she should?"

Mia did not answer for a moment. Then she said, "Most of the time, everyone deserves more than one chance. We all do things we regret now and then. You just have to carry them with you."

Lexie fell silent. Unconsciously, one hand crept down to her belly, where an ache was beginning to blossom.

"I'd better go home," she said at last. "School's almost over, and my mom will probably be back now."

Mia swept crumbs of eraser dust from the table and stood up. "Are you ready?" she said, with a gentleness that made Lexie ache.

"No," Lexie said. She laughed nervously. "But am I ever going to be?" She stood up. "Thanks for—well. Thanks."

"Are you going to tell her?" Mia asked, as Lexie gathered her things.

Lexie considered. "I don't know," she said at last. "Maybe. Not now. But maybe one day." She pulled her car keys from her pocket and lifted her purse. Beneath it was the pink discharge slip from the clinic. She paused, then crumpled it into a wad and tossed it into the garbage can, and then she was gone.

16

Mia was right: by the time the custody hearing began, there had been a series of news stories—in print and on television—on Bebe Chow and her fitness to be a mother. Some of them portrayed her as a hardworking immigrant who had come in search of opportunity and had been overcome—temporarily, her supporters insisted—by the obstacles and the odds. Others were less kind: she was unstable, unreliable, an example of the worst kind of mother. The last week of March, as the hearing began, the steps to the courthouse were crowded with journalists and tabloid reporters alike, all rabid for scraps of anything that emerged in the testimony.

Because the hearing was kept private, like all proceedings in family court, the news stories could continue to be sensational and simplistic, easy arguments for one side or the other. Only those in the hearing room—the McCulloughs, their lawyer, Mr. Richardson, Ed Lim, Bebe, and the judge himself—heard about all that had happened, in all its messy complexity.

And it was complicated, what had happened. It was a terribly awkward, agonizingly slow, painfully intimate story that unfolded over the course of that week, back and forth between Mr. Richardson and Ed Lim: one of them making a point for his client, the other expertly picking it up and turning it neatly on its head.

><

When the baby was found, she had been undernourished. Her fontanel was sunken in, a telltale sign of dehydration, and her ribs and the small bones of her spine had been visible under her skin, like a string of beads. At two months old, she had weighed only eight pounds.

(But the baby had refused to latch. Bebe had tried and tried until her nipples cracked and bled. She had cried, her breasts hard with milk she could not feed her child, the infant screaming on her lap, furiously turning her little face away, and at the sound of the baby's cries pink milk had gushed from her breasts and trickled down into her lap. After two weeks of this, Bebe's milk had dried up. She had spent her last seven dollars on formula and then her wallet was empty, except for a fake million-dollar bill someone had given her at work, for good luck.)

Severe diaper rash on the baby indicated that she had sat in soiled diapers for hours—if not days—on end.

(But Bebe had had no money for diapers. Remember that she had spent her last seven dollars on formula. She had done her best. She had taken the soiled diapers off, scraped them as clean as she could, refastened them around her daughter's waist. She had smeared Vaseline—the only thing she had—onto the angry red patches that blossomed on her daughter's buttocks.)

Neighbors had heard the baby squalling for hours

on end. "All day, all night," the neighbor from 3B had said. "Screaming when I left for work in the morning. Screaming when I came home at night." He had thought about calling the police, but didn't want to interfere. "I keep to my own business."

(But Bebe had cried, too. Yes, she had lain and sobbed, sometimes with the baby across her chest, frantically stroking her back and hair, sometimes alone, on the floor beside the dresser drawer she had used as a cradle, while the baby wailed alongside her, their voices floating to the roof in painful harmony.)

In her month and a half of turbulent motherhood, Bebe did not once seek help from a psychologist or a doctor.

(She should have, it is true. But she had no idea where to turn. Her English was middling at best; her reading comprehension minimal. She did not know how to find the social workers who might have helped her; she did not even know they existed. She did not know how to file for welfare. She did not know that welfare was a possibility. When she looked down, she saw no safety net, only a forest of skyscrapers stabbing upward like needles upon which she would be impaled. Could you blame her for tucking her daughter onto a safe ledge while she herself plummeted?)

Bebe had left her baby early in the morning on January 5, 1997, at the fire station on Kinsman Road. That night the temperature had dipped to thirty-one degrees. With windchill, it was seventeen. At two thirty A.M., when the firemen opened the door and discovered the baby, lying in a cardboard box, it had just begun to

snow, and everything was covered with a silvery, crystalline dusting.

(Although it had indeed been quite cold when Bebe
placed her baby on the steps of the fire station, the baby
had been wearing three shirts and two pairs of pants
and had been swaddled in four blankets—every baby
item Bebe had owned. Her little hands had been tucked
inside to keep them warm and a fold of blanket had been
drawn over her head to shield it from the wind. By everyone's best estimates, she had been outside for approximately twenty minutes when the fire chief opened
the door, and in the snow for perhaps two. Only a little
of the snow had begun to stick to the blankets, making
her look as if she had been sugared, or dipped in dia-
monds.)

Bebe had been in the country only two years by the
time her baby was born, and in Cleveland for barely one.
She had held three apartments in the time she'd been in
Cleveland, had broken the lease on one and had been
chronically late and short on rent on another, and had
never held a job that paid more than minimum wage.

(She had been embarrassed, every month, about
being behind. One month she had paid in full and then
hadn't had enough money for groceries and electricity:
what a thing, to choose between hunger and darkness.
After that, she had decided to pay what she could, and
on days when she got good tips she would write her
name on a piece of paper, fold a twenty inside, and slide
it under her landlord's door. She kept track of the balance on an old envelope that was always out on the
kitchen counter. The balance ran like this:

Sept $100 short
  9/8 paid $20
  9/13 paid $20
  9/18 paid $20
Oct $80 short so now $120 short
  10/3 paid $20
  10/14 paid $20
  10/26 paid $20
Nov $70 short so now $130 short

Once she was behind, how could she catch up? And what other kind of job could she get, speaking little English, having not even the equivalent of a GED?)

During her pregnancy, and until shortly before she had left her baby, Bebe had worked at a restaurant where one of the cooks had been arrested for dealing heroin. Prior to that time, several of the other staff members had suspected something between the two of them. There had been flirting. On at least one occasion, the cook in question had given Bebe a ride home at the end of the night. Was it not probable that Bebe, with such dubious associates, had also been involved in something illicit?

(The cook, Vinny, had indeed been dealing heroin. This cannot be denied. But his interest in Bebe had been purely platonic. He had pitied her, watching her belly swell, knowing that her rat of a boyfriend had taken off and left her high and dry. Ten months earlier, his sister had been in the same boat and every night, when he came home to the apartment they shared with their mother, Teresa looked grayer, the baby squalling across her lap or slumped on her shoulder like a little old man, the two of them there on the couch looking elderly and exhausted. Is it any wonder that every morning, when he saw Bebe, his heart would feel bruised? Was it wrong for him to joke with her, trying to make her smile as he could no longer make his sister smile, to give her a ride home when he saw her feet swelling until the laces of her shoes nearly split?

As for Bebe: she had found Vinny attractive, it is true. But her attraction came largely from his kindness to her, and the thought of a man—any man—touching her as the baby drummed her heels within filled her with repulsion. When Vinny was picked up by the cops, Bebe had felt a deep sadness for him, as if he had been a brother she would never see again.)

Bebe's current job as a waitress paid her the state minimum for tipped employees: $2.35 per hour. At fifty hours per week plus tips, her average take-home pay each month was $317.50. Could she reasonably hope to support a child, and provide all its necessities, on that income? Would she not be forced to seek welfare, and food stamps, and school lunches, would she and her child not become a drain on the community's resources?

(But there would be love, too, so much love. With that, you could get by with so little. It was enough for the basics: rent, food, clothes. How did you weigh a mother's love against the cost of raising a child?)

Mark and Linda McCullough, it was quite clear, had all the necessary resources for raising a child. Mr. McCullough had a steady, well-paying job; Mrs. McCullough had, for the past fourteen months, been a full-time mother to the baby and planned to be so indefinitely. They owned their own home in a safe, affluent neighborhood. Overall they were in the ninety-sixth percentile financially. While in their care, the baby had been well clothed, well fed, and well cared for. She had had regular medical checkups, plenty of socialization, and plenty of enrichment: library storytime, infant swim, mommy-and-me music classes. The McCullough home had been rigorously checked and certified as lead free.

Furthermore, the McCulloughs had shown themselves to be exceptionally devoted to raising a child. Records showed that they had tried to conceive children of their own for ten years, and had been waiting to adopt for another four. They had sought the advice of every medical expert in the greater Cleveland area—including the best fertility doctors at the Cleveland Clinic—and then engaged the most reputable adoption agency in the state. Did this not suggest that they would give the baby the most loving possible care, along with every opportunity?

(But the baby already had a mother. Whose blood flowed in her veins. Who had carried her in her womb for months, who had felt her kicking and flipping within, who had labored for twenty-one hours as she made her way faceup and screaming into the bright light of the delivery room, who had burst into ecstatic tears at hearing her child's voice for the first time, who had—even before the nurses had wiped the baby clean, even before they had cut the cord—touched every part of her child, her tiny flaring nostrils and the faint shadows of her eyebrows and the womb-slicked soles of her feet, making certain she was wholly present, learning her by heart.)

Should custody be returned to Bebe, she would, of course, be raising her child as a single, working mother. Who would care for her child while she was at work? Would not the child be better off in a home with two parents—one of whom did not work and would be home raising her full time—rather than in a day care for the majority of the day? And would not the child be better off in a home with a mother *and* a father, studies showing the importance of a strong male figure in a child's life?

(It came, over and over, down to this: What made someone a *mother*? Was it biology alone, or was it love?)

><

Back in the courtroom, Mr. Richardson was grateful that no one heard the last day, when Mrs. McCullough had been called to speak. She had come to the front—in family court, there was no witness box, just a chair, set to the side of the judge—and sat down, and he could see how nervous she was by the way she crossed and un-crossed her ankles, by the way she could not decide where to place her hands, on the arms of the chair or in the soft hammock of her skirt. It had not struck him be-fore that the witness box in court, for all its formality and imposingness, hid you from the waist down: that at least the world would not see your feet fidgeting, that as much as you might be judged, at least your legs would not.

Ed Lim took his time in rising to question her. He was a tall man, especially for an Asian: six feet, lean and rangy, with the build of a basketball player—and indeed, he had played starting forward for Shaker's varsity team back in the sixties. He and Mrs. McCullough had been only three years apart at school, lifelong Shaker residents and graduates, and before this case he had remembered her only as a shy, slightly plump freshman with long golden-brown hair. He'd been one of just two Asians in his class—the other had been Susie Chang; kids had teased that they would grow up and marry each other. They hadn't, of course; Susie had gone off to Oregon right after graduation, but in the end Ed had indeed met and married a nice Chinese girl in college, a first-generation kid like him. Mrs. McCullough, however, remembered none of this, not even Susie Chang, who'd been a cheerleader for a year alongside her.

"Now, Mrs. McCullough," Ed Lim said, setting his pen down at his table. "You've spent all your life here in Shaker, is that right?"

Mrs. McCullough acknowledged that it was.

"Shaker Heights High School, class of 1971. Did you go to Shaker schools all the way up?"

"From kindergarten. At Boulevard, back when it was still K to eight. And then the high school, of course."

"And then you attended Ohio University?"

"Yes. Class of 1975."

"And after that you moved back to Shaker Heights. Directly?"

"Yes, I'd been offered a job here, and my husband—my fiancé at the time—and I knew we wanted to raise a family here." She shot Mr. Richardson a quick glance at his table, and he gave her the merest nod. They'd talked about this in prep: the focus was to remind the judge, whenever possible, of how much she and Mr. McCullough wanted this baby, how family focused they were, how devoted they were to little Mirabelle.

"So you've really lived in Ohio your entire life." Ed Lim seated himself on the arm of his chair. "May Ling's parents, as we all know by now, came from Guangdong. Or perhaps you know it as Canton? Have you ever been there?"

Mrs. McCullough shifted in her seat. "Of course we plan to take Mirabelle there on a heritage trip. When she's a bit older."

"Do you speak Cantonese?"

Mrs. McCullough shook her head.

"Mandarin? Shanghainese? Toisan? Any dialect of Chinese?"

Mr. Richardson clicked his pen irritably. Ed Lim was just showing off now, he thought.

"Have you studied Chinese culture at all?" Ed Lim asked. "Chinese history?"

"Of course we're going to learn all about that," Mrs. McCullough said. "It's very important to us that Mirabelle stay connected to her birth culture. But we think the most important thing is that she has a loving home, with two loving parents." She glanced at Mr. Richardson again, pleased that she had managed to work this in. There are two of you, he had said; that might be a big advantage over a single mother.

"You and Mr. McCullough are clearly very loving. I don't think anyone has any doubts about that." Ed Lim smiled at Mrs. McCullough, and Mr. Richardson stiffened in his seat. He knew enough about lawyers to know when they were about to snap the trap shut. "Now, what exactly will you do to keep May Ling 'connected to her birth culture,' as you put it?"

There was a long pause.

"Maybe that's too big of a question. Let's back up. May Ling has been with you for fourteen months now? What have you done, in the time she's been with you, to connect her to her Chinese culture?"

"Well." Another pause, a very long one this time. Mr. Richardson willed Mrs. McCullough to say something, anything. "Pearl of the Orient is one of our very favorite restaurants. We try to take her there once a month. I think it's good for her to hear some Chinese, to get it into her ears. To grow up feeling this is natural. And of course I'm sure she'll love the food once she's older." Yawning silence in the courtroom. Mrs. McCullough felt the need to fill it. "Perhaps we could take a Chinese cooking class at the rec center and learn together. When she's older."

Ed Lim said nothing, and Mrs. McCullough prattled nervously on. "We try to be very sensitive to these issues wherever we can." Inspiration arrived. "Like for her first birthday, we wanted to get her a teddy bear. One she could keep as an heirloom. There was a brown bear, a polar bear, and a panda, and we thought about it and decided on the panda. We thought perhaps she'd feel more of a connection to it."

"Does May Ling have any dolls?" Ed Lim asked.

"Of course. Too many." Mrs. McCullough giggled. "She loves them. Just like every little girl. We buy her dolls, and my sisters buy her dolls, and our friends buy her dolls—" She giggled again, and Mr. Richardson's jaw tensed. "She must have a dozen or more."

"And what do they look like, these dolls?" Ed Lim persisted.

"What do they look like?" Mrs. McCullough's brow crinkled. "They're—they're dolls. Some are babies, and some are little girls—" It was clear she didn't understand the question. "Some of them take bottles, and some of them, you can change their dresses, and one of them closes her eyes when you lay her down, and most of them, you can style their hair—"

"And what color hair do they have?"

Mrs. McCullough thought for a moment. "Well—blond, most of them. One has brown hair. Maybe two."

"How about the doll that closes her eyes? What color are her eyes?"

"Blue." Mrs. McCullough crossed her legs, then uncrossed them again. "But that doesn't mean anything. You look at the toy aisle—most dolls are blond with blue eyes. I mean, that's just the default."

"The default," Ed Lim repeated, and Mrs. McCullough had the feeling of being caught out, though she wasn't sure why.

"It's not anything racist," she insisted. "They just want to make a generic little girl. You know, one that will appeal to everyone."

"But it doesn't look like everyone, does it? It doesn't look like May Ling." Ed Lim stood up, suddenly towering over the courtroom. "Does May Ling have any Asian dolls—that is, any dolls that look like her?"

"No—but when she gets older, and she's ready, we can buy her a Chinese Barbie."

"Have you ever seen a Chinese Barbie?" Ed Lim asked.

Mrs. McCullough flushed. "Well—I've never gone looking for one. Yet. But there must be one."

"There isn't one. Mattel doesn't make one." Ed Lim's daughter, Monique, was a junior now, but as she'd grown up, he and his wife had noticed with dismay that there were no dolls that looked like her. At ten, Monique had begun poring over a mail-order doll catalog as if it were a book—expensive dolls, with names and stories and historical outfits, absurdly detailed and even more absurdly expensive. "Jenny Cohen has this one," she'd told them, her finger tracing the outline of a blond doll that did indeed resemble Jenny Cohen: sweet faced with heavy bangs, slightly stocky. "And they just made a new one with red hair. Her mom's getting it for her sister Sarah for Hanukkah." Sarah Cohen had flaming red hair, the color of a penny in the summer sun. But there was no doll with black hair, let alone a face that looked anything like Monique's. Ed Lim had gone to four different toy stores searching for a Chinese doll; he would have bought it for his daughter, whatever the price, but no such thing existed.

He'd gone so far as to write to Mattel, asking them if there was a Chinese Barbie doll, and they'd replied that yes, they offered "Oriental Barbie" and sent him a pamphlet. He had looked at that pamphlet for a long time, at the Barbie's strange mishmash of a costume, all red and gold satin and like nothing he'd ever seen on a Chinese or Japanese or Korean woman, at her waist-length black hair and slanted eyes. *I am from Hong Kong,* the pamphlet ran. *It is in the Orient, or Far East. Throughout the Orient, people shop at outdoor marketplaces where goods such as fish, vegetables, silk, and spices are openly displayed.* The year before, he and his wife and Monique had gone on a trip to Hong Kong, which struck him, mostly, as a pincushion of gleaming skyscrapers. In a giant, glassed-in shopping mall, he'd bought a dove-gray cashmere sweater that he wore under his suit jacket on chilly days. *Come visit the Orient. I know you will find it exotic and interesting.*

In the end, he'd thrown the pamphlet away. He'd heard, from friends with younger children, that the expensive doll line now had one Asian doll for sale—and a few black ones, too—but he'd never seen it. Monique was seventeen now, and had long outgrown dolls.

Now, back in the courtroom, Ed Lim paced a few steps. "How about books? What kind of books do you read with May Ling?"

"Well." Mrs. McCullough began to think. "We read her a lot of classics. *Goodnight Moon,* of course. And *Pat the Bunny*—she loves that. *Madeline. Eloise. Blueberries for Sal.* I've saved all my favorites from when I was a child, and it's very special to get to share them with Mirabelle."

"Do you have any books that feature Chinese characters?"

Mrs. McCullough was ready for this one. "Yes, in fact, we do. We have *The Five Chinese Brothers*—it's a beautiful retelling of a famous Chinese folktale."

"I know that book." Ed Lim smiled again, and Mr. Richardson's shoulders grew tight. Whenever Ed Lim smiled, he was learning, you had to watch out. *You just can't tell what he's really thinking*, Mr. Richardson thought, and then, instantly chagrined, *What a terrible thing to think*. He flushed. "What do those five Chinese brothers in the book look like?" Ed Lim was asking.

"They're—they're drawings. They all look alike— I mean, a lot like each other, they're brothers, that's part of the story, no one can tell them apart—" Mrs. Mc-Cullough fumbled.

"They have pigtails, don't they? And little coolie hats? Slanty eyes?" Ed Lim didn't wait for Mrs. Mc-Cullough to respond. His daughter had seen this book in the school library in second grade and returned home deeply troubled. *Daddy, do my eyes look like that?* "Not exactly the image of Chinese people I'd want May Ling to have in 1998. What about you?"

"It's a very old story," Mrs. McCullough insisted. "They're wearing traditional costume."

"How about other books, Mrs. McCullough? Any other books with Chinese characters?"

Mrs. McCullough bit her lip. "I haven't really looked for them," she admitted. "I hadn't thought about it."

"I can save you some time," said Ed Lim. "There really aren't very many. So May Ling has no dolls that look like her, and no books with pictures of people that look like her." Ed Lim paced a few more steps. Nearly two decades later, others would raise this question, would talk about books as *mirrors* and *windows*, and Ed

Lim, tired by then, would find himself as frustrated as he was grateful. *We've always known,* he would think; *what took you so long?*

Now, in the courtroom, Ed Lim stopped in front of Mrs. McCullough's chair. "You and your husband don't speak Chinese or know much about Chinese culture or history. You haven't, by your own testimony, even thought about that entire aspect of May Ling's identity. Isn't it fair to say that if May Ling stays with you and Mr. McCullough, she will effectively be divorced from her birth culture?"

At this point, Mrs. McCullough burst into tears. In those early weeks she had fed Mirabelle every four hours, held her every time she cried, and watched her grow until her heels stretched her newborn rompers almost to the breaking point. It was she who had checked Mirabelle's weight regularly, who steamed peas and sweet potatoes and fresh spinach and pureed them and fed them to Mirabelle in doll-sized spoonfuls. When Mirabelle spiked a fever, it was she who spread a cold washcloth on her forehead, who pressed her lips to that little brow to test the heat. And when an ear infection turned out to be the culprit, it was she who fed antibiotic syrup drop by drop into Mirabelle's small pink mouth and let her lap it up like a kitten. She could not, she had thought as she bent to kiss the baby's flushed cheek, have loved this child more if it had come from her own flesh. All night—because feverish Mirabelle would not sleep except in motion—she cradled Mirabelle in her arms and paced the length of the room. By morning she had walked nearly four miles. It was she who, after breakfast, before bath time, and at bed, nuzzled Mirabelle's soft belly until the baby gurgled with laughter. She was the one who had caught Mirabelle in her arms as she stumbled to stand upright; she was the one to whom Mirabelle stretched out her own arms when she was in pain, or afraid, or lonely. She would know Mirabelle in pitch dark by one cry of her voice—no, one touch of her hand. No, one breath of her smell.

"It's not a requirement," she insisted now. "It's not a requirement that we be experts in Chinese culture. The only requirement is that we love Mirabelle. And we do. We want to give her a better life." She continued to cry, and the judge dismissed her.

"It's all right," Mr. Richardson said as she took her place beside him. "You did just fine." Inside, however, even he was beginning to feel a faint tremor of doubt. Of course Mirabelle would have a good life with Mark and Linda. There was no question about that. But would there be something—*something*—missing from her life if she were to grow up with them? Mr. Richardson was suddenly keenly conscious of Mirabelle, of the immense weight of the complicated world on this one tiny, vulnerable person.

On the courthouse steps, when the reporters stopped them, he made a brief, anodyne statement about having faith in the process. "I have complete confidence in Judge Rheinbeck, that he'll weigh all the issues and make a fair decision," he said.

The McCulloughs did not appear to notice this subtle

shift in his tone—in earlier statements he'd spoken with some force about how clear it was that they should receive custody, how obvious it was they would raise her best, how completely evident it was that Mirabelle belonged with the McCulloughs (she *is* a McCullough, he'd insisted). Nor did the newspapers, which ran stories titled LAWYER FOR ADOPTIVE PARENTS CERTAIN OF WIN. Mr. Richardson, however, was far less certain than the news stories made it sound.

At dinner that evening, when Mrs. Richardson asked how the day's hearing had gone, he said little. "Linda testified today," he said. "Ed Lim was pretty hard on her. It didn't look good." He meant *for Mrs. McCullough,* but as the words left his mouth an idea occurred to him, a way to spin this, and later that evening he would call his contacts at the paper. The following morning, the *Plain Dealer* would publish a story mentioning Ed Lim's "aggressive" tactics, how he had badgered poor Mrs. McCullough to the point of tears. Men like him, the article would suggest, weren't supposed to lose their cool—though it was never specified whether "like him" meant lawyers or something else entirely. But the truth was—as Mr. Richardson recognized—that an angry Asian man didn't fit the public's expectations, and was therefore unnerving. Asian men could be socially inept and incompetent and ridiculous, like a Long Duk Dong, or at best unthreatening and slightly buffoonish, like a Jackie Chan. They were not allowed to be angry and articulate and powerful. And possibly right, Mr. Richardson thought uneasily. Once the article came out, a number of people who had been neutral threw their support behind the McCulloughs; some who had been on Bebe's side found their passions cooling.

For now, the idea still forming in his mind, he said only, "We'll see how things shake out."

"I feel bad for her," Lexie said suddenly from the far end of the table. "Bebe, I mean. She must feel so awful."

"I'm sorry," said Izzy, "is this the same Bebe that you referred to last month as a negligent mother?"

Lexie flushed. "She should've taken better care of the baby," she admitted. "But I dunno. I wonder if she just got in over her head. If she didn't know what she was getting into."

"And that's why pregnancy is not something to be taken lightly," Mrs. Richardson cut in. "You hear me, Alexandra Grace? Isabelle Marie?" She lifted the dish of green beans and helped herself to an almond-sprinkled spoonful. "Of course having a baby is difficult. It's life changing. Clearly Bebe wasn't ready for it, practically or emotionally. And that might be the best argument for giving the baby to Linda and Mark."

"So one mistake, and that's it?" Lexie said. "I'm not ready to have a baby. But if I—" She hesitated. "If I got pregnant, you'd make me give it up, too?"

"Lexie, that would never happen. We raised you to have more sense than that." Her mother set the dish back in the center of the table and speared a green bean with her fork.

"Well, somebody's heart grew three sizes today," Izzy said to Lexie. "What's with you?"

"Nothing," Lexie said. "I'm just saying. It's a complicated situation, that's all." She cleared her throat.

"Brian was saying that even his parents don't agree about it."

Moody rolled his eyes. "The case that tore families all over Cleveland apart."

"John and Deborah are entitled to their own opinions," Mr. Richardson said. "As is everyone at this table." His gaze swept around the room. "Trip, what's this I hear about a hat trick in yesterday's game?"

After dinner, however, Mr. Richardson's thoughts were still clouded. "Do you think," he asked Mrs. Richardson as they cleared the table, "that Mark and Linda really know how to raise a Chinese child?"

Mrs. Richardson stared at him. "It's just like raising any other child, I should think," she said stiffly, stacking the plates in the dishwasher. "Why on earth would it be any different?"

Mr. Richardson scraped the remnants of egg noodles from the next plate into the disposal and handed it over. "Of course everything important is the same," he conceded. "But I mean, when that little girl gets older, she's going to have a lot of questions. About who she is, where she came from. She's going to want to know about her heritage. Will they be able to teach her that?"

"There are resources out there." Mrs. Richardson waved a dismissive hand, inadvertently flicking a few drops of stroganoff onto the counter. "I don't see why they can't learn it alongside her. Wouldn't that bond them all closer, learning about Chinese culture together?" She had vivid childhood memories of Linda swaddling her Raggedy Ann in an old kerchief and gently putting it to bed. More than anyone, she knew how fiercely Linda Mc-Cullough had always wanted a baby, how deep that longing to be a mother—that magical, marvelous, terrifying role—ran in her friend. Mia, she thought, ought to understand that better than anyone: Hadn't she seen that in the Ryans? Hadn't she, maybe, even felt it herself, hadn't that been why she'd run away with Pearl? She swabbed at the counter with her thumb, smudging the granite. "Honestly, I think this is a tremendous thing for Mirabelle. She'll be raised in a home that truly doesn't see race. That doesn't care, not one infinitesimal bit, what she looks like. What could be better than that? Sometimes I think," she said fiercely, "that we'd all be better off that way. Maybe at birth everyone should be given to a family of another race to be raised. Maybe that would solve racism once and for all."

She shut the dishwasher with a clang and left the room, the dishes inside still rattling in her wake. Mr. Richardson took a sponge and wiped the sticky counter clean. He should have known better than to bring it up, he realized: it was too personal for her; she couldn't see clearly; she was so close that she didn't even realize how unclearly she was seeing. For her it was simple: Bebe Chow had been a poor mother; Linda McCullough had been a good one. One had followed the rules, and one had not. But the problem with rules, he reflected, was that they implied a right way and a wrong way to do things. When, in fact, most of the time there were simply *ways*, none of them quite wrong or quite right, and nothing to tell you for sure which side of the line you stood on. He had always admired his wife's idealism, her belief that the world could be made better, could be made orderly, could perhaps even be made perfect. For the first time, he wondered if the same held true for him.

17

I t soon became clear, however, that Mr. Richardson was not the only conflicted party. The judge seemed to be waffling as well. A week passed after the hearing, then two, with no decision made. In mid-April, Lexie was due for a follow-up appointment at the clinic, and to both Pearl's and Mia's surprise, she asked Mia to accompany her.

"You don't have to *do* anything," she promised Mia. "I'd just feel better if you were there." The earnestness in her voice was persuasive, and on the afternoon of the appointment, after tenth period, Lexie parked her Explorer outside the house on Winslow. Mia started up the Rabbit and Lexie climbed into the passenger seat and they drove away together, as if she really were Pearl, as if Mia really were her mother taking her on this most intimate errand.

In fact, since the visit to the clinic, Pearl had felt a strange sense of reversal: as if, while she and Lexie slept under the same roof, Lexie had somehow taken her place and she'd taken Lexie's and they had not quite disentangled. Lexie had gone home in a borrowed T-shirt, and Pearl, watching her walk out the door in her own clothing, had had the eerie feeling of watching herself walk away. The next morning, she'd found Lexie's own shirt on her bed: laundered and carefully folded by Mia, presumably left there to be returned at school. Instead of tucking it into her bag, Pearl had put it on, and in this borrowed skin she'd felt prettier, wittier, had even been a bit sassy in English class, to the amusement of her classmates and her teacher alike. When the bell rang, a few kids had glanced back at her, impressed, as if they were noticing her for the first time. So this is what it's like to be Lexie, she'd thought. Lexie herself was back at school, wan and somewhat subdued and with dark rings under her eyes, but upright. "You stole my shirt, bitch," she said to Pearl, but affectionately, and then, "Looks good on you."

Days later, shirt returned and her own retrieved, Pearl still felt Lexie's confidence fizzing in her veins. So now, when presented with a rare empty house, Pearl decided to take full advantage. She left a note in Trip's locker; she told Moody that she'd promised to help her mother at home all afternoon. Mia, meanwhile, had told Izzy she had a shift at the restaurant—"Go do something fun," she'd said, "I'll see you tomorrow, okay?"—so no one was home when Trip and Pearl arrived at the house on Winslow after school and went upstairs to Pearl's bedroom. It was the first time Trip had been to her house, and to her it seemed momentous to be able to lie down with him in a place of her own choosing, instead of on the old worn-out couch in Tim Michaels's basement, surrounded by the PlayStation and the air hockey table and Tim's old soccer trophies, all the paraphernalia of someone else's life. This would be in her own space, in her own bed, and that morning, as she'd made it carefully, she'd felt a warm glow at the base of her throat, thinking of Trip's head lying on her pillow.

Moody, left to his own devices, had just shut his locker and was headed home when he heard someone calling his name. It was Tim Michaels, gym bag slung over his shoulder. Tim was tall and tough and had never been very kind to Moody: years ago, when Tim and Trip had been closer and he'd come over to the Richardsons' now and then to play video games, he'd nicknamed Moody *Jake*—"Jake, get me another Coke," "Jake, move your big head, you're blocking my view." Moody had dared to think it was affectionate, but then he'd heard the word at school and understood what it meant in Shaker slang. Dave Matthews Band was dope; Bryan Adams was jake. Getting to third base was dope; being grounded was jake. After that, he'd stayed upstairs when Tim came over, and was meanly glad when he and Trip began to drift apart. Now here was Tim calling Moody's name—his real name—and jogging down the theatre wing toward him.

"Dude," Tim said when he'd caught up to Moody. "You know anything about this mystery girl of your brother's?"

It took Moody a moment to parse this question. "Mystery girl?"

"He's been bringing some girl over to my place in the afternoons while I'm at practice. Won't tell me who she is." Tim shifted his gym bag to the other shoulder.

"Trip's not really a man of mystery, you know what I mean? I figure either it's someone totally sketch or he's really into her."

Moody paused. Tim was an idiot, but he wasn't imaginative. He wasn't the kind to make things up. A suspicion was beginning to form in his mind.

"You don't know anything about her?" he said.

"Nothing. It's been, like, two months now. I'm almost tempted to go over there one afternoon and catch them in the act. He hasn't said anything to you?"

"He never tells me anything," Moody said, and pushed the door open and went out onto the front lawn.

He was still fretting when he got home and found Izzy reading on the couch.

"What are you doing home so early?" he said.

"Mia had her other job this afternoon," Izzy said. She turned a page. "Where is everyone? Is Pearl not with you?"

Moody didn't answer. The suspicion was taking on an uncomfortable solid shape. "Some new project my mom's working on," Pearl had told him. "She just needs an extra set of hands." Yet there was Izzy—a perfectly good set of extra hands—at home, telling him Mia was out. Without answering Izzy, he dropped his bookbag on the coffee table and headed to the garage for his bike.

All the way to the duplex on Winslow, he told himself he was imagining things. That there was nothing going on here, that this was all a coincidence. But there, just as he'd expected, was Trip's car, parked across the street from the house. He stayed there, staring at Pearl's window, for what felt like hours, trying not to think about what was happening inside, but unable to look away. It looked so innocent, that modest little brick house, with its clean white door, the peach tree in the front yard ruffled with soft pink blossoms.

When Trip and Pearl emerged, they were holding hands, but that wasn't what shook him. There was an ease between them that, Moody was sure, could only come from being intimately comfortable with another person's body. The way their shoulders jostled as they came down the walkway. The way Pearl leaned over to close the zip on Trip's backpack, the way he leaned down to smooth a stray curl out of her face. Then both of them looked up and saw Moody, astride his bicycle on the sidewalk, and froze. Before either of them could respond, he jammed his foot onto the pedal and sped away.

It never occurred to Moody to confront his brother; this was only what he expected from Trip. All of his fury was saved for Pearl, and later that afternoon, when she tiptoed upstairs and rapped on his door, he was not in the mood to listen to her excuses.

"It just happened," she said, once she'd shut the door. Moody knew from her voice that she was telling the truth, but it brought him little comfort. He rolled his eyes at how much she sounded like a character on a bad teen drama and went back to tuning his guitar.

"Whatever," he said. "I mean, if you want to screw my loser brother—" Pearl flinched, and in spite of himself, he stopped. "You know he's just using you, right?" he said after a moment. "That's what he does. He's never serious about anyone. He gets bored and he moves on."

Pearl maintained a defiant silence. This time, she was

sure, was different. They were both right: Trip got bored easily, and seldom thought about girls once they were out of his sight. But he had never encountered a girl like Pearl before, who wasn't embarrassed to be smart, who didn't quite fit into the orderly world of Shaker Heights, whether she knew it or not. Over the past two months she had wormed into his mind at all hours of the day: in chemistry lab, during practice, at night when he normally would have fallen asleep quickly and dreamed banal dreams. The girls he'd grown up with in Shaker—and the boys, too, for that matter—seemed so purposeful: they were so ambitious; they were so confident; they were so certain about everything. They were, he thought, a little like his sisters, and his mother: so convinced there was a right and a wrong to everything, so positive that they knew one from the other. Pearl was smarter than any of them and yet she seemed comfortable with everything she didn't know: she lingered comfortably in the gray spaces. She thought about big things, he discovered, and in those afternoons after they'd been together, big things were what they ended up talking about: How bad he felt that he and Moody didn't get along ("We're brothers," he said, "aren't we supposed to be friends?"). How he wasn't sure, at seventeen, what he wanted to do with his life: everyone was asking; he was supposed to be thinking about college, he was supposed to *know* by now, and he didn't, not at all. There's time, Pearl had reassured him, there's always more time. Being with Pearl made the world feel bigger, even as being with him made Pearl feel more grounded, less abstract, more real.

"You're wrong about him," she said at last.

"It's fine," Moody said. "I guess if you don't mind being the latest of his conquests. I just thought you had more respect for yourself than that." If he looked up, he knew, he would see the pain in Pearl's eyes, so he kept his eyes pointedly on the guitar in his lap. "I thought you were smarter than the sluts who usually agree to do it with him." He thumbed one of the strings, nudged the tuning peg a little higher. "But I guess not."

"At least there's someone who wants me. At least I'm not going to spend high school as a frustrated virgin." Pearl fought the urge to cross the room and yank the guitar from Moody's hands and smash it against the desk. "And for your information, I'm not a conquest. You know what? I was the one who started it with him."

Moody had never seen Pearl angry before, and to his embarrassment his first reaction was to burst into tears. He didn't know what exactly he wanted to say—*I'm sorry, I didn't mean it*—only the ever-deepening regret at how things were turning out between them, the desperate and impossible desire to go back to the way things had been. Instead he bit the inside of his cheek to keep from crying, until the sharp, salty taste of blood spread over his tongue.

"Whatever," he said at last. "Just—do me a favor and let's not talk about it. Okay?"

As it turned out, this meant they stopped talking at all. The following morning, they walked separately to school for the first time, took seats on the opposite sides of the classroom in first period and every period after that.

More than anything, Moody told himself, he was disappointed in Pearl. That after all, she'd been shallow enough to pick Trip, of all people. He hadn't expected her to choose *him*—of course not; he, Moody, was not the kind of guy girls had crushes on. But Trip—that was unforgivable. He felt as if he'd dived into a deep, clear lake and discovered it was a shallow, knee-deep pond. What did you do? Well, you stood up. You rinsed your mud-caked knees and pulled your feet out of the muck. And you were more cautious after that. You knew, from then on, that the world was a smaller place than you'd expected.

In the middle of algebra, when Pearl was in the bathroom and no one else was looking, he opened her bookbag and pulled out the little black Moleskine notebook he had given her all those months ago. As he'd suspected, the spine hadn't even been cracked. That evening, in the privacy of his room, he tore the pages out in handfuls, crushing them into wads and tossing them into the garbage can. When the can was heaped with crumpled paper, he dropped the leather cover—empty now, limp, like the husk stripped from an ear of corn—on top and kicked the can under his desk. She never even noticed that it was missing, and somehow this hurt him most of all.

><

Lexie, meanwhile, was having romantic troubles of her own. Since coming home from the clinic, she'd been understandably skittish about sleeping with Brian again, and the strain was starting to show. She'd said nothing to him about the abortion, and it sat between them like a scrim, blurring everything. Brian's patience was increasingly wearing thin.

"What's with you," he grumbled one afternoon, when he'd leaned over to kiss Lexie and she had, once again, turned her face to offer her cheek instead. "You PMS-ing again?"

Lexie flushed. "You guys. You think everything's about hormones. Hormones and periods. If men ever got periods, believe me, you'd all be in a ball on the ground from cramps."

"Look, if you're pissed at me, just tell me what it is you think I've done. I'm not a damn mind reader, Lex. I'm not going to apologize at random."

"Who says I wanted an apology?" Lexie looked down at her hands, as if she might find a note scribbled on her palms, like a cheat sheet to guide her through. "Who says I'm even pissed at you?"

"If you're not pissed, why are you acting like this?"

"I just want some space, that's all. You don't have to be pawing me all the time."

"Space." Brian slammed his hands against the steering wheel. "For the past month I've given you nothing but space. You haven't even kissed me in like a week. How much more space do you need?"

"Maybe all of it." The words fell out of Lexie's mouth like stones. "I'm going off to Yale and you're heading to Princeton—maybe it's better this way."

Stunned silence filled the car as Lexie and Brian both picked over what she'd said.

"That's what you want?" Brian said at last. "Okay.

We're done, then." He clicked the unlock button on the car door. "See you around."

Lexie slung her bookbag over her shoulder and stepped out of the car. They had been parked on a quiet side street, a spot they'd used often when they wanted time alone. *He wouldn't just drive off,* she thought to herself. *This can't really be how it ends.* But as soon as she slammed the door shut, Brian started the car with a growl and drove away. He didn't look back, though Lexie thought she saw his eyes flick to the rearview mirror, just once, before he turned the corner.

Without thinking where she was going, she began to walk: down the sidewalk and around the corner and out to the main road, paths she'd driven often but seldom walked before. She and Brian had been friends since the eighth grade, had been dating for almost two years. She thought of everything they'd done together— screaming from way up in the bleachers at Indians games, watching from the middle school parking lot on the Fourth of July as the city shot fireworks high into the night sky. Homecoming, Brian slipping a rose corsage onto her wrist, an Italian dinner at Giovanni's neither of them knew how to pronounce, dancing in the gym to the Fugees until they were both beaded with sweat, then pressed in his arms during "I Don't Want to Miss a Thing," so close that their sweat mingled. Now all that was gone. She walked and walked, following the curve of the road, stopping now and then only to let cars pass by, and then she found her feet had taken her somewhere she hadn't expected, but that felt like the only place in the world she wanted to be: not home, but the duplex on Winslow. Through the upstairs windows she could see Mia hard at work on something, and Lexie knew that Mia would know just the right thing to say, would give her the space to think this through, to process what had just happened, what would happen next, why she'd just left what she'd thought was a perfect boyfriend, a perfect relationship, how it had all suddenly fallen apart.

When Lexie climbed the stairs and opened the door into the kitchen, Izzy was there, too, sitting at the table beside Mia, folding scraps of paper into cranes. Handfuls of them in all sizes lay on the table already, scattered across it like confetti. She shot Lexie a hostile look, but before she could open her mouth, Mia cut her off.

"Lexie. I'm glad you came."

She pulled out a chair and Lexie settled into it, her face so still that even Izzy could tell something was wrong. Lexie looked almost as if she were going to be physically ill. She had never seen her sister like this before.

"Are you okay?" she asked.

"Fine," Lexie said through dry lips. "I'm fine."

"You're fine," Mia said, squeezing Lexie's shoulder. "You're going to be fine." She pulled an extra mug from the cupboard and put the kettle on.

Without meeting Izzy's eyes, Lexie said, "Before you ask, Brian and I broke up."

"I'm sorry," Izzy said, and found that she really meant it. Brian had always been nice to her, letting her tag along for milkshakes once or twice at Yours Truly when he and Lexie had first started dating and she'd still been in middle school; giving her a ride home now and then when he'd passed her walking. She glanced at Lexie, then at Mia. "Do you—want me to leave?"

At the stove, Mia pretended to busy herself with opening a tea bag. Lexie shook her head. "Stay," she said. "It's fine. I'm fine. Just—stay."

After a moment, Izzy slid a square of paper across the table, and Lexie took it and began to follow her sister's lead: folding over, back, to the center, out, until at last she took hold of the corners and pulled and a crane bloomed like a pale flower in her hands.

><

"Judge Rheinbeck says he's not yet ready to make a decision," Mr. Richardson told Mrs. Richardson the last week of April. Harold Rheinbeck was sixty-nine, gray haired, a longtime boxing fan, and an enthusiastic recreational hunter, but he was a sensitive man, too, and well aware of the intricate emotional complexities of the case. Over the past month, since the hearing had ended, he had in fact spent nights lying awake for hours thinking about little May Ling–Mirabelle, as he thought of her—trying to be scrupulously fair, every time he heard one name he appended the other in his mind, and for him the two names had firmly blended into one. Because the baby herself was in the care of a sitter and not present—infants being notoriously indisposed to long hearings—Ed Lim had wisely blown up a photograph and placed it on his prep table, and everyone in the court had been staring at it every day. As a result, the judge pictured her small face as he mulled over each day's testimony, and the more he thought about it, the more undecidable the case became. He felt a sudden, intense sympathy for King Solomon, and each morning, short on sleep and uncomfortable in mind, he barked unfairly at his clerks and his secretary without even realizing why.

"It's agony," Mrs. McCullough said to Mrs. Richardson over a commiserating cup of coffee. They were, as usual, in Mrs. McCullough's home, to avoid scrutiny. "What else does he want? How can this be a hard decision?" The baby monitor on the table beside them crackled, and she adjusted the volume slightly higher. Both women fell silent, and the quiet sound of Mirabelle's sleeping breathing filled the kitchen.

"Can you think of anything else you could tell the judge?" Mrs. Richardson asked. "Things that give more context. Other factors for him to weigh." She leaned forward. "Can you think of anything else you and Bill haven't brought up? Reasons you'd be the better choice for custody? Or—" She hesitated, then plunged in anyway. "Or other reasons Bebe might be unfit? Anything at all."

Mrs. McCullough nibbled one fingernail. It had been her nervous habit as a child, and Mrs. Richardson noticed she'd been doing it again of late. "Well," she began, then stopped. "It's probably not true."

"This might be your last chance, Linda," Mrs. Richardson said gently. "Anything you've got, we'd better throw at them."

"It's only a suspicion. I don't have any proof." Mrs. McCullough sighed. "About three months ago, I noticed that Bebe seemed—plumper. Her face got rounder and rounder, I noticed that particularly, when she came with the social worker to pick up Mirabelle. And her—her chest. And the social worker told me something strange. She said that on one of their visits around then, Bebe had to run off to the bathroom suddenly. They were at the library and she suddenly handed Adrienne the baby and dashed off. Adrienne said she heard Bebe throwing up." Mrs. McCullough looked up at Mrs. Richardson. "It just made me wonder if she might have been pregnant. She seemed so incredibly exhausted then, too. I just had this hunch. There's a look women get—you can see it, if you look. All these years, all this time we were trying, and one after another of my friends got pregnant—every time, I knew before they told me. I knew every time you were pregnant. Didn't I, Elena?"

"You did," said Mrs. Richardson. "Every time, you knew. Before I'd said a word."

"And then, about a month ago, she suddenly went back to normal. Her face flattened out again. Back to being skinny and straight as a rail. I wondered." Mrs. McCullough took a deep breath. "I wondered if she might have been pregnant, and then ended it."

"An abortion." Mrs. Richardson settled back in her chair. "That's a big accusation."

"I'm not accusing," Mrs. McCullough insisted. "I told you, I don't have proof. Only a suspicion. And you said *anything*." She sipped her coffee, which had gone cold. "If she *had* had an abortion, would that change anything?"

"Maybe." Mrs. Richardson considered. "Having an abortion doesn't make her a bad mother, of course.

Though it would likely turn public opinion against her, if the news got out. People don't like to hear about abortions. And an abortion while trying to get back a baby you abandoned?" She drummed her fingers on the table. "At the very least, it would suggest that she was careless enough to get pregnant again." She took Mrs. McCullough's hand and squeezed it. "I'll look into it. See if there's anything that might help. If there is, we can bring it up with the judge."

"Elena," Mrs. McCullough sighed. "You always know what to do. What on earth would I do without you?"

"Don't say anything to Bill or Mark," Mrs. Richardson said, gathering her purse. "Let's not get their hopes up yet. Trust me. I'll take care of everything."

Bebe had not, in fact, been pregnant. Under the stress of the impending hearing, with news crews filming outside the restaurant one day and a journalist stopping her on the street to shove a microphone into her face the next, with a story about the case out every other day, it felt like, and her boss grumbling about the time she'd have to take off for the hearing—she had given in to junk food cravings: Oreos, French fries, once an entire bag of pork rinds, ballooning up fifteen pounds in a month. She'd put in extra hours to make up for the time she'd be taking off, working until two or three on the nights she closed and arriving at nine to open the next morning. That time, in her memory, existed only as a blur. And then she'd gotten food poisoning—a box of leftovers that had sat too long in the fridge—and thrown up right in the library, in front of the social worker. She hadn't been able to eat for days afterward, and when she recovered, she found that, with the hearing mere weeks away, she was too nervous to eat. By the time the hearing began she had lost the extra fifteen pounds plus ten more.

Mrs. Richardson, however, knew none of this. With no way to prove a negative, she began, logically enough, by searching for evidence of the positive. She could find anything out, she reminded herself. Even if she didn't know it herself, she had connections. The next morning, she pulled out her Rolodex and flipped to the M's: *Manwill, Elizabeth.*

She and Elizabeth Manwill had been roommates freshman year in college, and though they'd found other roommates in later years, they'd stayed in touch, through graduation and afterward. They had reconnected when Elizabeth moved to Cleveland and became the head of a medical clinic just east of Shaker Heights—the only clinic on the East Side, it happened, that provided abortions.

It was a small thing Mrs. Richardson wanted to ask: a small, illicit, slightly illegal thing. Could she check the clinic's records and see if Bebe Chow's name appeared in the list of recent abortions? "Unofficially. Off the record," Mrs. Richardson assured her friend, tucking the phone receiver against her shoulder and double-checking that her office door was shut.

"Elena," Elizabeth Manwill said, shutting her own office door. "You know I can't do that."

"It doesn't have to be a big thing. No one needs to know."

"It's confidential. Do you know how much the fines are for that? Not to mention the ethics of it."

Elizabeth Manwill had been friends with Mrs. Richardson for many years, and she owed Mrs. Richardson a great deal, though she herself hated to put it that way. She had shown up at Denison as Betsy, a painfully shy girl from Dayton, relieved to escape the constant teasing that had been her high school years, terrified that college might turn out to be the same. At eighteen, Elizabeth Manwill was an easy target for mockery: glasses perpetually sliding down her nose, forehead knobby with acne, clothes frumpy and ill fitting. Her new roommate looked just like the snotty girls who had made high school miserable: pretty, beautifully dressed, somehow at ease with the world, and that first night she had cried herself to sleep.

But Elena had taken her under her wing and transformed her. She'd lent her lipstick and Noxzema, taken her shopping, taught her new ways to style her hair. Walking to class with Elena, sitting beside her in the dining hall, Elizabeth had learned a new confidence as well. She began to speak as Elena did—as if she knew people wanted to hear her thoughts—and to hold herself taller, like a dancer. By the time they graduated, Elizabeth was a different person, Liz Manwill, who wore pantsuits and heels and architect's glasses that made her look almost as smart as she was, a person who would go on to run a clinic with ease. In the years that followed, Elena—now Mrs. Richardson—had continued to offer her assistance. With her many local connections, she had put in a good word when Elizabeth had applied to the clinic, and after Elizabeth had gotten the job and moved to town, had introduced her to all sorts of people, both professionally and personally. In fact, Elizabeth had met her husband at a cocktail party the Richardsons had thrown some years before; he had been a colleague of Mr. Richardson's. Mrs. Richardson had never asked, or even hinted, at repayment, and both of them were keenly aware of this.

"How is Derrick, by the way?" Mrs. Richardson asked suddenly. "And Mackenzie?"

"They're fine. Both of them. Derrick's been working too hard, of course."

"I can't believe Mackenzie is ten already," Mrs. Richardson mused. "How is she fitting in at Laurel?"

"She loves it. She seems so much more confident now. I think it makes a real difference, being at a girls' school, you know?" Elizabeth Manwill paused. "Thanks again for putting a word in."

"Betsy! Don't be ridiculous. It was my pleasure." Mrs. Richardson tapped her pen against her desktop. "What are friends for?"

"You understand, Elena, I'd love to help you. It's just if anyone found out—"

"Of course you can't *show* me anything. Of course not. But I mean, if I were to come and take you for lunch, and I just happened to glance over your shoulder at the list for the past few months, no one could possibly say you had shown me on purpose, could they?"

"And what if this woman's name is on there?" Elizabeth asked. "What good does it do? Bill can't use it in court."

"If it does, he'll look for other evidence. I know it's a huge favor, Betsy. He just needs to know if it's even worth digging. And if it's not? This goes no further."

Elizabeth Manwill sighed. "All right," she said at last. "I'm tied up the next few days, but how about Thursday?"

The two women scheduled a lunch date, and Mrs. Richardson hung up the phone. She would soon have this cleared up. Poor woman, she thought, thinking of Bebe with new generosity. If she had had an abortion, who could blame her? In the middle of this custody case, with only a dead-end job, and after what she'd been through with the first. No one had an abortion without regret, she thought; abortions were an action of last resort, when there was no better option. No, Mrs. Richardson could not blame Bebe, even as she still hoped the McCulloughs kept the baby. *But she can always have another*, Mrs. Richardson thought, *once she gets her life together*, and she propped her office door open again.

18

Mrs. Richardson's benevolent mood toward Bebe lasted until her lunch date with Elizabeth Manwill.

"Betsy," she said as she was buzzed into the office on Thursday. "It's been way too long. When did we last get together?"

"I can't remember. Holiday party last year, maybe. How are the kids?"

Mrs. Richardson took a moment to brag: Lexie's plans for Yale, Trip's latest lacrosse game, Moody's good grades. As usual, she glossed over the topic of Izzy, but Elizabeth didn't notice. Until that very moment she had planned to help Elena; Elena had done so much for her, after all, and anyway, Elena Richardson never stopped until she got what she wanted. She had even gone so far as to pull up the records Elena had asked for, a list of all the patients in the past few months who'd had a procedure at the clinic; they were in a separate window on her screen, behind a budgeting spreadsheet. But now, as Elena prattled on about her marvelous children, her husband's high-profile case, the new landscaping they planned to do in the backyard once the summer came, Elizabeth changed her mind. She had forgotten, until they were face-to-face, how Elena so often talked to her as if she were a child, as if she, Elena, were the expert in everything and Elizabeth should be taking notes. Well, she wasn't a child. This was her office, her clinic. Out of habit she'd picked up a pen at the sight of Elena, and now she set it down.

"It'll be strange having just three of them in the house next year," Mrs. Richardson was saying. "And of course Bill is so frazzled about this case. You remember Linda and Mark from some of our parties, no? Linda recommended that dog sitter for you a couple of years back. We're all hoping it's over soon, and that they get to keep their baby for good."

Elizabeth stood up. "Ready for lunch?" she said, reaching for her handbag, but Mrs. Richardson did not move from her seat.

"There was that one thing I wanted your advice on, Betsy," she said. "Remember?" With one hand she pushed the door shut.

Elizabeth sat down again and sighed. As if Elena could have forgotten what she wanted. "Elena," she said. "I'm sorry. I can't."

"Betsy," Mrs. Richardson said quietly, "one quick glance. That's all. Just to know if there's even anything to find out."

"It's not that I don't want to help you—"

"I would never put you at any risk. I'd never *use* this information. This is just to see if we need to keep digging."

"I would love to help you, Elena. But I've been thinking it over, and—"

"Betsy, how many times have we stuck our necks out for each other? How much have we done for one another?" Betsy Manwill, Mrs. Richardson thought, had always been timid. She'd always needed a good push to do anything, even things she wanted to do. You had to give her permission for every little thing: to wear lipstick, to buy a pretty dress, to put her hand up in class. Wishy-washy. She needed a firm hand.

"This is confidential information." Elizabeth sat up a bit straighter. "I'm sorry."

"Betsy. I have to admit I'm hurt. That after all these years of friendship, you don't trust me."

"It's not about trust," Elizabeth began, but Mrs. Richardson went on as if she hadn't been interrupted. After all she'd done for Betsy, she thought. She'd nurtured her like a mother and coaxed her out of her shell and here was Betsy now, at her big desk in her posh office at the job Elena had helped her get, not even willing to grant her a little favor.

She opened her purse and drew out a gold tube of lipstick and a palm-sized mirror. "Well, you trusted my advice all through college, didn't you? And when I told you you should come to our Christmas party all those years ago? You trusted me when I told you that you should call Derrick instead of waiting for him to call you. And you were engaged—what?—by Valentine's Day." With small precise strokes she traced the contours of her mouth and clicked the tube shut. "You got a husband and a child by trusting me, so I'd say trusting my judgment has worked out well for you every time before."

It confirmed something Elizabeth had long suspected: all these years, Elena had been building up credit. Perhaps she'd honestly wanted to help, perhaps she'd been motivated by kindness. But even so, she'd been keeping a running tally of everything she'd ever done for Elizabeth, too, every bit of support she'd given, and now she expected to be repaid. Elena thought she was owed this, Elizabeth realized suddenly; she thought it was a question of fairness, about getting what she deserved under the rules.

"I hope you aren't planning to take credit for my entire marriage," she said, and Mrs. Richardson was taken aback at the sharpness in her voice.

"Of course I didn't mean that—" she began.

"You know that I'll always help you any way I can. But there are laws. And ethics, Elena. I'm disappointed that you would even ask for such a thing. You've always been so concerned with what's right and wrong." Their eyes met across the desk, and Mrs. Richardson had never seen Betsy's gaze so clear and steady and fierce. Neither of them spoke, and in that pocket of silence, the phone on the desk rang. Elizabeth held the stare for a moment more and then lifted the receiver.

"Elizabeth Manwill." A faint murmur from the other end of the line. "You just caught me. I was about to step out for lunch." More murmuring. To Mrs. Richardson's ears, it sounded vaguely apologetic. "Eric, I don't need excuses—I just need this done. No, I've been waiting for this over a week; I don't want it to wait another minute. Look, I'll be right down." Elizabeth hung up and turned to Mrs. Richardson. "I have to run downstairs—there's a report I've been expecting and I've had to nudge it along every step of the way. One of the delightful parts of being the director." She stood up. "I'll just be a few minutes. And when I get back, we'll go for lunch. I'm starving—and I've got a meeting at one thirty."

When she had gone, Mrs. Richardson sat stunned. Had that really been Betsy Manwill talking to her like that? Implying that she was unethical! And that last little dig about *being the director*—as if Betsy were reminding her how important she was, as if to say *I'm more important than you now*. When she'd helped Betsy get this very job. Mrs. Richardson pressed her lips together. The door to the office had been pushed to; no one outside could see in. Quickly she came around the desk to Elizabeth's chair and nudged the mouse across its pad, and the black screen of Elizabeth's monitor flickered to life: a spreadsheet showing the year-to-date expenses. Mrs. Richardson paused. Surely the clinic had some kind of database of patient records. With a click she shrank the spreadsheet and like magic there it was: a window listing the patients in just the period she'd wanted. So Betsy had changed her mind at the last minute, she thought with a flash of smugness. What had she always said? Wishy-washy.

Mrs. Richardson leaned over the desktop and scrolled quickly through the list. There was no Bebe Chow. But a name at the bottom of the list, in early March, caught Mrs. Richardson's attention. *Pearl Warren.*

Six minutes later, Elizabeth Manwill returned to find Mrs. Richardson back in her own seat, composed and unruffled except for one hand clenched on the arm of the chair. She had reopened the budget spreadsheet and put the monitor back to sleep, and when Elizabeth sat down again at her desk that afternoon, she would notice nothing amiss. She would close the list with relief, proud of herself for standing up to Elena Richardson at last.

"Ready for lunch, Elena?"

Over saag paneer and chicken tikka masala, Mrs. Richardson put her hand on Elizabeth's arm. "We've been friends a long time, Betsy. I'd hate to think something like this would come between us. I hope it goes without saying that I understand completely, and I'd never hold this against you."

"Of course not," Elizabeth said, stabbing a piece of chicken with her fork. Since they'd left her office, Elena had been stiff and a bit cool. Elena Richardson had always been like this, she thought, charming and generous and always saying kind things, and then when she wanted something she was sure you couldn't say no. Well, she had done the impossible: she had said no. "Is Lexie still doing theatre?" she asked, and for the rest of the meal they made superficial chitchat about the common denominators of their life: children, traffic, the weather. This would, in fact, be the last lunch the two women ever had together, though they would remain cordial to each other for the rest of their lives.

So innocent little Pearl was not so innocent after all, Mrs. Richardson thought on her way back to the office. There was no doubt in her mind who the father was, of course. She had long suspected Pearl and Moody's relationship was more than friendly—a boy and a girl didn't spend so much time together at their age without *some-thing* happening—and she was appalled. How could they have been so careless? She knew how much emphasis Shaker placed on sex ed; she had sat on the school board committee two years before, when a parent complained that her daughter had been asked to put a condom on a banana during health class, for practice. Teens are going to have sex, Mrs. Richardson had said then; it's the age, it's the hormones, we can't prevent it; the best thing we can do is teach them to be safe about it. Now, however, that view seemed wildly naive. How could they have been so irresponsible? she wondered. More pressing: How had they managed to keep this from her? How could it have happened right under her very nose?

For a moment she considered going to the school, pulling the two of them out of class, demanding how they could have been so stupid. Better not to make a scene, she decided. Everyone would know. Girls in Shaker, she was sure, had abortions now and then—they were teenagers after all—but of course it was all kept very quiet. No one wanted to broadcast their failures in responsibility. Everyone would talk, and she knew how rumors would fly. That was the kind of thing, she knew, that stuck to a girl. It would tar you for life. She would speak to Moody that evening, as soon as she got home.

Back at her office, she had just taken off her coat when the phone rang.

"Bill," she said. "What's going on?"

Mr. Richardson's voice was muffled, and there was a lot of commotion in the background. "Judge Rheinbeck just delivered his decision. He called us in an hour ago. We didn't expect it at all." He cleared his throat. "She's staying with Mark and Linda. We won."

Mrs. Richardson sank into her chair. Linda must be so happy, she thought. At the same time, a thin snake of disappointment wriggled its way through her chest. She had been looking forward to ferreting out Bebe's past, to delivering the secret weapon that would end things for good. But she hadn't been needed after all. "That's wonderful."

"They're beside themselves with joy. Bebe Chow took it hard, though. Burst out screaming. The bailiff had to escort her outside." He paused. "Poor woman. I can't help but feel bad for her."

"She gave up the baby in the first place," Mrs. Richardson said. It was exactly what she'd been saying for the past six months, but this time it sounded less convincing. She cleared her throat. "Where are Mark and Linda?"

"They're getting ready for a press conference. The news teams got wind of it and have been showing up left and right, so we said they'd make a statement at three. So I'd better go." Mr. Richardson let out a deep sigh. "But it's done. She's theirs now. They just have to hold out until the story dies down and they can all go back to living their lives."

"That's wonderful," Mrs. Richardson said again. The news about Pearl and Moody settled on her shoulders like a heavy bag, and she wanted badly to blurt it out to her husband, to share some of its weight, but she pushed it away. This was not the moment, she told herself. Firmly she put Moody out of her mind. This was a moment to celebrate with Linda.

"I'll come down to the courthouse," she said. "Three o'clock, you said?"

Across town, in the little house on Winslow, Bebe was crying at Mia's kitchen table. As soon as the verdict had been announced, she'd heard a terrible keening, so sharp she'd clamped her hands over her ears and collapsed into a ball. Only when the bailiff took her arm to escort her out of the room did she realize that the wail was coming from her own mouth. The bailiff, who had a daughter about Bebe's age, took her to an anteroom and pressed a cup of lukewarm coffee into her hands. Bebe had swallowed it, mouthful by watery mouthful, digging her teeth into the Styrofoam rim every time she felt a scream rising in her throat again, and by the time the coffee was gone, the cup had been shredded almost to pieces. She did not even have words, only a feeling, a terrible hollow feeling, as if everything inside her had been scooped out raw.

When she had finished the coffee and calmed down, the bailiff gently pried the shards of foam from her hands and threw them away. Then he led her out a back entrance, where a cab was waiting. "Take her wherever she wants," he told the driver, passing him two twenties from his own wallet. To Bebe he said, "You gonna be okay, honey. You gonna be fine. God works in mysterious ways. You keep your chin up." He shut the cab door and headed back inside, shaking his head. In this way Bebe was able to avoid all the news cameras and crews that had lined up at the front entrance, the news conference that the McCulloughs were preparing for that afternoon, the reporters who had hoped to ask her whether, in the light of this decision, she would try to have another child. Instead, Ed Lim deflected their questions, and the cab sped away up Stokes Boulevard toward Shaker Heights, and Bebe, slumped against the window with her head in her hands, also missed a last glimpse of her daughter, carried down the hallway from the waiting room by a DCF social worker and placed into Mrs. McCullough's waiting arms.

Forty-five minutes later—there had been traffic—the cab pulled up in front of the little house on Winslow. Mia was still home, trying to finish a piece she'd been working on, and she took one look at Bebe and understood what had happened. She would get the details later—some from Bebe herself, when she'd calmed down; others from the news stories that would air that night and the newspaper articles that would print the next morning. Full custody to the state, with a recommendation that the adoption by the McCulloughs be expedited. Termination of visitation rights. A court order prohibiting further contact between Bebe and her daughter without the McCulloughs' unlikely consent. For now, she simply folded Bebe in her arms and took her into the kitchen, set a cup of hot tea before her, and let her cry.

The news was just beginning to spread at the high school as the last bell rang. Monique Lim got a page from her father, Sara Hendricks—whose father worked at Channel 5—got another from hers, and word traveled from there. Izzy, however, knew nothing of this until she arrived at Mia's after school, let herself in through the unlocked side door as usual, and came upstairs to see Bebe crumpled at the kitchen table.

"What happened?" she whispered, though she already knew. She had never seen an adult cry like that, with such an animal sound. Recklessly. As if there were nothing more to be lost. For years afterward, she would sometimes wake in the night, heart thumping, thinking she'd heard that agonized cry again.

Mia jumped up and shepherded Izzy back out onto the stairs, shutting the kitchen door behind her. "Is she—dying?" Izzy whispered. It was a ridiculous question, but in that moment she was honestly terrified this might be true. If a soul could leave a body, she thought, this is the sound it would make: like the screech of a nail being pulled from old wood. Instinctively, she huddled against Mia and buried her face against her.

"She's not dying," Mia said. She put her arms around Izzy and held her close.

"But is she going to be okay?"

"She's going to survive, if that's what you mean." Mia stroked Izzy's hair, which billowed out from beneath her fingers like plumes of smoke. It was like Pearl's, like her own had been as a little girl: the more you tried to smooth it, the more it insisted on springing free. "She's going to get through this. Because she has to."

"But how?" Izzy could not believe that someone could endure this kind of pain and survive.

"I don't know, honestly. But she will. Sometimes, just when you think everything's gone, you find a way."

Mia racked her mind for an explanation. "Like after a prairie fire. I saw one, years ago, when we were in Nebraska. It seems like the end of the world. The earth is all scorched and black and everything green is gone. But after the burning the soil is richer, and new things can grow." She held Izzy at arm's length, wiped her cheek with a fingertip, smoothed her hair one last time. "People are like that, too, you know. They start over. They find a way."

Izzy nodded and turned to go, then turned back. "Tell her I'm so sorry," she said.

Mia nodded. "See you tomorrow, okay?"

><

Lexie and Moody, meanwhile, came home to a message on the answering machine telling them the case was over. *Order some pizza,* their mother's staticky voice said. *There's cash in the drawer under the phone book. I'll be home after I file my piece. Dad won't be home until late—he's tying up paperwork after the hearing.* Did Pearl know yet, Moody wondered, but they'd barely spoken since their falling out, and he retreated to his room and did his best not to wonder what Pearl was doing. As he'd guessed, Pearl was out with Trip that afternoon, and learned the news only when she came home some hours later to find Bebe—quiet now—still at the kitchen table.

"It's over," Mia told her quietly, and that was all that needed to be said.

"I'm really sorry, Bebe," Pearl said. "I'm—I'm so sorry." Bebe didn't even look up, and Pearl disappeared into her bedroom and shut the door behind her.

Mia and Bebe sat in silence for some time, until it had grown quite dark and Bebe finally rose to go.

"She will always be your child," Mia said to Bebe, taking her hand. "You will always be her mother. Nothing will ever change that." She kissed Bebe on the cheek and let her go. Bebe said nothing, just as she had said nothing all this time, and Mia wondered if she should ask what she was thinking, if she should push her to stay, if Bebe would be all right. In her place, she thought, she'd rather not be forced to talk, and tact won out. Later she would realize that Bebe must have heard this differently. That she must have heard, in these words, a permission granted. She would wonder if Bebe might have told her what she was planning if she'd pushed harder, and whether she would have tried to stop Bebe, or if she'd have helped, if she'd known. Even years later, she would never be able to answer this question to her own satisfaction.

><

The press conference ran longer than expected—nearly every news outfit had questions for the McCulloughs, and the McCulloughs, dazzled by their good fortune, stayed to answer them all. Were they relieved to have the ordeal over? Yes, of course they were. What were their plans for the next few days? They would take some time to themselves, now that Mirabelle was home to stay. They were looking forward to their life together as a family. What were they going to make for Mirabelle's first meal back home? Mrs. McCullough answered: macaroni and cheese, her favorite. When would the adoption process be finalized? Very soon, they hoped.

A reporter from Channel 19, at the back of the crowd, raised her hand. Did they feel any sympathy for Bebe Chow, who would never get to see her daughter again?

Mrs. McCullough stiffened. "Let's remember," she said sharply, "that Bebe Chow wasn't able to care for Mirabelle, that she abandoned her, that she walked away from her responsibilities as a mother. Of course it saddens me that anyone would have to go through such a thing. But the important thing to remember is that the court decided Mark and I are the most appropriate parents for Mirabelle, and that now Mirabelle will have a stable, permanent home. I think that speaks volumes, don't you?"

By the time the conference had wound down, and the McCulloughs had taken Mirabelle home for good, it was almost five thirty. Mrs. Richardson, due to her husband's involvement in the case, could not write the *Sun Press*'s story on the decision, so Sam Levi had been assigned the story instead. In his place, Mrs. Richardson was to cover Sam's usual beat—city politics. It was nearly nine o'clock when Mrs. Richardson finally filed her stories and arrived home. Her children had scattered to their own devices. Lexie's and Trip's cars were gone, and on the counter Mrs. Richardson found a note: *Mom, went to Serena's, back ~11 L.* No note from Trip, but that was typical: Trip never remembered to leave notes. Ordinarily this was a source of annoyance, but this time Mrs. Richardson found herself relieved: with so many people in the Richardson house, there was usually an audience, and tonight she did not want an audience.

Upstairs, she found Izzy's door shut, music wailing from inside. She had gone upstairs even before the pizza had arrived and had been in her room since, thinking about Bebe, how utterly shattered she had seemed. Part of her wanted to scream, so she slid a Tori Amos CD into the player, turned up the volume, and let it do the screaming for her. And part of her had wanted to cry— though she never cried, hadn't cried in years. She lay in the center of her bed and dug her fingernails into her palms so hard they left a row of half-moons, to keep tears from falling. By the time her mother came past her doorway and down the hall, toward Moody's room, she had listened to the album four times and was just beginning on the fifth.

On an ordinary day, Mrs. Richardson would have opened the door, told Izzy to turn the volume down, made some disparaging comments about how depressing and angry Izzy's music always seemed to be. Today, however, she had more important things on her mind. Instead, she went down the hallway to Moody's room and rapped on the door.

"I need to talk to you," she said.

Moody was sprawled on his bed, guitar beside him, scribbling in a notebook. "What," he said without looking up. He didn't bother to sit up as his mother entered, which irritated her further. She shut the door and marched to the bed and yanked the notebook out of his hands.

"You look at me when I'm talking to you," she said. "I found out, you know. Did you think I wouldn't?"

Moody stared. "Found out what?"

"Did you think I was blind? Did you think I wouldn't even notice?" Mrs. Richardson slammed the notebook shut. "The two of you sneaking around all the time. I'm not stupid, Moody. Of course I knew what you were up to. I just thought you'd be a little more responsible."

In Izzy's room, the music clicked off, but neither Moody nor his mother noticed.

Moody slowly pushed himself up to a sitting position. "*What* are you talking about?"

"I know," Mrs. Richardson said. "About Pearl. About the baby." The shock on Moody's face, his stunned silence, told her everything. He hadn't known, she realized. "She didn't tell you?" Moody's gaze had unfocused slowly from her face, like a boat adrift. "She didn't tell you," Mrs. Richardson said, sinking down on the bed beside him. "Pearl had an abortion." She felt a pang of guilt. Would things have been different, she wondered, if he had known? When Moody still said nothing, Mrs. Richardson leaned over to take his hand. "I thought you knew," she said. "I assumed you'd talked it over and decided to end it."

Moody slowly, coldly, pulled his hand away. "I think you have the wrong son," he said. It was Mrs. Richardson's turn to be taken aback. "There's nothing between Pearl and me. It wasn't mine." He laughed, a tight, bitter cough. "Why don't you go ask Trip? He's the one screwing her."

With one hand he took the notebook from his mother's lap and opened it again, focusing on his own handwriting on the page to keep tears from escaping. It was true for him now, in a way it hadn't been before. She had been with Trip, he had made love to her and she had let him and this had happened. Mrs. Richardson, however, didn't notice. She rose, in a daze, and headed down the hall to her own room to think things over. Trip? she thought. Could that be? Neither she nor Moody was aware of the sudden quiet from Izzy's room, that Izzy's door was now open a crack, that Izzy, too, was sitting in stunned silence, absorbing what she'd heard.

><

Mrs. Richardson went to work early on Friday morning, leaving a half hour early to avoid facing any of her children. The night before, Lexie had come home close to midnight, Trip even later, and though normally she'd have scolded them for being out late on a school night, she had instead stayed in her room, ignoring their attempts to be stealthy on the stairs. She was trying to make sense of it all. Due to the extra stress she had allowed herself a second glass of wine, which had gone warm. Trip and Pearl? She understood, of course, why Pearl would fall for Trip—girls generally did—but what Trip might see in Pearl was another matter. She fell asleep puzzling over it, and woke no more illuminated. He was not, she reflected as she backed out of the garage, the kind of boy who usually fell for serious, intellectual girls like Pearl. She could admit this, even as his mother, even as she adored him. He had always been about surface, her beautiful, sunny, shallow boy, and on the surface she couldn't see what would draw him to Pearl. So did Pearl have hidden depths, or did Trip? This thought preoccupied her all the way into her office.

All morning she thought about what to do. Confront Trip? Confront Pearl? Confront them both together? She and her husband did not speak to the children about their love lives—she'd had a talk with Lexie and Izzy, when their periods had started, about their responsibilities. ("Vulnerabilities," Izzy had corrected her, and left the room.) But in general she preferred to assume that her children were smart enough to make their own decisions, that the school had armed them well with knowledge. If they were *up to things*—as she euphemistically thought of it—she didn't need, or want, to know. To stand in front of Trip and that girl and say to them, I know what you've been doing—it seemed as mortifying as stripping them both naked.

At last, midway through the morning, she found herself getting into her car and driving to the little house on Winslow. Mia would be there, she knew, working on her photographs. Mrs. Richardson opened the shared side door and entered without knocking. This was her house, after all, not Mia's; as the landlord, she had the right. The downstairs apartment was silent; it was eleven o'clock and Mr. Yang was at work. Upstairs, however, she could hear Mia in the kitchen: the rumble of a kettle coming to a boil, a whistle springing to life and then subsiding as someone lifted it from the stove. Mrs. Richardson climbed the steps to the second floor, noting the linoleum that was just beginning to peel at the corners of the treads. That would have to be fixed, she thought. She would have the entire staircase—no, the entire apartment—stripped bare and redone.

The door to the upstairs apartment was unlocked, and Mia looked up, alarmed, as Mrs. Richardson came into the kitchen.

"I didn't expect anyone," she said. The kettle gave a

faint whine as she set it back on the hot burner. "Did you need something?" Mrs. Richardson's gaze swept over the apartment: the sink with Pearl's breakfast dishes still stacked over the drain, the array of pillows that passed for a couch, the half-open door to Mia's bedroom, where a mattress lay on the carpet. It was such a pathetic life, she thought; they had so little. And then she spotted something familiar, draped over the back of one of the mismatched kitchen chairs: Izzy's jacket. Izzy had left it there on her last visit, and the casual carelessness of this gesture affronted Mrs. Richardson. As if Izzy lived here, as if this were her home, as if she were Mia's daughter, not Mrs. Richardson's own.

"I always knew there was something about you," she said.

"Pardon?"

Mrs. Richardson did not respond right away. *Not even a real bed,* she thought. *Not even a real couch. What kind of grown woman sits on the floor, sleeps on the floor? What kind of life was this?*

"I suppose you thought you could hide," she said to the kitchen table, where Mia had been carefully splicing a photograph of a dog and a man together. "I suppose you thought no one would ever know."

"I don't know what you're talking about," Mia began. Her knuckles clenched the handle of her mug.

"Don't you? I'm sure Joseph and Madeline Ryan do." Mia went silent. "I'm sure they'd like to know where you are. So would your parents. I'm sure they'd love to know where Pearl is, too." Mrs. Richardson shot

LITTLE FIRES EVERYWHERE • 357

Mia a glance. "Don't try to lie about it. You're a very good liar, but I know all about it. I know all about you."

"What do you want?"

"I almost didn't say anything. I thought, what's in the past is past. Maybe she's made a new life. But I see you've raised your daughter to be just as amoral as you."

"Pearl?" Mia's eyes went wide. "What are you talking about?"

"What a hypocrite you are. You stole that couple's child and then you tried to take a baby away from the McCulloughs."

"Pearl is *my* child."

"You had a little help making her, didn't you?" Mrs. Richardson raised an eyebrow. "Linda McCullough and I have been friends for forty years. She's like a sister to me. And no one deserves a child more than she does."

"It's not a question of deserving. I just think a mother has a right to raise her own child."

"Do you? Or is that just what you tell yourself so you can sleep at night?"

Mia flushed. "If May Ling could choose, don't you think she'd choose to stay with her real mother? The mother who gave birth to her?"

"Maybe." Mrs. Richardson looked at Mia closely. "The Ryans are rich. They wanted a baby so desperately. They'd have given her a wonderful life. If Pearl had gotten to choose, do you think she'd have chosen to stay with you? To live like a vagabond?"

"It bothers you, doesn't it?" Mia said suddenly. "I think you can't imagine. Why anyone would choose a different life from the one you've got. Why anyone might want something other than a big house with a big lawn, a fancy car, a job in an office. Why anyone would choose anything different than what you'd choose." Now it was her turn to study Mrs. Richardson, as if the key to understanding her were coded into her face. "It terrifies you. That you missed out on something. That you gave up something you didn't know you wanted." A sharp, pitying smile pinched the corners of her lips. "What was it? Was it a boy? Was it a vocation? Or was it a whole life?"

Mrs. Richardson shuffled the snippets of Mia's photographs on the table. Under her hands pieces of dog and pieces of man separated and mingled and re-formed.

"I think it's time you moved on," she said. With one hand she lifted Izzy's jacket from the chair and dusted it, as if it were soiled. "By tomorrow." She set a folded hundred-dollar bill on the counter. "This should more than make up for the rent for the month. We'll call it even."

"Why are you doing this?"

Mrs. Richardson headed for the door. "Ask your daughter," she said, and the door shut behind her.

19

Friday afternoon, when the bell rang at just after one, Pearl settled herself into seventh period and set her bag beside her chair. She was going to meet Trip at his car after school; he had put a note into her locker that morning. Lexie had left another after lunch: *Movie tonight? Deep Impact?* It was almost enough to make her forget that she and Moody were no longer friends. Every day they still saw each other in class, but most days he jumped up as soon as the bell rang and bolted out the door before she'd even had a chance to close her binder. Now there he was across the aisle, bent over his copy of *Othello*. She wondered if they'd ever get back to normal, if things would ever be the same between them. Sex changed things, she realized—not just between you and the other person, but between you and everyone.

She was still turning this insight over in her mind when the classroom phone rang. It was usually a question from the main office about something—a misplaced attendance sheet, an excuse for a tardy student—so she paid no attention until Mrs. Thomas hung up and came to crouch by her desk.

"Pearl," she said softly, "the office says your mother's here to pick you up. Take your things with you, they said." She went back to the board, where she was outlining the third act of the play, and Pearl puzzled over this as she packed her books away. Was there an appointment she'd forgotten? Was there some kind of emergency? Out of instinct, she shot a quick look at Moody in the next seat—the closest they'd come to a conversation in weeks. But Moody seemed as clueless as she was, and the last thing she remembered as she left the classroom was his face, their shared moment of confusion.

She came out of the science wing door and saw her mother parked by the curb, leaning back against the little tan Rabbit, waiting for her.

"There you are," Mia said.

"Mom. What are you doing here?" Pearl glanced over her shoulder, in the universal reaction of all teenagers confronted by their parents in a public place.

"Do you have anything important in your locker?" Mia unzipped Pearl's bag and peeked inside. "Your wallet? Any papers? Okay, let's go." She turned back toward the car, and Pearl jerked herself free.

"Mom. I can't. I have a biology quiz next period. And I'm meeting—I'm meeting somebody after school. I'll just see you at home, okay?"

"That's not what I mean," said Mia, and Pearl noticed the wrinkle between her mother's eyebrows that meant she was deeply worried. "I mean we have to go. Today."

"What?" Pearl glanced around. The oval lay quiet and

green before them. Everyone was inside, in class, except for a few students clustered—just off school grounds—at the nearby traffic triangle, smoking. Everything seemed so normal. "I don't want to leave."

"I know, my darling. But we have to."

Every time before, when her mother had decided to leave, Pearl had felt at most a twinge of regret—always over the minor things: a boy she'd admired from afar, a certain park bench or quiet corner or library book she hated to leave behind. Mostly, however, she had felt relief: that she could slide out of this life and begin anew, like a snake shedding its skin. This time all that welled up inside her was a mixture of grief and rage.

"You promised we would stay," she said, her voice thickening. "Mom. I have friends here. I have—" She looked around, as if one of the Richardson children might appear. But Lexie was off in the Social Room finishing her lunch. Moody was back in English class discussing *Othello*. And Trip—Trip would be waiting for her after school on the other side of the oval. When she didn't appear, he would drive away. She had a wild thought: if she could only run to the Richardson house, she would be safe. Mrs. Richardson would help her, she was sure. The Richardsons would take her in. The Richardsons would never let her go. "Please. Mom. Please. Please don't make us go."

"I don't want to. But we have to." Mia held out her hand. Pearl, for a moment, imagined herself transforming into a tree. Rooting herself so deeply on that spot that nothing could displace her.

"Pearl, my darling," her mother said. "I'm so sorry. It's time to go." She took Mia's hand, and Pearl, uprooted, came free and followed her mother back to the car.

$\bowtie$

When they got back to the house on Winslow, a few belongings were already packed: the couch had been stripped of its blanket and disassembled into a stack of pillows; the various prints Mia had tacked to the wall had been boxed. Mia was a fast packer, good at squeezing an improbably large number of things into a tight space. In their year in Shaker, however, they'd acquired more things than they'd ever had before, and this time many more things would need to be left behind.

"I thought I'd be finished by now," Mia admitted, setting her keys down on the table. "But I had to finish something. Fold up your clothes. Whatever will fit in your duffel bag."

"You promised," Pearl said. In the safe cocoon of their home—their real home, as she'd begun to think of it—the tears began to flow, along with a choking rush of fury. "You said we were staying put. You said this was *it*."

Mia stopped and put an arm around Pearl. "I know I did," she said. "I promised. And I'm sorry. Something's happened—"

"I'm not going." Pearl kicked her shoes onto the floor and stomped into the living room. Mia heard the door to her room slam. Sighing, she picked up Pearl's sneakers by the heels and went down the hallway. Pearl had flopped on her bed, math book spread in front of her, jerking a notebook from her bookbag. A furious charade.

"It's time."

"I have to do my homework."

"We have to pack." Mia gently closed the textbook. "And then we have to leave."

Pearl snatched the textbook from her mother's hands and threw it across the room, where it left a black smudge on the wall. Next went her notebook, her ballpoint, her history book, a stack of note cards, until her bookbag lay crumpled on the floor like a shed skin and everything that had been inside it had scattered. Mia sat quietly beside her, waiting. Pearl was no longer crying. Her tears had been replaced by a cold, blank face and a set jaw.

"I thought we could stay, too," Mia said at last.

"Why?" Pearl pulled her knees to her chest and wrapped her arms around them and glared at her mother. "I'm not going until you tell me why."

"That's fair." Mia sighed. She sat down beside Pearl on the bed and smoothed the bedspread beneath them. It was afternoon. It was sunny. Outside, a mourning dove cooed, the low hum of a lawn mower rose, a passing cloud cast them into shadow for a moment, then drifted away. As if it were simply an ordinary day. "I've been thinking about how to tell you for a long time. Longer than you can imagine."

Pearl had gone very still now, her eyes fixed on her mother, waiting patiently, aware she was about to learn something very important. Mia thought of Joseph Ryan, sitting across the table from her that night at dinner, waiting to learn her answer.

"Let me tell you first," she said, taking a deep breath, "about your Uncle Warren."

><

When Mia had finished, Pearl sat quietly, tracing the lines of quilting that spiraled across the bedspread. She had told Pearl the outline of everything, though they both knew all the details would be a long time in coming. They would trickle out in dribs and drabs, memories surfacing suddenly, prompted by the merest thread, the way memories often do. For years afterward, Mia would spot a yellow house as they drove by, or a battered repair truck, or see two children climbing up a hillside, and would say, "Did I ever tell you—" and Pearl would snap to attention, ready to gather another small glittering shard of her history. *Everything*, she had come to understand, was something like infinity. They might never come close, but they could approach a point where, for all intents and purposes, she knew all that she needed to know. It would simply take time, and patience. For now, she knew enough.

"Why are you telling me this?" she had asked her mother. "I mean, why are you telling me this *now*?"

Mia had taken a deep breath. How did you explain to someone—how did you explain to a child, a child you loved—that someone they adored was not to be trusted? She tried. She did her best to explain, and she had watched confusion wash over Pearl's face, then pain. Pearl could not understand it: Mrs. Richardson, who had always been so kind to her, who had said so many nice things about her. Whose shining, polished surface had entranced Pearl with her own reflection.

"She's right, though," Mia said at last. "The Ryans would have given you a wonderful life. They'd have loved you. And Mr. Ryan is your father." She had never said those words aloud, had never even allowed herself to think them, and they tasted strange on her tongue. She said it again: "Your father." Out of the corner of her eye she saw Pearl mouthing the words to herself, as if trying them out. "Do you want to meet them?" Mia asked. "We can drive to New York. They won't be hard to find."

Pearl thought about this for a long time.

"Not right now," she said. "Maybe one day. But not right now." She leaned into her mother's arms, the way she had when she was a child, tucking herself neatly under her mother's chin. "And what about your parents?" she said after a moment.

"My parents?"

"Are they still out there? Do you know where they are?"

Mia hesitated. "Yes," she said, "I believe I do. Do you want to meet them?"

Pearl tipped her head to one side, in a gesture that reminded Mia so strongly of Warren it made her catch her breath. "Someday," she said. "Someday maybe we could go and see them together."

Mia held her for a moment, buried her nose in the part of Pearl's hair. Every time she did this, she was comforted by how Pearl smelled exactly the same. She smelled, Mia thought suddenly, of home, as if *home* had never been a place, but had always been this little person whom she'd carried alongside her.

"And now we'd better pack," she said. It was three thirty. School was out, Pearl thought as she began to roll up her clothing. Moody would just be getting home. Trip would have given up on her by now—or would he be waiting for her still? When she didn't show up, would he come looking for her? She hadn't yet told her mother about Trip; she wasn't sure, yet, if she ever would.

There was a knock at the side door. To Pearl, it was as if she'd summoned Trip with her mind, and she turned to Mia, wide-eyed.

"I'll go and see who it is," Mia said. "You stay up here. Keep packing." If it was Mrs. Richardson, she thought—but no, it was Izzy, standing bewildered in the driveway.

"Why is the door locked?" she said. For months she'd been coming to help Mia every afternoon, and the side door had never before been locked. It had been open to her—to all the Richardson children, it occurred to her now—at any moment of the day, no matter what her trouble.

"I was—I was taking care of something." Mia had forgotten all about Izzy, and she tried to think of a plausible excuse.

"Is Bebe still here?" This was the only thing Izzy could think of that might make Mia shut her out and send her away.

"No, she's gone home. I just—I was busy."

"Okay." Izzy took a half step back from the doorway, and the storm door, which she'd been holding open with her foot, gave a faint shriek. "Well, is Pearl here? I—I wanted to tell her something." She had been trying to catch Pearl all day; in fact, she had tried to call Pearl the previous night—but had gotten only a busy signal: Mia, while comforting Bebe, had taken the phone off the hook, and had forgotten to put it back on. She'd tried over and over, until past midnight, deciding at last that she'd find Pearl at school in the morning. Pearl, she felt, ought to know what Moody had said about her, that her mother knew about Trip. But she didn't know which routes Pearl might take from class to class—would she take the main stairwell, with its crush of students, or the back one that led down to the English wing? Would she eat in the cafeteria, or in the Egress downstairs, or perhaps out on the lawn somewhere? Each time she guessed wrong, and Izzy was frustrated at missing Pearl again and again, even more frustrated at how poorly she seemed to know Pearl. Right after school, she promised herself, she would find Pearl and tell her everything.

Now, face-to-face with Mia, she could tell something was wrong, but wasn't sure what. Did Mia already know? Was Pearl in trouble? Was Mia, for some reason, angry at *her*, too?

Mia looked down at Izzy's anxious face and could not tell whether lying or telling the truth would hurt her more. She decided to do neither.

"I'll tell her you came by, okay?" she said.

"Okay," Izzy said again. With one hand on the doorknob she peeked up at Mia through her hair. Had she done something wrong? she wondered. Had she made Mia angry? Izzy, Lexie had always said, had no poker face, and it was true: Izzy never bothered to hide her feelings, didn't even know how. She looked so young at that moment, so confused and vulnerable and lonely, and this, more than anything, made Mia feel she'd failed her.

"Remember what I said the other day?" she said. "About the prairie fires? About how sometimes you need to scorch everything to the ground and start over?" Izzy nodded. "Well," Mia said. A long moment unraveled between them. She could not think of a way to say goodbye. "Just remember that," she finished. "Sometimes you need to start over from scratch. Can you understand that?" Izzy wasn't sure she did, but she nodded again.

"See you tomorrow?" she said, and Mia's heart cracked. Instead of answering, she pulled Izzy into her arms and kissed her on the top of her head, the same place where she often kissed Pearl. "See you soon," she said.

Pearl heard the door close, but it was a few minutes before Mia came back upstairs, her feet slow and heavy on the steps.

"Who was it?" she asked, though she had a good idea by now.

"Izzy," Mia said, "but she's gone," and she turned into her bedroom to pack.

They had done this so many times before: two glasses stacked, their handful of silverware corralled inside, glasses nested into bowls, bowls nested into pot, pot nested into frying pan, the whole thing wrapped in a paper grocery sack and cushioned with whatever food would keep—a sleeve of crackers, a jar of peanut butter, half a loaf of bread. Another bag held shampoo, a bar of soap, a tube of toothpaste. Mia wedged their duffel bags into the footwells and laid a stack of blankets on top. Her cameras and her supplies went into the trunk, along with the dishes and toiletries. Everything else—the gateleg table they'd painted blue, the mismatched chairs, Pearl's bed and Mia's mattress and the tussock of pillows they'd called a couch—would be left behind.

It was almost dark by the time they'd finished, and Pearl kept thinking about Trip and Lexie and Moody and Izzy. They would be home now, in their beautiful house. Trip would be wondering why she hadn't come to meet him. She would never get to see him again, she thought, and her throat burned. Lexie would be perched at the counter, twirling a lock of hair around her finger, wondering where she was. And Moody—they would never have the chance to make up.

"It isn't fair," she said as her mother put the last of their things in a paper grocery bag.

"No," Mia agreed. "It's not." Pearl waited for a parental platitude to follow: *Life isn't fair,* or *Fair doesn't always mean right.* Instead Mia held her close for a moment, kissed her on the side of the head, then handed her the grocery sack. "Go put this in the car."

When Pearl returned, she found her mother in the kitchen setting a plain manila envelope on the kitchen counter.

"What's that?" Pearl asked, interested in spite of herself.

"Something for the Richardsons," Mia said. "A good-bye, I guess."

"A letter? Can I read it?"

"No. Some photographs."

"You're just leaving them here?" Pearl had never known her mother to leave any of her work behind. When they left an apartment, they took everything that was truly theirs with them—and Mia's photos were the most important. Once, when they hadn't had enough space in the trunk of the Rabbit, Mia had jettisoned half of her clothing to make room.

"They're not mine." Mia took her keys from the counter.

"Who else's could they be?" Pearl insisted.

"Some pictures," Mia said, "belong to the person who took them. And some belong to the person inside them. Are you ready?" She flicked off the lights.

>>><<<

Across town, Bebe sat on the curb in the shadow of a parked BMW and watched the McCulloughs' house across the street. She had been sitting there for some time, and now it was seven thirty, and inside, her daughter must be having her bath. Linda McCullough, she knew, liked to keep to a schedule. "I always find that regular habits make for a calmer life," she had told Bebe more than once, especially on the days Bebe was late for her visitation. As if, Bebe thought, as if she were just offering her own opinion on the subject, free of judgment, as if she were expressing a preference for apples over pears.

The light in the upstairs bathroom clicked on, and Bebe pictured it: May Ling holding on to the white porcelain edge of the bathtub, one hand stretching to touch the water as it tumbled from the faucet. The street was quiet now, lights glowing softly in the living rooms, an occasional blue flicker from a TV, but when she closed her eyes she could almost hear her daughter laughing as a spray of droplets flecked her face. May Ling had always loved water; even in those hungry days, she had calmed when Bebe had lowered her into the kitchen sink for a bath, and when Bebe had lost the energy even for this—afraid the baby would wriggle from her hands, afraid she might simply lie down on the scuffed linoleum and let the child slip beneath the surface—May Ling had screamed all the more. Mrs. McCullough, she was sure, must have an array of bath products at her disposal: all those lotions and soaps and creams made just for babies, rich with shea butter and almond oil and lavender. They would be lined up along the edge of the tub—no, on a fancy glass rack, safely out of reach of inquisitive little hands—and there would be toys, too, bins of them, not just an old yogurt cup for rinsing her hair, but ducks and wind-up frogs. Dolphins. Boats and airplanes. Miniature versions of the marvelous life May Ling would have with the McCulloughs.

After the bath, Mrs. McCullough would wrap May Ling in a fluffy white towel, so plush that when she unwound it there would be a perfect imprint of a little girl in it, right down to her thumbprint navel. She would brush May Ling's hair—which was straight when dry but wavy when wet, just like her mother's—and coax her damp limbs into pajamas. And then she would give May Ling her bottle and put her to bed. Bebe watched the light in the bathroom go out and, in a moment, saw the light at the back of the house—May Ling's room—go on. May Ling would fall asleep, milk-sated and warm, in that cozy crib, snug under a hand-knit coverlet, a wall of crib bumpers shielding her from the hard slats of the sides. She would fall asleep and Mrs. McCullough would turn on the night-light and close the door, and when she went to bed herself, she would already be looking forward to the morning, when she would come in and find Bebe's daughter there waiting for her.

Bebe leaned her head against the BMW and waited for the light in her daughter's room to go out.

>×<

Izzy came home from Mia's to an empty house. Her parents, of course, were still at work, but one of her siblings was usually around. Where was Lexie? she wondered. Where was Moody? Trip, she decided, must be out with Pearl—she hoped she could catch Pearl before her mother arrived home.

As it happened, Trip and Moody had arrived home earlier—Moody right after school, and unexpectedly, Trip a short while later. Trip seemed grumpy and at loose ends, and Moody suspected—correctly—that he'd planned to meet Pearl and something had gone amiss.

"Bad day?" Trip grunted. "She stood you up," Moody went on, clucking his tongue. "Sucks, man. But I mean, what did you expect."

"What are you talking about?" Trip said, turning to Moody at last, and Moody felt a mean thrill shoot through him.

"Did you think you were the only one?" he said. "You think anyone's dumb enough to save themselves for *you*? I just can't believe you didn't catch on sooner." He laughed, and it was then that Trip dove at him. They hadn't scrapped like this in years, since they were boys, and with a sudden sense of relief Moody laughed again even as Trip socked him in the stomach and they toppled onto the floor. For a few moments they scuffled on the tile, their shoes leaving streaks on the cabinet doors, and then Trip got Moody into a headlock and the fight was over.

"You shut up," Trip hissed. "Just shut the fuck up." Since the first time he'd kissed Pearl, he'd wondered what she saw in him, had wondered if she might—sooner or later—decide she'd made a mistake choosing him. It was as if Moody had somehow peered into his brain and spoken all his fears out loud.

Moody sputtered and pulled at Trip's arm and Trip, finally, let him go and stormed off. After half an hour of aimless driving, he headed to Dan Simon's house. In the days before Pearl, he and Dan and some of their hockey teammates had spent hours hunched around Dan's Nintendo playing GoldenEye, and this afternoon he hoped that video-game haze would distract him from what Moody had said, from wondering if it was true. Moody, meanwhile, headed to Horseshoe Lake, where he thought about all the things he wished he'd said to his brother, today and over all the years.

Izzy, home alone, turned Mia's words over and over in her head. *Sometimes you need to start over from scratch.* At five, Mia had not yet arrived to prepare dinner, and an uneasy feeling grew in the pit of her stomach. It only intensified when her mother called at five thirty. "Mia can't come today," she said. "I'll pick up some Chinese food on the way home." When Moody finally came home, at a little past six, she ran downstairs.

"Where is everyone?" she demanded.

Moody shrugged off his flannel shirt and tossed it onto the couch. He had sat at the lake for hours, throwing rocks into the water, thinking about Pearl and his brother. *Look what you did to her,* he thought furiously. *How could you put her through that?* He had thrown every rock he could find and it was still not enough. "How would I know," he said to Izzy. "Lexie's probably over at Serena's. Who knows where the fuck Trip is." He stopped. "What do you care? I thought you liked being alone."

"I was looking for Pearl. Have you seen her?"

"Saw her in English." Moody went into the kitchen to get a soda, with Izzy trailing after him. "Not since then. She left class early." He took a swig.

"Maybe she's with Trip?" Izzy suggested. Moody swallowed and paused. Izzy, noticing that he did not contradict her, pressed her advantage. "Is that true, what you said last night about Pearl and Trip?"

"Apparently."

"Why did you tell Mom?"

"I didn't think it was a secret." Moody set the can down on the counter. "It's not like they were subtle about it. And it's not my job to lie for them."

"Mom said—" Izzy hesitated. "Mom said Pearl had an abortion?"

"That's what she said."

"Pearl didn't have an abortion."

"How would you know?"

"Because." Izzy couldn't explain, but she was sure she was right about this. Trip and Pearl—that she could believe. She had seen Pearl watching Trip for months, like a mouse watching a cat, longing to be eaten. But Pearl, pregnant? She thought back. Had Pearl seemed unusual at all?

Izzy froze. She remembered the day she'd gone to Mia's and Lexie had been there. What had Lexie said? That she'd come over to see Pearl, that Pearl was helping her with an essay. Lexie, usually so coiffed, was disheveled and wan, hair in a limp ponytail, and Mia had been so quick to shoo Izzy away. She thought back further. Lexie, coming home the next afternoon in Pearl's favorite green T-shirt, the one with John Lennon on the front. In one hand she'd clutched a plastic bag with something inside it. She'd stayed in her room all evening, skipping dinner—again, unlike Lexie, who had an appetite—and had been in a sour mood for weeks afterward. Even now, Izzy thought, her sister seemed less effervescent, less gregarious, as if a damper had been closed. And she and Brian had broken up.

"Where's Lexie?" she said again.

"I told you. I think she's at Serena's." Moody grabbed Izzy's arm. "Keep your mouth shut about Trip and Pearl, okay? I don't think she knows."

"You are such a fucking idiot." Izzy shook herself free. "Pearl wasn't pregnant. You realize Mom and her mom are probably going to kill her, and you threw her under the bus for no reason?"

Moody blanched, but only for a moment. Then he shook his head. "I don't care. She deserved it."

"She *deserved* it?" Izzy stared.

"She was sneaking around with Trip. *Trip*, of all people, Izzy. She didn't even care that—" He stopped, as if he had pressed too hard on a fresh bruise. "Look, she decided to sleep around. She deserves whatever she gets."

"I cannot believe you." Izzy had never seen her brother act this way. Moody, who had always been the most thoughtful person in her family; Moody, who had always taken her side even if she chose not to take his advice. Moody, the person in her family she'd always trusted to see things more clearly than she could.

"You realize," she said, "that Mom is probably going to blame Mia for all of this."

Moody shifted. "Well," he said, "maybe she should have kept a closer eye on her daughter. Maybe she should have raised her to be more responsible."

He reached for his can of soda, but Izzy got it first. The cold metal smashed into his cheekbone, and a spray of fizz and froth hit him squarely in the face. By the time he could see again, Izzy was gone, and he was alone, except for the can rolling slowly away across the wet kitchen tile.

><

Serena's house was on Shaker Boulevard, by the middle school, nearly two miles away. Forty minutes later, Serena answered the doorbell to find Izzy, breathless, on the front steps.

"What are you doing here, freak?" Lexie said, coming down the stairs behind Serena.

"I need to ask you something," Izzy said.

"Ever heard of the telephone?"

"Shut up. It's important." Izzy pulled her sister by the arm into the living room and Serena, familiar with Richardson family dynamics, retreated to the kitchen to give them some privacy.

"What," Lexie said when they were alone.

"Did you have an abortion?" Izzy said.

"What?" Lexie's voice dropped to a whisper.

"When Mom was out of town. Did you?"

"It's none of your fucking business." Lexie turned to go, but Izzy barreled ahead.

"You did, didn't you. That time you said you slept over at Pearl's."

"It's not a crime, Izzy. Tons of people do it."

"Did Pearl go with you?"

Lexie sighed. "She drove me. And before you start getting all moralistic and self-righteous—"

"I don't care about your morals, Lex." Izzy flicked her hair out of her face impatiently. "Mom thinks Pearl's the one who had it."

"Pearl?" Lexie laughed. "Sorry, that's just funny. Virginal, innocent little Pearl."

"She must think that for a reason."

"I made the appointment under Pearl's name," Lexie said. "Whatever. She didn't mind." She turned to go, then wheeled around again. "Don't you dare tell anyone about this. Not Moody, not Mom, not anyone. Got it?"

"You are so fucking selfish," Izzy said. Without saying good-bye, she pushed past Lexie into the front hallway, where she nearly knocked Serena over on her way out the door.

It took her another forty minutes on foot to reach the little house on Winslow, and by the time she got there she knew something was wrong. All the lights upstairs were off and there was no sign of the Rabbit in the driveway. She hesitated for a moment on the front walk, poking at the peach tree, where the blossoms were shriveling and turning brown. Then she went around to the side of the house and rang the doorbell until Mr. Yang answered.

"Is Mia here?" she said. "Or Pearl?"

Mr. Yang shook his head. "They leave maybe five, ten minutes ago."

Izzy's heart went leaden and cold. "Did they happen to say where they were going?" she asked, though she already knew the truth: she had missed them, and they were gone.

Mr. Yang shook his head again. "They don't tell me." He had peeked out from behind the curtains just in time to see Mia and Pearl backing carefully out of the driveway, the Rabbit piled high with bags and boxes, and driving off into the growing darkness. They had been good people, he thought sadly, and he wished them a safe journey, wherever they were headed.

A note, Izzy thought wildly; there must be a note. Mia would not have left without a good-bye. "Can I go up and check their apartment for something?" she said. "I promise, I won't bother anything."

"You have a key?" Mr. Yang opened the door and let Izzy clomp up the stairs. "Maybe the door locked?" It was, in fact, and Izzy knocked several times and rattled the doorknob before giving up and coming back down.

"I don't have key," Mr. Yang said. He held the storm door open as Izzy rushed outside. "You ask your mommy, she have the key."

It took Izzy twenty-five minutes to walk home, where—although she would never know it—Mia and Pearl had dropped off their keys just a short time earlier. It took her another half an hour to find her mother's spare keys to the Winslow house in the catchall drawer in the kitchen. She was quiet, ignoring the half-eaten carton of lo mein and orange chicken left on the counter for her, careful not to disturb her brothers or her parents, who by then had dispersed to their various corners of the house. By the time she returned to Winslow Road, it was nine thirty, and Mr. Yang—who on weekdays rose at 4:15 in order to drive his school bus route, and liked to keep a regular schedule—had already gone to bed. So no one heard Izzy come in through the side door, unlock the door to Mia and Pearl's apartment, and step inside at last, knowing deep down that she was too late, that they were gone for good.

><

By nine the next morning, the Richardson house was nearly empty as well. Mr. Richardson had gone in to the office to catch up, as he often did on Saturday mornings; the recent developments in the McCullough case had set him behind in everything else. Lexie was asleep across town in Serena's queen-size bed. Trip and Moody had both gone out: Trip to distract himself with a pickup game at the community center, Moody on his bike to Pearl's house, where he intended to apologize but instead—to his consternation—found a locked door and no Volkswagen. And on Saturday mornings, Izzy knew, Mrs. Richardson always went to the rec center pool to swim laps. Her mother was such a creature of habit that Izzy didn't even bother to peek into her bedroom. She was certain she had the house to herself.

It was unfair, all of it, deeply unfair: that was the one thought that had pulsed through Izzy's mind all night. That Mia and Pearl had had to leave, that they'd finally made a home and now they had been driven away. The kindest people she knew, the most caring, the most sincere, and they'd been chased away by her family. In her mind she cataloged the many betrayals. Lexie had lied; she'd used Pearl. Trip had taken advantage of her. Moody had betrayed her, on purpose. Her father was a baby stealer. And her mother: well, her mother had been at the root of it all.

She thought of Mia's house, glowing golden and warm. All her life she'd felt hard and angry; her mother always criticizing her, Lexie and Trip always mocking her. Mia hadn't been like that. With Mia she'd been different, in a way she hadn't known she could be: in Mia's accepting presence she'd become curious and kind and open, as if under a magic spell. She had felt, finally, as if she could speak without immediately bumping into the hard shell of her sheltered life, as if she suddenly saw that the solid walls penning her in were actually bars, with spaces between them wide enough to slip through. Now Izzy tried to imagine going back to life as it had been before: life in their beautiful, perfectly ordered, abundantly furnished house, where the grass was always cut and the leaves were always raked and there was never, ever any garbage in sight; in their beautiful, perfectly ordered neighborhood where every lawn had a tree and the streets curved so that no one went too fast and every house harmonized with the next; in their beautiful, perfectly ordered city, where everyone got along and everyone followed the rules and everything had to be beautiful and perfect on the outside, no matter what mess lay within. She could not pretend that nothing had happened. Mia had opened a door in her that could not be shut again.

And then she thought about the first day she'd met Mia, what Mia had asked her: *What are you going to do about it?* It was the first time Izzy had ever felt there *was* something she could do about anything. Now she remembered what Mia had said to her the last time they'd seen each other, the words that had been echoing through her head ever since: how sometimes you needed to start over from scratch. Scorched earth, she had said, and at that moment Izzy decided what she was going to do.

She had spent the night planning and now that it was time, she hardly thought at all. It was as if she were standing outside herself, watching someone else do these things. Their father always kept a can of gasoline in the garage, to fill the snow blower, and to power the generator if the power went out during a storm. With the jerry can Izzy made a neat circle on her sister's bed, then her brothers'. The gasoline made a dark, oily blotch on Lexie's flowered comforter, on Trip's pillow, on Moody's plaid sheets. By the time she'd finished in Moody's room the can was empty, so she contented herself with setting it outside the closed door of her parents' bedroom. Then she replaced the keys to the Winslow house in the catchall drawer and removed the box of matches.

Remember, Mia had said: *Sometimes you need to scorch everything to the ground and start over. After the burning the soil is richer, and new things can grow. People are like that, too. They start over. They find a way.* She thought of Mia now and her eyes began to burn and she scraped the first match against the side of the box. On her shoulder she had her bookbag stuffed with a change of clothes, all the money she owned. They couldn't be far ahead, she thought. There was still time to find them. The sandpaper grated under the match head like nails on a chalkboard and there was a whiff of sulfur and the tip flared bright, and Izzy dropped it onto her sister's flowered comforter and ran out the door.

20

After the fire trucks had gone, the shell of the Richardson house now gaping and blackened and steaming gently, Mrs. Richardson pulled her bathrobe tightly around herself and took stock. There was Mr. Richardson on what had been their front walkway, consulting with the fire chief and two policemen. There were Lexie and Trip and Moody, perched on the hood of Lexie's car across the street, watching their parents, awaiting instruction. It had not been lost on Mrs. Richardson that Izzy was missing, and—she was sure—this was what her husband was discussing with the policemen right now. He would be giving them a description, asking them to help find her. *Isabelle Marie Richardson*, she thought with a mixture of fury and shame. *What on earth have you done?* She said as much to the policemen, to the firemen, to her children and her abashed husband. "Reckless," she said. "How could she do this?" Behind her, one of the firemen placed the charred remnants of the jerry can into the truck—to send to the insurance company, she had no doubt. "When Izzy comes back," Lexie murmured to Trip, "Mom is going to *slaughter* her."

It was only when the fire chief asked where they

would be staying that Mrs. Richardson saw the obvious solution.

"At our rental house," she said. "Over on Winslow Road, near Lynnfield." To her puzzled husband and children, she said only, "It was vacated yesterday."

It took some maneuvering to fit three cars into the narrow driveway at the Winslow house, and while Lexie finally parked her Explorer by the curb, Mrs. Richardson had a sudden fear that the apartment would not be empty after all: that they might go upstairs and open the door and find Mia and Pearl still there, placidly eating their lunches at the table, refusing to leave. Or perhaps Mia would have left behind some kind of statement: a mess to clean up, broken windows or smashed walls, one last middle finger to her landlords. But when the Richardson family had stowed all four cars at last and paraded up the steps—much to Mr. Yang's confusion—there was no sign of anyone upstairs, just a few pieces of discarded furniture. Mrs. Richardson nodded in approval and relief.

"It looks so different," Lexie murmured. And it did. The three remaining Richardson children clustered together in the doorway between the living room and the kitchen, so close their shoulders nearly touched. In the kitchen the cupboards were empty, the two mismatched chairs pushed neatly under the rickety table. Moody thought of how many times he'd sat at that table beside Pearl, doing homework, eating a bowl of cereal. Lexie scanned the living room: only a few throw pillows stacked on the carpet, bare walls now except for some stray thumbtack holes in the plaster. Trip glanced toward the bedroom, where through the open door he could see Pearl's bed, stripped of its sheets and blankets, reduced now to a bare mattress and frame.

Perfectly serviceable, Mrs. Richardson thought. Two bedrooms, one for the adults and one for the boys. The girls—for she was still certain Izzy would be back with them shortly—could sleep on the three-season porch. A bathroom and a half—well, they would have to share. It would only be for a little while, until they could find something more suitable, until their house could be repaired.

"Mom," Lexie called from the kitchen. "Mom, look at this."

On the counter lay a large manila envelope, thick with papers. It could have been left behind by mistake—some of Mia's paperwork or Pearl's schoolwork, perhaps, overlooked in their hasty departure. Even before Mrs. Richardson touched it, though, she knew this was not the case. The paper was like satin under her fingers, the flap carefully fastened but not gummed, and as she pried the fastener open with a fingernail and opened the envelope, the remaining Richardsons clustered around her to see what it contained.

There was one for each of them. Mia had stacked them neatly inside: half portraits, half wishes, caught on paper. Each of the Richardsons, as Mrs. Richardson carefully laid the photos out on the table in a line, knew which was meant for them, recognized it instantly, as they might have recognized their own faces. To the others it was just another photo, but to them it was unbearably intimate, like catching a glimpse of your own naked body in a mirror.

A sheet of paper sliced into strips, thin as match-sticks, woven to form a net. Suspended in its mesh: a rounded, heavy stone. The text had been sliced to un-readable bits, but Lexie recognized the pale pink of it at once—the discharge form from her visit to the clinic. On one strip ran the bottom half of her signature—no, her forged signature: Pearl's name in her own hand-writing. She had left the slip at Mia's, and Mia had trans-formed it for her. Lexie, touching the photo, saw that beneath the weight of the rock, the intricate net bulged but did not break. It was something she would have to carry, Mia had said to her, and for the first time, she felt that perhaps she could.

A hockey chest pad, lying in the dirt, cracked through the center, peppered with holes. Mia had used a hammer and a handful of roofing nails, driving each one through the thick white plastic like arrows, then prying it out again. It's all right to be vulnerable, she had thought as she made each hole. It's all right to take time and see what grows. She had filled Trip's chest pad with soil and scattered seeds on it and watered it pa-tiently for a week until from each hole, burgeoning up through the crack, came flashes of green: thin tendrils, little curling leaves worming their way up into the light. Soft fragile life emerging from within the hard shell.

A flock of miniature origami birds taking flight, the largest the size of an open palm, the smallest the size of a fingernail, all faintly striped with notepaper lines. Moody recognized them at once, even before he saw the faint crinkles that textured each one: the pages from Pearl's little notebook, which he had given and then taken back, which he had destroyed and crumpled and thrown away. Although Mia had flattened the pages, the wrinkles still rippled across the birds' wings as if the wind were ruffling their feathers. The birds lay over a photograph of sky like a scattering of petals, soaring away from a pebbled leather ground toward higher and better things. *You will, too,* Mia had thought as she set the birds one by one up in their paper sky.

The next photograph had begun when Mia, sweeping, found one of Mr. Richardson's collar stays under the dresser. She had kept it: he had plenty of others, a whole boxful on top of his dresser, every day tucking one into the point of each collar to keep it stiff. Turning the little steel strip over and over between her fingers, she remembered an experiment she'd done in science class as a child. She had rubbed it with a magnet and then floated it in a dish of water, let it spin this way and that as it slowly settled with its point toward north. The resulting long exposure caught a bow-shaped blur, like the ghostly wings of a butterfly, then the bright line of the collar stay as it found its bearing and grew still. Mr. Richardson, looking at the silver arrow aligned and gleaming and certain in the clouded water, touched the collar of his shirt, wondered which way he was facing now.

And last, and to Mrs. Richardson most startling of all: a paper cutout of a birdcage, shattered, as if something very powerful inside had burst free. Looking closer, she saw it was made of newsprint. Mia had sliced each word out neatly with a razor to form the gaps between the bars. It was one of her own articles, Mrs. Richardson was sure, though with all the words gone there was no way to tell which one: the write-up of the Nature Center fund-raiser, the report on the new community colonnade, the progress of the "Citizens on Patrol" project, any one of the pieces she'd dutifully churned out over the years, any one of the stories that had, despite her intentions, built the bulk of her career. Each splintered bar bent gracefully outward, like the petal of a chrysanthemum, and in the center of the empty cage lay one small golden feather. Something had escaped this cage. Something had found its wings. Mia, assembling this photograph, could think of no better wish for Mrs. Richardson.

They did not realize that one photo was missing until Mrs. Richardson lifted the last to reveal a bundle of negatives. The message was clear: Mia would not try to sell them; she would not share them or hold them for some future leverage. *These are yours,* the stack seemed to say, *these are you. Do what you will with them.* Inside were their portraits, inverted and reversed, all the dark made light and the light made dark. But one did not match any print in the box: Izzy had removed that print the night before, when she had come into the empty apartment and found Mia and Pearl gone and only the envelope of photos left behind as a farewell. She'd known it was hers immediately: a black rose dropped on a cracked square of pavement, the petals cut from black boot leather—her beloved boots, which had made her feel fierce, which her mother had thrown away—the outside petals from the scuffed toes, the inner, darkest petals from the tongue. A bootlace, tip fraying, stretched out long for a stem. Yellow snippets of stitching, unpicked from around the sole, to form the delicate threads of its heart. Toughness rendered tender, even beautiful. Izzy had slipped it into her bag before closing the envelope again and turning out the lights and locking the door behind her. Her family, left with just the negative, could view only its tiny inverse: a pale flower fading to moon white within, a dark gray slab behind it like a cloudy night sky.

It was not until late that afternoon that Mr. Richardson checked the voice mail on his cell phone and got the news. In the staticky recording, Mark McCullough was sobbing so hard Mr. Richardson could barely understand him. The night before, he and Linda, both exhausted from the verdict, the press conference, the gauntlet of the entire ordeal, had fallen into the kind of sleep they hadn't had for months: deep, dreamless, and uninterrupted. In the morning they woke groggy, drunken from so much rest, and Mrs. McCullough had glanced at the clock on her nightstand and realized it was ten thirty. Mirabelle usually woke them at sunrise, crying for breakfast, for a new diaper, and she knew as soon as she saw the red numbers on the clock that something was very wrong. She had leapt from bed and run into Mirabelle's room without even putting on her slippers and her robe and Mark McCullough—still blinking in the strong morning light—had heard her screaming from the other room. The crib was empty. Mirabelle was gone.

It would be a full day before the police could piece together the clues and figure out what had happened: the unlocked sliding door to the back patio—such a safe neighborhood, not that kind of place; the latch on the inside and out, covered with fingerprints. Bebe's absence from work; Bebe's empty apartment; and finally, a ticket, booked in Bebe's name, for a flight to Canton at 11:20 the night before. After that, there was almost no chance, the McCulloughs were told, that they could trace her. China was a large country, the inspector told them without a trace of irony. Bebe would have reached Canton by then and who knew where she might go? A needle in a haystack. You could burn all your money, he'd told them, trying to track them down.

Almost a year later—when the Richardsons' new house was nearly rebuilt, when the McCulloughs had spent not all their money, but tens of thousands of dollars, on detectives and diplomatic wranglings with little result—Mrs. McCullough and Mrs. Richardson had lunch together at the Saffron Patch. They had seen each other through the past months of turmoil as they had seen each other through decades of ups and downs, and would continue to see each other over the various hills and valleys yet to come. "Mark and I have applied to adopt a baby from China," Mrs. McCullough told Mrs. Richardson, as she scooped chicken tikka masala onto a mound of rice.

"That's wonderful," Mrs. Richardson said.

"The adoption agent says we're ideal candidates. She thinks they'll have a match for us within six months." Mrs. McCullough took a sip of water. "She says that coming from China, the odds of the baby's family trying to regain custody are almost nil."

Mrs. Richardson leaned across the table to squeeze her old friend's hand. "That will be a very lucky baby," she said.

This was what would haunt Mrs. McCullough most: that Mirabelle hadn't cried out when Bebe had reached into the crib and lifted her up and taken her away. Despite everything—despite the homemade food and the toys and the late nights and the love, so much love, more love than Mrs. McCullough could have imagined possible—despite it all, she still had felt Bebe's arms were a safe place, a place she belonged. This next baby, she told herself, coming from an orphanage, would never have known another mother. She would be theirs without question. Already Mrs. McCullough felt dizzy with love for this child she had yet to meet. She tried not to think about Mirabelle, the daughter they'd lost, out there somewhere living some other, foreign life.

><

That final night, as they pulled away from the Richardsons' house, Pearl had dropped the keys into the Richardsons' mailbox with a clatter and climbed back into the car and finally voiced the question that had been clinging to the tip of her tongue.

"What if those are the pictures that were going to make you famous?"

They would not be—that would be the idea just beginning to sparkle in Mia's mind as she flicked on the headlights, a wisp of an idea, not yet coalesced into an image, let alone words. As it happened, the Richardsons would never sell those photos. They would keep them and the photos would assume the status of uneasy family heirlooms, something later generations would wonder about when at last that dusty box in the attic was found and opened: where those photographs had come from, who had made them, what they meant.

For now, Mia eased the car into first gear. "Then I'll owe them much, much more than the price of the photos." She guided the Rabbit past the duck pond, across Van Aken and the Rapid tracks, toward Warrensville Road, which would take them to the highway, out of Cleveland, and onward.

"I wish I'd had a chance to say good-bye." Pearl thought about Moody, about Lexie and Trip, the threads that still bound her to each of them in different ways. Over the years, over the course of her life, she would try repeatedly to untangle these threads, and find each time that they were hopelessly intertwined. "And Izzy. I wish I'd gotten to see her one last time."

Mia was quiet, thinking of Izzy, too. "Poor Izzy," she said at last. "She wants to get out of there so badly."

An idea began to form in Pearl's mind in wild golden loops. "We could go back and get her. I could climb up the back porch and knock on her window and—"

"My darling," Mia said, "Izzy is only fifteen. There are rules about that kind of thing."

But as the car sped down Warrensville Road and toward I-480, Mia allowed herself a brief fantasy. They would be driving down a two-lane road, some back highway, the kind Mia favored: the kind that wove its way through small towns composed of a store and a café and a gas pump. Dust would billow in the air as they went by, like golden clouds. They would come around a curve and out of that golden mist they would see a shadowy figure by the roadside, arm out, one thumb up. Mia would slow the car and as the dust settled they would see her hair first, a billow of gold on gold, recognizing that wild hair, that golden wildness, even before they saw her face, even before they could stop and fling the door wide and let her in.

><

Saturday morning, as Mia and Pearl crossed into Iowa, Izzy—the smell of smoke still clinging, faintly, to her hair—climbed aboard a Greyhound bus headed for Pittsburgh. Across town her family was just now gathering on the bank of the duck pond, watching the firefighters douse the Richardson house, flame by flame. She had, folded in her back pocket, an address she had found in her mother's files, which she had rifled through late the previous night, after packing her bag. *George and Regina Wright. Bethel Park, Pennsylvania.* There had been a phone number, too, but Izzy knew a phone call would not give her the answers she needed. The file on her mother's desk—neatly labeled M.W. in her mother's careful writing—had been quite full, and she had read everything, sitting in the lamplight in her mother's office chair, while everyone slept quietly upstairs. Below the Wrights' address she'd copied another: *Anita Rees, the Rees Gallery.* It was somewhere in New York City. Mia, she knew, had started there when she was not much older than Izzy. She wondered what it would be like.

Maybe one of these people would help her find Mia, wherever she might be headed. Maybe they would send her back to her parents. And if they did? She would leave again. She would leave again and again until she was old enough that no one could send her back. She would keep searching until she found what she was looking for.

Pittsburgh beckoned, and beyond it, New York: Mia's past, but her future. They would lead her to Mia somehow.

Now, settling into a seat and leaning her head against the window, she imagined how it would go. She would spot Mia from behind first—but of course she would recognize her immediately. Izzy knew her outline like a shape she'd traced over and over until she knew it by heart. She would find Mia and when Mia turned she would open her arms, she would take Izzy in and take her with her, wherever she would go next.

✕

That last night, as Mrs. Richardson settled down to sleep in the Winslow house for the first time, she began to think, as she would for a long time, of her youngest child. The noises of the house were foreign to her—the hum of the fridge, the faint rumble of the furnace downstairs, the squeak of a branch rubbing the slate roof overhead—and she rose and went outside and sat on the steps of the little duplex, her bathrobe wrapped tightly around her. Under her feet the cement stoop was cool and slightly damp, as if a fog had just lifted.

All day long she had been fuming at Izzy, both internally and aloud. Ungrateful child, she had said. How could she do this. What she wasn't going to do when they found her. She would be grounded for life. She would be sent to boarding school. Military school. A convent. She had half a mind to let the police have her: let her learn about consequences in jail. Her husband and children, used to her flares of fury at Izzy, nodded quietly, let her rant. But this was different from other times.

This time Izzy had crossed every line, and now—each member of the family was slowly realizing—she might never be back.

The police were searching for Izzy, of course; they'd put out an alert for her as a runaway and a possibly endangered child, and in the days to come Mrs. Richardson would give them photos for bulletins and posters, would track Izzy's friends and classmates one by one, searching for clues about where she might have gone. But the ones who might have known, she realized, had already gone. All up and down the street the houses looked like any others—but inside them were people who might be happy, or taking refuge, or steeling themselves to go out into the world, searching for something better. So many lives she would never know about, unfolding behind those doors.

It was nearly midnight, and a car drove down Winslow quickly, its high beams on, as if it had somewhere important to be, then disappeared into the darkness. She probably looked crazy to the neighbors, she thought, sitting out there on the steps in the dark, but for once she did not care. The anger she had stoked all day had burned away, like the heat of the afternoon burning off as evening fell, leaving her with one thought, cold and crystalline and piercing as a star: Izzy was gone. Everything that had infuriated her about Izzy, even before she'd taken her first breath, had been rooted in that one fear, that she might lose her. And now she had. A thin wail rose from her throat, sharp as the blade of a knife.

For the first time, her heart began to shatter, thinking of her child out there among the world. Izzy: that child who had caused her so much trouble, who had worried her so much, who had never stopped worrying her and worrying at her, whose restless energy had driven her, at last, to take flight. That child who she thought had been her opposite but who had, deep inside, inherited and carried and nursed that spark her mother had long ago tamped down, that same burning certainty that she knew right from wrong. She thought, as she would often for many years, of the photograph from that day, with the one golden feather inside it: Was it a portrait of her, or her daughter? Was she the bird trying to batter its way free, or was she the cage?

The police would find Izzy, she told herself. They would find her and she would be able to make amends. She wasn't sure how, but she was certain she would. And if the police couldn't find her? Then she would look for Izzy herself. For as long as it took, for forever if need be. Years might pass and they might change, both of them, but she was sure she would still know her own child, just as she would know herself, no matter how long it had been. She was certain of this. She would spend months, years, the rest of her life looking for her daughter, searching the face of every young woman she met for as long as it took, searching for a spark of familiarity in the faces of strangers.

ACKNOWLEDGMENTS

When I was on book tour for *Everything I Never Told You,* an audience member once asked, "I counted, and you thanked sixty-five individual people in your acknowledgments—why did you thank so many people?" I explained that although my name is the only one on the cover, many, many people helped me along the way, and this book wouldn't exist without them. That's even more true the second time around.

Thank you as always to my superagent Julie Barer and everyone at The Book Group—so grateful to be part of Barer Nation. My unflappable editor, Virginia Smith Younce, made this a better, richer book through her expert guidance, and Jane Cavolina straightened out my time line and italics with supreme patience. Juliana Kiyan, Anne Badman, Sarah Hutson, Matthew Boyd, Scott Moyers, Ann Godoff, Kathryn Court, Patrick Nolan, Madeline McIntosh, and the entire team at Penguin Press and Penguin Books did a fantastic job of getting this book out into the world—thank you for having my back again.

My faithful writing group, the Chunky Monkeys (Chip Cheek, Calvin Hennick, Jennifer De Leon, Sonya Larson, Alexandria Marzano-Lesnevich, Whitney Scharer, Adam

Stumacher, Grace Talusan, and Becky Tuch) were the first readers of this book; their cheerleading helped me finish, and our email chains were more like lifelines. Ayelet Amittay, Anne Stameshkin, and my MFA cohort: as always, you lead the way. Jes Häberli and Danielle Lazarin, I'm sending you a van of donuts. And my non-writer friends have kept me sane and grounded through this crazy ride; in particular, I can't believe Katie Campbell, Samantha Chin, and Annie Xu still put up with me.

Huge thanks go to my readers—both of this novel and of the first. To those of you who emailed me, wrote me letters, handed me notes at readings, or chatted with me at the signing table: thank you. I can't tell you how grateful I am. Many thanks to my Twitter friends as well: you remind me every day how smart, funny, and kind people can be. Thanks, too, to several artists whose work influenced Mia's, including Kent Rogowski and Cindy Sherman.

And finally, the last and biggest thanks to my family. Lily and Yvonne Ng encouraged my writing habit from my earliest days; I wouldn't be here without you—figuratively or literally. My husband, Matt, believed writing was my job long before I did, and kept telling me so. Thank you for everything you do. And my son, still my best creation: this be the verse, but I'm doing my best.

A PENGUIN READERS GUIDE TO

LITTLE FIRES
EVERYWHERE

Celeste Ng

A Letter from
Celeste Ng

Dear readers,

When I first began *Little Fires Everywhere*, I knew I wanted to write about my beloved hometown of Shaker Heights, Ohio. I started with a story about troubled families—the wealthy Richardsons and their complicated family dynamics, mysterious Mia and her daughter, and the secrets they all carry with them— and set the story in my hometown.

Shaker Heights, I realized, is full of fascinating contradictions. It's a wealthy, highly regulated city— one of the first *planned* communities in the United States—and the belief in planning is so strong that the city even planned for diversity in everything from the appearance of its houses to the racial makeup of its population. It was founded on utopian principles and even today brims with idealism and a sense of exceptionalism. And despite all this, of course, Shaker Heights still struggles with the same race and class issues as the rest of the nation.

Like many places in our country, Shaker Heights is full of idealistic, altruistic people—of all races—who are good at heart and sincerely want to do the right thing. Yet when personally affected by the issues, even idealists often end up making selfish choices with far-reaching effects. It's human nature, yet I wanted to explore how—and how often—we justify it to ourselves when we cross moral lines. Where do we follow the rules, and where do we justify breaking them? Do our pasts determine what we deserve in the future? And is it ever possible to leave your past behind? These are some of the questions I hope the novel raises.

It wasn't that long ago that my debut novel, *Everything I Never Told You*, hit bookshelves, and I want to thank readers like you for embracing it so warmly. It wouldn't have succeeded without the support of enthusiastic readers like you. After working on *Everything I Never Told You* for six years, to have it enter the world to such a loving reception still feels like a dream. (Really: thank you.) I hope that *Little Fires Everywhere* will similarly capture your imagination, spark spirited discussions, and win your heart.

Thank you for reading,

Celeste

A Conversation with

Celeste Ng

Tell us a bit about Shaker Heights. Do you see it as representative of Every Town, USA, or is there something you feel makes Shaker Heights stand apart?

Growing up, I always thought that my hometown was pretty much just like everywhere else—I think most people do. And in many ways, Shaker Heights is a lot like suburbs everywhere: it's placid and idyllic and full of well-intentioned families.

But when I went away to college, I discovered that Shaker Heights really was unusual in a lot of ways. I thought it was normal—or at least not unusual—to have a race relations group at your high school, and to live next door to people of different races. I thought it was weird to put your garbage on the curb and normal to get fined if you didn't mow your lawn. Yet Shaker Heights is not exactly Stepford, either: the town truly values diversity, in everything from actively encouraging an integrated population to insisting on variation in the designs of the houses.

As I researched, I learned more about the history of the city and how deeply ingrained its idealism is: right from the beginning, Shaker Heights wanted to be a little utopia, and they take that more seriously than any community I've ever seen. I sometimes sum up the town's goal as to be just like everyone else, only better—and in that sense, Shaker Heights is both a lot like many towns across the country and totally different from any other place I know.

You were born in Pittsburgh and when you were nine years old, your family moved to Shaker Heights, where you lived until you went college. How much did you draw from your own adolescent and teen years while writing the book?

I was a high schooler at the time the book is set, and I had a lot of fun sending the teens in the novel to my old haunts. (I've consumed more fries in that diner—and spent more quarters in the jukebox there—than I can count, and I visited it again to sample the fries while writing the book. Purely for research purposes, obviously.) So much of the scene-setting comes from memory, but I did need a refresher. Meghan Hayes, the Local History Librarian at the Shaker Heights Public Library, helped me find old yearbooks, issues of *Shaker* magazine, and copies of the *Shakerite*, the high school newspaper—invaluable references for what we wore, what we were talking about at the time, what slang we used.

We meet many characters who have a supposedly color-blind mindset that they use to justify their words and actions, or lack thereof. What do you hope readers will take away from these viewpoints and conversations?

The novel is set in 1997 and 1998, which is two decades ago, yet doesn't feel that far away. It's easy to forget how the conversation around race at that time mostly involved discounting or ignoring it—I think of the blithe (yet often problematic) Benetton ads of that era that perfectly captured the "Skin color doesn't matter! We're all one!" mentality.

Now we're starting to be aware of the problems with not "seeing race": ignoring race means ignoring

6

longstanding problems and history, as well as ignoring important aspects of a person's identity. I hope readers, encountering that allegedly race-blind mindset in these pages, will reflect on the ways our views have changed—and on the ways they haven't changed as much as they might need to.

Can you talk about the inspiration for Mia's art? Why did you choose to have her be a photographer?

I've always been interested in art; I would have done a minor in art history if I could have. Photography is particularly interesting to me because it's often seen as objective—after all, the camera captures what it sees— but it's also inherently subjective: so much depends on the framing of the photograph, deciding what gets included and what gets left out, how it's shown. It's a peculiar combination of technology and human perspective and that makes really rich material for fiction.

I knew a little bit about photography from art history, but to create Mia's art, I read more about the history of the medium. I also looked at the works of contemporary photographers and artists who use photographs in their work, so I could get a sense of what these artists were doing and why. Then came the fun part: making up Mia's photographs. They're all pure invention, but were inspired by the ways contemporary artists experiment with altering their photographs. For various reasons (which will be clear after you've read the book!) she's very concerned with the idea of starting over, so nearly all of her work has to do with change or transformation in some way.

In a case of art influencing real life, writing this novel has sparked my own interest in learning photography. My dad was an amateur photographer, and I have some of his old cameras, so I'm starting to take some photographs of my own.

The exchange about dolls in the courtroom will resonate with any parent or child who has looked for a toy or book that looks like them but can't find it, or what they do find is outdated. Was this an experience you had growing up? How have things changed now that you're a parent?

My mother was aware of this issue way before it entered the main cultural conversation. Anytime she found a book with Asian characters, she would buy it for me—which I now realize was her way of trying to show me myself on the page. Often the choice was between bad representation—as in the classic *Five Chinese Brothers* book mentioned in the novel—and no representation at all. She was never able to find Asian dolls, though, so she would buy me dark haired dolls when she could. When American Girl finally introduced its "American Girl of Today" dolls in 1995, my mother bought me the Asian one, even though by that age I was out of the doll stage. I think it was as much for her sake as for mine. (I still have it.)

As a mother myself, I'm now aware of this issue from the other side. When my son was small, he spotted an Asian boy baby doll in a toy store, and I snapped it up. If he wants an older Asian boy doll, though, I'm not sure what I'll do. And it's still difficult to find representations of East Asian children in books—though there are more now than there were thirty years ago!—and my son is biracial, so even East Asian characters don't exactly look like him. On the positive side, this is a topic of conversation in the literary world right now, and I hope that more publishers will put out books featuring diverse children, so that more kids can see themselves represented on the page.

The stories of mothers—Mrs. Richardson, Mia, Bebe, Linda McCullough—interweave and clash in different, sometimes shocking, sometimes deeply moving ways. At the heart of the court case is the difficult question of who "deserves" to be a mother. Why did you want to tackle this subject?

I think a lot about these issues because I'm both a mother and a daughter: what motherhood is, what my relationship to it is, what society expects of women who are mothers, or who aren't. How we're "supposed" to go about this whole business of motherhood. I have friends who've conceived easily, who've struggled to conceive, who've adopted or gone through invasive IVF procedures or used surrogates, or who've decided not to conceive—and the main constant in all of their experiences seems to be judgment. Motherhood seems to be a no-win battle: however you decide to do (or not do) it, someone's going to be criticizing you. You went to too great lengths trying to conceive. You didn't go to great enough lengths. You had the baby too young. You should have kept the baby even though you were young. You shouldn't have waited so long to try to have a baby. You're a too involved mother. You're not involved enough because you let your child play on the playground alone. It never ends.

It strikes me that while all this judgment goes on, the options available to women become fewer and fewer. I'm not even (just) talking about the right to choose—across the U.S., women have less access to birth control, health care, reproductive education, and post-partum support. So we give women less information about their bodies and reproduction, less control over their bodies, and less support during and after pregnancy—and then we criticize them fiercely for whatever they end up doing. This seems not only unfair to me but a recipe for societal disaster. I don't have answers here, but I wanted to raise questions about what we expect of mothers and who we think "deserves" to be a mother and who doesn't—and why we think that question is ours to decide.

This book, like Everything I Never Told You, takes place at a time before everyone has a cell phone and is instantly interconnected. Do you feel that having your characters and their stories exist before technology took over our lives allows them to act and think with more freedom?

As many of my readers probably know, I'm a social media junkie—I can often be found procrastinating on Twitter when I'm supposed to be writing. Generally, I'm grateful to be living in our interconnected world: I get to connect with people all over the globe; virtually any information I need is available to me at the click of a button; and when I'm away from home, my friends and family are in my pocket, seconds away by video call or text. For a writer who spends most of the day at home and inside her own head, that sense of connectedness and community is a godsend.

But all this connectedness has a downside: it leaves less space for mystery. If I want to know where a friend is, I can check her Facebook or Twitter feed or see if she's checked in on Foursquare or—if it comes to that—ping her phone and ask her to share her location. Information is hard to erase from the internet, too: whatever you said or did in the past follows you like a tail dragging along behind you. That has its own potential for fiction, but in *Little Fires Everywhere* I needed some shadowy places where mysteries could lurk, where secrets could stay hidden and pasts could be—at least temporarily—shed.

Questions for Discussion

1. Shaker Heights is almost another character in the novel. Do you believe that "the best communities are planned"? Why or why not?

2. There are many different kinds of mother-daughter relationships in the novel. Which ones did you find most compelling? Do mothers have a unique ability to spark fires, for good and ill, in us?

3. Which of the Richardson children is most changed by the events of the novel? How do you think this time ultimately changes Lexie's life? Trip's? Moody's? Izzy's?

4. The debate over the fate of May Ling/Mirabelle is multilayered and heartbreaking. Who do you think should raise her?

5. How is motherhood defined throughout the book? How do choice, opportunity, and circumstances impact different characters' approach to motherhood?

6. Mia's journey to becoming an artist is almost a beautiful novella of its own. Mia's art clearly has the power to change lives. What piece of art has shaped your life in an important way?

7. Pearl has led a singular life before arriving in Shaker, but once she meets the Richardsons, she has the chance to become a "normal" teenager. Is that a good thing?

8. What ultimately bothers Elena most about Mia?

9. The novel begins with a great conflagration, but its conclusion is even more devastating. What do you think happens to Elena after the novel ends? To Mia and Pearl? To Izzy? Do you think Izzy ever returns to Shaker and her family? Why or why not?

10. Celeste Ng is noted for her ability to shift between the perspectives of different characters in her work. How does that choice shape the reader's experience of the novel?

11. We see how race and class underline the experiences of all the characters and how they interact with each other. In what ways are attitudes toward race and class different and the same today as in the late 1990s, when the book is set?

12. Izzy chooses "This Be the Verse" to sum up her life. Is what the poem says accurate, in the context of Izzy's experience?

13. What does the title mean to you? What about the book's dedication?